The Dressmaker of Dachau

The Dressmaker of Dachau

Mary Chamberlain

W F HOWES LTD

This large print edition published in 2016 by
W F Howes Ltd
Unit 5, St George's House, Rearsby Business Park,
Gaddesby Lane, Rearsby, Leicester LE7 4YH

1 3 5 7 9 10 8 6 4 2

First published in the United Kingdom in 2015
by HarperCollins*Publishers*

A CIP catalogue record for this book is available
from the British Library

ISBN 978 1 51001 796 2

Typeset by Palimpsest Book Production Limited,
Falkirk, Stirlingshire

For the little ones – Aaron, Lola, Cosmo, Trilby – and their Ba.

PROLOGUE

The April sun cast shafts of light onto the thick slubs of black silk, turning it into a sea of ebony and jet, silver and slate. Ada watched as Anni ran her hand along the fine, crisp edges of the jacket, tracing the rich, warm threads and fingering the corsage as if the petals were tender, living blooms.

She was wearing it over a thick wool jumper and her cook's apron, so it pulled tight around the shoulders. *No*, Ada wanted to say, *not like that. It won't fit.* But she kept her mouth shut. She could see from Anni's face that the jacket was the most beautiful thing she had ever possessed.

Anni was holding the key to Ada's room in one hand and a suitcase in the other.

'Goodbye,' she said, throwing the key on the floor and kicking it towards Ada.

She walked away, leaving the door open.

ONE

LONDON, JANUARY 1939

Ada peered into the broken mirror propped up on the kitchen dresser. Mouth open, tongue to attention, she plucked at her eyebrows with a pair of rusty tweezers. Winced and *ouched* until only a thin arc was left. She dabbed on the witch hazel, hoped the stinging would fade. Dunked her hair in clean, warm water in the old, cracked butler sink, patted it dry with a towel and parted it along the left. Eighteen years old, more grown up this way. Middle finger, comb and straighten, index finger, crimp. Three waves down the left, five down the right, five each herringbone down the back, pin curls and a Kirby grip tight to her skull, leave it to dry.

Ada was taking her time. She opened her handbag and fished around until she found her powder, rouge and lipstick. Not too much, in case she looked common, but enough to make her fresh and wholesome like those young girls from the Women's League of Health and Beauty. She'd seen them in Hyde Park in their black drawers and white blouses and knew they practised on a Saturday afternoon in the playground of Henry

5

Fawcett's. She might think about joining them. It was good to be supple, and slender. She could make the uniform herself. After all, she was a dressmaker now, earned good money.

She rubbed her lips together to spread her lipstick, checked that the waves were holding their grip as her hair dried, picked up the mirror and carried it into the bedroom. The brown houndstooth skirt with the inverted pleats and the cream blouse with the enamel pin at the neck – that was smart. Good tweed, too, an offcut from Isidore, the tailor in Hanover Square. Just fifteen she was when she started there. Gawd, she was green, picking up pins from the floor and sweeping away fabric dustings, plimsolls grey from the chalk and her hand-me-down jacket too long in the arm. Dad said it was a sweatshop, that the fat capitalist who ran it did nothing but exploit her and she should stand up for her rights and organize. But Isidore had opened her eyes. He taught her how fabric lived and breathed, how it had a personality and moods. Silk, he said, was stubborn, lawn sullen. Worsted was tough, flannel lazy. He taught her how to cut the cloth so it didn't pucker and bruise, about biases and selvedges. He showed her how to make patterns and where to chalk and tack. He taught her the sewing machine, about yarns and threads, how to fit a new-fangled zipper so it lay hidden in the seam and how to buttonhole and hem. *Herringbone, Ada, herringbone.* Women looking like mannequins. It was a world of enchantment. Beautiful hair and glistening gowns. Tailored knickers even. Isidore had shown Ada that world, and she wanted it for herself.

She wasn't there yet. What with Mum demanding a share for her keep and the bus to work and a tea cake in Lyons with the girls on pay day, there wasn't much over at the end of the week.

'And don't think you can come into this house and lord it around,' Mum raised a stained finger at Ada, knuckles creased like an old worm, 'just because you pay your way.' Still had to do her share of the dusting and sweeping and, now she was trained up, the family's dressmaking too.

Ada knew this life of scrimping and nit-combs and hand-me-downs was not what she was meant for. She damped her finger and thumb with her tongue, folded down her Bemberg stockings with the fitted toe and heel and rolled them up, crease by crease, *careful you don't snag,* so the seam sat straight at the back. *Quality* shows. *Appearances* matter. So long as her top clothes looked good, nobody could touch her. Lips pinched, nose in the air, *excuse me.* Airs and graces, like the best of them. Ada would go far, she knew, be a *somebody* too.

She propped the mirror on top of the mantel-piece and combed her hair so it settled in chestnut waves. She placed her hat on her head, a brown, felt pillbox that one of the milliners at work had made for her, nudging it forward and to the side.

She slipped her feet into her new tan court shoes and, lifting the mirror and tilting it downwards, stood back to see the effect. Perfect. *Modish.* Groomed.

Ada Vaughan jumped over the threshold, still damp from the scrubbing and reddening this morning. The morning sky above was thick, chimney pots coughing sooty grouts into the air. The terrace stretched the length of the street, smuts clinging to the yellow stock and to the brown net curtains struggling free from the open windows in the city-hobbled wind. She covered her nose with her hand so the murk from the Thames and the ash from the tallow melts wouldn't fill her nostrils and leave blackened snot on the handkerchiefs she'd made for herself and embroidered in the corner, *AV.*

Clip-clop along Theed Street, front doors open so you could see inside, respectable houses these, clean as a whistle, good address, you had to be a *somebody* to rent here, Mum always said. Somebody, my foot. Mum and Dad wouldn't know a somebody if he clipped them round the ear. Somebodies didn't sell the *Daily Worker* outside Dalton's on a Saturday morning, or thumb their rosaries until their fingers grew calouses. Somebodies didn't scream at each other, or sulk in silence for days on end. If Ada had to choose between her mother and father, it would be her father every time, for all his temper and frustrations. He wasn't waiting for Heaven but salvation in the here and now, one last push and the edifice of prejudice and privilege would crumble and everyone would have the world that Ada yearned for. Her mother's salvation came after death and a lifetime of suffering and bleeding hearts. Sitting in the church on Sunday, she wondered how anyone could make a religion out of misery.

Clip-clop past the fire station and the emergency sandbags stacked outside. Past the Old Vic where she'd seen *Twelfth Night* on a free seat when she was eleven years old, entranced by the glossy velvet costumes and the smell of Tungstens and orange peel. She knew, just knew, there was a world enclosed on this stage with its painted-on scenery and artificial lights that was as true and deep as the universe itself. Make-up and make-belief, her heart sang for Malvolio, for he, like her, yearned to be a *somebody*. She kept going, down the London Road, round St George's Cross and onto the Borough Road. Dad said there was going to be a war before the year was out and Mum kept picking up leaflets and reading them out loud, *When you hear the siren, proceed in an orderly fashion . . .*

Ada clip-clopped up to the building and raised her eyes to the letters that ran in black relief along the top. 'Borough Polytechnic Institute'. She fidgeted with her hat, opened and shut her bag, checked her seams were straight, and walked up the stairs. Sticky under her arms and between her thighs, the clamminess that came from nerves, not the clean damp you got from running.

The door to Room 35 had four glass panels in the top half. Ada peered through. The desks had been pushed to one side and six women were standing in a semicircle in the middle. Their backs were to the door and they were looking at someone in the front. Ada couldn't see who. She wiped her palm down the side of her skirt, opened the door and stepped into the room.

A woman with large bosoms, a pearl necklace and grey hair rolled in a bun stepped forward from the semicircle and threw open her arms. 'And you are?'

Ada swallowed. 'Ada Vaughan.'

'From the diaphragm,' the woman bellowed. 'Your name?'

Ada didn't know what she meant. 'Ada Vaughan,' her voice crashed against her tongue.

'Are we a mouse?' the woman boomed.

Ada blushed. She felt small, stupid. She turned and walked to the door.

'No, no,' the woman cried. 'Do come in.' Ada was reaching for the door-knob. She put her hand on Ada's. 'You've come this far.'

The woman's hand was warm and dry and Ada saw her nails were manicured and painted pink. She led her back to the other women, positioned her in the centre of the semicircle.

'My name is Miss Skinner.' Her words sang clear,

like a melody, Ada thought, or a crystal dove. 'And yours?'

Miss Skinner stood straight, all bosom, though her waist was slender. She poised her head to the side, chin forward.

'Say it clearly,' she smiled, nodded. Her face was kindly, after all, even if her voice was strict. 'E-nun-ci-ate.'

'Ada Vaughan,' Ada said, with conviction.

'You may look like a swan,' Miss Skinner said, stepping back, 'but if you talk like a sparrow, who will take you seriously? Welcome, Miss Vaughan.'

She placed her hands round her waist. Ada knew she must be wearing a girdle. No woman her age had a figure like that without support. She breathed in *Mmmmm,* drummed her fingers on the cavity she made beneath her ribs, opened her mouth, *Do re mi fa so.* She held tight to the last note, blasting like a ship's funnel until it left only an echo lingering in the air. Her shoulders relaxed and she let out the rest of the air with a *whoosh.* It's her bosoms, Ada thought, that's where she must keep the air, blow them up like balloons. No one could breathe in that deep. It wasn't natural.

'Stand straight.' Miss Skinner stepped forward, 'Chin up, bottom in.' She threaded her way through the group, came to Ada and pushed one hand against the small of her back and with the other lifted Ada's chin up and out.

'Unless we stand upright,' Miss Skinner rolled

her shoulders back and adjusted her bosom, 'we cannot project.' She trilled her *rrrs* like a Sally Army cymbal. 'And if we cannot project,' Miss Skinner added, 'we cannot pronounce.'

She turned to Ada. 'Miss Vaughan, why do you wish to learn elocution?'

Ada could feel the heat crawl up her neck and prickle her ears, knew her face was turning red. She opened her mouth, but couldn't say it. Her tongue folded in a pleat. *I want to be a somebody.* Miss Skinner nodded anyway. She'd seen the likes of Ada before. Ambitious.

'I thought you were one of the customers,' the Hon. Mrs Buckley had said, 'when I saw you standing there, looking so smart.' Taken for one of the customers. *Imagine.* She was only eighteen years old when she'd started there last September. Ada had learned fast.

The Hon. Mrs Buckley traded under the name 'Madame Duchamps'. Square-hipped and tall, with painted nails and quiet earrings, she dazzled with her talk of *couture* and *atelier* and *Paris, pah!* She would flip through the pages of *Vogue* and conjure ballgowns and cocktail dresses from bolts of silks and chenilles which she draped and pinned round slender debutantes and their portly chaperones.

Ada had learned her trade from Isidore and her nerve from Mrs B., as the other girls all called her. Where Isidore had been wise and kind and funny, *genuine*, Mrs B. was crafted through artifice. Ada was sure the Hon. Mrs Buckley was neither an Hon. nor a Mrs, and her complexion was as false as her name, but that didn't stop Mrs B. What she didn't know about the female form and the lie of a fabric was not worth writing on a postage stamp.

Mrs B. was a step up from Isidore. *Paris.* That was the city Ada aimed to conquer. She'd call her house 'Vaughan'. It was a modish name, like Worth, or Chanel, but with British *cachet.* That was another word she'd learned from Mrs B. *Cachet.* Style and class, rolled into one.

'Where did you learn all this French, madame?' The girls always had to call her 'madame' to her face.

Mrs B. had given a knowing smile, her head pivoting on the tilt of her long neck. 'Here and there,' she said. 'Here and there.'

Fair dues to Mrs B., she recognized in Ada a hard worker, and a young woman with ambition and talent. Aitches present and correct without aspiration, *haspiration*, Ada was made front-of-house, Madame Duchamps's instore fresh-faced mannequin, and the young society ladies began to turn to her to model their clothes, rather than Mrs B., whose complexion and waistline grew thicker by the day.

'Mademoiselle,' Mrs B. would say. 'Slip on the evening gown.'

'The *douppioni*, madame?'

Midnight blue with a halter neck. Ada would lean into her hips and sway across the floor, swirl so her naked back drew the eye, and that eye would marvel at the drape of the fabric as it swallowed the curve of her figure, out and in, and fanned in a fishtail. She'd turn again and smile.

'And now the chiffon.'

Veils of mystery and a taffeta lining, oyster and pearl and precious lustres. Ada loved the way the clothes transformed her. She could be fire, or water, air or earth. Elemental. Truthful. *This* was who she was. She would lift her arms as if to embrace the heavens and the fabric would drift in the gossamer breeze; she would bend low in a curtsy then unfold her body like a flower in bloom, each limb a sensuous, supple petal.

She was the centre of adoration, a living sculpture, a work of art. A creator, too. She would smile and say, 'But if you tuck it here, or pleat it there, then *voilà.*' With a flourish of her long, slim fingers and that new, knowing *voilà*, Ada would add her own touch to one of Mrs B.'s designs and make it altogether more modern, more desirable. Ada knew Mrs B. saw her as an asset, recognized her skills and taste, her ability to lure the customers and charm them with an effortless eloquence, thanks to Miss Skinner's skilful tutoring.

'If you cut on the bias,' Ada would say, holding up the dress length on the diagonal to a customer, 'you can see how it falls, like a Grecian goddess.'

Draped across the breast, a single, naked shoulder rising like a mermaid from a chiffon sea.

'*Non, non, non.*' Mrs B. tut-tutted, spoke in French when Ada pushed the limits of decency. 'That will not do, Mademoiselle. This is not for the *boudoir*, but the ball. Decorum, decorum.'

She'd turned to her client. 'Miss Vaughan is still a little inexperienced, *naïve*, in the subtler points of social correctness.'

Naive she might be, but Ada was good publicity for Madame Duchamps, *modiste*, of Dover Street, and Ada had hopes that one day she could be more than an asset but a partner in the business. She had developed a respectable following. Her talent marked her out, the flow and poise of her design distinguished her. She conjured Hollywood and the glamorous world of the stars and brought them into the drawing rooms of the everyday. Ada *became* her designs, a walking advertisement for them. The floral day dress, the tailored suit, the manicured nails and the simple court shoes, she knew she was watched as she left the shop and sauntered west down Piccadilly, past the Ritz and Green Park. She would *clip-clop* along, chin in the air, pretending she might live in Knightsbridge or Kensington, until she knew she was free of curious eyes. Then finally she turned south, *clip-clopped* over Westminster Bridge and into Lambeth and past the sniggering urchins who stuck their noses in the air and teetered behind her on imaginary heels.

★   ★   ★

15

Late April, black rain fell in turrets and drummed on the slate roofs of Dover Street. Torrents, scooped from the oceans and let loose from the heavens, thundered down to earth and soaked deep into the cracks between the paving, fell in dark rivers along the gutters, eddied in dips in the pavements and in the areas of the tall, stuccoed houses. It splattered off the umbrellas and sombre hats of the pedestrians and soaked the trouser legs below the raincoats. It seeped into the leather of the shoes.

Ada reached for her coat, a soft camel with a tie belt, and her umbrella. She'd have to bite the bullet today, turn left right away, pick up the number 12 in Haymarket.

'Good night, madame,' she said to Mrs B. She stood under the door frame, then out into the sodden street. She walked towards Piccadilly, looking down, side-stepping the puddles. A gust of wind caught her umbrella and turned it inside out, whipped the sides of her coat so they billowed free and snatched her hair in sopping tentacles. She pulled at the twisted metal spokes.

'Allow me, please,' a man's voice said as a large umbrella positioned itself above her head. She turned round, almost brushed the man's face, an instant too close but long enough for Ada to know. His face was slim, punctuated by a narrow, clipped moustache. He wore small, round glasses and behind them his eyes were soft and pale. *Duck egg blue*, Ada thought, airy enough to see through. They chilled and stirred her. He stepped back.

'I apologize,' he said. 'I was only trying to protect you. Here, you hold this.' He passed over his umbrella and took hold of hers with his free hand. He sounded continental, Ada thought, a sophisticated clip to his accent. Ada watched as he bent it back into shape.

'Not quite as good as new,' he said. 'But it will take care of you today. Where do you live? Do you have far to go?'

She started to answer, but the words tangled in her mouth. Lambeth. *Lambeth.*

'No,' she said. 'Thank you. I'll get the bus.'

'Let me walk you to the stop.'

She wanted to say yes, but she was frightened he'd press her on where she lived. The number 12 went to Dulwich. That was all right. She could say Dulwich, it was respectable enough.

'You're hesitating,' he said. His eyes creased in a smile. 'Your mother told you never to go with strange men.'

She was grateful for the excuse. His accent was formal. She couldn't place it.

'I have a better idea,' he went on. 'I'm sure your mother would approve of this.' He pointed over the road. 'Would you care to join me, Miss? Tea at the Ritz. Couldn't be more English.'

What would be the harm in that? If he was up to no good, he wouldn't waste money at the Ritz. Probably a week's wages. And it was in public, after all.

'I am inviting you,' he said. 'Please accept.'

17

He was polite, well-mannered.

'And the rain will stop in the mean time.'

Ada gathered her senses. 'Will? Will it? How do you know?'

'Because,' he said, 'I command it to.' He shut his eyes, stretched his free arm up above his head, raising his umbrella, and clenched and opened his fist three times.

'*Ein, zwei, drei.*'

Ada didn't understand a word but knew they were foreign. 'Dry?' she said.

'Oh, very good,' he said. 'I like that. So do you accept?'

He was charming. Whimsical. She liked that word. It made her feel light and carefree. It was a diaphanous word, like a chiffon veil.

Why not? None of the boys she knew would ever dream of asking her to the Ritz.

'Thank you. I would enjoy that.'

He took her elbow and guided her across the road, through the starlit arches of the Ritz, into the lobby with its crystal chandeliers and porcelain jardinières. She wanted to pause and look, take it all in, but he was walking her fast along the gallery. She could feel her feet floating along the red carpet, past vast windows festooned and ruched in velvet, through marble columns and into a room of mirrors and fountains and gilded curves.

She had never seen anything so vast, so rich, so shiny. She smiled, as if this was something she was used to every day.

'May I take your coat?' A waiter in a black suit with a white apron.

'It's all right,' Ada said, 'I'll keep it. It's a bit wet.'

'Are you sure?' he said. A sticky ring of heat began to creep up her neck and Ada knew she had blundered. In this world, you handed your clothes to valets and flunkeys and maids.

'No,' the words tripped out, 'you're right. Please take it. Thank you.' Wanted to say, don't lose it, the man in Berwick Street market said it was real camel hair, though Ada'd had her doubts. She shrugged the coat off her shoulders, aware that the waiter in the apron was peeling it from her arms and draping it over his. Aware, too, that the nudge of her shoulders had been slow and graceful.

'What is your name?' the man asked.

'Ada. Ada Vaughan. And yours?'

'Stanislaus,' he said. 'Stanislaus von Lieben.'

A foreigner. She'd never met one. It was – she struggled for the word – exotic.

'And where does that name come from, when it's at home?'

'Hungary,' he said. 'Austria-Hungary. When it was an empire.'

Ada had only ever heard of two empires, the British one that oppressed the natives and the Roman one that killed Christ. It was news to her that there were more.

'I don't tell many people this,' he said, leaning towards her. 'In my own country, I am a count.'

19

'Oh my goodness.' Ada couldn't help it. A *count*. 'Are you really? With a castle, and all?' She heard how common she sounded. Maybe he wouldn't notice, being a foreigner.

'No.' He smiled. 'Not every count lives in a castle. Some of us live in more modest circumstances.'

His suit, Ada could tell, was expensive. Wool. Super 200, she wouldn't be surprised. Grey. Well tailored. Discreet.

'What language were you talking, earlier, in the street?'

'My mother tongue,' he said. 'German.'

'German?' Ada swallowed. Not all Germans are bad, she could hear her father say. Rosa Luxemburg. A martyr. And those who're standing up to Hitler. Still, Dad wouldn't like a German speaker in the house. *Stop it, Ada.* She was getting ahead of herself.

'And you?' he said. 'What were you doing in Dover Street?'

Ada wondered for a moment whether she could say she was visiting her dressmaker, but then thought better of it.

'I work there,' she said.

'How very independent,' he said. 'And what do you work at?'

She didn't like to say she was a tailoress, even if it was bespoke, ladies. Couldn't claim to be a *modiste*, like Madame Duchamps, not yet. She said the next best thing.

'I'm a mannequin, actually.' Wanted to add, an *artiste*.

He leant back in the chair. She was aware of how his eyes roamed over her body as if she was a landscape to be admired, or lost in.

'Of course,' he said. 'Of course.' He pulled out a gold cigarette case from his inside pocket, opened it, and leant forward to Ada. 'Would you like a cigarette?'

She didn't smoke. She wasn't sophisticated like that. She didn't know what to do. She didn't want to take one and end up choking. That would be too humiliating. Tea at the Ritz was full of pitfalls, full of reminders of how far she had to go.

'Not just now, thank you,' she said.

He tapped the cigarette on the case before he lit it. She heard him inhale and watched as the smoke furled from his nostrils. She would like to be able to do that.

'And where are you a mannequin?'

Ada was back on safer ground. 'At Madame Duchamps.'

'Madame Duchamps. Of course.'

'You know her?'

'My great-aunt used to be a customer of hers. She died last year. Perhaps you knew her?'

'I haven't been there very long,' she said. 'What was her name?'

Stanislaus laughed and Ada noticed he had a glint of gold in his mouth. 'I couldn't tell you,' he said. 'She was married so many times, I couldn't keep up.'

'Perhaps that's what killed her,' she said. 'All that marrying.'

It would, if *her* parents were anything to go by. She knew what they would think of Stanislaus and his great-aunt. Morals of a hyena. That was Germany for you. But Ada was intrigued by the idea. A woman, a *loose* woman. She could smell her perfumed body, see her languid gestures as her body shimmied close and purred for affection.

'You're funny,' Stanislaus said. 'I like that.'

It had stopped raining by the time they left, but it was dark.

'I should escort you home,' he said.

'There's no need, really.'

'It's the least a gentleman can do.'

'Another time,' she said, realizing how forward that sounded. 'I didn't mean that. I mean, I have to go somewhere else. I'm not going straight home.'

She hoped he wouldn't follow her.

'Another time it is,' he said. 'Do you like cocktails, Ada Vaughan? Because the Café Royal is just round the corner and is my favourite place.'

Cocktails. Ada swallowed. She was out of her depth. But she'd learn to swim, she'd pick it up fast.

'Thank you,' she said, 'and thank you for tea.'

'I know where you work,' he said. 'I will drop you a line.'

He clicked his heels, lifted his hat and turned. She

watched as he walked back down Piccadilly. She'd tell her parents she was working late.

Martinis, Pink Ladies, Mint Juleps. Ada grew to be at ease in the Café Royal, and the Savoy, Smith's and the Ritz. She bought rayon in the market at trade price and made herself some dresses after work at Mrs B.'s. Cut on the bias, the cheap synthetic fabrics emerged like butterflies from a chrysalis and hugged Ada into evening elegance. Long gloves and a cocktail hat. Ada graced the chicest establishments with confidence.

'Swept you off your feet, he has,' Mrs B. would say each Friday as Ada left work to meet Stanislaus. Mrs B. didn't like gentlemen calling at her shop in case it gave her a bad name, but she saw that Stanislaus dressed well and had class, even if it was *foreign* class. 'So be careful.'

Ada twisted rings from silver paper and paraded her left hand in front of the mirror when no one was looking. She saw herself as Stanislaus's wife, Ada von Lieben. Count and *Countess* von Lieben. 'I hope his intentions are honourable,' Mrs B.'d said. 'Because I've never known a gentleman smitten so fast.'

Ada just laughed.

'Who is he then?' her mother said. 'If he was a decent fellow, he'd want to meet your father and me.'

'I'm late, Mum,' Ada said. Her mother blocked

the hallway, stood in the middle of the passage. She wore Dad's old socks rolled down to her ankles, and her shabby apron was stained in front.

'Bad enough you come home in no fit state on a Friday night, but now you've taken up going out in the middle of the week, whatever next?'

'Why shouldn't I go out of an evening?'

'You'll get a name,' her mother said. 'That's why. He'd better not try anything on. No man wants second-hand goods.'

Her mouth set in a scornful line. She nodded as if she knew the world and all its sinful ways.

You know nothing, Ada thought.

'For goodness sake,' Ada said. 'He's not like that.'

'Then why don't you bring him home? Let your father and I be the judge of that.'

He'd never have set foot inside a two-up two-down terrace that rattled when the trains went by, with a scullery tagged on the back and an outside privy. He wouldn't understand that she had to sleep in the same bed with her sisters, while her brothers lay on mattresses on the floor, the other side of the dividing curtain Dad had rigged up. He wouldn't know what to do with all those kids running about. Her mother kept the house clean enough but sooty grouts clung to the nets and coated the furniture and sometimes in the summer the bugs were so bad they had to sit outside in the street.

24

Ada couldn't picture him here, not ever.

'I have to go,' Ada said. 'Mrs B. will dock my wages.'

Her mother snorted. 'If you'd come in at a respectable time,' she said, 'you wouldn't be in this state now.'

Ada pushed past her, out into the street.

'I hope you know what you're doing,' her mother yelled for all the neighbours to hear.

She had to run to the bus stop, caught the number 12 by the skin of her teeth. She'd had no time for breakfast and her head ached. Mrs B. would wonder what had happened. Ada had never been late for work before, never taken time off. She rushed along Piccadilly. The June day was already hot. It would be another scorcher. Mrs B. should get a fan, cool the shop down so they weren't all picking pins with sticky fingers.

'Tell her, Ada,' one of the other girls said. Poisonous little cow called Avril, common as a brown penny. 'We're all sweating like pigs.'

'Pigs sweat,' Ada had said. 'Gentlemen perspire. Ladies glow.'

'Get you,' Avril said, sticking her finger under her nose.

Avril could be as catty as she liked. Ada didn't care. Jealous, most likely. *Never trust a woman*, her mother used to say. Well, her mother was right on that one. Ada had never found a woman she could call her best friend.

The clock at Fortnum's began to strike the quarter hour and Ada started to run, but a figure walked out, blocking her way.

'Thought you were never coming.' Stanislaus straddled the pavement in front of her, arms stretched wide like an angel. 'I was about to leave.'

She let out a cry, a puppy whine of surprise. He'd come to meet her, before work. She knew she was blushing, heat prickling her cheeks. She fanned her hand across her face, thankful for the cool air. 'I'm late for work,' she said. 'I can't chat.'

'I thought you could take the day off,' he said. 'Pretend you're sick or something.'

'I'd lose my job if she ever found out.'

'Get another,' he said, shrugging his shoulders. Stanislaus had never had to work, couldn't understand how hard she'd struggled to get where she was. Ada Vaughan, from Lambeth, working with a *modiste*, in Mayfair. 'How will she find out?'

He stepped forward and, cupping her chin in his hand, brushed his lips against hers. His touch was delicate as a feather, his fingers warm and dry round her face. She leant towards him, couldn't help it, as if he was a magnet and she his dainty filings.

'It's a lovely day, Ada. Too nice to be cooped up inside. You need to live a little. That's what I always say.' She smelled cologne on his cheeks, tart, like lingering lemon. 'You're late already. Why bother going in now?'

Mrs B. was a stickler. Ten minutes and she'd dock

half a day's wages. Ada couldn't afford to lose that much money. There was a picnic basket on the pavement beside Stanislaus. He'd got it all planned.

'Where had you in mind?'

'Richmond Park,' he said. 'Make a day of it.'

The whole day. Just the two of them.

'What would I say to her?' Ada said.

'Wisdom teeth,' Stanislaus said. 'That's always a good one. That's why there are so many dentists in Vienna.'

'What's that got to do with it?'

'It's a toff's complaint.'

She'd have to remember that. *Toffs* had wisdom teeth. *Somebodies* had wisdom teeth.

'Well,' she hesitated. She'd lost half a day's wages already. 'All right then.' Might as well be hung for a sheep as a lamb.

'That's my Ada.' He picked up the picnic basket with one hand, put his other round her waist.

She'd never been to Richmond Park, but she couldn't tell him that. He was sophisticated, travelled. He could have had his pick of women – well-bred, upper-class women, women like the debutantes she clothed and flattered and who kept Mrs B. in business. Ahead of her the park gates rose in ornate spears. Below, the river curled through lush green woods to where the distant, dusty downs of Berkshire merged into slabs of pearl and silver against the sky. The sun was already high, its warm rays embracing her as if she was the only person in the world, the only one who mattered.

They entered the park. London was spread before them, St Paul's and the City cast in hazy silhouette. The ground was dry, the paths cracked and uneven. Ancient oaks with blasted trunks and chestnuts with drooping catkins rose like forts from the tufted grassland and fresh, spiky bracken. The air was filled with a sweet, cloying scent. Ada crinkled her nose.

'That's the smell of trees making love,' Stanislaus said.

Ada put her hand to her mouth. *Making love*. No one she knew talked about that sort of thing. Maybe her mother was right. He'd brought her here for a purpose. He was *fast*. He laughed.

'You didn't know that, did you? Chestnuts have male and female flowers. I guess it's the female that gives off the smell. What do you think?'

Ada shrugged. Best ignore it.

'I like chestnuts,' he went on. 'Hot chestnuts on a cold winter's day. Nothing like it.'

'Yes.' She was on safe ground. 'I like them too. Conkers, and all.'

And all. Common.

'Different sort of chestnut,' he said.

How was Ada to know? There was so much to learn. Had he noticed how ignorant she was? He didn't show it. A gentleman.

'We'll stop here, by the pond.' He put down the hamper and pulled out a cloth, flicking it so it filled with air like a flying swan, before falling to the earth. If she'd known she was going to have to sit on the ground, she'd have worn her sundress with the full skirt, enough to tuck round so she didn't show anything. She lowered herself, pulled her knees together, bent them to the side and tugged her dress down as best she could.

'Very ladylike,' Stanislaus said. 'But that's what you are, Ada, a real lady.' He poured two beakers of ginger beer, passed one to her and sat down. 'A lovely lady.'

No one had ever called her lovely before. But then, she'd never had a boy before. *Boy*. Stanislaus was a man. Mature, experienced. At least thirty, she guessed. Maybe older. He reached forward and handed Ada a plate and a serviette. There was a proper word for serviette, but Ada had forgotten it. They never had much use for things like that in Theed Street. He pulled out some chicken, *what a luxury*, and some fresh tomatoes, and a tiny salt and pepper set.

'*Bon appétit*,' he said, smiling.

Ada wasn't sure how she could eat the chicken without smearing grease over her face. This was all new to her. *Picnics*. She picked at it, pulling off shards of flesh, placing them in her mouth.

'You look a picture,' Stanislaus said. 'Demure. Like one of those models in *Vogue*.'

Ada began to blush again. She rubbed her hand over her neck, hoping to steady the colour, hoping Stanislaus had not noticed. 'Thank you,' she said.

'No,' Stanislaus went on, 'I mean it. The first time I saw you I knew you had class. Everything about you. Your looks, the way you held yourself, the way you dressed. Chic. Original. Then when you told me you *made* the clothes. Well! You'll go far, Ada, believe me.'

He leant on one elbow, stretched out his legs, plucked a blade of grass and began to flutter it on her bare leg. 'You know where you belong?' he said.

She shook her head. The grass tickled. She longed for him to touch her again, run his finger against her skin, feel the breeze of a kiss.

'You belong in Paris. I can see you there, sashaying down the boulevards, turning heads.'

Paris. How had Stanislaus guessed? House of Vaughan. Mrs B. said *maison* was French for house. *Maison Vaughan.*

'I'd like to go to Paris,' Ada said. 'Be a real *modiste*. A couturier.'

'Well, Ada,' he said, 'I like a dreamer. We'll have to see what we can do.'

Ada bit her lip, held back a yelp of excitement.

He pushed himself upright and sat with his elbows on his knees. He lifted one arm and pointed to the deep bracken on the right. 'Look.' His voice was hushed. 'A stag. A big one.'

Ada followed his gaze. It took her a while, but she spotted it, head proud above the bracken, the fresh buds of antlers on its crown.

'They grow them in the spring,' he said. 'A spur

for every year. That one will have a dozen by the end of the summer.'

'I never knew that,' Ada said.

'Bit of a loner, this time of year,' Stanislaus continued. 'But come the autumn, he'll build a harem. Fight off the competition. Have all the women to himself.'

'That doesn't sound very proper,' Ada said. 'I wouldn't want to share my husband.'

Stanislaus eyed her from the side. She knew then it was a silly thing to say. Stanislaus, man of the world, with his much-married aunt.

'It's not about the women,' he said. 'It's about the men. Survival of the fittest, that's what it's about.'

Ada wasn't sure what he meant.

'Wisdom teeth,' Ada said.

Mrs B. raised a painted eyebrow. 'Wisdom teeth?' she said. 'Don't try to pull the wool over my eyes.'

'I'm not.'

'I wasn't born yesterday,' Mrs B. said. 'You weren't the only one skiving off. Nice summer's day. I've given Avril her marching orders.'

Ada swallowed. She should never have let Stanislaus persuade her. Mrs B. was going to sack her. She'd have no work. How would she tell her mother? She'd have to get another position, before the day was out. *Guess what, Mum? I've changed my job.* She'd lie, of course. *Mrs B. didn't have enough work for me.*

'You knew there were big orders coming in. How did you think I was supposed to cope?'

'I'm sorry,' Ada said. She cupped her hand around her cheek, as Stanislaus had done, remembered the cool tenderness of his touch. *Stick with the excuse.* 'It was swollen. It hurt too much.'

Mrs B. harrumphed. 'If it had been any one of the other girls, you'd be out on your ear by now. It's only because you're good and I need you that I'll let you stay.'

Ada dropped her hand. 'Thank you,' she said. Her body relaxed into relief. 'I'm very sorry. I didn't mean to let you down. It won't happen again.'

'If it does,' Mrs B. said, 'there'll be no second chance. Now, get back to work.'

Ada walked towards the door of Mrs B.'s office, hand poised on the handle.

'You're really good, Ada,' Mrs B. called. Ada turned to face her. 'You're the most talented young woman I've known. Don't throw away your chances on a man.'

Ada swallowed, nodded.

'I won't be so tolerant next time,' Mrs B. added.

'Thank you,' Ada said and smiled.

Ada stretched her slender fingers, took a cigarette and drew it to her lips. Legs crossed and wound round each other like the coils of a rope. She breathed in, inclined her head with the smile of a saint, and watched as the plumes of smoke furled from her nostrils. She leant forward and picked up her Martini glass. The Grill Room. Plush, red seats, golden ceilings. She glanced in the mirrors and saw herself and Stanislaus reflected a thousand times. They became other people in the infinity of glass, a man in an elegant suit and a woman in Hollywood cerise.

'You're very beautiful,' Stanislaus said.

'Am I?' Ada hoped she sounded *nonchalant*, another word she'd picked up at Mrs B.'s.

'You could drive a chap to distraction.'

She uncurled her legs, leant forward and tapped his knee. 'Behave.'

A whirlwind romance, that's what *Woman's Own* would call it. A swirling gale of love that snagged her in its force. She adored Stanislaus. 'It's our anniversary,' she said.

'Oh?'

'Fourteenth of July. Three months.' Ada nodded. 'Three months since I met you that day in April, in the pouring rain.'

'Anniversary?' Stanislaus said. He smiled, a crooked curl of his lip. Ada knew that look. He was thinking. 'Then we should go away. Celebrate. Somewhere romantic. Paris. *Paree.*'

Paris. *Paree.* She longed to see Paris, hadn't stopped thinking about it, since that day in Richmond Park.

'How about it?'

She never thought he'd suggest going away so soon. Not now, with all this talk of Hitler and bomb shelters. 'Isn't there going to be a war?' she said. 'Perhaps we should wait a bit.'

'War?' He shook his head. 'There's not going to be a war. That's just all talk. Hitler's got what he wants. Claimed back his bits of Germany. He's not greedy. Believe me.'

That wasn't what her father said, but Stanislaus was educated. He was bound to know more.

'You said you wanted to go,' Stanislaus continued. 'You could see some real French couture. Get ideas. Try them out here. You'd soon make a name for yourself.'

Ada opened her mouth to speak but her tongue rucked up like a bolster. She bit her lip and nodded, calculating quickly. Her parents would never let her go to Paris, not with all this talk of war, much less let her go with a *man*. They knew she was courting, but even so. She knew they wouldn't like a foreigner. She told them he brought her home each night, made sure she was safely back. She told him her parents were invalids and couldn't have visitors. She'd have to miss work, invent some excuse for going away otherwise she'd get the sack. What would she say to Mrs B.?

'Do you have a passport?' Stanislaus said.

A passport. 'No,' she said. 'How do I get one of those?'

'This isn't my country.' Stanislaus was smiling. 'But my English friends tell me there is an office which issues them, in Petty France.'

'I'll go tomorrow,' Ada said, 'in my lunch hour.

I'll get one straight away. Will you wait for me?'
She'd tell her parents Mrs B. was sending her to
Paris, to look at the collections, to buy new fabrics.
She'd ask Mrs B. if she would *really* let her do
that.

Only the man in Petty France said she needed a
photograph, and her birth certificate, and seeing
as how she was under twenty-one, her father
needed to complete the form. They could issue it
in twenty-four hours but only in an emergency,
otherwise she'd have to wait six weeks.

'But,' he added, 'we don't advise travel abroad
right now, Miss, not on the Continent. There's
going to be war.'

War. That was all anyone talked about. Stanislaus
never mentioned war, and she liked him for that.
He gave her a good time.

'Can't worry about what's not here.'

The man frowned, shook his head, raised an
eyebrow. Perhaps she was being a bit silly. But
even if war was coming, it was months away yet.

She sniffed and put the papers in her handbag. She couldn't ask her father to fill out the
form. That would be the end of the matter.
She'd never told Stanislaus how old she was, and
he'd never asked. But if he understood she was a
minor, he might get cold feet and lose interest in
her. She was a free spirit, he'd said, he'd spotted
it the first time they met. How could she tell him
otherwise?

The solution came to her that afternoon, watching Mrs B. make out the bill for Lady MacNeice. Ada's father wrote with a slow, careful hand, linking the arms and legs of his letters in a looping waltz. Ada had always been entranced by the way he choreographed his words, had tried to copy him when she was young. It was an easy hand to forge, and the man at Petty France would be none the wiser. She knew it was wrong, but what else could she do? She'd get her likeness taken tomorrow, in her lunch hour. There was a photographer's shop in Haymarket. It would be ready at the weekend. She'd go to the public library on Saturday, fill in the form, take it in person on Monday. It would be ready in a few weeks.

'Then it has to be the Lutetia,' Stanislaus said. 'There is simply no other hotel. Saint-Germain-des-Prés.' He squeezed her hand. 'Have you ever been on a boat?'

'Only on the river.' She'd been on the Woolwich ferry.

'Don't worry,' he said. 'August is a good month to sail. No storms.'

Ada had it worked out. She'd have to tell her parents, but she'd do it after she'd gone. Send them a postcard from Paris so they wouldn't call the police and declare her a Missing Person. She'd have hell to pay when she got back, but by then Stanislaus and she would be engaged in

36

all likelihood. She'd tell Mrs B. she was going to Paris on a holiday and would she like her to bring back some fabric samples, some *tissus*? She'd say it in French. Mrs B. would be grateful, would tell her where to go. *That's kind of you, Mademoiselle, giving up your holiday.* It would give her something to do in Paris, and she could pick up ideas. In the meantime, she'd bring the clothes she planned to take to Paris with her to work, one at a time. She sometimes brought sandwiches for lunch in a small tote bag. It was summer, and the dresses and skirts were light fabrics, rayon or lawn. She knew how to fold them so they wouldn't crease or take up space. She would hide everything in her cupboard at work, the one where she hung her coat in winter and kept a change of shoes. Nobody looked in there. She would need a suitcase. There were plenty in Mrs B.'s boxroom which was never locked. She'd borrow one. She had the keys to the shop. Come in early on the day, pack quickly. Catch the bus to Charing Cross, in good time to meet Stanislaus by the clock.

'Paris?' Mrs B. had said, her voice rising like a klaxon. 'Do your parents know?'

'Of course,' Ada had said. She had shrugged her shoulders and opened her hands. *Of course.*

'But there's going to be a war.'

'Nothing's going to happen,' Ada said, though she'd heard the eerie moans of practice sirens along with everyone else, and watched the air-raid shelter being built in Kennington Park. 'We don't want war. Hitler doesn't want war. The Russians don't want war.' That's what Stanislaus said. He should know, shouldn't he? Besides, what other chance would she have to get to Paris? Her father had a different view about the war but Ada didn't care what he thought. He was even considering signing up for the ARP for defence. *Defence*, he repeated, just so Ada wouldn't think he supported the imperialists' war. He even listened now as her mother read aloud the latest leaflet. *It is important to know how to put on your mask quickly and properly* . . .

'But they're going to evacuate London,' Mrs B. said. 'The little kiddies. In a few days. It was on the wireless.'

Three of her younger brothers and sisters were going, all the way to Cornwall. Mum had done nothing but cry for days, and Dad had stalked the house with his head in his hands. *Pah!* Ada thought. This will blow over. Everyone was so pessimistic. Miserable. They'd be back soon enough. Why should she let this spoil her chances? *Paris.* Mum would come round. She'd buy her something nice. Perfume. Proper perfume, in a bottle.

'I'll be back,' Ada said. 'Bright and early Tuesday morning.' *Engaged.* She had been dreaming about the proposal. Stanislaus on one knee. *Miss Vaughan, would you do me the honour of* . . . 'We're only going for five days.'

'I hope you're right,' Mrs B. said. 'Though if you were my daughter, I wouldn't let you out of my sight. War's coming any day now.' She waved her hands at the large plate-glass windows of her shop, crisscrossed with tape to protect them if the glass shattered, and at the black-out blinds above.

'And your fancy man,' she added. 'Which side will he be on?'

Ada hadn't given that a thought. She'd assumed he was on their side. He lived here, after all. But if he spoke German, perhaps he'd fight with Germany, would leave her here and go back home. She'd follow him, of course. If they were to be married, she'd be loyal to him, stay by his side, no matter what.

'Only in the last war,' Mrs B. went on, 'they locked the Germans up, the ones who were here.'

'He's not *actually* German,' Ada said. 'Just speaks it.'

'And why's he over here?'

Ada shrugged. 'He likes it.' She had never asked him. No more than she had asked what he did for a living. There was no need. He was a count. But if they locked him up, that wouldn't be so bad. She could visit and he wouldn't have to fight. He wouldn't die and the war wouldn't last forever.

'Perhaps he's a spy,' Mrs B. said, 'and you're his cover.'

'If that's the case,' Ada said, hoping her voice didn't wobble, 'all the more reason to enjoy myself.'

'Well,' Mrs B. said, 'if you know what you're

doing . . .' She paused and gave a twisted smile. 'As a matter of fact, there are one or two places you might care to visit in Paris.' She pulled out a piece of paper from the drawer in her desk and began to write.

Ada took the piece of paper, *Rue Dorsel, Place St Pierre, Boulevard Barbès.*

'I haven't been to Paris for so long,' she said. There was a wistfulness in her voice which Ada hadn't heard before. 'These places are mostly in Montmartre, on the Right bank.' Stanislaus had talked about the Seine. 'So be careful.'

Their hotel was on the Left bank, where the artists lived.

Charing Cross station was a heaving tangle of nervy women and grizzling children, cross old people, worried men checking their watches, bewildered young boys in uniforms. Territorial Army, Ada guessed, or reservists. Sailors and soldiers. The occasional ARP volunteer elbowed his way through the crowd, *Keep to the left.* People took them seriously now, *Air Raid Precaution,* as if they really did have a job to do. A train to Kent was announced and the shambles surged forward, a giant slug of humanity. Ada stood her ground, shoved back against the crowd, banged her suitcase against other people's shins. *Watch out, Miss.* The frenzy of the scene matched her mood. *What if he wasn't there? What if she missed him?* She realized that she had no way of contacting him. He didn't

40

have a telephone. He lived in Bayswater, but she didn't know his address. A woman pushed past her with two children, a boy in grey short trousers and a white shirt, a girl in a yellow, smocked dress. In fact, Ada thought, she knew very little about Stanislaus. She didn't even know how old he was. He was an only child, he'd told her. Both his parents were dead, as was his much-married aunt. She had no idea why he had come to England. Maybe he *was* a spy.

This was daft. She shouldn't go. She hardly knew him. Her mother had warned her. White slave trade. Stick a pin in you so you fainted and woke up in a harem. And all these people. Soldiers. ARP. There really *was* going to be a war. Stanislaus was wrong. Maybe he was a spy. The enemy. She shouldn't go.

She spotted him. He was leaning against a pillar in a navy blue blazer and white slacks, a leather grip at his feet. She took a deep breath. He hadn't seen her. She could turn round, go home. There was time.

But then he saw her, grinned, pushed himself forward, lifted his bag and swung it over his shoulder. *A spy.* A sharp prickle of heat crept up Ada's neck. She watched as he wove his way towards her. It would be fine. Everything would be all right. He was a handsome man, despite his glasses. An honest man, anyone could see that. A man of means too. Nothing to worry about. Silly of her. His face was creased in a broad smile. He walked faster, pleased to see her. This, Paris, was happening to *her*, Ada Vaughan, of Theed Street, Lambeth, just by the Peabody buildings.

The Gare du Nord was full of the same sweating turmoil as Charing Cross, except the station was hotter and stuffier, and the crowds noisier and more unruly. Ada was transfixed. *Why don't they line up? Why do they shout?* She was tired from the journey, too. She hadn't slept the night before, and there wasn't a seat to be had on the train to Dover. The crossing had made her queasy and the view of the white cliffs receding into a faint stripe of land had unsettled her in ways she hadn't expected. Worry hammered in her head. *What if war did come? What if they were stuck here?* She couldn't ignore the scrolls of barbed wire on the beaches ready to snare and rip the enemy. The hungry seagulls hovering over the deserted pebbles and bundles of scabby tar waiting for their morsels of flesh. The battleships in the Channel. Destroyers, Stanislaus called them, hovering hulks of metal, grey as the water.

Then Stanislaus had given her a ring.

'I hope it fits.' He pushed it onto her third finger. A single band of gold. Not real gold, Ada could tell that straight away.

'You'd better wear it,' he said. This was not how she imagined he would propose, and this, she knew, was not a proposal. Her stomach churned and she leant over the side of the ship.

'I've booked the room under Mr and Mrs von Lieben.'

'*The* room?' Her voice was weak.

'Of course. What else did you think?'

She wasn't that kind of a girl. Didn't he know that? She wanted to save herself for their wedding night. He wouldn't respect her otherwise. But she couldn't run away. She had no money. He was paying for all of this, *of course* he'd expect something in return. Mrs B. had hinted as much.

Stanislaus was laughing. 'What's the matter?'

She leant over the side of the ship, hoping the breezes would sweep out the panic lodged inside her head like a cannon ball. She was not ready for this. She thought he was a gentleman. Those society women, they were all loose. That's what her father always said. Stanislaus thought she was one of them. Didn't he see it was all a sham? The way she dressed, the way she spoke. A sham, all of it. She took a deep breath, smarted as the salty air entered her lungs. Stanislaus placed his arm round her shoulders. *Free spirit.* He pulled her close, cupped her face in his hand, tilted it towards him, and kissed her.

Perhaps this was what it took, to become a woman.

The hotelier apologized. They were so busy, what with all these artists and musicians, refugees, you know how it is, *Monsieur, Madame* . . . The room was small. There were two single beds, with ruched covers. Two beds. What a relief. There

43

was a bathroom next to the bedroom, with black and white tiles and a lavatory that flushed. The room had a small balcony that looked over Paris. Ada could see the Eiffel Tower.

By night, Paris was as dark as London. By day, the sun was hot and the sky clear. They wandered through the boulevards and squares and Ada tried not to pay attention to the sandbags or the noisy, nervous laughs from the pavement cafés, or the young soldiers in their tan uniforms and webbing. She fell in love with the city. She was already in love with Stanislaus. Ada Vaughan, here, in Paris, walking out with the likes of a foreign count.

He held her hand, or linked her arm in his, said to the world, *my* girl, said to her, 'I'm the happiest man.'

'And I'm the happiest woman.'

Breeze of a kiss. They slept in separate beds.

Left bank. Right bank. Montmartre. *Rue Dorsel, Place St Pierre, Boulevard Barbès.* Ada caressed the silks against her cheek, embraced the soft charmeuse against her skin and left traces on velvet pile where she'd run her fingers over. Stanislaus bought her some moiré in a fresh, pale green which the *monsieur* had called *chartreuse.* That evening Ada crossed the length across her breasts, draped the silk round her legs and secured it with a bow at her waist. Her naked shoulder blades marked the angles of her frame and in the bathroom mirror she could see how the eye would be drawn along

44

the length of her back and rest on the gentle curve of her hips.

'That,' Stanislaus said, 'is genius.' And ordered two brandy and chartreuse cocktails to celebrate.

Ada stared with hungry eyes at the Chanel *atelier* in the rue Cambon.

'Bit of a rough diamond, she was,' Stanislaus said. Sometimes his English was so good Ada forgot he was foreign. 'Started in the gutter.'

He didn't mean it unkindly, and the story Stanislaus told gave Ada heart. Poor girl made good, against the odds.

'Mind you,' Stanislaus winked, 'she had a wealthy male admirer or two who set her up in business.'

Distinctive style. A signature, she thought, that's the word. Like Chanel. *A signature*, something that would mark out the House of Vaughan. And help from an admirer, if that's what it took too.

'Paris,' she said to Stanislaus, as they strolled back arm in arm through the Luxembourg Gardens, 'is made for me.'

'Then we should stay,' Stanislaus said, and kissed her lightly again. She wanted to shriek *Yes, forever.*

On their last morning they were woken by sirens. For a moment Ada thought she was back in London. Stanislaus pushed himself off his bed, opened the metal shutters and stepped onto the balcony. A shard of daylight illuminated the carpet and the end of her bed, and Ada could see, through the open doors, that the blue sky was no longer fresh and washed. They must have overslept.

'It's very quiet out there,' Stanislaus called from outside. 'Unnatural.' He came in through the open door. 'Perhaps it was the real thing.'

'Well, we're leaving today.'

They were going home and Stanislaus hadn't proposed, nor had he taken advantage of her. That would count for nothing if she had to tell her parents. She would lie. She had it worked out. Mrs B. had sent her to Paris with one of the other girls, for work. They'd shared a room. The hotel was ever so posh.

'Get up,' Stanislaus said. His voice was clipped, agitated. He was pulling on his clothes. Ada swung her legs over the side of the bed.

'Wait here,' he said. She heard him open the lock, shut the door behind him. She sauntered into the bathroom and turned on the taps and watched as the steaming water fell and tumbled in eddies in the bath, melting the salts she sprinkled in. How could she go home to a galvanized tub in the kitchen? A once-a-week dip with the bar of Fairy?

An hour passed. The water grew cool. Ada sat up, making waves that washed over the side and onto the cork mat on the floor. She stepped out, reached for the towel, wrapped herself in its fleece, embracing the soft tufts of cotton for the last time. Paris. *I will return.* Learn French. It wouldn't take long. She had already picked up a few phrases, *merci, s'il vous plait, au revoir.*

She stepped into the bedroom and put on her slip and knickers. She'd organize a proper *trousseau* for when she and Stanislaus married. He'd have to pay, of course. On her wages, she could barely afford drawers. She'd buy a *chemise* or two, and a *negligee*. Just three days in Paris and she knew a lot of words. She glanced at the bedside clock. Stanislaus had been gone a long time. She flung open the wardrobe doors. She'd wear the diagonal striped dress today, with the puffed sleeves and the tie at the neck. It had driven her mad, matching up all the stripes, so wasteful on the fabric, but it was worth it. She looked at herself in the mirror. The diagonals, dark green and white, rippled in rhythm with her body, lithe like a cat. She sucked in her cheeks, more alluring. She was grateful that Stanislaus left the room when she dressed in the morning, or undressed at night. A true gentleman.

There was a soft knock on the door – their signal – but Stanislaus barged in without waiting for her to reply. 'There's going to be war.' His face was ashen and drawn.

Her body went cold, clammy, even though the room was warm. War wasn't supposed to happen. 'It's been declared?'

'Not yet,' Stanislaus said. 'But the officers I spoke to in the hotel said they were mobilized, ready. Hitler's invaded Poland.'

There was an edge to his voice which Ada had never heard before.

War. She'd batted off the talk as if it were a wasp.

47

But it had hovered over her all her life and she had learned to live with its vicious sting. It was the only time her father wept, each November, homburg hat and funeral coat, words gagging in the gases of memory, his tall frame shrinking. He sang a hymn for his brother, lost in the Great War. Brave enough to die but all they gave him was the Military Medal, not good enough for the bloody Cross. He had only been seventeen. *Oh God, our help in ages past . . .*

War. Her mother prayed for Ada's other uncles whom she'd never met, swallowed in the hungry maws of Ypres or the Somme, missing presumed dead, buried in the mud of the battlefields. A whole generation of young men, gone. That's why Auntie Lily never married, and Auntie Vi became a nun. That was the only time her mother swore, then. Such a bleeding waste. And what for? Ada couldn't think of a worse way to die than drowning in a quagmire.

'We have to go home,' she said. Her mind was racing and she could hear her voice breaking. War. It was real, all of a sudden. 'Today. We must let my parents know.' She hoped now they hadn't got her postcard. They'd be worried stiff.

'I sent them a telegram,' Stanislaus said, 'while I was downstairs.'

'A telegram?' Telegrams only came when someone died. They'd go frantic when they saw it.

'They're invalids,' Stanislaus said, 'they must know you're safe.'

She had forgotten she'd told him that. Of course.

'That was,' she stumbled for the word, 'that was very kind. Considerate.'

She was touched. Stanislaus's first thought had been of her, in all of this. And her parents. She felt bad now. She'd told him they were house-bound. She might even have said bedridden. She'd really be in for it now, when she got home. All those lies.

'I sent it to Mrs B. The telegram. I didn't have your address. She can let your parents know. I trust that's OK,' Stanislaus said and added, before she could answer, 'Who's looking after them? I hope you left them in safe hands.'

She nodded, but he was looking at her as if he didn't approve.

They packed in silence. Officers in blue uniforms milled round the hotel lobby. There were soldiers too. Ada had never seen so many. The other guests, many of whom Ada recognized from the restaur-ant, argued in groups or leant, waving and shouting, against the reception desk. Ada was aware of the musk of anxious men, the lust of their adrenalin.

'Follow me.' Stanislaus took her bag. They pushed their way through the crowded lobby and out through the revolving doors.

'Gare du Nord,' he said to a bell boy, who whis-tled for a taxi. The once deserted street with its eerie silence was now full of sound, of scurrying

49

people and thunderous traffic. There were no cabs in sight. Ada had no idea how far it was to the station. She could feel her head begin to tighten. What if they were stuck here in France? Couldn't get home? At last, a taxi hove into view, and the bell boy secured it.

'You didn't pay,' she said to Stanislaus, as they pulled away from the hotel.

'I settled earlier,' he said. 'When I sent the telegram.' She shut her eyes.

A solid wall of people filled the street, men, women and children, old and young, soldiers, policemen. Most of them were carrying suitcases, or knapsacks, all heading in the same direction, to the Gare du Nord. The people were silent, save for the whimper of a baby in a large pram piled high with bags, and the shouts from the police. *Attention! Prenez garde!* No one could move. All of Paris was fleeing.

They had to walk the last kilometre or so. The taxi driver had stopped the cab, shrugged, opened the door, '*C'est impossible*'.

'It's hopeless,' Ada said. 'Is there another way?' People were crowding in behind them now. Ada looked quickly at a side street but saw that that was as thick with people as the main avenue.

'What shall we do?'

Stanislaus thought for a moment. 'Wait for the crowds to pass,' he said. 'They're just panicked. You know what these Latin-types are like.' He tried to smile. 'Excitable. Emotional.'

50

He used their bags as a ram, beat a path to the side. 'We'll have a coffee,' he announced. 'Some food. And try later. Don't worry, old thing.'

Ada would have preferred a cup of tea, brown, two sugars. Coffee was all right, if it was milky enough, but Ada wasn't sure she could ever get used to it. Far from the station, the crowds had finally thinned. They found a small café, in the Boulevard Barbès, with chairs and tables outside.

'This is where we were,' Ada said, 'when I bought the fabric. Just up there.' She pointed along the Boulevard.

Stanislaus sat on the edge of his seat, pulled out his cigarettes, lit one without offering any to Ada. He was distracted, she could see, flicking the ash onto the pavement and taking short, moody puffs. He stubbed out the cigarette, lit another straight away.

'It's all right.' Ada wanted to soothe him. 'We'll get away. Don't worry.'

She laid her hand on his arm but he shook it off.

The waiter brought them their coffee. Stanislaus poured in the sugar, stirred it hard so it slopped on the saucer. She could see the muscles in his jaws clenching, his lips opening and shutting as if he was talking to himself.

'Penny for them.' She had to get him out of this mood. 'Look on the bright side, maybe we'll get to stay in Paris for another day.' She didn't know what else to say. It was not what she wanted, her parents going out of their minds, Mrs B. livid. She could picture her now, gearing up to sack her. She'd done that with one of the other girls who didn't come back from her holidays on time. *Do you think I run a charity?* Right pickle they were in but they were stuck, for the time being. She had no one to turn to, only Stanislaus. The waiter had left some bread on the table, and she dipped it into her coffee, sucking out the sweetness.

'Is there anyone who can help us?' she said.

'How?'

'I don't know.' She shrugged. 'Get us home.' The French wouldn't do that, she was sure, they had enough of their own kind to look after. Stanislaus turned in his seat, put his elbows on the table, and leant towards her. His forehead was creased and he looked worried.

'The truth is, Ada,' he said. 'I can't go back. I'll be locked up.' She drew a breath. Mrs B. had said something like that and all. Ada corrected herself, Mrs B. had said something like that *too*. Mustn't drop her guard, not now, in case Stanislaus left her. *You're not who I thought you were.*

'Why?' Ada said. 'You're not a German. You only speak it.'

'Austria, Hungary,' he said, 'we're all the enemy.'

Ada put her hands in her lap and pulled at her cheap ring, *up, down, up down.* She was stranded. She'd have to go back alone. She wasn't sure she could do that, find the right train. What if they made an announcement and she didn't understand? They did that all the time on the Southern Railway. *We regret to have to inform passengers that the 09.05 Southern Railways train to Broadstairs will terminate at . . .* She'd be stuck. In the middle of a foreign country, all by herself, not speaking French. And even if she got to Calais, how would she find the ferry? What if it wasn't running anymore? What would she do then?

'What will you do?' Her voice came through high and warbling.

'Don't worry about me,' he said. 'I'll be all right.'

It was already late in the afternoon. The waiter came out and pointed at their cups.

'*Fini?*'

Ada didn't understand so she shook her head, wished he'd leave them alone.

'*Encore?*'

She didn't know what it meant, but nodded.

'I can't abandon you,' she said. 'I'll stay here. We'll be all right.' For a moment, she saw them, hand in hand, sauntering through the Tuileries.

Stanislaus hesitated. 'The thing is, old girl.' His voice was slow and quavering and for a fleeting moment he didn't sound foreign, she'd got so used to his accent. 'I have no money. Not now. With the war. I won't be able to wire.'

Ada couldn't imagine Stanislaus without money. He'd never been short of a bob or two, always flashed it round. Surely they wouldn't be poor for long? And anyway being poor in Paris with Stanislaus would be different from being poor in

Lambeth. She felt a surge of love for this man who had swept her off her feet, a warm, comfortable glow of optimism.

'We don't need money,' she said. 'I'll work. I'll look after us.'

The waiter reappeared with two more cups of coffee and placed them on the table, tucking the bill under the ashtray.

'*L'addition,*' he said and added, '*la guerre a commencé.*'

Stanislaus looked up.

'What's he say?' Ada said.

'Something about the war. *Guerre* is French for war.'

The waiter stood to attention. '*La France et le Royaume-Uni déclarent la guerre à l'Allemagne.*'

'It's started,' Stanislaus said.

'Are you sure?'

'Of course I'm bloody sure. I may not know much French, but I understood that.'

He stood up abruptly, knocking the table so their coffee spilled in the saucers. He stepped to the side, as if he was leaving, then turned and sat back down again.

'Would you stay with me?' he said. 'Here, in Paris? We'd get work, the pair of us. Won't be short of money for long.'

Ada had been so sure a few moments ago, but now a wave of panic tightened round her head and fear clawed at her stomach. War. *War.* She wanted to be home. She wanted to sit in the kitchen at the back of the house with her parents and brothers and sisters. She wanted to smell the dank musk of the washing as it dried round the cooking range, to listen to the pots boiling potatoes for tea, to hear her mother thumb the rosary beads and laugh at her father as he mimicked her, *Hail Marx, full of struggle, the revolution is with thee, blessed art thou among working men . . .*

But there was no way she could get home, not by herself. She nodded.

'Would you mind,' Stanislaus said, 'if we used your name?'

'Why?'

'My name's too foreign. The French might lock me away.'

'I don't mind.'

'I'll get rid of my passport,' he was talking fast. 'Pretend I lost it. Or it was stolen. I could be anyone then.' He laughed and the gold in his tooth glinted in the evening sun. He fished in his pockets for some coins to pay the waiter and picked up their bags.

'Come,' he said.

'Where?'

'We have to find somewhere to stay.'

'The hotel,' Ada said. 'We'll go back there.'

Stanislaus put his arm round Ada, and rested his chin on top of her head. 'They're full. They told me. We'll find somewhere else. A little pension house.'

★   ★   ★

55

The room had a bed with a rusty iron frame and sagging mattress covered in stained ticking, a small table, a chair with a broken seat, and some hooks on the wall. The wallpaper had been torn off at some point, but stubborn shreds stuck in corners and above the wainscoting, bumping and rippling with the slumbering bugs beneath.

'I can't stay.' Ada picked up her case and stepped towards the door. Stanislaus had never been poor, didn't understand how low they had fallen.

'I don't know where you'll go then,' Stanislaus said. 'With no money. The hotels will be full. The army have commandeered them.' He sat on the bed, releasing a small cloud of dust. 'Come here.' His voice was soft, tempting. 'It's just till we get back on our feet. I promise you.'

They'd find jobs, move up in the world. She'd done it before, she could do it again.

'What will you do?' she said. 'What job will you look for?'

He shrugged. 'I don't know. I'm not used to working.'

'Not used to working?'

'I've never had to,' he said. She had forgotten. He was a Count. Of course Counts didn't work. They were like Lords and Ladies. Bloody parasites, her father called them. Getting rich on the backs of the poor. For a moment Ada saw him from a different angle, as someone alien. She saw something else too: he was lost, didn't know what to do. He was an innocent and she the streetwise urchin. She felt sorry for him. Pity. She could hear her father snorting. *Pity? Would they ever take pity on you? Did the Tsar pity the peasants? Got what he bloody deserved.*

Ada stood up. She was still wearing the striped dress. A bit crumpled, but she pulled it taut over her body and fished in her handbag for her lipstick. She dapped some on, rubbed her lips together.

'I'll be back,' she said. She had to take charge. She knew where she was going.

Walked into the very first establishment, and landed herself a job. Ada couldn't believe her luck. But she supposed that's what she was: lucky. The wages weren't much, but the work was plentiful. Monsieur Lafitte ran a thriving business. Wholesale, retail, and tailor. He was a congenial man who reminded her of Isidore. He spoke French very fast, but slowed down for Ada, took pains to help her learn the language. Ada filled the vacancy left by Monsieur Lafitte's apprentice, who had enlisted in the army, leaving him with more work than he could handle himself. Although Ada longed to invent new drapes and cuts, and from time to time would suggest a new detail – the twist of a collar, the turn of a pocket – he'd frown and wag his finger. *Non.*

Within a week she and Stanislaus had moved from the filthy room to a small attic, closer to the shop and the better end of the Boulevard Barbès. Between Monsieur Lafitte and the concierge,

Madame Breton, her French became passable and she was talking to customers even.

Ada couldn't quite believe there was a war. It was too quiet, didn't seem real, even though there were more soldiers on the streets and in the bars and cafés. There were stockpiles of sandbags on the corners, and shelters built in the parks and squares. Men and women walked about with gas masks slung over their shoulders.

'Even the prostitutes,' Stanislaus said. 'I wonder how they do it, with those on?'

They hadn't been issued with masks, but Stanislaus conjured two for them, tapping his nose, *ask no questions.* 'I'm in business.' She loved him, with his mystery and his charm and his strange, foreign accent that waxed and waned depending on how excited he was.

From time to time a siren wailed, but nothing came of it and at night the neighbourhood was black and impenetrable. Cloth was scarce, good cloth at least, and Ada began to cut the garments with a narrower fit and a shorter length, and a seam allowance that skimped and scraped.

'What do you do all day when I'm not here?' She and Stanislaus were sitting in the Bar du Sport. They'd been in Paris two months now and were regulars, had taken to having a glass of red wine at night before they ate dinner there. It was a far cry from cocktails at Smith's, but Ada made an effort to dress up. Monsieur Lafitte let her have

58

the remnants and offcuts and, with the new vogue for plain styles and shorter hems, Ada had run up a presentable winter frock for going out and some simple skirts and blouses. Monsieur Lafitte had given her some old clothes that, he said, had belonged to an uncle of his, now deceased, which Ada had remodelled for Stanislaus. Madame Lafitte had given her a winter coat which she had adjusted. Stanislaus would need a coat soon and Monsieur Lafitte had hinted that he might be able to lay his hands on some surplus army fabric. They made ends meet, and Stanislaus had money again.

They had recaptured something of the old days, but with a difference. Now they were man and wife. Not legally, but as good as.

'I'll be gentle,' he'd said the first time, 'and wear a rubber.'

'A what?'

'A johnny. What do you call them?'

Ada didn't know. She'd heard bits and pieces from the girls at Mrs B.'s, but nobody had ever sat her down and said this is what happens on your wedding night. Her mother had talked about the sacrament of marriage and Ada thought it something so holy that babies could be made in ways they couldn't if you weren't married. Stanislaus had laughed. *This bit is for this, and that for that.* She knew it was wrong, not being married, but it seemed natural, sidling close so her body soaked up his male smell and her flesh rippled and melted in his warmth. She knew he'd propose, once the war was over in a few months, make an honest woman of her.

'Are you sure you don't want to go home?' Stanislaus said. Ada shook her head. She was in Paris, with him, and wouldn't wish to be anywhere else in the world. Besides, she hadn't heard from home, even though Stanislaus had said he'd sent another telegram. *All safe. Working in Paris.* Telegrams cost money, she knew, but even so, they could have sent *something*.

After they had eaten, once the evenings had drawn in, there wasn't much to do. There was a blackout, and the streets were empty, the cafés hidden behind closed doors and shuttered blinds. They played rummy, and pontoon. Ada tried to read French, but it was hard-going. The newspapers, as far as she could make out, were full of news about Germany and Russia, speculation about the Americans and complaints about the behaviour of British troops in France. They didn't have so much to talk about now. Stanislaus said she wouldn't understand his business, so she stopped asking. He wasn't interested in her work. What was exciting about turning up a hem and economizing on a cut? She missed home at those moments, her brothers and sisters. Mum and Dad. She even missed the girls at Mrs B.'s. At least they could have had a laugh.

In December, Stanislaus's business began to

take him away for the night. Two or three times a week. Long, lonely evenings with nothing to do. The old iron radiator in their room creaked and tapped. Ada never got used to it, was sure an intruder was there, padding around, waiting to strike. It was all right when Stanislaus was with her, but on those nights when he was out late, she went to bed early to keep warm, with a small candle by the side, *go away, don't come near me*, until she fell asleep. The radiator didn't give much heat and was turned off at ten, so the room grew bitter and cold by dawn. Sometimes a fine layer of ice formed overnight on the bowl of water they kept on the table.

She hoped one day they could afford better lodgings, with a small kitchen, so she could prepare their own food and not always have to eat at the Bar du Sport. She'd have to learn to cook. She knew how to make a mutton stew but it needed pearl barley and Ada wasn't sure you could buy that here. There was other food she could try to make, French food. Omelette, for instance, or a soufflé. She could see herself whisking the eggs, the way she'd seen the cook at the Bar du Sport do.

The kitchen would have an airer too, so that when she did their laundry she could hang it up to dry, and not drape it over the bedstead. Perhaps they'd have a little parlour, with a table and a red chenille cloth, and a mirror. She'd keep it pretty, with fresh flowers, if she could get them, in a jam jar. Her wages weren't much, but with both of them earning money, they'd live a simple life.

But something was changing.

'The thing is, Ada,' he said. 'I need to be in the mood.'

She respected that to begin with, but now it didn't seem right. She touched his face, ran her fingers along his nose to the tickle of his moustache, tapped a rhythm on his lips.

Stanislaus shoved her hand away. 'No, Ada,' he said. 'Not now.'

She heard his breathing, heavy and hard, felt the air squall from his mouth.

'Do you love me?' she said.

'Stop it, Ada.'

He threw back the bed covers and stood up. Ada heard him pull on his trousers, swearing at the buttons in the dark, yank his shirt from the back of the chair, pick up his shoes with an angry slap and slam the door. She lay still on the bed. She shouldn't have said that, shouldn't have thrown herself at him. Her mother said no man respects that. Men like to do the chasing. She'd say she was sorry. He'd come round.

The Stanislaus she met in London had thrilled her with his honeyed talk and feathered touch. He had changed. The war had changed him, the business had changed him. He was out, night after night. She'd have to make more of an effort, make herself more alluring. A new lipstick, if she could afford it. She looked young for her age, she knew.

Her cheeks still had the plumpness of youth. She'd try to look older, more mature. Perhaps that's what Stanislaus wanted, an older woman, an experienced woman. Her hair had grown long. She'd roll it in a pleat round her head, like some of the sophisticated women she'd seen in Paris. He'd love her then. Nobody said marriage would be easy.

Christmas-time she bought Stanislaus some new handkerchiefs and a pipe. Wrapped the presents in newspaper and tied them with a ribbon from Madame Lafitte.

'Thank you, Ada,' he said, putting the gifts on the floor beside the bed. Stanislaus had made her a stocking, one grey sock bulging with walnuts and a small bottle of perfume.

'L'Aimant,' she read. 'Coty.' *Loving.* She knew it. He just couldn't say it. Some men were like that. She dabbed the perfume behind her ears. It was too sweet for her taste, but she liked that he'd thought of her, had taken the trouble to make a stocking, even if it was only full of nuts. Dad did the stockings at home. Brussels sprouts more likely, and a couple of spuds. *Ha ha, got you there.* But he made sure there was an orange in the toe, or a spinning top, and Mum always made them a new outfit for Christmas.

She'd never spent Christmas away from home. She'd have given anything to be back in Theed Street today. Go to Mass, while Dad cooked breakfast. Bacon and egg and fried bread. Then he and the boys would go to the King's Arms for their jug of porter while she and Mum got the meal ready.

Lunch in the Bar du Sport didn't feel or taste like Christmas dinner at home. They'd splashed out on a bottle of wine. *Vin du Pays.* It was thick and heavy, a dark, ruby red. It reminded her of Ribena, and Ada didn't much care for it, but Stanislaus knocked it back as if it was fruit juice and then had a couple of brandies to chase it down.

He patted his stomach, winked at her. 'Nothing like a good meal, is there, Ada?' he said. 'Fancy a game of rummy?'

'That would be nice, Stanislaus,' she said, pushing herself away from the table. Mum would be bringing in the Christmas pudding now. If Dad had got his bonus, he'd get a drop of brandy from the chemist and pour it over. *Turn out the lights.* Put a match to the brandy and bring the pudding to the table in a ball of flaming blue.

'You smell good,' Stanislaus said, opening the door to their room and pulling her towards him. The alcohol was fusty on his breath.

'Are you tipsy, Stanislaus?'

'Just merry, Ada. Merry,' he said. 'Why shouldn't a man get merry at Christmas?'

He crossed his arms around her, squeezed her close. Maybe she should have worn perfume before.

He released his grip and flopped on the bed,

patting the place next to him. Ada took off her dress and stockings and lay down beside him. His eyes were shut and he'd fallen asleep, *put-putting* through velvet lips, one arm raised above his head. Ada watched him as the daylight faded. She should get up, pull the curtains, turn on the light. But the room was quiet, soft in the twilight, and Stanislaus was sleeping. She ran the back of her hand down his cheek, caressing the soft flesh of his skin, the sharp scratch of his whiskers.

He grabbed her wrist, pinching it tight so she yelped. 'Lay off, Ada,' he said. 'I've told you before.' He looked at her as if she was a stranger, then shoved her onto her back. 'Is this what you want?'

He reached for the rubber, fitted it with clumsy fingers, thrust himself into her and pulled away without a sound. He rolled over and fell asleep.

Ada buried her head in the pillow. This wasn't *love,* not like it used to be.

Winter filtered into spring, fizzing flecks of green in the parks and on the trees. Despite the bitter cold, there had been something safe about the winter, tucked beneath the long thick blanket of the blackout. Now the later evenings and brighter days were like a searchlight illuminating everything and Ada jumped whenever an aeroplane droned above. There were more planes flying overhead, and soldiers on the move along the streets and boulevards, *boots, boots*. Ada picked up a newspaper almost every day and Monsieur Lafitte brought his wireless into the shop. Madame Lafitte said that she'd seen British tanks near the Belgian border when she went to visit her sister, lumbering monsters that churned up the roads. Her sister said that the British had sent thousands of men, so they were expecting trouble. Ada couldn't imagine that number. So many young men in uniforms. Who had made them all?

Stanislaus shrugged. 'What will be, will be,' he said. 'We can't stop it.' He was back to his old self, relaxed, happy.

But Ada fretted. War marched with hobnail boots, *left right, left right*. The streets around the Boulevard Barbès filled with refugees, haunted faces in shabby clothing pushing their possessions in a child's pram. Stanislaus didn't seem to notice. Nothing worried him. He was a continental, that's why. Continentals were relaxed. He looked foreign, neat ears close to his skull, short fair hair, his clipped moustache in the centre of his lip, a bit like Hitler, she often thought, though that was the fashion these days. Milky eyes framed by his glasses. He always wore them. She couldn't imagine his face without them. It must have been such a come-down for him, living like this.

'For you, madame.' He pulled a round box from behind his back and presented it to her. She undid the ribbon and pulled out a hat, a lemon straw pillbox with a spotted black veil. 'Your Easter bonnet.'

It didn't go with her winter outfits, and the weather wasn't warm enough yet to put on her summer dress, but Stanislaus had gone out of his way to purchase the hat when goodness knows this kind of raffia was hard to come by now.

She put it on, the veil drawn across her face. A grown-up hat, a woman's hat. 'Thank you,' she said.

'Shall we, as the French say, *faire une promenade*?'

Ada giggled. Stanislaus rarely spoke French, at least not with her. It was always English and even so he often got his 'v' and 'w' muddled, and could never pronounce 'th', however many times she tried to show him. Sometimes he was in a good mood, sometimes not. He'd taken to putting the bolster down the middle of the bed, his side, hers.

Two weeks after Easter, Germany invaded Norway, *neutral* Norway. There was news of resistance and fighting, of British troops sent in to help. Endless *blah blah* on the wireless about the Maginot Line and what to do if Germany invaded France. Refugees needed to be vetted. Sympathizers would be shot. It was the duty of France to stand up and fight back.

Her neighbours' faces were pinched and Monsieur and Madame Lafitte looked gaunt and frail. A smell began to permeate the Paris air. It oozed from the pores of women and mouths of screaming babies, from grown men and from the hairs of dogs pissing on the lamp-posts. Ada sniffed it in her nostrils, on her clothes, from Stanislaus as he lay on his side of the bed at night. Ada knew it now, the stale onion of fear.

There was talk of rationing. She wondered whether Stanislaus would change his mind, if she could persuade him to leave. They should go home, find a way to England. Monsieur Lafitte was hinting that it was time he retired, now the work was getting thin, and he didn't want to start making army uniforms, not at his age. What if she lost her job? What then?

'You shouldn't be here,' he said one day. 'A young girl like you. It's too dangerous. Go home. While you can.'

She thought of where her parents lived, close to the river with its docks and ports, of her younger brothers and sisters, living goodness knows where in the country, of her Mum, thin with worry, and Stanislaus out till late, leaving Ada with nothing to do but gnaw at her anxieties like a fox in a trap.

Stanislaus came back one night in May with a bloodied nose and broken lip, his spectacles twisted and crooked on his nose.

'Pack,' he said. 'We have to leave.'

'What happened?'

He splashed water from the basin on his face. Drops fell onto the table, washed pale and pink. There was blood on the towel he dried himself with.

'What happened?' Ada said again. 'Did someone hit you?'

'It doesn't matter,' he said. 'Just pack. Now.'

She moved to dab at his cuts with the cloth but he grabbed her hand and forced it away.

'Pack,' he shouted. 'Now.'

She knew he only raised his voice when he was worried. Perhaps someone had thought he was a German.

'Are you listening? We must go.'

He took her suitcase from the top of the wardrobe and flung it on the bed. She opened it, took out a dress from the cupboard, started to fold it. He snatched it from her, threw it into the case.

'No time for that.' He scooped up the rest of her clothes, grabbed her hat and shoved it in, yanked her underwear from the bedpost where it had been drying, tossed it on top and slammed the case shut. 'Come on.'

He hadn't packed a thing. She followed him down the stairs, racing, two at a time. She'd trip if she tried to keep up. She held the banister to steady herself. 'But where—'

'Shut up,' he said.

The concierge had gone home for the night, the blind pulled down, her office dark and vacant. They walked out of the building, through the courtyard, into the street, and up to a black car parked nearby, a car she'd never seen before. He lifted the boot, put the suitcase inside and opened the passenger door.

'Get in.'

She climbed inside, the leather seat chill against her bare legs. Stanislaus pulled at the starter handle until the car chugged to life, climbed in beside her and drove off, the shaded lights throwing narrow triangles on the road in the pitch-black midnight. Her stomach tightened in a ball and her mouth tasted of metal, of fear.

'Where are we going?'

'Belgium.'

'Belgium?'

'Belgium's neutral.' She was right. They thought he was a German. She wanted to say how sorry she was. She couldn't see him in the dark, but she knew his lips were closed and tight and he was not going to talk to her about it. He was a brave man.

'Where did you get the car?'

'I borrowed it.'

Then she remembered. 'My samples,' she said. 'I left my samples. We have to go back.'

'Forget it.'

'Please, Stanislaus.'

He laughed, a cruel, mocking 'Ha, ha'. She had never known him like this.

There was no traffic on the road and they sped through Paris, the unlit streets and suburbs unfolding behind them. Maybe they could go back later, when this crisis had blown over. Madame Breton would keep them for her. That's what concierges did.

'Do you know the way?' Ada said.

'I'd better.'

'How long will it take?'

'Five hours, six. Who knows?'

Six hours was a long time. He was driving fast.

'Will they catch us?'

'Who?'

'Whoever is after you.'

He said nothing. They sat in silence. She closed her eyes. She was tired. The *burr* of the engine and the rocking motion of the car were soothing, even though her stomach churned and her head spun with questions. Something had happened, something serious. What if they were caught? She'd be in for it too.

She must have fallen asleep because it was dawn, a soft, grey light that mottled through tall trees and drew faint stripes across the road.

'Glad you slept,' he said in a bitter tone.

Ada stretched her legs and arms, clenched and unclenched her hands. The road ahead was straight, the countryside flat. 'Where are we?'

'Picardy,' he said. 'Somewhere.'

Her father used to sing, *Roses are shining in Picardy*. It was one of his favourite songs. That and *Tipperary*. She wanted to hear it now, a longing so acute it lunged like a knife. She could hear him singing, his voice sweet and tender, and she began to sing with him in her head, a soft, mournful duo, *in the hush of the silver dew. Roses are flowering in Picardy, but there's never a rose like you.*

Stanislaus turned and faced her. 'Where did that come from?'

'It was a wartime song,' she said. 'The soldiers sang it in the trenches. I expect you Germans sang the same kind of songs.'

His knuckles tightened on the wheel and the muscles in his jaw flexed. 'I am not a German.'

'I know.' She was cross, tired. A silly mistake. But still, he didn't have to speak so sharp. She wasn't the enemy.

'Do you think they'll fight again here?'

'Shut up.'

She slunk back in her seat, stared out of the window, tears pricking her eyes. She had no idea where they were and there didn't seem to be any road signs. They passed a platoon of troops, dressed in khaki, helmets and rifles at the ready.

'They're British,' Ada said. 'Stop, I want to talk to them.' Ask where they were going, what they were doing. Perhaps they'd look after her. Take her home.

'Please stop,' she said again.

'Don't be stupid,' he said, adding, 'you're a fucking liability, you know that, don't you?'

He'd never sworn before. She turned in her seat and watched them disappear through the rear window.

The car began to slow down.

'No.' His foot pumped the pedal on the floor and he shifted the gears on the dashboard, making angry grinding sounds. The car spluttered and stopped.

'No.' He was screaming.

He got out and slammed the door. Ada watched him open the boot, felt the car shudder as he banged it shut again. He walked round to her side, and flung open her door.

'Out,' he said.

'What's happened?'

'We have no petrol.'

'What will we do?'

'Walk,' he said.

Ada stepped onto the running board and jumped to the ground. She looked down the road behind her, but the soldiers were out of sight. She could run, catch them up.

He grabbed her hand and began to pull.

'My case,' she said. 'I need my case.'

'No time for that. It'll slow us down.'

'But my shoes,' Ada said. 'I can't walk in these shoes.' She only had the shoes that she had travelled in to France, all that time ago, simple courts with high, stacked heels. She had worn them constantly and there was a hole in one of the soles. They were comfortable enough, but not for walking.

'Then take them off,' he said. He would not let go of her hand and his pace was fast.

'How far is it?'

'Ten kilometres. Fifteen.'

'What's that in miles?'

'Seven,' he said. 'Roughly. Ten.'

Ten miles. Ada had never walked so far in her

73

life, and here she was, trotting to keep up with him.

They stopped once when Stanislaus needed to relieve himself. Ada was glad for the pause. She had a stitch, and sat down on the side of the road, slipping off her shoes. They were old and worn, but at least they weren't rubbing. She wiggled her toes. She had no idea what time it was, but the sun was already high in the sky. They had passed several platoons of soldiers. She wanted to call out to them, *Good luck, boys!* To ask them for help, to take her home, but Stanislaus told her to keep quiet, threatened to silence her, once and for all, if she made a sound. There were other people on the road, walking like themselves, or on bicycles, men with their girlfriends or wives sitting on the crossbar. One couple had a baby, and another a young child strapped into a chair over the rear wheel. From time to time a car passed, piled with luggage. Well-to-do people, she thought, who had found a way round petrol shortages. She wondered who Stanislaus had borrowed the car from.

He was tense, but then he had responsibilities. He was doing his best. He had to protect them. They'd be all right, she knew. She was lucky. *They* were lucky. Nothing would happen and it was exciting, in its way, running away like this. She regretted having to leave the samples behind, but there was nothing much else in the suitcase that she really wanted to bring back to England with her. The clothes she'd packed – Stanislaus had packed – were worn and stretched. If they were going home, she'd be on her feet again in no time, could make herself some nice new outfits. That's if Mrs B. gave her her old job back. And if she didn't? She'd get another job, just as she had in Paris. Or maybe they'd stay in Belgium. She didn't know anything about Belgium. She pulled out her hankie and wiped her nose. At least she still had her handbag and had had the foresight to slip in her lipstick and comb before they left. Her purse and passport were always there, in the side pocket.

'Not far,' Stanislaus said. He looked happier now, held out his hand to help her up. His moods didn't last long.

'Perhaps,' he went on, 'when we get to the border, you could do the talking? Your French is better than mine.'

'What do I have to talk about?'

'I got rid of my passport, remember? You'll have to say it got lost, or was stolen, or mislaid in our rush to leave. Something. I have to get out of France.'

'But it doesn't say I'm married on it. It's not a married woman's passport. I'd be on yours if I really was your wife.'

'You'll think of something.'

The crowds were thickening now and Ada could see what looked like a queue ahead that snaked away to two officers whom she could see standing in the distance by a sentry box.

'Is this it?' she said. 'Belgium?'

Stanislaus nodded, put his arm round her waist, pulled her close.

Most people were speaking French, but there were some other languages Ada had never heard before. Soldiers walked up and down, making sure the line was orderly and calm. French soldiers, Ada thought. They moved slowly, inch by inch. Stanislaus fished in his pocket, and handed over a franc to a young boy pushing a trolley with baguettes and a steel churn that glinted in the sun. She was thirsty, and hungry, grateful for the bread and the water, even though she wished the metal cup for the water had been a little cleaner. But then the French never thought about those things.

The line moved slowly. More people came up behind them. There must be hundreds, Ada thought, thousands. It was as if half of Europe were escaping. Her shoes were pinching now. She longed to sit down, or better, lie flat with her head on a soft, feather pillow. They'd be here all day at this rate, all night. The guards took their time, inspecting the paperwork, asking questions, eyeing the refugees. They were opening suitcases, pulling out a cotton dress, a cummerband, the snatched relics of a former life. Stanislaus stood beside her, worry creased in his forehead.

They inched forward. She'd say Stanislaus was her brother. A bit simple. She'd tap her head.

Muddled. Would he mind? Or perhaps he could be deaf and dumb? *My brother can't talk. Someone stole his passport.* Would he snap at her afterwards, *What do you take me for?* Or would he say, *Well done, Ada, I knew you'd think of something.* She rehearsed the lines in her head, in her best French. What if she forgot them? Or they saw through her? *He's not your brother. Come with me, monsieur, mademoiselle.* She'd have to warn him, *Don't say a word.* She worried that he looked suspicious with his face cut and bruised like that.

Slowly, slowly. Most of the people were let through but some were turned away. There was a large family, a grandmother and her two sons and a daughter, or perhaps a wife, grandchildren. There must have been around ten of them all together. The children were knock-kneed with socks scrolled down their skinny legs, the boys in grey flannel shorts, the girls in smocked dresses. They stood still, eyes wide, watching, while one of the fathers pointed to their documents, to the children. The guard shook his head, beckoned over another man with braid on his uniform. Ada couldn't hear what they were saying. One of the sons took the guard's hand, pumped it, smiling and they walked to the other side, to Belgium. Ada breathed with relief. If that family could get through, she and Stanislaus would be all right. She followed each refugee, one by one, as the guard let them pass, smiling with them, for them. Families, single women, old men. Edging forward.

They were two away from the border post. An elderly couple was ahead of them. He was wearing an overcoat tied round the middle with string, and she wore a black skirt with an uneven hem that draped at the back over her thick, fat ankles. Everyone looked dowdy in the war, dressed in old clothes, patched and darned. Perhaps they were saving their best for the armistice. The guard stamped their documents and Ada watched as they shuffled away.

Almost their turn. A young man was in front of them. He looked about her age. His cheeks were flushed and smooth, unmarked by whiskers. Close-up, the guard looked stern, bored. A hard man. If they didn't let Stanislaus through, she thought, what would happen? Would they arrest him? Take him to prison? If he started talking, they'd know she had lied. She'd be in for it then, too. Perhaps they'd have to stay in France. They could hide. Change their names. No one would know. They should never have come anyway. They could turn around, now, go back to Paris.

Ada shifted her weight to relieve the pressure off her blister and stepped on a small, brown teddy bear lying on the ground. It was woollen, soft, stuffed with kapok, sewn together down the side, smooth even stitches. Perhaps someone had made a pullover for her husband, knitted a toy for the baby with the leftover two-ply. Ada looked around. There was no baby in sight. She'd keep it, a good luck charm. She put it in her bag.

The guard had taken the young man's documentation, was studying it, twisting it upside down, to the side. He returned the papers and pointed left, to a small bureau a few yards along.

'*Mais*—' the young man began, his shoulders slumped. He was close to tears. But the guard wasn't listening, was beckoning to Ada and Stanislaus. The youth picked up his knapsack, slung it over his shoulder, and walked towards the office.

They stepped forward. Ada ran through the lines in her head. *My brother, someone stole*—

'*Nationalité?*'

She wasn't sure if she should show her passport. It was right here, in her hand, a small, dark blue book. She squeezed her bag instead with the soft teddy inside, *Wish me luck.*

'*Nous sommes anglais.*'

The officer lifted his chin, studied their faces. She dared not look at Stanislaus. Her armpits were wet. She began to sweat behind her knees and in the palms of her hands.

The guard said nothing, waved them through with a flick of the wrist, summoned the next in line, a large family with five children.

Walked through, just like that. The strain had made her dizzy, but she was almost disappointed too. No one had given her the chance to say the words she'd practised over and over in her head. Stanislaus wouldn't know how clever she could be.

'We made it,' he said.

They were in Belgium.

The relief brought with it exhaustion. Her legs ached, her back hurt, another blister had formed on her heel. She wanted this to be over. She wanted to go home, to open the door, *Hello, Mum, it's me.* She wasn't sure she had the strength to walk another yard, and she had no idea where they were.

'Are we far from the sea?' she said.

'Sea?' He laughed. 'We're a long way from the sea.'

'Where do we go?'

'Namur.'

'Why?'

'No more,' he said, winking. 'Get it?'

'Where is it? Is it on the way?'

The family that had been behind them in the queue jostled forward, scratching her legs with the buckle of a suitcase, pushing her closer to Stanislaus. She leant towards him.

'I want to go home,' she said. 'To England. Can't we go back now?'

'Maybe.' His voice was distant. 'Maybe. But first Namur.'

'Why? I want to go home.' She wanted to say, *this minute.* Stamp her feet, like a child.

'No,' he said. 'Namur.'

'Why Namur?'

'Business, Ada,' he said. She couldn't imagine what business could be taking them there.

'Promise me.' There was panic in her voice. 'After. We go home.'

He lifted her hand, kissed her knuckles. 'I promise.'

They hitched a lift to Mons and caught a crowded train to Namur that stopped at every station and red light. It was evening by the time they arrived. The baguette was all Ada had eaten since they'd left Paris eighteen hours ago and she felt faint and weak. Stanislaus took her by the elbow, guided her away from the station, down the side streets. She had no idea where they were going, or whether Stanislaus knew the way but they stopped by a small café above which was a painted sign, '*Pension*'.

'Wait here,' he said. 'I'll organize it.'

She sat at a table and chair outside. This side of the street was in the shade but she was too tired to walk to the other side, where the last of the May sun was shining. Stanislaus came out.

'Everything,' he said, 'is organized. Madame will give us a simple meal, and while we're eating her daughter will arrange the room.' As he spoke, Madame appeared with two glasses of beer which she placed in front of them.

Stanislaus picked up his glass. 'To you, Ada Vaughan. Namur.'

She touched her handbag with the teddy bear, and held the glass so it chinked with his and smiled at him. *Lucky.*

Paté and bread, sausage. The beer was cloudy and sweet, and she drank two long glasses. It made her light-headed, and she was glad for it. She hadn't been tipsy since before the war. The early days with Stanislaus seemed like another age now, at the Café Royal, a Martini or two, with a cherry on a stick. Content and flushed with love, they'd sashayed down Piccadilly to the number 12, where he'd kiss her under the lamp-post, tender lips to hers. She'd suck peppermints on the way home so her breath didn't smell. It was like that just now. Stanislaus's mood had evaporated, his worries – *their* worries – over. *Namur. No more.* No more temper or brooding silences. He was in good heart again, but he swung so quickly from light to dark. It worried her. His moods made her change too. When he was sunny so was she, nimble toes and bubbling breath. But when his mood turned cold it choked her like a fog.

They went upstairs after dinner. She was unsteady on her feet, could smell herself tart and musty from the day, her hair sticky with dust and sweat. Madame had left a jug of water and a wash bowl on the table and had laid out a towel and a flannel.

'I must,' her words slurred, 'wash.'

Stanislaus nodded and walked to the window, looked out over the street with his back to her. Ada wet the flannel and rubbed. She heard her mother in her head, saw herself as a child standing by the sink in the kitchen at home. *Up as far as you can go, down as far as you can go.* She giggled into the cloth, and found herself crying, a lunge of homesickness and fear, as if

82

she was tumbling deep into a canyon and couldn't stop herself.

She was aware of Stanislaus catching her as she fell, laying her on the bed and fumbling with the buttons on his flies. Her head was spinning, her eyes heavy. She just wanted to sleep. She felt him open her legs, enter her with an impatient thrust, sharp rips of pain that made her cry out. He lifted himself off her and lay by her side. Her legs were wet. He'd kept his shirt on, she could see, even through the blur of beer.

It was dark when she woke. Then she heard it. The distant blast of an explosion, the boom of heavy guns. The curtains had been left open and through the window the night sky streaked white and vermilion.

'Stanislaus.' She groped for him next to her. The bed was empty, the sheets cold and smooth. She sat up, awake, panic gripping her body, short of breath.

'Stanislaus.' His name echoed round the empty room. Something was wrong, she knew. She fumbled for her clothes, pulled them on, *please God let him come back*. There were steps outside. It must be him. *Just went out for a cigarette*. She opened the door but it was Madame who was walking up the stairs, her way lit by a small oil lamp.

'Mademoiselle,' she was panting from the climb. 'The Germans are here. You must come, to the basement.'

'My husband,' Ada said. 'Where is my husband?'

'Follow me,' Madame said, lighting the way for them both. She held up the long skirt of her nightdress with her free hand.

'But my husband.' Dread clamoured, a shrill, persistent klaxon. 'My husband. He's not here.'

They had entered the café now. The room was dark. Ada could make out the tables and chairs, the glisten of bottles behind the bar. Madame opened a trap door and began to lower herself down.

'Come,' she said.

Ada looked for Stanislaus in the gloom, listened for his breathing, smelled the air for his scent, but her nostrils filled with the tang of stale beer and burnt sugar.

'Mademoiselle. Now. You must come now. We are in danger.' A hand tugged at her ankle. Stanislaus wasn't in the room. He was out there, in the night, by himself, in danger. A boom thundered in the distance. The hand tugged again at her foot so Ada lost her balance and had to steady herself on a chair.

'I'm coming,' she said.

She looked for the glow of his cigarette in the cellar, his shadow in the vaults. *You took your time, Ada.* Madame closed the trap door, and switched on a single bulb which shed a dim light through the darkness. The cellar was full of barrels stacked five high, and a pair of porters' trolleys. The earth floor smelled of mushrooms. Madame had brought down a sheet of linoleum and two hard-backed chairs. There was a hamper next to one, with bread and cheese. She had prepared for this day, knew that war was coming. Ada should have known too.

'My husband,' Ada began to whimper. 'He's not here.'

'Your husband?'

'Yes. Where is he?'

'Your *husband*?'

'Yes. *Mon mari*.' Ada wondered if Madame was deaf, or simple. 'The man who was with me last night. Moustache, glasses. My husband.'

'Yes, yes,' the woman said. 'I know who he is. He left yesterday evening.'

Ada limped to the chair and sat down, blood thundering through her head. 'He left?' Her voice was frail.

'*Oui*,' Madame said. 'He went to meet his wife. They were going to Ostend, for the ferry, to England. I said I thought he'd be lucky, the transport's not what it was. Can't get the fuel, see? But he insisted.'

'No,' Ada said. 'There's some mistake.'

'No,' the woman sounded almost cheery. 'He was adamant. Said he had to get back to England.'

Stanislaus had left? To meet his *wife*? England, where he'd face jail? It made no sense.

'But what about me?' Ada said.

'He said you had other plans. You would know what to do.'

The strength left her body, flesh slumped and numb. This had to be some other person Madame was talking about. In the morning, when it was light, she'd go and look for him. He was out there, lost. Perhaps he was hurt. She'd find him. The German guns were still far away, although they sounded near enough.

The road ran above the cellar. She could hear cars rolling by, footsteps clipping the cobbles, the squeak of a barrow and the brisk bell of a bicycle. There was a wooden trap door to the street through which the delivery men lowered the barrels. Ada could see daylight through the joins.

'You must not go out,' Madame said. 'The last war . . . the Germans. Such horrors.' She held her down, gnarled hand on Ada's arm, corrugated fingers round her wrist.

Ada shook her off. 'He may be waiting,' she said. 'Outside. We have to let him in.'

'He has gone.' Madame was shaking her head. She doesn't know Stanislaus, Ada thought. Or she misunderstood him. He spoke terrible French.

She could hear voices, muffled, urgent speech which she couldn't quite catch. The town was awake and alive and Stanislaus was part of it.

She freed herself from Madame's hold, grabbed her handbag, climbed the stepladder and pushed open the trap from the cellar into the café. The morning light flooded in, motes of dust dancing in the sunlight. Ada glanced back at Madame standing by the chair, holding a cloth napkin across her lap.

'*Vous êtes folle!*' Madame said, shaking her head.

Ada pulled the bolts on the street door and slipped outside. The light was fresh and the sun glowed low and warm. On this side of the house the street was silent and empty, as if an army of ghouls had passed through and cleared the souls away. There was a smell in the air, a sweet balsam from a tree which overhung the road with newborn foliage. She thought of Stanislaus, so long ago, *the smell of trees making love*. Her blister still hurt, and she plucked some leaves and shoved them into the heel of her shoe, *clip-clopped* round the corner with a limp.

The buildings were tall, redbrick walls with roofs that soared and curled. Ada turned and walked down another street. Empty. There was no sign of the Germans anywhere. A man on a bicycle was coming towards her and for a moment Ada was sure it was Stanislaus. He cycled by, a fair-haired man with a leer, turning round as he passed to stare. Ada clutched at her collar. She had buttoned it askew in her rush last night, the top gaped open, her slip showed. *Dressed in a hurry. Woman of the night.* She waited until the man had passed, re-organized her dress, began to run in case he returned, her blister rubbing raw as her shoe jolted on the cobblestones.

The street opened into a large square filled with hundreds of people. Ada stopped, drew her hands to her face, covered her nose. The smell of fear she first learned in Paris filled this square too, its dread tasted sour on her tongue, its keening echoed round her ears. Faces cast with determination, eyes fixed ahead, elbows out, dragging suitcases and children. They shouted and cried, pushed bicycles or prams laden with possessions. There was an old lady in a wheelbarrow, her hair straight and white, her face gaunt and drawn, tears draining down her hollow cheeks, bony knuckles clutching the sides as her son struggled to keep the barrow steady. Cars honked in irritation as they tried to push through the crowds. A dray horse breathed in the terror, straining on the creaking shafts of the cart. Tempers were short all round. She'd seen it before, in London, in Paris. Only now it was real. The Germans were coming. Belgium should have been safe.

She'd never find Stanislaus in this crowd. Perhaps he did get away or perhaps he had been caught, shot, his body already festering behind enemy lines. She shut her eyes and tried to rid herself of the thought, tried to make sense of everything, of *him*. How could he have a wife? They had spent every day together since they left London. He always came home, however late it was. Ada would have known. Madame was wrong. But why else leave Paris so fast? Why come to Belgium, why Namur? Why here?

The crowd pushed against her. She recognized where they were, close to the train station. The people must be heading there. She wanted to be free of them, to think. She tried to turn and stand against the force. No one noticed her, no one cared. She was alone in the middle of a thousand frightened, fleeing people. There was no Stanislaus. She had no idea where to go, or what to do. She had no one to turn to. She let the crowd carry her with them. Perhaps they knew where they were going. Perhaps they knew where it was safe.

Paris. She could go back to Paris. Monsieur Lafitte, Madame Breton. They would take care of her. She'd explain why she left without warning. *Bit of bother that Stanislaus got himself into. They thought he was a German.*

And then a truth smacked her hard across the face. What if Stanislaus was German? What if Mrs B. had been right all along? He was a spy, and she his alibi. She tried to turn again but the pressure of the crowd was too strong. Move to the side, she thought, to the side, forward and to the side. The crowds were thinner there.

A man trod on her toe and she yelped.

'*Excusez moi, mademoiselle,*' he said. '*Excusez moi.*' He didn't linger, his eyes hard focused on the space ahead.

Ada reached the edge of the square and stood beneath an arcade away from the crowd. What had he been doing in London? She never asked. Took her to Paris. Said there'd be no war, said he couldn't go back to England. She promised him she'd stay. They were a nice young couple and she was his cover. Where did he get his money from? What sort of business was he in? Did he love her?

She had been a fool. Taken in. And then Belgium, Namur. *No more*. Of course. He knew the Germans were coming, he must have. That was who he went to join, not his wife, he had no wife. That was a codeword. Spies used them. Of course she'd never seen his passport, he couldn't show it to her. He'd give himself away. *You do the talking, Ada, when we get to the border.* Left her here, discarded her, after he was done with her. Purpose served, mission complete.

An aircraft overhead emitted a steady rhythmic drone, like a giant wasp. It flew low enough that Ada could make out a swastika on its tail, the cross on its side, and the ghostly shape of its pilot in the cockpit. Moments later there was an explosion, close enough to make the ground shudder. The crowd screamed and scattered. She heard the frightened whinnies of the horses, the cries of children, could see people falling, trampled on the ground. She stood at the edge of the square, frozen. Another aircraft came into view and Ada realized that it had spotted the crowds, was lining up to attack them. She pushed her way through the arcade, into a side street. Ran and ran as another bomb hurtled down, closer this time, its force rocking the ground so she tripped and fell. *Get up, get up.* She knew she had to run, get out of the open streets and find protection. She heard a heavy rumble. Ahead of her a building was crumbling down, a giant with shattered knees, falling in a thick fog of grit. She must go back to Madame, to the cellar, shelter.

She pushed herself onto her feet and looked round. The sky was filled with dust, sticky, grey grouts that clogged her nose and fell like ash on her hands and in her mouth. She tried to push them out but they coated her tongue and sat like blotting paper, mopping up her spittle. She had no idea where the *pension* was or what it was called or which street it was on. She had lost her bearings. Her foot was sticky. She had cut her knee when she fell and blood was trickling down her calf and into the side of her shoe. Her blister throbbed. She pulled off her shoes. Have to run. Get away. Perhaps the *pension* was to the right. She had cut across the square. Up the road, first on the right, but the street veered back on itself and twisted round again. She was going round in circles.

The crowds had fled for shelter. Another plane droned off in the distance and there was a sharp crack of gunfire. The plane came into view and Ada watched, transfixed, as the long, black bomb fell behind a row of houses nearby. The ground juddered. She heard the tinkle of shattered windows, felt a shard of glass brush her arm, watched a cloud of thick, black smoke billow from a neighbouring street. There were more planes

now, and more bombs, coming faster and faster.
Nowhere was safe. There was broken glass all
round and her feet were bare. She slipped her
shoes back on, wincing at her blisters, and ran
away from the blast, down another street she didn't
recognize, *away* and *away,* her mind racing in time
with her legs, praying for the first time for months.
Please God, please God . . .

Round a corner. Two of them. Standing there,
in full view, staring at her.

Les Soeurs de la Bienveillance. Heavy black cloaks
and white starched wimples. She recognized the
habit. It was the same order that her Auntie Vi
had joined fifteen years ago.

'Please,' she said. She could feel the words
tumbling out, pushing for space, begging to be
heard over the roar of the bombers. 'Please. Help
me. *Aidez moi.* My name is Ada. My aunt is a
Sister, one of you, Sister Bernadette of Lourdes,
perhaps you know her? She served her novitiate
here, in Belgium.' Or was it France? Ada couldn't
remember. She was only little at the time. 'I'm
lost. My husband—' What could she say? 'I'm
alone.'

'Your husband?' One of the nuns said.

She had to stick with her lie. 'Yes,' she spoke
quickly. The gunfire and explosions had stopped.
Smoke and dust clung like a shroud, and the smell
of broken masonry and burning filled the air. This
might be her only chance. 'I've lost my husband.'

She felt sick, and her head began to spin. When she came to, she was sitting on the ground, her head held down between her knees.

'Madame,' one of the sisters was saying. 'Madame, you cannot stay here. It isn't safe.'

'Help me,' Ada said. Her voice was far away, a distant rap in her head. 'I have nowhere to go.'

The nuns lifted her to her feet, one on each side, a firm grip on her elbows. 'Come with us.'

She leant on them for support, legs moving, one before the other, but her bones had turned to sponge and she had no strength left.

She was aware of an eerie quiet, clouds of rising smoke in the clear blue sky, a river gleaming in the sunlight, and a castle high on the hill. She was aware, too, of uneven cobbles and broken glass and, beyond, an archway with wrought iron writing, *La Résidence de Saint-Joseph*. The nuns led her inside, into a large hall with a marble chequerboard floor and a life-size statue of St Joseph standing in the centre. He balanced a lily in the crook of an arm and held the other up in a blessing. One nun went off down a corridor and the other led her to a long wooden settle.

'*Asseyez-vous*,' she said. '*Attendez*.'

Ada sat. She was still dizzy and faint. The noise of the bombs and the falling debris echoed in her head. She hadn't had a proper meal for days, not a meal with meat and potatoes; nor had she had a good night's sleep. She eased off the first shoe,

93

and then the second. Her feet were filthy, blood-ied and black from the road. She clutched her handbag close to her. It was scuffed and dusty and bulging from the teddy bear stuffed inside. The bear was bringing her luck, had kept her alive so far. She fished inside for her compact and lipstick. *Must look a fright.*

She heard the rattle of beads, the swish of heavy skirts, and smelled the bland talcum of nuns. One from this morning was carrying a tray. Another nun, tall and thin, walked with an air of authority. She must be the head. What did Auntie Vi say they were called? Reverend? Mother? Good Mother. There was an older nun behind her with a stern, red face and round, horn-rimmed glasses. The nun who rescued her this morning placed the tray beside her on the settle. There was a glass of water and some bread. The tall nun approached Ada, her arms outstretched in greeting.

'*Je suis la Bonne Mère,*' she said. Ada tried to stand but her knees buckled. The Good Mother sat next to her, pointed to the tray. *Mangez.* Ada drank the water, felt it soothe her throat. She broke off a piece of bread and stuffed it into her mouth.

'You are English,' Good Mother said. 'You have lost your husband.'

Ada nodded.

'Your name?'

'Ada Vaughan.'

'And you are the niece of our beloved *Soeur* Bernadette de Lourdes?'

94

Ada nodded again. Her lips trembled. She had never been so alone, or so frightened.

'Remind me,' Good Mother went on, 'what was your aunt's name, before she took Holy Orders?'

'Auntie Vi,' Ada said. She corrected herself. 'Violet. Violet Gamble.'

'And when did she enter?'

'I can't remember,' Ada said. She knew she was being tested. She could be an impostor. If she gave the wrong answer, they'd send her away, back out to the street. 'I was only little when she left but it must have been about fifteen years ago. Maybe ten.' She added, 'I think she was here.'

'And where did she come from?' The other red-faced nun said. She spoke in English, with an Irish accent. She sounded strict, as if Ada was telling a fib.

'London,' Ada said. 'Walworth. 19 Inville Road, Walworth.'

This red-faced nun nodded at the Good Mother.

'Please help me,' Ada said.

'How?' the Good Mother said. 'We look after old people. We must think of them.'

'I'll work for you.' Auntie Vi had said they always have lay people in to do the cleaning, wash the dishes, make the beds. Ada could do that. They had to keep her. 'Let me stay, please. I'll do anything. I have nowhere to go.'

The Good Mother patted Ada's hand, stood up and walked to the corner, beckoning the other

95

nun to follow. They turned their backs to Ada and leant their heads close. Ada couldn't hear what they were saying, nor was she sure she would understand if she did. The Good Mother spoke fast.

They returned after a few minutes. 'We can shelter you.' She shrugged. 'But for how long?' she rolled her hands so the palms faced upwards. '*Je ne sais pas*. If the British help us, drive the Germans out, a few days perhaps. And then, you must leave.'

Ada nodded. She'd be safe here, safer than at the *pension*. Besides, she'd never find the pension, not now, with the bombs and the smoke.

'Thank you, *Bonne Mère*,' Ada said. 'Thank you so much.' The British would be here soon. It would be all right. They'd send her back to London, to Mum and Dad.

The Good Mother nodded, and tucked her hands behind her scapular. 'Sister Monica,' she said, tilting her head towards the other nun who was scowling at Ada, 'is in charge of our novitiates. I shall leave you with her. I have much to do now.' She turned on her heel and marched down the corridor.

'She's not the only one with much to do,' Sister Monica said in a tight voice. 'And no time to do it.'

'I can help,' Ada said, though all she wanted was to sleep.

'You? How?'

'I can sew. And clean, and—'

Sister Monica snorted, and began to walk away, calling over her shoulder. 'Well, come on then. Follow me. Good Mother says I'm to make a nun of you.'

Ada stood up, nestling her handbag under her arm. 'Make a nun of me?'

'She said to dress you up like one of us.' She hissed, 'A sacrilege. Not to mention the danger. What if the Germans win? Eh?'

There were two tall doors at the end of the corridor marked '*Privé*'. Sister Monica led the way through them, up a long flight of wooden steps, down another corridor and into a large room full of open shelves on which were stacked folded piles of garments, linen and towels.

'You need a bath,' Sister Monica said, thrusting a towel into Ada's arms and pointing to a door opposite. 'But don't bother dressing when you're done. Wrap this round you,' she handed over a long, white shift, 'and come back in here. Don't take all day. No more than two inches of water in the bath, and mind you clean it after you.'

A large tub on claw feet, tiled floor and walls. No mirror. Just as well. She wouldn't want to see what she looked like. She turned the tap. The pipes screamed as steaming water belched out. The bath wasn't run that often, Ada thought. The pipes were full of air, like the pump at home. She undressed and lowered herself into warm water, wincing as it hit the raw of her blisters, watching as it dissolved the dirt. She lay back, wetting the ends of her hair. If she shut her eyes, she could sleep.

Sister Monica was hammering at the door. 'Come out now. I don't have time to wait for you.'

Ada rubbed her body with the towel, pulled the shift over her head. It rucked on her damp skin. She felt better for the bath, and the food, more herself.

'Sit there,' Sister Monica said, pointing to a chair. She held a large pair of scissors in her hands. Ada stared at the shears.

'Don't even argue,' Sister Monica went on. 'I've got the measure of you, Ada Vaughan.'

She sat on the chair and Sister Monica tugged at her hair. She heard the scratch of the blades as they sliced and watched as a chestnut lock floated past her to the floor. She'd known that nuns shaved their heads, but if it was only for a few days, why did *she* have to? She'd be back in England soon enough and she'd look ridiculous. Clumps of hair swilled from her shift and onto the floor.

'Now,' Sister Monica said, 'stand over there.' Ada felt her head. It wasn't shaved, but the hair was short. It felt dry and sharp, like stubble. Her hair lay below her, long waves of rich amber like fallen leaves. Cruel. A cruel cut. She'd have to wear a hat while it grew back. She could have made a turban from one of the samples she'd left in Paris, that would've been all right. But now she'd have to go out with tufts, unless she found a scarf to cover her head.

Sister Monica was rifling through the shelves, pulling out items of folded clothing. 'You'll wear Sister Jeanne's habit,' she said. 'She died last week. These are your drawers. They go on first.' She held up a large square of calico, divided halfway down. 'You step in and pull the tapes. Waist. Legs.'

Ada stepped in. The drawers were vast. 'Do you have a smaller pair?'

Sister Monica snorted. 'I suppose you'll want tailored French knickers next.' Ada said nothing. 'Now this.'

Bodice and underskirt, tunic and scapular, belt and rosary. Serge, black. Sister Jeanne had been a large nun and Ada was lost in her clothes. The shoes and stockings were several sizes too big.

'And now,' Sister Monica said, 'the wimple.' She rammed it on Ada's head, pulling it hard so it sat tight round her skull. 'And you button it here.' Her fingers scratched at Ada's chin as she forced the padded button through a tight hole in the starched linen.

'One more thing,' Sister Monica said. 'When you have your monthlies, you come to me and ask for the padding. And is that a wedding ring I see?' She pointed. Ada nodded. 'Give it to me.'

Ada slipped the ring off and handed it to the nun.

'And will you tell me why it's left a green mark on your finger?'

Ada knew it hadn't been real gold.

'You see,' Sister Monica said, her eyes drawn tight into that knowing *I've got the measure of you*. 'Sister Bernadette told me all about your family. I remembered. Vaughan is your maiden name. Married indeed. You're a fallen woman, a harlot, and I told the Good Mother as much.'

She was helpless. Why had she lied? She couldn't tell the truth now, no one would believe her, no one would sympathize. She wanted to get away from Sister Monica, find the Good Mother. Ada could explain herself to her. She had been kind.

'Give me your passport,' Sister Monica said. 'We'll take care of it.'

Ada opened her handbag, pulled out the teddy bear and her passport. Sister Monica tucked it in her pocket.

'We'll have to burn the bag,' she said. 'In case the Germans come.'

Ada wanted to protest, but didn't dare. She handed it over.

'And the teddy,' Sister Monica said.

This was a lucky bear, though Ada dare not say that to this nun. She shook her head, groped in the side of her tunic, found the pocket, and shoved the bear inside.

The floor juddered, and moments later Ada heard the boom. The Germans were bombing again, nearby. Sister Monica crossed herself, and grabbed Ada's hand. They ran down the corridor. The thick skirts made moving difficult. Through the *Privé* doors, along and into a large dormitory smelling of disinfectant, with what must have been two dozen old men lying on their backs or sitting on the side of their beds. The room opened at both ends and through the far doors Ada could see a nun pushing a bed out and, beyond her, another. They were evacuating the ward, lining up the beds to be wheeled into the lifts.

'Help them,' Sister Monica said. Ada took her cue from a young woman who was assisting one of the old men to walk. She went to the nearest bed, put her arms round the back of a fragile man, felt his weight as he leant on her for support. He smelled of urine and had the fusty breath of morning teeth. He groped for a stick and shuffled away. She went to the next bed. This man was larger and Ada almost buckled under his weight. She held his elbow as he walked. They followed the others, making slow, painful steps down the steep, stone staircase to the vaults beneath.

Sometimes the explosions were so close the ground shuddered with their impact. At other times, there was silence, punctuated only by the rat-a-tat of distant gunfire. Ada slept in the deceased Soeur Jeanne's bed, followed her routine. Up at five, Angelus, prayers, Mass. The scab on Ada's knee stung when she knelt. She'd been here four days now, ticking off time. Work all day. Washing the old women, combing their thin, white hair, shaving the men and cleaning their privates. The bedpans were the worst. Sometimes the old men wet the bed and Ada had to pull off the sodden sheets and mop up the mess. *Please God*, Ada thought, *let the Germans go away. Let me go home.* She was grateful to the Good Mother for taking her in, but she knew she couldn't do this for much longer, especially not with Sister Monica. *Sister Spiteful*, Ada called her.

Most of the time they spent in the basement of the building. The Good Mother said it was for the best, until the Germans left and the explosions stopped. She told them what was happening every day after the Angelus, picking up the news from the priest who heard it on his wireless. Ada counted the days. *Five.* The Germans had broken through the Allied defences in the Ardennes. Ada didn't know where that was, but she knew it was serious. *Six. Eight.* Brussels had fallen. *Nine.* Antwerp had fallen. Ada clamped her hands over her ears. *Ten.* Heavy fighting. *Fourteen. Sixteen.* More than two weeks. It might go on forever. Let it stop. Let it go away. What if their boys couldn't hold the Germans? What would happen? She didn't want to live in a basement as a nun, to listen to the Good Mother every day, leading them in prayer when they could be out there doing something, fighting back, like the soldiers she'd passed, those British lads, though she wasn't sure she would be brave enough.

The stiff, hard linen of the wimple scratched her head and chafed against her chin. Once she caught a glimpse of herself in the glass of a window. Black and shapeless. The habit was hot and Ada was tempted to take off one of the underlayers but dared not in case Sister Spiteful found out. There were a number of English nuns in the convent, as far as Ada could tell, but they all had to speak French, so she wasn't sure how many there were, or who was who. She had no one to talk to. She missed Stanislaus.

Then the Good Mother told them that the King of Belgium had surrendered, and the army too, after eighteen days of brave resistance. The country was now under German rule. They must carry on with their vocation to care for the poor, the sick and the old, regardless. Ada was about to ask *what about me?* but the door bell rang, and rang again. Its clamour bounced round the little makeshift chapel in the basement where they were gathered. The stations of the cross trembled and the candles beneath them flickered.

The Good Mother signalled for the nuns to sit. There were voices in the distance, coming closer. Boots on the floor above, *one two, one two*, thudding on the stone stairs and along the corridor. The Good Mother stood by the altar looking above their heads, waiting. The chapel doors were thrown open and banged back against the wall. Two German soldiers entered, boots gleaming, grey uniforms pristine and pressed, their collars closed tight and studded with insignia. Ada was sure there must be more outside. They marched up to the altar. One of them took off his cap and tucked it under his arm. He turned to face them, spoke in French.

Ada's throat was dry and it was difficult to swallow. Here she was, a British woman, with the Nazis so close she could touch them. *The enemy.* Her legs were quaking and she pressed her hands down hard on her thighs to keep them still. The nun next to her thumbed her rosary beads, her face ashen. Another, in front, was quivering and Ada wondered if she was crying. She couldn't understand what the German was saying: he spoke good French but she couldn't follow it all. He talked about passports, strangers, enemies. British. For their protection. Safety. Gather their belongings. Assemble out in the front.

He nodded to the Good Mother, held up his arm. 'Heil Hitler,' and with his colleague turned and marched back through the chapel between the lines of pews. The steel caps on their boots sparked on the cold, flagstone floor.

The Good Mother waited until they had left the chapel and shut the door behind them. It gave a soft, reverend click. She took a deep breath. 'Let us pray.'

The nuns bent to their knees, heads bowed in their hands. Silent prayer. Ada liked prayer-time as a chance to daydream, but today she prayed in earnest, in desperation. This was war. Proper war. Not the phoney war she'd had in Paris with Stanislaus, as if nothing could happen. Now it was here, and she was alone in a strange country, for no reason except her own stupidity. She should have gone back to England at the start, when it was possible. Now Stanislaus had left, and she was a long way from home. *Please God, please God, save me.* She added, *save us all.* The Good Mother pushed herself away from the altar rail and stood up.

'Soeur Brigitte, Soeur Augustine,' she said, her voice softer than Ada had ever heard it. She signalled for them to stand. 'Soeur Thérèse, Soeur Josephine, Soeur Agatha, Soeur Clara.'

One by one the nuns stood.

'Soeur Clara,' the Good Mother repeated, looking at Ada. She had forgotten. She had been given a name. Clara. She hated it. It wasn't her.

'We have five nuns who are British,' she said, 'and Sister Clara, who has a British passport. The Germans are our masters now. For everybody's sake, we must obey them. We cannot lie to them, pretend you're Belgian.' She took another deep breath, staring at the closed doors. The nuns sat still, save for the swish of their wimples as they brushed against their chests with every breath they took. It was a while before she spoke. 'God bless you, and may God look after you.'

Sister Monica walked down the aisle to Ada. 'You too,' she said.

'I don't understand,' Ada said.

'The Germans are rounding up the British.' Sister Monica's voice was breaking and Ada could see she was biting her lip, fighting back tears. She didn't think Sister Spiteful was capable of feeling. 'They are making you prisoners of war. You must go with them. Do nothing that will betray you or the others. Do you understand? Their lives depend on you keeping silent.'

Ada shook her head. 'Why me?'

'We lied, may God forgive us. Told them you are a nun. If they find out—' Behind Sister Monica's glasses her eyes looked small and plaintive. *The horrors*, Madame had said. Her father, too: *The Germans ate babies, you know that?* 'The consequences would be fatal and on your conscience forever.'

'And you?' Ada said. 'Aren't you coming?'

'No,' Sister Monica shook her head. 'I have an Irish passport.' She took Ada's hand and squeezed it, an unexpected gesture of tenderness. 'You can use Soeur Jeanne's bag and Holy Bible.'

Ada followed her out of the chapel, one hand on her rosary, the other pressed against the good luck teddy bear deep inside her pocket.

Her old fears – how to get home, with no money, no clothes – were small and trifling now. New ones had arrived, weighty sacks of anxiety that Ada carried on her back, heavier by the day. She was trapped. They were trapped. Escape was out of the question. This would be her life forever, living as Sister Clara under the Nazis, looking after the old, in this geriatric home in the middle of Munich.

Sister Brigitte had managed to prise open the tiny window in the attic but now it wouldn't close. It didn't matter, Ada thought, the room was hot and stuffy, just below the roof. You could hear the pigeons in the early morning scratching for a foothold, cooing to their mates. The six nuns shared the room. There were two sets of bunk beds and they took it in turns to sleep. It worked out all right, since half of them worked at night and swapped beds with the others who worked by day.

Ada had never known such weariness. It made her jumpy and tearful, like her Auntie Lily who'd suffered with her nerves ever since the Zeppelins in the First War gave her alopecia. She dared not think of home, even though Sister Brigitte said to focus on the happy things before the war, to cheer themselves up. Sister Brigitte had become their leader, their new Good Mother. They'd even started calling her that. She wasn't very old. Ada guessed she couldn't be much more than thirty. But she was calm and wise and a clever negotiator. She held her ground when she needed to, gave way when it was prudent. She had got them mats for their beds and permission to hear Mass when the priest came. Father Friedel was ancient. He should have been in this geriatric home too. He could just about remember the Latin, *In nomine Patris, et Filii et Spiritus Sancti*, shuffling round after the doctor with his big priest's bag, unable to remember the quick from the dead.

Ada and Sister Brigitte and a mousy nun called Sister Agatha worked the day shifts in the geriatric wards. That was the hardest, when the old people were awake and needed feeding and cleaning, medicines administered, ulcers drained. The patients smelt musty, laid in their cots with bony knuckles and wormy hands. Ada had to cut their toenails, tough horn that curled into their flesh. She had to lay their bodies out when they died, pallid and grey without the pulse of blood. She'd lift up a stiffened arm till it cracked against the shoulder blade and wipe the soapy rags against the grain of sagging skin. Left arm. Right. Tilt the body forward, scrub the back, lay it down, right leg prised free of the groin, scrubbed in the privates, left leg. In between the toes. Cut the nails, straighten flat, ready to meet their Maker.

Ada didn't know how much longer she could stand it. Living with cadavers with stiffened limbs and congealed blood, with the smell of putrefaction and formaldehyde all round her. She wanted to run her fingers along beating tendons, to gaze into sparkling eyes, not close the lids on lustreless voids. She wanted soft tissue and pulsing blood and the hope that came with life and breath. She had just turned nineteen. She was young, wanted to live in the world, but death surrounded her, imprisoned her. So many dead, feeble, demented. Father Friedel at the gravesides, sprinkling holy water on the coffins.

Eight in the morning until eight at night, day after day, week after week. Supper. Rest. *Rest?* That was when they did their own laundry, calico drawers and underskirts, weighty with water, mildewed before they dried, draped over the ends of the bunks, their monthly paddings stained and brown, wimples limp and grey. Ada mended the stockings. Sister Brigitte had got some four-ply yarn from the guard and a needle, and Ada was glad to weave the stitches, web and warp, in, out. It took her mind off things, reminded her of the work she used to do, of a life she once had. And prayers. Always prayers. She'd shut her eyes and try to sleep while they prayed, blocking out Sister Brigitte's pious drone, rocking on her knees, thinking of Stanislaus.

She hadn't thought they'd last the journey in that cattle truck, all the way from Namur, through France and into Germany. The June air had been thin, the light poor, and it had grown hotter by the day. She had been wedged between Sister Brigitte and another prisoner, a man from Glasgow who swore and fidgeted, his elbow digging into her when he turned. More people were pushed in every time the train stopped. In the end no one could move. Ada tried to shift her feet, up on tiptoes, down, could feel her ankles swelling even in Sister Jeanne's outsize shoes. There was a tall man in the corner of the truck who took command. He was English, spoke posh, and Ada could imagine him in another life back home, a big boss, perhaps an army man, or a doctor.

'We're off to the seaside,' he bellowed, 'in a charabanc. Let's have a sing-song. Altogether now, *Ten green bottles sitting on the wall.*' It cheered Ada at first, '*and if one green bottle should accidentally fall.*' But as the days went on, the voices grew frail and the carriage silent, broken by fretful tears and a screaming baby. Fear swung like a gibbet, questions rotting unanswered in its stark, steel frame. The man tried to get them to move, *keep the blood circulating,* to make space for the infirm, to let some sit or lean against the side. They'd shove to the back or the front. Ada's toes were stepped on, painful pinches that she stopped feeling after a day. They had no water, had to sleep standing while the wheels screeched and the brakes screamed.

'We should be grateful and thank the Lord,' Sister Brigitte said when they arrived in Munich six days later and understood what they had to do. 'Our vocation is to help the elderly infirm, no matter where they are.' She looked at Ada then. 'Or who.' Sister Monica must have told her, *get the measure of her.* Mustn't say a word out of place, Ada thought.

Ada didn't agree with Sister Brigitte. These people were the enemy, after all, no matter how old or sick they were.

There had been one bucket in that carriage. People stood in their soiled clothes, weeping with shame.

Ada's nostrils clogged with her own fetid stench, her throat and mouth dry as sand. *Clackety clack, clackety clack.* The train had stopped. There was shouting outside. The sides of the trucks had been let down and the prisoners blinked in the light, took deep breaths like gasping fish, stumbled over the bodies of the dead and dying inside. The station sign read 'München'. 'Bavaria,' Sister Brigitte had hissed, 'Catholic'. As if it made a difference. Ada had no idea where Bavaria was, and didn't care. She wanted to run away, or die. Let them shoot her, blast her apart, far from here. But she was too weak to run and too scared.

They weren't allowed to talk when they were working in the home, not to themselves, or anybody. Even though it wasn't a prison, they were prisoners, forced labourers, with guards everywhere. The old-age home was a large establishment, men only, former army officers and retired people, professionals, *somebodies*, who could pay their way. The healthy ones were free to come and go and walk round. Widowers, for the most part, who had no idea how to look after themselves once their wives had died and didn't want a housekeeper. They had a comfortable sitting room and a spacious dining hall, and a large conservatory with doors which opened to the air. The infirm ones were much older, lived in the hospital attached. The guards came into their wards, pointing batons and shouting at them and all the other women working there, Polish women, a large 'P' pinned to their threadbare clothes. They were forced to scrub the wards, do the heavy laundry, dig the graves and work the vegetable patch.

'Courtesy costs nothing,' Sister Brigitte said in one of her nightly homilies. 'Even if we're not allowed to talk to them. The Polish women are prisoners too, like us. Forced to work like slaves, against their will. So smile at them. Allow them to pass. Nod your acknowledgement. Remember, they're as frightened and lonely as we are.'

More frightened, Ada thought, the way they turned frantic eyes to make sure no guard had seen, shook their heads at her, *Don't make trouble for us. Don't make it worse.*

The nuns were allowed to take the sick old people into the garden, to push their beds outside and let them soak in the sun and breathe the air. The summer had been hot, but now it was October and the temperatures dropped to freezing at night. There was no heating in their room and Ada wondered what it would be like in the dead of winter, with the draughts from the window that wouldn't shut, and a single blanket on the bed.

'We're lucky to be alive,' Sister Brigitte said, 'and busy. The devil makes work for idle hands.'

The old people were fed well. Those who were fit helped the prisoners in the gardens. They grew vegetables, but the SS took most of the produce and there was little for them. The feeble were tied to their beds, liquid dribbled into their mouths.

The nuns ate cabbage soup and dumplings and Ada put on weight.

'Can I have a word, Sister Clara?' Sister Brigitte said one evening in late October as they climbed the stairs to their attic room. Ada wondered what she'd done. Perhaps she talked in her sleep, or swore. Given away secrets, not that she had many left. Sister Brigitte knew she wasn't a real nun, and maybe she knew what Sister Monica guessed, that she hadn't been a real wife, either. Or perhaps she had some news. Ada knew she'd spoken to the guard – not *spoken*, because she didn't speak German – but drawn a red cross and pointed. 'Because,' she explained to them, 'they can let our families know.'

Perhaps there was news of Stanislaus. He was here, in Germany, had traced her, had come to save her. *I lost my way that night, Ada. Come back to me.* She would, too. Forgive him. Just a misunderstanding.

'I can't help noticing,' Sister Brigitte said. She sat on the lower bunk, tapped the space next to her for Ada to sit. 'That you haven't had your monthlies. Is there anything you need to tell me?'

Ada shrugged. 'It's the shock.' Her mother used to say it does that to women. 'And the worries. And the tiredness.'

'And do you feel sick?'

'Only when I have to lay them out. I can't stand the bodies, you see. The smell.'

'You were married?' Sister Brigitte wasn't listening to what Ada was saying, otherwise she wouldn't ask such silly things.

'Yes, but—' Ada stopped herself. She couldn't say *not really,* in case Sister Brigitte didn't know the truth.

'And the marriage was consummated?'

This was nothing to do with Sister Brigitte.

'When was the last time you were *with* your husband?'

Ada wanted to say *Be quiet.*

'Are you expecting a baby?' Sister Brigitte's question made her shiver.

She hadn't given it a moment's thought. A baby. Of course not. But the evening he left in Namur. She had been woozy, Stanislaus had been on top of her. She'd felt him thrust inside her. It had hurt. She had been damp when he moved away, had bled a little. He hadn't worn a rubber.

Ada sat on the bunk, staring at her folded hands. Now Sister Brigitte had raised the possibility, it made sense. No periods. She'd put on weight. She'd even felt fluttering inside her. What did they call it? Quickening. She'd thought it was something she'd eaten, or swallowed.

'Didn't you know?' Sister Brigitte said. Ada shook her head, stunned. How could she have a baby? Where could she have one? Where could she keep it?

'What am I going to do?' She heard her own

114

voice thin as a reed, felt her stomach floundering. *Pregnant.* What if the Germans found out?

She couldn't be pregnant. She only did it that one time without a rubber. No one gets pregnant that easily, everybody knows that. *A baby.*

'You're very quiet,' Sister Brigitte said, patting Ada's knee. 'God will show us the way.'

'Us?'

She had put them all in danger. They'd all pay for it when she had the baby and the Germans found out she wasn't a nun; that the nuns had lied and covered for her. She began to panic.

'I could say I was raped,' Ada said. It was obvious what to do. 'By a soldier. That might make it all right.'

'It would be a lie.'

'Maybe I need to tell one then,' she said. She swallowed hard. She'd become good at lying. 'Would they let me keep the baby?'

'When you make a lie,' Sister Brigitte said, 'you have to live it and sooner or later, the truth comes out. The lie, and living the lie.'

'But the baby?'

Sister Brigitte shook her head. 'Perhaps a good German family can adopt it.'

'Take my baby?'

'Sister Clara, we can't keep the baby. How will we hide it? Keep it quiet?'

She couldn't give up the baby, not to the Germans. She'd escape. Take some of the old people's clothes, or the other prisoners' clothes.

115

Rags. She wouldn't look like a nun then. She'd have to get past the guards. Pretend she was one of the Poles. They slept somewhere else at night. Slip away, when no one was looking. Maybe there was a German who'd take pity on her. Help her get home. Or find Stanislaus. He'd come back to her then, take care of them both. *Always wanted a son, Ada.*

But she'd never find him. She'd been a fool, believing him. She should have stood up to him that night in Namur, their last night, before the Germans came. *I'm too tired, Stanislaus, too tired.* Now here she was, a prisoner of war, and in the family way. Alive only because she was living like a nun, living a lie.

And if she did escape, what if she was caught? Sister Brigitte and the others would suffer. She could see the guard cracking his baton. *Where has she gone? Tell us.* Sister Brigitte wouldn't flinch. But the others would. Mousy Sister Agatha especially. And if she stayed, and they found out? What then? It was hopeless. There was no way out.

'Let's kneel and pray,' Sister Brigitte said. Ada eased herself off the bunk and sank to her knees. She calculated she must be about five months gone. Pregnant. Imprisoned. She shut her eyes. Hot, angry tears rolled down her cheeks.

The stone floor was cold. The balls of her bare feet were numb, her toes frozen, curled round the edge of the slab. Her legs were deadweights

116

on her body. Moonlight brightened the landing below, an oblong of white against the black of the stairwell.

She swung forward, teetered, pulled back.

There were fifteen risers on this flight, fifteen on the flight below. She had counted them. The house in Theed Street only had twelve but it had been enough for their neighbour to fall and miscarry.

Her shift was thin and Ada shivered. She gripped the rail with one hand, pressed against the wall with the other. A single push.

It was a mortal sin, but it wasn't just for her. It was for everyone, for the other sisters who would suffer. *Count.* On three, she told herself, on three.

She arched her back, hands firm against the side. All she had to do was swing, and let go. What if she broke a bone instead? Cracked her head open?

One.

She lifted one foot, then the other. These steps were stone. The stairs in Theed Street were wood. Their neighbour only had a few bruises and a bump on her forehead.

Two.

She took a deep breath. It was a long way to the pocket of moonlight on the landing below. The flight was steep and dark.

A door opened far below and she heard voices. She leaned forward, lost her footing, the shift tangling round her legs. She tried to stop her fall, felt her head crash on a step, her back crack against the wall, her arm buckle beneath her, her body ricochet from side to side. She heard herself scream, a piercing yell that sounded far away. A light snapped on.

She was lying crooked on the stairs, one leg straddled across the other. She hadn't fallen far. Five steps, at the most, though it had felt like more.

'*Was ist los*?'A German soldier stood over her, one boot close to her face, the muzzle of his gun pointing down. Her head throbbed and there was a shooting pain in her side. She tried to talk, heard herself barking as she gasped to catch her breath.

'Sister Clara,' Sister Brigitte's voice was above her, 'are you all right?'

The soldier moved his boot onto a lower tread.

'She fell,' Sister Brigitte said as she ran down the stairs. 'She sleepwalks, that's all.'

Ada could see Sister Brigitte waving her hand, dismissing him. The soldier hesitated, turned and walked back down the stairs.

'You've at least one cracked rib,' Sister Brigitte said, 'if not two. And a nasty bump on your temple. But at least you haven't lost the baby.'

The pain jarred every time she breathed. She lay on her back. She couldn't turn, it hurt too much. All this for nothing. Perhaps the shock would do it. Perhaps that's how it worked. You lose the baby *after*. She'd thumped it round enough. Surely it would loosen its grip, flush itself away.

'Poor little mite,' Sister Brigitte was feeling Ada's stomach. 'He must have thought he was on a helter-skelter.'

Did Sister Brigitte believe the story she'd told the soldier? Sleepwalking. Tripped on her shift. Lost her balance. Perhaps she did, she couldn't see that Ada had done this deliberately. Sister Brigitte called the baby 'he'. *He*. As if the baby was already a person. Ada wished she had died. Broken her neck, burst her skull. But the stairs were too narrow. She'd got wedged. She was still here, alive, in Nazi Germany, with sore ribs and a throbbing head. And a baby growing inside her. Ada felt sick.

'It's all right,' Sister Brigitte was saying. 'I know what I'm doing. I'm a trained nurse. Just lie here and keep still.'

Ada lay awake all night, hoping the pains would start, the blood would trickle along her thighs, the sheet sticky beneath her. Her ribs hurt when she breathed. She heard the pigeons scratching on the attic roof, their soft *coo-coo* as the grey dawn filtered through the tiny skylight. She missed her mother, wished she was here with her. Not that her mother would have approved, her not married, and *this*. She'd have to fib. *Tripped down the stairs. An accident.* Her mother would know what to do. *Rest. Keep still.* Perhaps she'd have the bed to herself. Cissie would have to sleep on the floor, or the chair bed in the front room, where Uncle Jack had slept before he died.

Cocoa. She'd drink cocoa with lots of sugar, swirling eddies in the cup, velvet vapours.

She was aware of Sister Brigitte leading the prayers, washing her hands and face, tiptoeing out of the room. She woke as Sister Brigitte slipped an arm behind her. 'Just sit up and lean forward,' Sister Brigitte said.

Ada pushed herself up, wincing with every move. She could feel Sister Brigitte pulling up her shift, exposing her naked breasts. Ada crossed her arms in front.

'Well, there's a modest one,' Sister Brigitte was laughing. 'You don't think I haven't seen it all? Stretch out your arms.' She felt as if her skeleton was being pulled apart. Sister Brigitte wrapped her chest in a winding cloth, round and round and round.

'It won't make it better,' she said. 'But at least you can stand. You have to work.'

'I can't.'

'You have no choice. Offer it up.' She looked hard at Ada, crooking her arm. Ada gripped it, pulled herself off the bed. Sister Brigitte took Ada's chin and turned her face so she could look her straight in the eye. 'That was a sinful thing to do. I trust you won't do anything so wicked again. Pray to the Lord to forgive you.'

Sister Brigitte knew the truth. Of course. Ada shook her head. She had no idea what to do now.

★   ★   ★

120

She felt the skirt of her tunic snag as she walked past the old man. She'd seen him before. A widower, one of the healthy ones who lived like kings in the residential part of the home, waited on hand and foot. She stopped and turned. He had caught it on the end of his walking stick. He was laughing, a tall man in a dark grey loden waistcoat buttoned to the neck, a pale shirt and green moleskin trousers. He was handsome, in a way. His hair was white and his eyes the same translucent blue as Stanislaus. For one giddy moment, Ada wondered if he and Stanislaus were related.

'You're a very pretty nun,' he said. Ada felt the heat rising up her neck and hoped the wimple hid her blush. 'What's your name?'

Ada looked round her. They were forbidden to talk. There was no one in sight, apart from the patients. 'You speak English,' Ada whispered.

'A little,' he said. 'But you forget a language if you don't use it. What's your name?'

She was about to say *Ada*. So easy to be tricked. 'Sister Clara.'

'Sister Clara,' he said. 'And before, before you were a nun?'

She wasn't sure if she should tell. Did nuns do that? But it felt good to speak English. The silence was unbearable during the day.

'It's all right,' he said, as if he could read her thoughts. 'You can tell me.'

She looked round her. They were alone. 'Ada.'

'Ada,' he said, 'short for Adelheid. It's a very German name. Did you know that?'

She shook her head. No one was at the near door, or the far door. She wanted to keep talking. 'And your name?'

He shook his stick free of her tunic and pulled himself up tall. 'I am Herr Professor Dieter Weiss.'

'That's a lot of names,' Ada wanted to giggle. She hadn't laughed, she realized, for months. She winced. Her ribs hurt. They were still alone, no guard to crack his whip and shout, *Es ist verboten, zu sprechen.*

'Herr is German for Mister, Professor is German for professor, Dieter is my Christian name and Weiss is my family name.'

'I've never met a Professor,' Ada said. She liked this old man. He had a name. It made him a person, not a sack of flesh she had to wash and feed.

Herr Weiss smiled. 'I am retired now, but I used to teach at the Gymnasium. You English would call it a High School, or a Grammar School.' He lifted his stick and pointed at the window where Ada could see one of the soldiers leaning against a tree smoking. 'These are my boys. I taught them all. Barely out of breeches.'

'What did you teach?'

'History,' Herr Weiss said, 'German history. Would you sit and talk with me?' Ada looked round her. 'It's not allowed.'

'Why isn't it allowed?'

Ada shrugged. 'It isn't.'

'But this establishment is my home now. I will talk with whomever I wish in my own home.' He waved his stick at the figures through the window. 'Don't worry about them. I still have respect, as their former teacher.'

He laughed. His teeth were clean and even, his face shaved and fresh. He didn't smell like the others. Ada needed to sit.

'Follow me,' he said, 'to the conservatory. We will blazen it out.'

'Blazen?'

'Is that not the word? What do I mean?'

'Brazen, perhaps,' Ada said. 'It means to be bold.'

'You see?' He took her by the elbow, steered her down the corridor. 'You are good for me already.'

Ada let him guide her. *Helping an old man, Commandant, that's all, just along to the summer room.* Then it struck her. If he would teach her German in return, if she could learn to speak it, she'd be all right, be able to get round. And who knows? Maybe she could get away. She held his stick while he lowered himself into a chair.

'Mr Weiss,' she said. 'Mr *Professor* Weiss. If I help your English, you could teach me German.'

He grabbed his stick and stomped it hard on the floor. 'You forget, my dear. You are the prisoner. I am your gaoler. You don't bargain with me.'

Ada had been sure he would say yes. She turned

123

to walk away, but her tunic snagged again. This time, she felt the stick slap against her leg. She stopped.

'But if you *ask* me would I teach you German, then perhaps the answer would be different.'

He was used to having his way, Ada could see. A man in charge, but a man, nonetheless, who found her pretty. Humour him. Let him look big.

'Would you teach me German, please?'

He leant forward, squeezed her hand. 'Sister Clara, it would be my pleasure. And you will improve my English.'

The guard who had been smoking outside entered the conservatory. Ada wasn't sure, but he looked like the one who had found her on the stairs a few nights ago. She hadn't noticed how young he was. He didn't shave yet and his skin had the smoothness of a boy. He could have been her younger brother. She pulled her hand away, rested it on Herr Weiss's shoulder, as if she had been soothing him.

'Hans,' Herr Weiss said, 'you will order her to teach me English. Every day.'

Ada could not look the soldier in the eye. She began to tremble, clenched her fists so her hands stayed still. It was dangerous to want, even something as ordinary as a conversation. He could say no. Scream in German. She might not know the words, but she grasped their meaning: *I have the power of life and death.*

The soldier shrugged, said something, Herr Weiss

replied. The soldier pulled his heels together, raised his arm. 'Heil Hitler.'

'Heil Hitler.'

'He has to confirm with the Commandant,' Herr Weiss said. 'But you will come to me in the evenings, after your work, Sister Clara. My little hobby must not interfere with your duties to the Reich.' He thrust his arm into the air. 'Heil Hitler.'

Ada swallowed. She was sure he expected her to reply, *Heil Hitler*. She couldn't, wouldn't. And the evenings, after work. She was too tired then, far too tired. But this, she knew, was an order. He took her hand again, squeezed it, rubbed his thumb inside her palm.

Christmas 1940 had long passed. Remember the date, Sister Brigitte had said. We must remember the date. Now it was another year, 1941. Ada was glad Soeur Jeanne had been plump. She was eight months pregnant now, filling the ample habit, although she couldn't imagine how. She wasn't even eating for one, let alone two. Cabbage soup. Once or twice a little cheese that Herr Weiss slipped her. But where was the goodness in all of that? Herr Weiss had slipped his hand round her waist two evenings ago as they walked towards the sitting room, telling her about the Luftwaffe, bombing London, the City. Cold, clear January nights when the stone churches gleamed like ghosts and the pilots let free their explosives, illuminating the streets below. The British will surrender, he said, after this. The City was close to *her* home, though she couldn't tell Herr Weiss that. One wayward bomb, that's all it would take. Just one. Did they come up the river to the City? Or down? Herr Weiss didn't know.

Did he guess, fingering her body? She wasn't big. Sister Brigitte said that first time you never are. You don't show. Thank the Lord. Ada had wriggled free from Herr Weiss as her baby kicked out.

Was her baby hungry, too? He must want to live, this little boy. Clinging on for sheer life. He had survived so much in his short, unborn existence. Worry hammered in her head, devoured her like a devil at the Last Judgement.

'God will provide,' Sister Brigitte said.

Ada didn't have Sister Brigitte's faith. She wasn't brave like her, either. She wished she had more courage. Each day could be her last, and it terrified her. She could irritate a nervous guard, let something slip with Herr Weiss. He could be tetchy. The British had bombed Bremen, he told her. *We will avenge.* He could also be tender. Uncomfortable, his hand lingering on hers, his stick brushing her leg, a little higher. She had to watch herself. Life and death. They never let them forget.

She had called the baby Thomas in her mind. *Thomas,* the Germans spelled it the same, though they pronounced it different. Little Thomas, Tommykins. She tried not to love him, little

Tomichen. If he was born sickly, or even dead, she'd grieve, but she wouldn't be sorry. But if he was alive, what then? She tried not to think about that. But how could she avoid it? She felt the shape of his elbow or knee at night as she lay in bed, breathed his hiccups as her own, knew when he slept, when he woke. Despite herself, she was falling in love with this unborn baby. *It's all right*, she whispered to him, her hand rubbing circles on her stomach. *It'll be all right. I'll look after you.* Her child, another life that would carry hope and love in his songs. In all this death and darkness, he was joy, and the future. He was all she had. She couldn't just sweep that away, brush it under the carpet like dirt. She loved this child, Stanislaus's child, their child.

She hadn't felt right that February evening.

'Something I ate,' she said. 'My stomach's rumbling.' She'd had nothing since breakfast. Uncomfortable. The baby was asleep, lay well down in her stomach, pressed against her bladder. He'd been asleep for nearly two days now, while her stomach had churned round him. *He's getting ready*, Sister Brigitte had said. *Saving his strength.*

Sister Brigitte checked her. 'No pain?' she said. 'Remarkable. You're almost fully dilated.' Ada felt her scratching round inside. 'Let's help it along.' Her waters broke, ran and ran, dripped over the side of the bed. What if they dripped through the floor, flooded the ceiling below?

'Slowly, slowly,' Sister Brigitte said. Sister Agatha stood with her ear pressed to the door on the look-out. She'd wedged a chair against the handle, was saying a prayer, *Blessed Virgin Mary, let the guards play cards, let them stay away.* They never checked the nuns. What could nuns get up to at night, by themselves, upstairs in the attic? But you never know. They might hear something.

'Shhh,' Sister Brigitte said. 'Scream quietly.'

The pains came fast now, like a storm surge, one after the other. Sister Brigitte had told her to breathe through the pain, sing a song in your head, sing anything.

She was as bright as a butterfly and as proud as a queen.

'Push.'

Was pretty little Polly Perkins of Paddington Green.

'Push.'

He eased out of Ada in the early hours of that cold February morning and lay puny and purple on her breast. Sister Brigitte wrapped him in an old towel she had smuggled out, put the placenta in the slop bucket to be flushed away in the morning, and cleaned Ada up as best she could.

She had also baptized the baby. 'To be on the safe side,' she said. Thomas. *Tomichen.* Tommykins.

'A nice saint,' Sister Brigitte said.

'And now?' Ada said. She would have to own up. *Take me, not them. Kill me, not them. Spare the baby. Please spare my baby.*

My baby. Ada had not expected this rush of love,

this avalanche of passion. She stroked his temple, watched the soft valley on the top of his head, the pucker of his lips and the up–down of his jaw as he lay against her. He was asleep, so delicate, so quiet. Sister Brigitte took him from her, swaddled the towel round him, laid him on the edge of the bunk and left the room. Sister Agatha took Ada's bloodied shift, helped her dress and sit up on the bed, next to Thomas.

Sister Brigitte returned a little later, with Father Friedel. He entered the attic, his rheumy eyes adjusting to the gloom.

'A baby. We found a baby. Ada,' Sister Brigitte said, nodding at Ada, emphasizing the words she had to repeat. 'Your German's better than mine. Tell Father how we found this newborn baby. Just *outside* the back door. Tell him how we took him in. Ask him to take the baby in his bag. Say *he* found it in his Baby Box, at his church.'

Ada knew that Sister Brigitte had dreamed up this plan. Sister Agatha was in on it too. She had to give her baby up. Give him to the priest. Send him away. Hope and pray that someone kind found him. Her baby, her *Tomichen*.

She swallowed. Her German was basic, but Herr Weiss had taught her how English was once German, so if she didn't know a word, she should try the English.

'Baby,' she began. '*Wir haben gefunden. Vor der Tür.*'

Ada pulled the edge of the towel away from his

129

face. She had to remember this tiny memory. 'Baby box.' Her voice was frail, the words too difficult to say.

Father Friedel looked confused. Her mother had told her about them once, how you opened a flap and put the baby inside. Ada drew the motion of a hatch opening in the air, of a bundle being deposited, of the hatch closing.

'*Ja, ja,*' Father Friedel said. '*Ein Babyklappe.*'

Ada had no idea if that was right, but she nodded.

'Tell him,' Sister Brigitte said, 'that no one must know. That he must take the baby now, while he sleeps. Put him in his bag. Say nothing.'

If Father Friedel was discovered, that would be the end for them. And Thomas. Ada pointed to the baby, and the bag. '*Still,*' she said, pressing her fingers on her lips. '*Nicht ein Wort.*' She motioned to the door.

'*Ja, ja,*' Father Friedel said. Ada wasn't sure he understood, wasn't sure he would ever understand, but he was their only hope of smuggling Thomas out, of giving him some chance of life.

Ada pushed herself off the bed. She knew she must not show how exhausted she was, that she had just given birth to this baby boy. Sister Brigitte stepped forward and took the priest's bag. She placed it on the bunk and opened it, pushing the stole to one side, the crucifix and oil to the other. She lifted Thomas up, and placed him inside. Father Friedel looked on, smiling.

He's demented, Ada thought. Doolally. Dear God. Sister Brigitte shut the case.

'Wait,' Ada said. She fished deep inside her pocket and pulled out the little teddy bear. Opening the case, she tucked the bear inside the swaddled towel and leant over and kissed Thomas on his forehead, smooth as wax.

'This is for luck,' she whispered. 'I will come back, my little Tomichen. I will find you.' She lifted the stole out from the side, and the crucifix, and laid them across the baby. Perhaps if the soldiers made Father Friedel open the bag, they'd see the cross and the stole and look no further.

'We called him Thomas,' she said.

'He must go,' Sister Brigitte said.

'Please,' Ada said in English. 'Please. Take care of him.' She couldn't say that in German. The most important words and she couldn't make herself understood. He was only three hours old. Her precious child. She knew she couldn't linger now. She'd have a lifetime for that. She snapped the lock and handed the bag to the priest.

The priest shrugged, adjusted his grip on the handle with his left hand and held up his right in a blessing. *In nomine patris* . . .

Sister Brigitte followed him out. Ada heard their footsteps on the stone stairs. Fifteen to the landing, fifteen down again. They faded in the distance. A door clicked shut. She threw herself on the bunk, buried her face in the coarse mat and howled.

★   ★   ★

131

The next morning, Sister Brigitte fished out the winding cloths from where she'd hidden them under her mattress and bound them round Ada's stomach.

'You will not talk about this,' she said, pulling the cloth tight. 'Is that understood?'

Sister Brigitte had never had a child wrenched from her, never had to watch as her baby was swaddled and smuggled away. She would never understand Ada's anguish, not knowing where Thomas was, whether he was alive or dead. She would never know her desolation. Ada had never felt so alone.

'You must offer it up,' Sister Brigitte was saying, 'as atonement. And besides,' she yanked the cloth round again, 'our lives depend on your silence.'

'But Father Friedel—' Ada said.

'Father Friedel knows nothing,' Sister Brigitte said. 'Not a word.' She slipped her arm behind Ada. 'Can you stand?'

Ada pushed her feet to the floor, leaning on Sister Brigitte for support.

'You should've been in bed for ten days,' she said, as if Ada was the one insisting on walking. 'To rest and recover. But these,' she patted the bands round Ada's stomach, 'should make sure you don't have a prolapse.'

A *prolapse*. That was what old women got, why they smelt of piss. Ada shuddered.

'I can't hide you away anymore. Are your breasts sore? Has your milk come in?'

Tomichen. Tommykin. Ada tried to conjure his face, puckered and pink with swollen eyelids, but the detail had faded even though it had only been two days. She'd know his scent, though, she was sure. He smelled of her, of the inside cushion of her flesh. She shut her eyes, clawing back the lost memory of him.

'Sister Clara, will you answer me please?'

'I'm sorry,' Ada said. 'I just can't help thinking.'

'You have to stop thinking,' Sister Brigitte said, her voice sharp, 'or you'll go mad. Now, take my arm and we'll try the stairs.'

Ada's legs had lost their gristle and her knees buckled. She had never known a fatigue so profound. She stood at the top of the flight. If she fainted now, she'd pull Sister Brigitte with her. She gripped the rail on the side, and sidled her foot forward.

Once the summer came, Herr Weiss took to waiting for Ada in the conservatory. It was a large lean-to structure facing the garden, with wicker chairs that lined the wall. During the winter they'd met in the communal sitting area but Herr Weiss had complained that it was too noisy, even though, as far as Ada could hear, nobody spoke but themselves.

'But here,' he'd said, patting the seat next to himself, 'we are alone. You and I.' He'd reached over and squeezed her hand like he always did.

'Tell me more about yourself,' he asked her one

night. 'Before you entered your convent. I like to imagine you then.'

She could barely remember what she had been like in London or Paris, or that she'd ever been happy. She'd grown even thinner than she was before she was pregnant. Sister Jeanne's habit hung in long, loose swathes. If she had a needle and thread, she could have taken it in, fitted it more closely, but now she didn't care. She knew she must look a fright. She could feel her skin had become scaly, her face blotchy and lined.

'I was a tailor,' she said. 'Ladies.'

'And what did you make?'

'Ball gowns, and day dresses, suits and skirts, blouses and collars.' She tried to recall the splendour of her creations, but the list came out flat and dogged, like a lie that had fallen out of grace.

He took her hand and placed it in his groin. 'Did you ever wear those gowns?'

Ada tried to pull her hand away but he pressed it harder to himself.

'I would sometimes act as a mannequin,' she said, heaving and swallowing her phlegm. He was doing this, this *revolting* thing.

'You must have looked lovely.'

His hand was clenched tight over hers, and beneath it his penis grew hard.

'Tell me how you looked.'

'Herr Weiss,' she said. 'Please. *Bitte.*'

He laughed. 'You don't enjoy it?' he said, squeezing her knuckles so hard that she cried out.

'I want to see you in a ball gown, the crack of your cleavage, the dip of your back. I want to watch you as you slink towards me. Talk to me.'

That world, that other Ada, was a long way away. She shut her eyes. The elemental beauty, its drama and grace fell from her memory like flesh from a cadaver. All she had now were the rattling bones.

'Talk to me,' Herr Weiss was shouting now.

'Pink,' she said, panic gripping like vice. 'One was pink.' She thought of her and Stanislaus together reflected in the mirrors at the Café Royal in London. They had looked good together. 'Cerise. Cut on the bias. Do you know what I mean?'

He shook his head, *no*. His eyes were shut and he was rubbing himself against the palm of her hand.

'You cut at an angle to the selvedge,' her breath was thin, her words short and strangled, suffocated by what he was making her do. 'Forty-five degrees. Precise. It gives it a stretch. Makes it drape. Accents the body. Folds over the hips, pauses on the stomach.'

Herr Weiss gave a groan, panted and released his grip. Ada slipped her hand free, leant back in the seat away from him.

'Go,' he said. 'I will see you tomorrow.'

She stood up and backed away, groping behind her until she found the door. Her mouth tasted of iron and every pulse in her body hammered inside her. She couldn't tell Sister Brigitte about this. She'd accuse Ada of leading him on. She wasn't a real nun, after all. Had she encouraged him? She couldn't see how. What kind of old man would want to do this filthy thing? It was disgusting.

But what if he made her do more? If she refused, he would punish her. He had the power. She was the prisoner. The thought made her shudder. An old man. It was repulsive. And she a nun, or supposed to be one. Perhaps she could play on that. *Herr Weiss, I have taken a vow of chastity.*

She had to sit next to him every evening now, he insisted. She had no choice. Ada manoeuvred herself as far away in her seat as was possible, kept her hands taut and hidden behind her scapular.

'You see,' he said, a few weeks later, pulling her hand free and pressing it deep into his groin, 'while I have vigour, I am alive.'

Ada shut her eyes, tried to ignore what she could feel.

'The old men,' he said, 'without vigour, without manhood.' He tapped his head, spiralling his finger, 'a little twisted up here. That happens, you know. When you get old.'

You warped old man, Ada thought. As if this would keep you from going demented.

'They aren't productive,' Herr Weiss was saying. 'They just take. They don't give. Nothing more than parasites. Just like the imbeciles. And Jews. And queers.'

'I don't understand.' Ada wasn't sure who he was talking about or what he was saying.

Herr Weiss appeared not to hear. 'Why should we keep them alive? A waste of time and money.'

He squeezed her hand, laid it gently to the side, and patted it. 'Perhaps not this week, my dear,' he said, as if all of this had been her idea. 'I'm not in the mood, it seems.' He smiled, and leant back in his chair. 'But you see, don't you? While I am vigorous, no one will put me on the list.'

Ada withdrew her hand and tucked it away. 'List?' she said.

'In a manner of speaking,' he said. 'Those whose life is not worth living. The retarded. The deformed. What life do they have? Better to put them out of their misery. A merciful death.'

'You kill them?'

'I like to think of it as horticulture. That's what I told my boys.' He pointed his stick at the window, though no guards were in view. 'You want a tree to grow strong and tall? Then you concentrate on the strongest boughs, and cut off the deadweight. You have to be scientific, not sentimental. Eugenics. That is the future.'

Ada tried to swallow but her mouth was dry and her tongue balled in her throat. She thought she would choke. She coughed, a painful spasm that clawed through her body.

'The German people are like a tree,' Herr Weiss went on, 'which must be freed of parasites and weaklings. Sickly babies. The old and infirm. The vile scum that saps our vigour.'

'Babies?' Ada said. 'What babies?'

'Puny ones,' he said, stamping his stick on the ground. 'Incurables. Orphans. Delinquents. Unwanted. All of them.'

Thomas. A shard of fear, sharp as glass. She had to know. Father Friedel, he would tell her. He must. Under oath, in the confessional. Despite what Sister Brigitte said, she needed to ask him. But she hadn't seen him, not for a while.

'Father Friedel?' she said, panic in her voice. 'Where is Father Friedel?'

'Friedel?' Herr Weiss snorted. 'What do you want with him? He's dead, didn't you know?'

'No,' Ada said. She couldn't stop herself. She wanted to cry. 'No.'

Herr Weiss faced her, his body coiled for action, pale blue eyes narrowed for aim. 'What's he to you?'

Thomas's feeble body, once pink with life, lay blue and marbled in her mind.

'Nothing,' she said. She shut her eyes. *Pull yourself together. Act normal.* 'Just you talking about people dying. I thought, naturally, of the Last Sacrament. Father Friedel. He used to be here all the time.'

Ada could see Herr Weiss relax. 'He was beheaded,' he said.

Ada gagged. She slapped her hand across her mouth.

'A few weeks ago,' Herr Weiss said. 'For preaching against it. Called it murder. How can we abandon it? Why should we? *Aktion T4*. It makes perfect

138

sense.' He leant back in the chair and shut his eyes, a smile of satisfaction stretched across his face. He waved his hand in dismissal.

Her Thomas, her beautiful, innocent Thomas, slaughtered. Had Father Friedel been caught? She thought he was senile, but he must have guessed. If so, he must have kept quiet about where he found the baby. Had died to save her baby. Little Thomas was small, and frail. He was placid, too, hadn't cried once or made a sound, just lain on the mattress with closed eyes. Perhaps he was simple. Would that be so bad, if he didn't live to see the horrors of this world?

And Stanislaus. Sitting pretty somewhere, Hungary, Austria, Germany. He wasn't suffering. Not like her. Not like Thomas, his son. How could he have abandoned her? Did he have no heart, no feelings? He must have known she'd be caught, how she'd be treated. Ada had never been a bitter person, never rancorous. But Stanislaus was her *lover*. She felt rage burn deep inside, like lava in the belly of the earth, suffocating reason with its fumes. She'd never felt like that before.

Sister Brigitte was leading night prayers. Ada slipped silently past her and knelt down by her bunk in the twilight. Perhaps Thomas was alive. Perhaps Father Friedel had given him to a family, a good family, who didn't believe in all this Aktion T4, or whatever it was called. That family loved him, they were caring for him. She buried her face in her hands, and for once was grateful for the nuns' soft mantras that she could mumble without thought. *Blessed are they who mourn . . .*

'*Sie.*' The guard poked her with his baton. '*Herkommen. Folgen.*' He marched ahead, through the doors. He walked fast, and Ada had to trot to keep up. She had no idea where he was taking her. Along the corridor, out of the building, into the January morning. It was almost dawn. It was the first time she had left the building since she had arrived here. It was 1942. They'd been here for nearly eighteen months, and it was almost a year since she'd given birth to Thomas. There was snow on the ground and the sky hung heavy and jaundiced. She must have been seen with Herr Weiss on one of their nightly meetings. One of the guards had spotted her touching him. It was forbidden. Or perhaps he had tired of her, told the guards to get rid of her, to make her disappear like they did with the Poles.

There was a truck ahead of them and the guard ordered her to sit in the back. She was alone. She wasn't sure if it was the cold or fear that made her shiver, sharp judders that rocked her bones and set her teeth on edge. Two soldiers emerged from behind one of the buildings, smoking and joking. One climbed into the cab, the other into the back of the truck with Ada, pulling his greatcoat around him and pushing his fingers into thick, leather gloves. The truck jerked into motion and drove out of the gates into the city.

They were in the centre of Munich, Herr Weiss had told her. They passed along streets with tall buildings on either side, past cathedrals with towering spires and large, spacious squares. In time, the houses thinned and gave way to fields and trees. Ada wrapped Sister Jeanne's outsize habit round her twice, grateful for the spare swags of thick serge, folded the scapular over her hands, curled and uncurled her toes to keep them from freezing. They passed through villages with squawking chickens and coils of smoke unfurling from the chimneys. A dog began to bark, broke free from its leash, followed them for a while, then fell back, cocking his leg against a tree, urine steaming in a steady flow that melted and yellowed the snow.

Where were they taking her? She was alone. She wanted to be with the other nuns. Strength in numbers. They held hands sometimes, she and Sister Brigitte and Sister Agatha. Took care of each other. No need to say a word. *We understand.* What would Ada do now, by herself? In a prison, or worse?

Ahead there was what looked like a factory. Long, low buildings and a tall chimney belching acrid, black smoke. They passed some gates. *Arbeit macht frei.* She wondered what they made there. *Work makes free.* Not for her, not here, not now. Lucky them. The road skirted the factory. They passed a road sign. 'Dachau', Ada read, as they pulled up at a large house with tall walls and double gates on the edge of the compound.

The soldier opened the tail flap, and jumped down. '*Runter!*'

Ada lowered herself onto the tarmac. He grabbed her arm and pushed her towards the gates that enclosed the house. Another soldier opened them and marched her into a vestibule at the front of the house. He turned, shut the doors behind him and locked them. The room was lit only by a small, circular window through which sickly shafts of light limped to the floor. There was a low shelf with boots of various sizes and shapes. Black knee-high army boots, shiny and polished, two pairs of ladies' boots, one pair neat and brown, the other suede with a fur trimming and a crepe rubber sole. There was a pair of galoshes, and a small pair of child's boots. The walls were painted a cheerless grey and the room was unheated. It was cold and damp and Ada could see her breath.

The door to the interior opened and an emaciated man entered the vestibule. His jacket was filthy and striped, with a large yellow star sewn on the front. He looked like he hadn't shaved for days.

'*Komm her,*' he said, his voice flat and dead. He led her into the main hall of the house, a vast, square room panelled in dark wood, lit by a large stained-glass window over the staircase. A striking, slender woman leant against the newel post, a long cigarette holder in her hand. Her day dress, Ada could see, was wool crepe, the colour of ruby port, with a white poplin sailor's collar trimmed in lace.

It had been a long time since Ada had seen such elegance. For one moment Ada floated free on a gossamer of beauty and yearning and she smiled. The woman pushed herself away from the post and sauntered towards her, the heels of her shoes tapping softly on the polished parquet floor.

'I am told you are a ladies' tailor,' she said in German, eyeing Ada in her shabby habit, adding with a sneer, 'though it seems unlikely.'

'I am,' Ada said. It was Herr Weiss. That was why she was here. He was the only person who knew.

'You speak German?'

'A little.'

'You only need to understand it. Come.'

Ada followed her into a small room off the scullery. A large table filling most of the space held a piece of paper, a pair of scissors, some tailor's chalk, a pin cushion, a tape measure and some black fabric, moiré, Ada guessed, from its sheen. Underneath the window was a sewing machine, a hand-turned one, not a treadle. In another corner there was an ironing board and an electric iron. These people were rich. In the far corner there was an old easy chair.

The woman lifted the piece of paper off the table and waved it in front of Ada. It was a photograph, torn from a newspaper, of a woman in evening dress.

'You will make me that dress,' she said, 'by this evening.'

'This evening? Madame, it's—' she was about to say 'impossible' but the woman interrupted her, her tone sharp as a bayonet.

'This is the house of the Commandant, the Obersturmbannführer Weiss. You do not argue with me.'

She must be Frau Weiss. Her husband had to be related to Herr Professor Weiss. Herr Weiss had told them who she was, what she did. Ada wondered what else they knew about her.

'Those are my measurements,' the woman said, pointing to a dressmaker's dummy in the far corner of the room. 'If the clothes fit that, they fit me. I do not try them on until they are finished.'

Ada wanted to say that clothes could not be made on a stiff, wooden dummy. They had to be tuned to ripple with the body as it moved, to drape when it stood in repose. She wanted to ask if there was a pattern, or another photograph of the dress. This was too grainy to see the detail.

'The squat little Jew who was here before failed to understand that,' the woman was saying. 'I will not have you touch me.' Ada had thought this woman was beautiful at first, but her mouth was hard and her flawless skin too brittle for kindness. The woman turned, paused by the door. 'Six o'clock, sharp,' she said. 'Everything you need is there.'

Ada heard the key turn in the lock behind her.

* * *

Even with a pattern and a willing customer, Ada would find it hard to complete a formal gown in a day. She stared at the photograph. The dress was tight, with a cowl neck set proud from the shoulders, and three-quarter-length sleeves. It wasn't a complicated design, though those necks could be tricky, with the fabric cut on the cross and rolled, and shoulders were always awkward. The bodice and skirt needed to fit perfectly. It was the sort of dress that in the right hands, with the right dressmaker, could look a hundred pounds. Badly made, it would look like an off-the-peg number. Frau Weiss, Ada could see, would never buy a ready-made.

She laid out the moiré on the table, running her finger over the soft watered marks that shimmered in the light, radiating subtle shades of black. People thought black was a dead, dull colour, but it had as many hues and lustres as blue or red. The moiré wasn't silk, but rayon, an unhappy fabric, she could hear Isidore say, that sheds its fibres like a weeping widow. There were at least five yards, more than enough to make the dress. Enough, even, for a cocktail hat or headpiece. Ada lifted the cloth and draped it over the dummy. There was no muslin to make a toile first. She'd have to do without it.

She rolled up her sleeves, placed the tape measure round her neck, stuck pins from the cushion down her scapular and set to work. Perhaps she should be grateful. Perhaps this had been a gift from Herr Weiss.

★   ★   ★

By three o'clock the dress hung lifeless on the dummy. Frau Weiss hadn't appeared all day. Even if the measurements were exact, Ada knew the dummy was no substitute for the real thing. You had to walk in the dress, breathe life into its empty form, so the fabric was at one with the flesh and skin.

Ada paused. It was quiet outside. She slipped the scapular over her head, pulled off the heavy tunic and the underskirt and shift, stood shivering in her calico drawers. Silence. She stepped out of her drawers and into the dress, twisting as she pulled it up and over her body so the neck lay obliquely on her shoulders and the bodice snug round her breasts. The rayon was smooth as balm against her skin, like brushed silk against her thighs. Ada stood on tiptoes, as if on heels, pirouetted once, twice. There was no mirror but she saw herself with long, wavy hair, the moiré shining light and dark against the evening sun, her skin pale and innocent against its sheen. It was a brief glimpse of her old life, of elegance and beauty and freedom, what her life could still have been if she hadn't met Stanislaus.

A dart needed taking in, and the seam could pucker if the tension wasn't right. She felt the collar which lay proud and even, touched her shoulders where the sleeve would go. Tighten the seam there. She held the back together with her hand. Fasten the hooks here, and here. There were voices outside. Ada froze.

She eased herself as fast as she could out of the dress, stepped back into her shift and drawers. Men's voices, indistinct. She tugged up her underskirts and pulled down her tunic, wrapping the belt twice round her waist. She left the scapular off. It only got in the way. She picked the dress up from the floor and took it over to the sewing machine as the voices drifted into the distance.

Her hands shook as she adjusted the pins and threaded the machine. Pin, tack and sew. If she had been caught wearing the dress, she knew the punishment would have been serious. She pressed the seams and whipped them, put the dress back on the dummy, fitted the sleeves so they didn't pucker, adjusted the length. She had no organza to line the hem and turn it so it draped soft as a breeze. *Then herringbone*, Ada, *herringbone*. Hooks and eyes, fifteen should do it. The natural light was fading. There was a single bulb over the table that Ada switched on from the plug on the wall. It gave out a dim glow but if she held the work close she could see. Final press, not too hard at the hem. There was a box of hangers under the table and Ada selected one and hung the dress from the picture rail.

Even in the poor light of the room, Ada knew it was a masterpiece. When this war is over, she thought, the House of Vaughan will live.

She eyed the remnant of fabric. There was some interfacing left and the moiré was firm. Perhaps a rose. It wouldn't take long, fitted to a small skull

147

cap that would grip snug and which Frau Weiss could pin to her hair with a Kirby grip, if they had them in Germany.

For the first time since he was born, nearly a year ago, Ada had not thought of Thomas. He'd be one year old in a few weeks. 19 February, 1942. *Happy Birthday, Tomichen.*

The man in the jacket with the yellow star collected the dress in the evening, held it by the hanger at arm's length.

'Excuse me,' Ada said. 'The lavatory?'

He pointed to a bucket by the door, switched off the light and turned the lock behind him. The room was pitch-black. She heard his footsteps fade. A baby was wailing in the distance. Ada remembered the child's boots in the vestibule. The cry was faint but now that Ada had heard, it did not go away. The child must be in the room above hers. How long had the little thing been crying? Her eyes adjusted to the dark and moonlight filtered through the window bars, casting shadows across the table. She could hear doors opening and shutting, footsteps, a woman's voice – Frau Weiss – calling out. The doorbell rang, a deep sonorous *clang*, more voices, laughter, the doorbell again. A party. Her room was close to the kitchen and the doors let in gobbets of noise as people entered and left. She could hear glasses, the hollow *pung* of popping champagne corks, laughter growing louder and louder, while above her the child yelled.

Ada relieved herself in the bucket, and sat on the stool by the sewing machine. She'd had no food since yesterday, and nothing to drink except a swig of water since this morning. Had they told Sister Brigitte where she was? She'd worry otherwise, fret that Ada had done something silly, had run away. Herr Weiss would be kept waiting too. He wouldn't tolerate that, he lost his temper easily. He'd be in the dayroom, stomping his stick on the floor, demanding. The guards wouldn't be pleased.

Except that Herr Weiss must know. Given permission for her to leave for one day. The voices were growing thinner, and the child was silent. Must have cried itself to sleep, poor little mite. They would come to get her soon. There were noises from the scullery, cutlery and plates being washed, glasses tinkling in soapy water. The party was over. They would collect her now, take her back to Munich.

But the house grew silent and the room cold and no one came. Ada moved to the old easy chair in the corner. The seat cushions were lumpy and the springs broken but it was softer than the stool and she could lean back. It smelt musty. She was tired and hungry. She missed Sister Brigitte and the other nuns, their warmth and the soft *put-put* of their breath as they slept. She wanted to talk to them. Not that she liked them very much, but they shared what she shared, feared what she feared and for all that Ada didn't believe in God, she knew they prayed for the same thing. They were on the same side, and they had each other.

In the morning the man in the striped jacket unlocked the door and pointed to the bucket.

'Follow me.'

She lifted the pail and he led her out through the scullery to an outdoor lavatory. A climbing rose had been planted against the wall, covered in plump red rosehips. It thrived in that soil, must catch the sun. Ada went inside. From the stains in the bowl, and the smell, Ada knew the lavatory had not been cleaned for years. The man turned away as she emptied the receptacle, then walked her back into the scullery, handing her a chipped enamel bowl half-full of beige slop. The old Ada had never liked porridge, could only eat it if it was smothered in sugar but now *this* Ada, a different Ada, swallowed it greedily. He waited while she ate.

'Who are you?' she said. He pressed his lips together.

'Can you talk?' He shook his head. *Das ist nicht gestattet.* Wagged his finger. *Verboten.*

He led her back to the room where Frau Weiss was waiting for her. She had a bolt of fabric over one arm and what looked like a ladies' magazine in her hand. Ada wondered if the Germans had rationing, like the French. This woman seemed short of nothing.

She placed the fabric on the table and, flicking

150

open the magazine, handed it to Ada. 'This,' she said, pointing to an image of a ladies suit, and then to the material on the table.

Ada picked up the picture. The jacket had a fitted waist and was fastened up to the neck with a straight line of studs down the centre. The skirt was an A-line flair. Dull as ditchwater. So was the fabric, donkey-grey with a dun check. Frumpy. But Ada could see that buttoned to the side, with a mandarin collar, two trim pocket flaps to match, and a pencil skirt with a kick pleat at the back, the suit would be young, *modisch*. She had learned the word from Herr Weiss. Just like the English, only spelt differently. Frau Weiss was pulling out lining fabric and threads. She had not said a word about the dress, but Ada knew that she must have been pleased with it, otherwise she would have sent her away.

Ada looked at her. 'Madame,' she took a deep breath. 'Perhaps,' she pointed to the picture, 'buttoned here, pocket there. More *modisch*.' Ada waited for a shout, but Frau Weiss was listening. 'Do you have a pencil and paper?' Ada went on. 'I want to show you.'

Frau Weiss left the room and returned. Ada was not good at drawing, but she could manage a design if she sketched it in stick form, lean and angular. She saw Frau Weiss play with a smile. She was a vain woman.

'I need the suit for tomorrow.' *Ja.* She turned and left the room.

Lined, too. Ada would have to stay up all night.

She picked up the magazine, and closed it. The Nazi insignia was on the front, with the words *NS Frauen-Warte*. Ada ran her finger over the letters. She couldn't read German, but she guessed at *Frau*. There was a photograph on the cover of a large German woman in a long, embroidered pinafore dress and white blouse sitting on a bench knitting a sock. A chubby toddler played in a cot by her side. The caption to the photograph was written in a strange, old-fashioned script. The child on the cover looked about the same age as Thomas, sitting in his cot, smiling, his hair neatly cut and parted.

The child upstairs was crying again. Why didn't Frau Weiss pick the baby up? She would never have let her baby cry like this, for hours on end. He'd give himself a hernia. The Frau must be hard as nails. It went with vanity.

Ada was let out twice that day, taken into the scullery and given watery soup and coarse, black bread, which she and the man ate standing up, in silence. Back to her room where she cut and draped and sat and sewed. She needed weights for the jacket so it would hang to perfection. The windows had curtains, rotting fabric that hung in swathes from the rusty curtain rail. Ada felt the hems. She fished out the tiny leads that weighted them down, took a couple. She'd sew them later into the jacket bottoms. When the house was quiet, she slipped on the suit, marked where it pulled or puckered, adjusted the darts. Weights in place and the linings French tacked. Although the wool was dull, it was soft against her skin, and the lining was smooth. Frau Weiss would never know that she had tried it on, that the fibres of the lining that had caressed Ada now clung to the Frau like cobwebs. She liked that idea.

She fell asleep in the easy chair. As dawn approached, Frau Weiss entered the room and took the suit without a word.

The routine was the same as the day before. She emptied her bucket, ate the watery gruel, returned to her room.

This time, the man brought in a basket of clothes and shoved it into her arms. 'To mend,' he said.

Ada could barely get her arms round the overflowing basket. She pulled out the items. Socks for darning and ladies' hose, with fine ladders at the top, just below the suspender line, for mending. Cardigans and jumpers with frayed cuffs or worn elbows, trousers with missing buttons, a skirt with a broken zipper, blouses with open seams, dresses in need of hemming, brassieres without hooks. There was a blanket with loose edges, a jacket with torn lining, a large, tweed great-coat which Ada could only imagine was there for turning and a child's ripped romper suit.

What kind of a housewife must she be, letting the mending all pile up, turning a minor chore into a major one? Some women couldn't sew, Ada knew, and Frau Weiss must be one of them, but she should have made an effort. She must be a real slut, Ada thought, surprised at the viciousness of her thoughts, surprised that she cared. This would take Ada days and days to finish. She wondered whether she would ever return to the geriatric home, to Sister Brigitte and the others, whether she would ever see beyond this room and the lavatory, would ever speak English again. Would ever talk again, would ever get home, be free.

Ada lost track of the days, began to count in menstrual cycles. At least with the old people Sundays were different and they could mark time, but here every day was identical. Ada was let out for food and the lavatory. She was given a wash bowl and rag. At some point a package arrived with a fresh wimple, drawers and shift. It must have come from the Red Cross. Sister Brigitte had got through to them, after all. Perhaps a letter would come soon, too.

What had Sister Brigitte said? *Remember the dates. Remember.* Ada started to keep a tally, chalked them on the underside of the table. It was summer now, the end of July 1942. She'd been here seven months, had watched the snow become rain and the rain give way to the sun. Her fingers sweated in the heat as she sewed. She had to keep wiping them on an old piece of towelling so she didn't leave greasy marks on Frau Weiss's fine spun lawns and tulles.

154

One hot day the door opened and Herr Weiss entered, smart in a white shirt and loden waistcoat, his stick tapping on the floor.

'Nönnchen,' he said. 'My nephew told me you were here.'

She was right. Herr Weiss had arranged this, was connected to the Obersturmbannführer, whom Ada had not yet laid eyes upon. She tensed, her fingers tight inside her palms, her teeth clamped hard against her jaw.

'Come, my little Sister Clara*lein*,' he walked towards her, the metal tip of his stick tap-tapping on the stone floor. 'Aren't you pleased to see me?'

Why had he come now? After all these months? What did he want?

'You don't smile when you see your old professor?' He ran his stick along the ground, flicked the hem of her habit. 'Is it not good to hear English again?'

Be polite. Don't ask for trouble. She smiled, a small lilt of her lips. He beamed back, placated.

'I have forgotten what it sounds like.'

He laughed. 'You never forget your native language. It rests deep inside you, always. Shall we sit down, you and I?'

Ada always made her bed in the morning, placing the cushions back on the chair, folding up Sister Jeanne's old habit and hiding it beneath. She had invented little routines to bring order to her life, something ordinary that reminded her of another world, that gave her some control.

'There is only one chair,' Herr Weiss said,

pointing to her bed, limping his way across the room towards it. *Tap, tap.* He was more stooped than she remembered. An old man.

'I'll sit on the stool,' she said. A safe distance away.

'As you will,' he said, 'as you will.'

She sat down, tension slipping free, her muscles smoothed flat. Calm down, she told herself. He was here for a talk, for an English lesson. Nothing more.

'And how do you find it here?' he said.

'As prisons go,' Ada said, 'not bad.' It was the truth. She could be washing old bodies, dead ones, or dying ones with sagging scrotums and fingers that clawed at the covers. She might not have enough food or clothes or a decent bed, and she worked all hours, but it was work she could take pride in. Even though Frau Weiss never praised her, much less showed her gratitude, she knew she appreciated her skill.

'I thought you would approve,' Herr Weiss said. 'I would have come to see you sooner, but I wanted you to settle first.'

He was wily, cunning. They were alone in this room, with no one to interrupt. The scissors were on the table, within her reach. If he came towards her she could rush and grab them. Her heart was hammering. Could she do it? He might be old but he was strong, *vigorous.* She was thin and weak. No match.

'Come, my dear,' he was saying. 'You don't look

happy. Life could be worse, believe me.' He pushed himself up from the chair, and lifted his stick from where he had leant it against the arm. 'Next time I come, I would like a little gratitude. But for now, dinner will be served and my nephew is a stickler for punctuality.'

He clicked his heels together and bowed. 'I believe,' he said, 'we have wild boar with an excellent French claret. Vintage, 1921. Our German wine is good, but doesn't have the body of the French. Good evening, Sister Clara.' He spun on his heel and tap-tapped from the room, turning at the door. 'We have much to celebrate. The Russians are in retreat.' He smiled, bowed. 'Until next time.'

She listened as his footsteps drifted along the corridor into silence. She rubbed the heel of her hand into one eye. After all these months she thought she was free of Herr Weiss, free of his slimy charm, his bony fingers pressed against hers, pushing them hard into his loins while he writhed and groaned beneath her. She was sick at the memory and at the future it waved in front of her. She wondered if the war would ever end, whether she would ever start a new life. What would be left? *Who* would be left? She didn't hear much about the war. Frau Weiss never spoke about it. But if the Russians were in retreat, that must mean something. She didn't know much about geography, or politics, but she remembered her father saying how vast Russia was. Not just Russia. The

Union of Soviet Socialist Republics. She could hear him saying, *Imagine, Ada, the most powerful country on earth, and socialist. Paradise.* If they were in retreat, Germany must be the most powerful country now. What did Herr Weiss call it? The Third Reich.

She longed to hear her father's voice. *You had it bad, Ada girl.* To start up where she left off, before she met Stanislaus, back at Mrs B.'s. To have made a different choice that night they met in London. *No thank you. I must get home. I can't join you for tea at the Ritz.* Where would she be now? Miss Vaughan, our most accomplished *modiste.* She might have met a husband. Loyal, not treacherous like Stanislaus. One of her own kind.

Instead, she was trapped in this prison, at the whim of Herr Weiss, ruining her eyesight and her looks. This was slave labour, she knew – but at least she *was* sewing, *was* creating. A *modiste.* Perhaps when the war was over, if it was ever over, she'd go to Paris again. She'd have experience, after all. She didn't have to say where she'd got it. *House of Vaughan.* She'd need someone to back her, like Coco Chanel had, someone who'd see her talent. *Modiste extraordinaire.* What did they call those old-time magicians who turned metal into gold? Alchemists. That's who she was, that's what she'd do. That's what this was, her war. Metal. She'd turn it to gold. Some time. Maybe. She *must* hope. She'd lost her lover, her family, her child, but she wouldn't lose this.

She rushed to the bucket, dry, painful heaves of bile. There was nothing inside her to vomit except misery.

She stumbled back to the stool. She was powerless. If she was ever freed from this place, she would never let another person have such control over her life.

She picked up her sewing and bent over the table, squinting at the needle. Above her, the child began to scream. Ada heard Thomas in those cries, saw his tiny face pucker in misery before the priest's bag closed over him. She couldn't get him out of her head, her baby boy, her abandoned baby boy, all alone. It made Ada want to scream too. *What's wrong with you, Frau Weiss?* What mother lets her baby suffer like this? He needs comforting. Or gripe water. Hours and hours, until Ada heard the yells shudder to a halt and silence close over. She'd rather be flogged every day than listen helpless to the child's anguish. She'd rather Herr Weiss with his lewd, vile needs.

She'd rather die.

She stared at her scissors, fingered the blade. How long would it take to bleed to death? One hour? Twelve? Hanging would be quicker. She could make a rope, easy as anything. Hang it from the ceiling lamp. Move the table, stand on the stool beneath, kick it away. The light flex looked skimpy. Wouldn't take her weight. She wanted to be sure she would die.

She returned the scissors to the table. Is this

what they wanted? Work her to death? Drive her out of her mind? What happened to the person who'd been here before her? Did that woman go mad from the silence and loneliness? The worry? The screaming baby? Did it remind her of her own children?

She looked again at the light flex. She pushed the stool towards the table and climbed on top. It wobbled and Ada squatted to save her balance.

This was madness. She didn't even have the courage to throw herself off a table.

No, damn it. She would survive. They wouldn't have that victory. She'd talk to herself, keep herself company. Make up stories with happy endings. Recite poems she'd learned at school. *The wind was a torrent of darkness among the gusty trees.* Who wrote that? *The moon was a ghostly galleon tossed upon cloudy seas.* She couldn't remember. There was no one to ask. *The road was a ribbon of –* Noyes, Alfred Noyes – *a ribbon of moonlight over the purple moor.*

'And the highwayman came riding,' Ada shouted.

'Riding, riding. The Highwayman came riding, up to the old inn-door.'

That September, the September of 1942, Frau Weiss introduced Ada to her friends, stout women and slim ones too, none as squeamish as Frau Weiss but fussy nevertheless. They arrived with pictures circled in the *Wiener Bunte Mode* or the *NS-Frauen-Warte*. Simple designs. Stolid, practical

160

clothes which lacked flair and inventiveness. Ada adapted a neckline, a hem-length, adding or removing a trim to make it different, unique, to emphasize the woman beneath and not the mother. From time to time they would come with photos of glamorous women called Zarah Leander or Emmy Göring, whom Ada guessed were actresses or film stars. They pointed to the pictures for Ada to copy.

They weren't like the clients who came to Mrs B., upper-class women, gracious with the servants. *That's breeding for you,* Mrs B. had said. These German ones had money, but no *class.* Thick Bavarian accents. Their husbands would be shop-keepers. Or pharmacists. Doctors, even. *Führer* this and *Führer* that. A river of words that meandered through places Ada had never heard of: Wannsee, Stalingrad, El Alamein; and eddied in pools round people she did not know: Johannah, Irma. That *Fräulein.* A model, for goodness sake. A photog-rapher. Here in Munich. Who did the *Führer* think he was kidding? Why didn't Magda Goebbels have a word with him? Ada listened hard, trying to glean some news from home in the currents of talk – General Government – Luftwaffe – London. But the topics flowed past on a tide of gossip about other women, not the war. That *Fräulein's* com-plexion. Too perfect. She must come by powder. Lipstick too. *She* didn't seem to be suffering in the war economy, taking her belt in a notch or two like the rest.

They preened in front of each other. They didn't see her as she cut and moulded the fabric round their bodies, tucking here, pinning there. Silk had been commandeered, you couldn't get stockings, or butter. But Frau Weiss served them coffee, real coffee, *from a little man she knew*, and she would give a smile and serve some cake sweetened with sugar, real sugar. Pranced round them, *Do help yourselves, bitte schön*, proud to be generous with her cakes and coffee, gracious in sharing her little secret with them, her nun, her dressmaker. Ada knew an upstart when she saw one, could see through Frau Weiss's phoney ways and false demeanour. If it wasn't for Ada and her skills, none of these women would play court to Frau Weiss.

They all looked good in Ada's clothes. This was her magic, her special talent, steaming and stretching the fabric so it fitted like skin, smoothed out the bumps, glorified the line. They didn't care how her head throbbed at night, how her eyes saw double in the morning, how her stomach cramped with hunger. *Sehr feminin. Modisch.* They entered her room like peasants and left like queens. *Ich könnte ein Filmstar wie Olga Chekhova sein.* Ada knew that they needed her. She saw them as they were: naked and vulnerable, their glamour only empty airs and graces, plain women, no different from Ada or the Poles. Without Ada, they were nobodies.

She hated them. Every time they entered her

room a deep, visceral loathing bubbled like brimstone in the pit of her stomach. Frau Weiss, cold as stone, indifferent to the suffering of others. *Immoral,* she could hear her mother say. *Amoral.* She hadn't always seen eye to eye with her mother, but that was over now. She'd make it up to her, become successful. *House of Vaughan.* She'd make her mother beautiful. Give her good foundations, girdle, brassiere, drape her in crepe de Chine and the finest charmeuse. *Watch your back,* Isidore would say, *charmeuse. A wily fabric.* Untrustworthy. Unreliable. She could see herself in her workshop, a bright attic with windows floor to ceiling, like those artists' houses on the Great West Road. A tailor's dummy in the corner, one of those expandable ones, that you could adjust. A double rail for her creations, one on top of the other, with a pole and hook to lift the dresses up and down. An oriental carpet on the floor, Thomas playing in the middle, making bridges with his Meccano.

What happened to Tommy's father, Ada? He died. Horrible death. In the war. I don't like to talk about these things.

These women, these *German* women, Herr Weiss, all of them, keeping her here like a slave, a woman without feelings.

Sometimes she felt dizzy. She was hungry and tired and the autumn air had a bite which gnawed her bones. She'd been wearing the same clothes since she'd arrived in January. The edges had softened and frayed, but the fabric was stiff with dirt, chafed when she moved. She could not stop work without feeling the back of Frau Weiss's hand across her cheek or the welt of a strap across her back, even through the thick serge of her habit. She dreaded Herr Weiss's return, expecting to hear the lock click, the door open, and the old man come in. She had begun to tremble, uncontrollable shudders that sent the needle ripping through her skin, or the scissors skidding through the fabric, until the gong was sounded for dinner and Ada could relax.

Autumn turned to winter. Frost coated the window panes and opened the pores of the building so the damp fungal of the bricks blew through the air, made the place smell like a cellar. Ada was given a blanket. She had taken to pulling the cushions off the chair and laying them on the floor. It was draughty, but at least she could stretch flat. Sister Jeanne's tunic hung in filthy rags and smelled of sweat and dirt, but Ada was used to the stink, had learned how to lie so the spare cloth was on top of her. She was mostly warm at night, trying not to think of home, the bed she shared with Cissie, the tiny front parlour which doubled as the dining room at Christmas. Sister Brigitte used to say *Imagine you are home and safe, think of those you love and who love you.* She could see the spread laid out, the haunch of ham and the liver paste, pork pie and sliced brawn, luncheon meat and cold beef, sausage rolls and ox tongue, black pudding and chitterlings, and a mountain of Scotch eggs, her favourites. Her mother and Auntie Lily squeezing through with cups of tea while her father stood to the side with a bottle of Watneys or a jar of porter, picking tobacco from his lips. It must be close to Christmas now. She fished out her tailor's chalk and wrote 1942 on the underside of the table. December. She had been in this house nearly one year, in Germany for nearly two and a half.

She turned in her bed, dragging the spare habit round her. The front door at home was painted black, like all the other doors in Theed Street. She could see her mother on her hands and knees, cloth stiff with the Cardinal's, scrubbing and rubbing till the doorstep shone. *Waste of time. Who cares?* Ada's eyes misted up and she tried to squeeze away the memory, but it stayed like a stubborn spot, grew larger until she was there, crossing the road on the balls of the feet so her heels didn't scuff between the cobbles, onto the pavement. Dry land, she'd say, when she was little and still at school and could imagine the road an ocean and she a billowing ship sailing away, *for a year and a day.* She turned left, past bleak-black houses and absent lives that stretched no further than a ha'penny bus ride, past the corner shop with its yellow and black enamel hoardings for Lyons Tea and Colman's mustard and OMO painted onto the wall, and the pram on its brake, with the baby fast asleep. Mum always peered into prams and Ada couldn't see why, but now she understood. She was a mother too now, but her baby was away, lost and alone. She could feel her heart weighed down in chains, dragged round in shackles.

Love and pain, despair and hope, the future and the past. She tried not to let them drift through her mind at night, tangle like cat's cradle as she lay on the dusty cushions on the floor. But the thoughts were stubborn, like silk, *Thomas and home*. She drifted to sleep, woke with a start. *Stanislaus*. Hold onto hope, she told herself.

The mornings were icy when she emptied her pail. The man in the striped jacket was no longer there. He'd left in the spring, and there was another who took his place, a middle-aged man whose skin hung in swags on his frame. He must have been a big man once, well fed. He winked at her when no one was looking, blew her a kiss. She had smiled.

After him came a cadaverous man, tall, stooped, clumsy. He bit his lip, looked away from Ada, as if he saw his own misery reflected in her. Frau Weiss let her out one morning and told her to cut down his body from the rafters of the outhouse where he slept. He had torn his jacket into shreds and knotted them together, tightened one end round the beam and the other round his neck. She had found the yellow star ripped off and pressed into his waste bucket. He'd only been there a week.

Ada lost count of the men who came and went. Another Red Cross parcel arrived. There was no letter. It contained two new wimples, underclothes and a tunic. Ada wondered why they still bothered. She would rather wear ordinary clothes. The new tunic fitted better, but she kept the old one as a blanket.

Ada's fingers grew numb and clumsy with the cold. Frau Weiss and her friends brought Donegal tweeds for their winter walking skirts, and dark green loden for their coats, cashmere for their dresses, chenille for the evening. Ada clutched the warmth from the wool, soothed her chapped hands with the lanolin from the tweed. There was some cashmere left over and Ada fashioned herself a pair of fingerless gloves which she used for working, and a pair of mitts and bedsocks from the offcuts of tweed for sleeping in at night. She kept them hidden by day, stuffed in the bottom of her remnant basket. *Hide a tree in a forest.*

Spring came late that year in 1943. Endless days of dull clouds and chilly rain which surrendered in a sudden and gave way to May. It became unseasonably hot. Frau Weiss had beads of sweat on her forehead, passed Ada a parcel of linen, a dull slub of fabric which she wanted fashioned into slacks. *Linen gets cross,* she heard Isidore say, *Stay out of its way.* Ada took off her scapular and tunic and her wimple which made her scalp sweat and itch. She had to cut her own hair. Without a mirror, she had no idea what it looked like. She

167

set to work in her shift and underskirts, aware of how her hands looked gnarled, her arms wasted, her veins bulged.

One morning towards the end of the month the door opened and Frau Weiss stood there hand in hand with a small boy, a toddler. He had fair hair and blue eyes, looked glum and solemn. In one hand he held a small, brown knitted bear. Ada watched his face turn from curiosity to terror at the sight of her. He began to scream. This was the child who cried himself to sleep each night.

Thomas. Her Thomas.

'*Nein*,' Frau Weiss said, slapping his hand. 'Stop crying. You are not a baby.'

Ada stepped towards him, squatted down to his level, held out her arms. She knew she shouldn't, but she couldn't stop. This was only natural. This was her son.

Frau Weiss scooped the child up, pushing Ada with her foot and sending her sprawling across the floor.

'Never touch my child! Never talk to him!' She kicked Ada in the back. 'Never!' She kicked again, catching Ada's ribs. 'Never! *Nie!*' She was shouting, the child was screaming.

'*Das ist eine Hexe*,' she yelled, grabbing the child by his chin and forcing him to look at Ada, 'sub-human.'

She put the child on the floor. 'You will not fear her. You are better than her. You must be a man.' Ada could see the beads of sweat breaking out on

Frau Weiss's forehead, and her hands trembling as she rested them on the little boy's head.

Ada knew then. Frau Weiss was frightened of *her*. You made me your prisoner, Ada thought, your slave, but I've got the measure of you, Frau Weiss. You need to be cruel to survive. Cruelty will destroy you before it destroys me. You hate yourself and despise me for it. Once I've gone, who will make you feel important? Who will make you look beautiful?

And what if I turn on you? I have the shears in my hand, one lunge, that's all it would take before your blood would spout like a geyser and you would writhe like a serpent beneath my feet. I would have Thomas then, clutch him tight and never let him go. It would be worth it, to feel his body close to mine, to soothe his fears and wipe away his tears.

'Put your clothes on, nun,' Frau Weiss said. She wagged her finger at the child. 'We will make a man of you, Joachim.' She swept out of the room, locking the door behind her, leaving Joachim behind. The child banged at the door, his face red and blotchy, his cries so violent he began to choke and retch.

'*Mutti, Mutti.*'

Ada pulled on her tunic, fixed the wimple round her head, put on the scapular and placed the poplin she was about to cut flat on the table, her head ringing with the toddler's wails.

She knew if she spoke it would be the child who

would suffer. Frau Weiss called him Joachim, but Ada wasn't fooled. If he was the Frau's natural son, his pain would pull at her gut. The umbilical cord, Ada knew, was never cut between a mother and her child. The passion Ada felt for this baby was proof enough that he was hers, he was her Thomas.

When this war was over, when the Germans were defeated and Hitler destroyed, she'd show Frau Weiss what a mother's love could do. Scoop Thomas into her arms, *Don't cry. Mummy's here.* Take him home. Find a nice little place for them both. A little cottage in the country. She'd gone to Kent one summer with the Children's Country Holiday Fund. Roses round the door, hollyhocks in the garden, thatch on the roof. Pretty as a picture. That's where they'd go. They'd be happy. She'd take him there. If Stanislaus ever found them, she'd tell him, *Stay away. What kind of a father were you? We don't need you.*

'*Mutti*,' Joachim whimpered, eyes wide in terror at the sight of Ada.

Ada tried to ignore him. She knew that Frau Weiss must have told him stories about her, a witch, *vermin*, knew if she stepped close he would grow hysterical. Sing, she thought, sing.

'*She was as beautiful as a butterfly, and as proud as a Queen,*

'*Was pretty little Polly Perkins of Paddington Green.*'

She went back to her work, cut through the fabric and marked the darts. Second verse, out loud, all together now:

'*Her eyes were as black as the pips of a pear,*
'*No rose in the garden her cheeks could compare.*'

Thomas stopped crying. Ada saw, from the corner of her eye, that he had pulled his fingers away from his eyes and was staring at her. A large sob forced itself through his small body. Ada carried on singing.

'*Her hair hung in ringlets so beautiful and long*
'*I thought that she loved me but found I was wrong.*'

Another loud sob filled the air, like a final convulsion. She sang again, loud enough for Thomas, but not so loud that Frau Weiss would hear.

'*She was as beautiful as a butterfly, and as proud as a Queen,*
'*Was pretty little Polly Perkins of Paddington Green.*'

She stopped singing. Thomas stood sniffing by the door, staring at her. She began to pin the darts. He began to cry so Ada sang again.

'*When I asked her to marry me she said "Oh, what stuff"*
And told me to drop it, for she'd had quite enough.'

The child was silent once more. She wanted to smile at him, talk to him, *ich bin deine Mutti, Tomichen. I wouldn't hurt you. You like music, huh? Don't be frightened of me.* Ada heard Frau Weiss's footsteps and she entered the room, yanked the child's arm and dragged him away.

Ada still counted the months in cycles, ticking them off with the chalk underneath the table, next to where she marked the years. She'd been here eighteen months. June 1943. Long days and nights that stretched to dawn while Ada sewed linen into skirts and lawn into blouses, smocked cotton into swimming costumes, fashioned parachute silk into negligees and knickers. If she didn't get them done, Frau Weiss beat her with the buckle end of the belt, or whatever came to hand. The silk snagged on her fingers so she had to fold it over the table, stab the needle *down in, up out*, lest her chapped skin dragged a thread and puckered the clothing. She'd lift the negligees to her face, stroke them against her cheeks, holding them up with the backs of her hand balled tight so the fingers didn't catch the gentle membranes. They were soft and warm as a baby's hand, *her* baby's hand, her *Tomichen*.

She had to make Thomas's clothes now. He was no longer a baby, but a little boy, in shirts and jackets, shorts and rompers. She took extra care with them, embroidered a small car on the bib, or baby bears on the braces. He still screamed at night. Ada wondered what terrors he had to visit in his dreams. During the day, she could hear him on the lawn behind her room. He had a bicycle with squealing brakes which she saw one morning when she emptied her pail and had peered round the rose bush into the garden. It was a small child's bike, black and low, with thick rubber wheels and stabilizers. He must have learned to ride it. He would be clever. He had left it out overnight, laid on its side on the grass, where it slept like a wounded clock.

She hoped she'd see him outside, playing in the garden. She could hear his chatter, his squeals and laughter, but he was always pulled inside when Ada went out. By September, as the nights drew in again, and the first of the frosts pinched the golden haws and coated the grass with the crunch of ice, she knew she would not see him again, not that summer.

Ada woke with a start. She could hear a dull hum, like a sewing machine, or a bee, a deep, steady chug and above it the hiss of air. It was coming closer, growing louder.

An aeroplane. Overhead. The sound circled, grew faint, and then swelled again. There was more than one. Who did they belong to? A faint light flickered and Ada heard the boom of an explosion. It was in the distance, but the sounds repeated. *Boom, boom.* She remembered Belgium, Namur, Stanislaus. It seemed a lifetime away, another world again. The night sky began to glow like a rich, copper scuttle. It couldn't be the Germans, Ada knew. It must be ours. *Ours.* Our boys. Dare she hope? The war would be over soon. She could go home. Perhaps she'd be home by Christmas. Christmas, 1943. It was only three months away.

In the morning, Frau Weiss said nothing but Ada could see she was angry. The bombing had been far away, probably Munich. Had they bombed the centre? Was Sister Brigitte safe? Perhaps the old man, Herr Weiss, was hurt, or dead. If only, Ada thought, *if only.*

Frau Weiss flung a dress on the table, swiping Ada across the face as she did so.

'A pin,' she screamed. 'You left a pin.' She was holding it in her fingers and began to jab at Ada, hitting the palms of Ada's hands as she lifted them to defend herself.

'I don't need you,' she went on. 'None of us need you. Don't you think we have German dressmakers of our own? They are the best in the world. Do you think I like having my clothes made by you?'

She was wearing a simple blue frock Ada had made, which highlighted the angles of her body, stark squares and triangles that camouflaged the flamboyance of the cut and elevated Frau Weiss into a higher realm. She looked sublime, ethereal, transformed by Ada's art from a dull chrysalis to a ravishing beauty. Frau Weiss needed Ada. She liked Ada making her clothes. She liked showing her off to her friends, sharing her with them. No other dressmaker could match Ada. Ada understood this. She knew Frau Weiss understood it too, hated herself for the weakness it showed.

'Next time,' Frau Weiss said, 'and you go to the camp.' She stomped to the door, slapping Ada hard again with the back of her hand as she passed. 'You disgust me.'

The Polish prisoners in the geriatric home came

from the camp. They hadn't looked healthy. Ada wondered if the camp had anything to do with the black smoke that she saw in the sky when she went outside to empty her bucket. The smell reminded her of that place in the Cut, back home, where they rendered fat. She guessed it came from the factory. Maybe it was where they processed meat, pork or even horse, given how difficult Frau Weiss said it was to get good beef.

When Frau Weiss and her friends talked about the camp in front of Ada, they said it was full of Bolsheviks and Jews, gypsies and queers. Troublemakers. Frau Weiss spat out the words, vermin, *Untermenschen*. Ada knew plenty of Jews and Bolsheviks. She could hear her father, sitting in the Windsor chair with the broken spokes in the kitchen back home in London, *If anyone calls you a Bolshie, Ada my girl, you say yes, and proud of it.* Home was a century ago. Her life had once had horizons. The war had shrunk them, shriveled her memories and buried them along with her dreams. Her world now was nothing more than this filthy room with its dirty windows and rusty bars.

The only thing she had done wrong was to believe Stanislaus. Her cheeks burned, hot as lava. What if she was stuck here for the rest of her life? What if the war never ended? Or the Germans won? What would she do? She grabbed Frau Weiss's dress and flung it across the room. She picked up the scissors and hurled them at the dummy, threw the tailor's chalk at the window, slung the pin cushion on the ground. She clasped her hands to her head, pressed them against her skull and screamed, rocking her body from side to side.

There was blood on her finger. She must have snagged it on the pins. She sucked at the bleeding. The pin. A painful scratch every time Frau Weiss turned. A pin, of course. She laughed. A *pin*, amidst all this bombing. Fancy that. It was always the little things, the straw that broke the camel's back, the flea that wore the elephant down.

There was more than one way to fight a war. She pulled off her clothes and stepped into the dress, fine worsted wool, black and slinky to the touch. She pressed it against her skin, followed the line of her body from her breasts to her thighs. Her bones jutted out and the dress was loose on her frame, but Ada was a woman again, possessing the dress, like a cat spraying scent. Frau Weiss would never know.

She rubbed her hand across the welt on her face. There was blood. Frau Weiss's ring must have caught her cheek.

No one opened her door to let her out that day at the end of September, not long after the first bombing raid in 1943. There were strange voices in the house, urgent noises, the scrape and thump of furniture being moved, footsteps past her door, through the kitchen and scullery. The sun began to warm the room, shining through the window, catching motes of dust in its rays. Ada guessed it must be afternoon. She was hungry and thirsty. The house grew silent, hollow and empty. Dusk crept in and night fell. Ada turned on the light switch and nothing happened. There was no electricity. She had been left, alone.

She tried to sleep but her feet tangled with the blanket. She shook them off with a panicked kick. She tried her usual trick, her mantra: *Thomas. Home. Stanislaus. Modiste.* She was closed in. The walls moved towards her, the ceiling pressed down. Planes droned and circled overhead. Ada waited for the vermilion to light her room, for the thud of the bombing. Once or twice the explosions landed close, shaking the house and rattling the windows. She screwed her eyes tight.

She could be bombed, suffocated in the rubble, buried alive. She sat up, screaming, but her cries bounced back. She lay down again. Her head lolled off the cushion, pulling her onto the icy, stone floor. Her stomach hurt. She was going to die here, locked away in a workroom, lost forever. Who knew she was here? Her leg cramped and she jumped up, walked round until the spasm passed. She would hang herself, cut her wrists. She could do it this time. She would have to. Starvation was a painful death.

Please don't bomb me. Let me live. She wondered what could be left of Munich now. She guessed the Germans must be doing the same to England.

She tried not to think of her family. They would survive. Like her. *Lucky*.

In the morning the lock turned with a noisy wrench and a portly woman in a dull black skirt and brown twin-set entered the room. Ada had never seen her before.

'You,' she said, pointing at Ada. 'Stand when I talk.' Ada pushed herself off her bed. She felt unsteady, a little faint. 'I am Frau Weiter. I give the orders now. Empty that,' she pointed to the bucket.

Ada was glad to get out, to breathe the crisp, fresh autumn air, to see the latest prisoner in the striped jacket. But there was no one in the scullery as she walked through, nor in the yard outside. The water from the cistern gushed down, splashing the floor and tiles. She peered round the rose bush but the lawn was empty. Had Frau Weiss left, taken Thomas?

His bike was gone. Next to it, in the mud, was a small knitted teddy bear.

'You,' Frau Weiter said as Ada returned, 'get out of that nun's habit.' She threw a limp, grey shift on the floor and pointed at it. 'You're no different from the other prisoners. Why should you have privileges?'

Ada picked up the shapeless drag of cotton. It was thin, its fibres lifeless.

'From now on,' Frau Weiter said. 'I am in charge.

My husband is the new Commandant here. You help the cook. You launder and you iron. You mend and sew. You do whatever we ask. You do not talk. Put that on, then go.' She pointed towards the open door and the scullery beyond, and left the room.

Ada wondered what had happened. She stepped out of her habit and pulled the dress over her head. This flimsy, soulless garment frightened her. It was what the Polish prisoners had worn. Is that what she had become? Like them? They came from the camp. She folded her habit, laid it on the bed, and walked towards the scullery.

The cook was not a prisoner, Ada could see. She was well fed, a round woman with a thick waist, grey hair and beads of sweat on her forehead and nose. The armpits of her blouse were wet and dark.

Frau Weiter called her Anni. They had long conversations. Ada understood that she had been her cook for many years. She understood too that Obersturmbannführer Weiss had been sent to Poland. The woman and child had wanted to stay on in the house. Frau Weiter tutted. Why should she be allowed special treatment, when it was obvious that Obersturmbannführer Weiter and her needed the Commandant's house? When there was such pressure on decent housing now? Of course the woman had to find accommodation elsewhere, go back to her own people.

Anni never smiled, but she made good food which Ada helped prepare, peeling, chopping,

179

shredding. Liver soup. Roasted boar. Cabbage rolls. Sauerkraut. *Apfelstrudel. Topfenstrudel. Auszogne.* No wonder Anni was so round and Frau Weiter so stout. And her husband, Obersturmbannführer Weiter. A vast man with a meaty gut that hung over his belt. His jacket puckered at the buttons, the sleeves strained on their seams. Ada had never met a really fat person, had never known what gluttony was until now, or why it was a sin. *Glands*, her mother used to say. *It's because of their glands. They can't help it.* The Weiters ate five times a day in the dining room, a fresh tablecloth for every meal.

Linen, with broderie anglaise borders twelve inches deep. The stitching was harder even than buttonholes, the eyelets were small and needed fine threads and needles. The work made Ada's eyes sore and her head pound. Monogrammed initials on the towels, *EW,* hand-sewn and hemmed, sheets and pillowcases. Drawn threads on the guest towels and tray clothes, whitework embroidery on the coasters and placemats. The Weiters were messy eaters and sleepers. They demanded fresh linen every day and Ada had to boil up the stained sheets and tablecloths in the copper, scrub them with borax and carbolic until her hands were raw, wring them out and hang them to dry on the washing lines in the yard, vast sails that billowed in the wind. The bombing and the war meant that soap was hard to come by, fuel too, to boil the water, but the Weiters refused to go without fresh laundry, screamed at Ada if she missed a day, threatened to send her to the camp, get someone else to do her work.

Ada took her time putting out the laundry, or taking it in, watched as the autumn swelled and mellowed in the garden and the flowers died back into the soil, the leaves rotted on the ground. Another year had passed. *Dust to dust, earth to earth.* There were berries on the trees and shrubs which the birds feasted on. The climbing rose by the lavatory had a fine crop of hips, garish orange haws which made her smile. She picked some and stuffed them into her pocket. She'd look at them in the evenings when she was alone. They would remind her of the garden, of a place where life carried on, hopeful and oblivious.

Frau Weiter wore dirndls, woollen ones for winter, velvet for best, cotton for summer with tailored bodices that emphasized her fleshy bosom. Fussy blouses with tie pulls round the neck and sleeves. She liked them embroidered from top to hem with edelweiss and gentian and other mountain flowers. She was a dirty, piggish woman, soiled her clothes every day, soup on the skirt, gravy on the blouse, fat on the bodice. She had sweaty feet that made her stockings stiff, dribbled piss and worse in her knickers. Washing and mending, sewing and ironing, tough, fiddly work to smooth the gathers in her dirndls without pressing them flat. Up at dawn and not asleep before the early hours. *Do this. Do that.* Frau Weiter's clothes that

181

made her look like one of Anni's bread dumplings. Or a pantomime dame. Ada laughed inside. Hair pulled back in a bun, Frau Weiter. She could be a man, dressed up. Widow Twanky.

Anni only spoke to Ada to give orders. But Anni left a good scraping in the saucepans, turned a blind eye if Ada licked the spoon or ran her finger round the mixing bowl before she washed them up. Little treats that broke the monotony of the watery soup that Ada had to eat every day. Anni had flushes, surges of fire that turned her neck red, exploded under her arms. She'd fling open the doors and windows, fan her face with her hands. There was an American client at Mrs B.'s who wore pads under her arms. *The change*, she'd mouthed to Mrs B., as if Ada was too young to understand this conspiracy of age, *that time of life*.

Ada thought of that. She had some towelling and scraps of soft cotton, remnants from her dress-making. It didn't take her long. Two semicircles. Ribbon. She had some brassiere buckles left over from Frau Weiss and attached them to the tapes, enough for two pairs.

Anni let her out in the morning and Ada gave her the shields, pointing to her armpits, fanning her face in a pretence of heat. She mouthed, *for the sweat.* Anni took the pads. Who knows, Ada thought, if she'll report her to Frau Weiter for this. Ada didn't care. It made her feel alive, a kindness, *just returning the favour, dear.* She was peeling potatoes when Frau Weiter appeared, still in her nightdress.

182

'Nun,' she said, 'bring a bucket and come with me.' Ada followed, through the doors into the hall. It was the first time she had been back there since her arrival nearly two years ago. It was Christmas 1943, and a tall fir tree stood in one corner with small candles attached to its branches. There was a carpet on the floor now, and a heavy, carved oak sideboard with two ugly low wooden chairs on either side. Frau Weiter marched Ada up the stairs, past the large window, along the corridor and into their bedroom. The smell hit Ada before she saw its cause: Herr Weiter lay naked on the bed, surrounded by vomit.

'Clean him,' Frau Weiter said, pointing to the mess on the floor. 'And then the rest.'

It wasn't just vomit. He lay moaning in his own excrement. Ada dry-heaved and gagged as she cleaned him up, Frau Weiter hovering behind her.

'There,' she said. 'And there. More there.' Prising open every fold and crease of flesh, wiping away the stinking remains, feeling his skin clench back over her fingers like vast, pulsing gums. *Pig*, Ada thought. Ate so much Christmas dinner it had made him ill. Serve him right.

The bedding. The bedroom. The bathroom. She cleaned all morning, washed all afternoon. Frau Weiter didn't hit Ada the way Frau Weiss had but Ada despised her more. She was a slut and a slob, a glutton and an idler. Ada hated the way her wrists hung in rings over her lumpy hands, the way she humped her body across the room like a

183

slug over grass, the way she laughed with Anni, *ho ho*, and pinched her cheeks, *We are so good to you, Annerl,* the folds on her chin wobbling in their own free time.

That evening, when Anni locked Ada up for the night, she slipped a package in Ada's pocket. There was a glass of milk on the table. Ada pulled out the package. A slice of Stollen, wrapped in grease-proof paper. *Danke. Frohe Weihnachten.* Happy Christmas.

Ada sat on the easy chair, holding the cake, and sobbed.

She kept the rosehips in a drawer. They had dried and shrivelled, the colour had lost its lustre. She hadn't done this since she was a child and they'd nicked the rosehips from the posh houses in West Square, but she remembered. She spread out the greaseproof paper from the cake, split open the haws, and laid out the fine hairs inside. Frau Weiter wore a slip next to her skin, gathered at the waist and secured with hooks at the side. Each gather formed a pouch and Ada poked the tiny hairs deep inside them. She held up the shift. Nothing showed. She reached for the next one.

She rolled the last hip in her hand. There were plenty more on the bush. *More than one way to fight a war,* she reminded herself.

Frau Weiss's friends still came to see her, fabric over their arms, photographs in their hands. Ada had to make their clothes on top of all her other chores. She knew if she refused they'd send her to the camp. Frau Weiter didn't need Ada, not the way Frau Weiss did. She wanted to ask the women what happened to Frau Weiss and the child, but knew she must not say a word. She listened to their talk. Obersturmbannführer Weiss was now in charge of another camp, Neuengamme. Near Hamburg, from what she could make out. But they never mentioned Frau Weiss by name, or little Thomas. Germany was doing well. The war would be over soon.

The trees began to glow with tiny, green buds. She put away her tweed mittens, which she still used for the night, and the cashmere gloves for the day. The moths had eaten holes in the palms and the edges were beginning to fray. The wool had felted with dirt. How long would this war go on? She scored off another month on her calendar under the table. March, 1944. She had been in this house for over two years. Her headaches were bad and sometimes she couldn't see her stitches. The buttonholes and eyelets were the worst. She had to hold them close to her eyes so she caught the loops and returns in straight, even rows.

Early one morning in April that year, before she'd had time to change out of her habit that she still slept in at night, there was Herr Weiss. Sometimes she wondered – hoped – that he had died. She had stopped listening for his tread along the corridor in the evenings, the steely *tap-tap* of his cane. With his nephew gone, she thought he would not return. But now he stood there, his mouth set in a crooked smirk, nodding. He had come for his reward. She had been hemming a sheet and allowed it to fall to the floor, the scissors on her lap clattering to the ground.

'Herr Weiss,' she said. 'I wasn't expecting you.'

'I said I would be back.'

He fished inside his jacket and pulled out a diary. 'I made a note,' he said. 'Do you know what day it is?'

Ada shook her head.

'It is the *Führer*'s birthday. April 20th, 1944.'

He smiled again and tapped his way across the room. His limp was more pronounced, and he grimaced as he moved. His breath came in sharp gasps. He had been ill, Ada could see.

'You do good work,' he said, pointing his cane at the dresses and suits hanging from the picture rail round the room. 'Do you know what they call you here?'

Ada shook her head.

'They call you the Dressmaker of Dachau,' he said. 'You are the talk of the town. It is quite a society we have here. Influential, you know. Not just Dachau. But Munich, Berlin. I am told that word has even reached the *Führer* himself.' He laughed, a gruff wheeze that ended in a film of spittle on his lips. 'I exaggerate. The *Führer* is too busy to bother with such trivialities.'

He fluttered the dresses up with his cane, revealing their faultless seams and flawless whipping underneath. He smiled at Ada, as if she were a child. 'I have a friend,' he said. 'She is looking for a new dressmaker. Someone who has to be discreet. So I think, who is more discreet than my *Nönnlein*?'

He sauntered over to the armchair and lowered himself into it, placing the cane on the floor by his feet. 'Come,' he said, patting his knee. 'You should be pleased to see me.'

Ada knew what was to come. She picked up her stool.

'No, my dear,' he said. 'Leave your stool. Come, sit close to me.'

She could sit on the floor, grab his cane if he tried something. She drew near, and he grasped her hand and pulled her down so she was forced to sit on his lap. She swallowed hard. He had never done this before. They had always sat side by side. But they were alone and Ada knew her screams would not be heard, would not matter.

He stroked her hand. 'Have you missed me?'

Ada said nothing.

'I've missed you.' He pulled her hand towards his groin, and grinned like a rutting goat. 'You can tell.'

Ada tried to ball her fist. That way she wouldn't feel him.

'*Nönnlein*,' he said, prising open her fingers. 'I have some news.'

He took his hand away and, placing his arms

187

round her, pulled her close. He had a cluster of white bristles on his cheek and another below his bottom lip. She could smell alcohol on his breath, and saw the veins threaded on his cheeks, his faded eyes a smoky absinthe. His lips were cracked. She hoped he wouldn't kiss her.

'I am leaving,' he said. 'Today. I will go away. I may never see you again.'

Her muscles slackened. *Thank goodnesss.*

'But before I go,' he said, stroking her face with the back of his hand. 'I want what is owed me.' Ada swallowed. 'For all of this,' he waved his arm at the surroundings, pointing to the dresses hanging round the wall, 'and what may yet pass.'

He was squeezing her waist, his fingers splayed wide so they brushed against her breast. 'I just have to say the word,' he went on, 'and this could vanish. Have you heard of Ravensbrück?' He was pulling at her habit, lifting it higher, touching her leg. 'It is for women. Criminals. Jews. Poles. Gypsies. *Lesbians.*' He spat the word. She felt drops of spittle on her cheek. He was groping her thigh. Ada tried to cross her legs but he forced them apart. 'A long way from here.'

'Please,' she said. 'I have taken Holy Orders.'

'I know,' he said. 'I would not violate a *nun*,' he added, his words dragging across his teeth, '*if* that is who you are.' The blood hurled itself through her body, forcing her heart to pump it round. Stay calm, *calm.* How could he know? He has to believe she is a nun.

'Then don't do this.'

He pushed her free of his lap, but held onto her arm, gripping it tight. He was surprisingly strong, too strong for Ada. 'You haven't learned, have you? You don't tell me what to do. *Nun.*' He shook her arm, looked at her through bitter eyes. 'Take your clothes off.'

'Please,' Ada said. 'Please, no.'

He squeezed her wrist, licked his lips. 'On second thoughts,' he said, 'your naked body would disgust me.'

He let go of her.

'You are too thin. There is no *woman* about you. Take off everything except your shift.'

Ada's fingers shook as she pulled the scapular over her head and unhooked her habit. He was watching her, his skin tight across his face in a rictus of craving. He'd discover she wasn't a virgin, and then what? Would he send her to Ravensbrück, put her in a brothel? He picked up his cane.

'And leave on your wimple. Your hair will not be your crowning glory.' He laughed, a smutty rumble in his throat.

'Now, come closer.' He leant forward and seized her arm, pulling her on top of him once more. She froze while he fumbled with his flies, rubbed himself against her, fingered her through the shift.

'Help me.' He yanked her hand close to his penis and groaned. It was over.

He pushed her away as the gong sounded for

breakfast. 'I will have an appetite now,' he said. 'Anni provides an excellent spread for Obersturmbannführer Weiter and his charming wife. *Schlackwurst*. Liverwurst. Cheese. Fresh rolls. Honey. Coffee. *Sekt*. Goodbye, Sister Clara.' He stood up, tucked his shirt in his trousers, buttoned his flies and picked his cane off the floor.

'I will put in a word for you with my friend.' He walked out of the room, locking the door behind him.

He had soiled her shift. She picked up a remnant of cloth and rubbed at the stain. She was shivering. She reached for her habit, pulled it over her head. She would never see him again. She was hungry.

It was a deep, rotten fatigue that drilled into her muscles and drained her brain. Ada would sink onto her makeshift bed in the early hours and drag herself up at dawn, too tired to weep or dream. She still kept tabs of the time but the rest of that spring and summer passed by in heavy, tedious work. Frau Weiter made her wash their *Federbetten*, thick eiderdowns stuffed with feathers that they used in the winter. Ada had to beat out the clumps of down with a stick while Frau Weiter sat and watched. *More. It needs more. Put your back into it.* She barely had the strength to pick up the stick. She had to take down the curtains in every room, heavy brocades that kept out the winter draughts, and wash them free of years of dust, hang them out so they could dry and air in the summer sun, gather them in and press them smooth, ready.

'Put on your clean dress,' Frau Weiter said one morning in the autumn as Ada was hanging up the clean brocade curtains for the winter. 'Make sure your hands and face are washed.'

Ada did as she was bid. Frau Weiter locked her in her room. Ada waited, watching through her window as the sun rose high in the sky, then dipped behind the houses. She'd had neither breakfast nor a midday meal and her stomach seized with cramps, painful vices that squeezed her guts. She had chores to complete. She'd be up all night, catching up with the laundry and ironing. The door opened and Frau Weiter entered, followed by another woman whom Ada had not seen before, and two Scottie dogs. Frau Weiter kept a distance from the other woman, disapproval snarling round her mouth, nose on high.

One of the dogs came up to Ada, sniffed her ankles, wagged its stump of a tail. Its breath was warm against her skin, its nose cold and wet. Ada longed to stroke it, feel the silky warmth of its fur, have it jump against her, whimpering delight, its tongue quivering to lick her, the affection of another living being.

'Negus,' the woman said. '*Kommt!*' She patted her thigh and the dog turned and walked towards the woman. Ada wanted to say, *It's all right. I don't mind.* Yearned for the little animal who said, *You're there. Another human.* Even the dogs had a name.

191

'*Sitz*,' the woman said, raising her finger to the dog. Ada couldn't help casting her eye over the woman. Slim, large breasts, full-bodied. Her hair was mousy, neither short nor long, set in waves. Her face was round and plain. She was young, attractive enough, but hers was not a face of beauty, not a face that would last the years. Her complexion was clear, set off by a hint of lipstick. *Lipstick*. None of the women had lipstick these days.

She was wearing a white suit. The skirt was straight and to the knee, the jacket short, with a peplum and a deep collar. She wore it buttoned, straining round her bosom, and beneath Ada could spot the top of a thin knitted jumper. You could see her in the market in the Cut, *Five pound of potatoes, a couple of onions, four apples, cookers.* Her and Widow Twanky, if the Widow could wipe off that smear of disdain, or get the costers to do it for her. *Stepped in horse shit, missus? You oughta look out.* Such an ordinary-looking woman, one who didn't make the best of herself.

'This is the nun,' Frau Weiter said, 'the dressmaker you've heard about.'

The woman looked round the room. Ada was making an evening dress for one of Frau Weiss's friends, a bottle-green creation, with a halter neck. It was hanging from the rail, and Ada was waiting before she hemmed it. *Let it drop, Ada, let it drop,* Isidore used to say. *Skill shows in the hemline.* She had some fabric on the table, a floral cotton which

192

another of Frau Weiss's friends had commandeered for a blouse and, folded next to it, the
pattern which Ada had cut out.

'*Ja,*' the woman said. 'I trust she is as good as
everyone says.'

She opened the parcel she was carrying, revealing
a bolt of black silk. She pushed it over the table
towards Ada. Ada drew it closer, running her
fingers across the top, feeling its slubs and ribs,
its sheen and strength. *Douppioni.* She had not felt
silk of this quality since Mrs B.'s.

'I need an evening dress,' she said. 'I am told
you are the best.'

It was a compliment, and Ada flushed, currents
of glory that surged through her body. Nobody
had praised her, not like this. Woman to woman.
She felt ashamed, did not recognize herself. Some
craven creature clamouring for approval. This
woman throwing crumbs of flattery which Ada
scooped with relish, like a starving sparrow. *Thank
you. Much obliged.*

'I have three dressmakers,' the woman was saying
to Frau Weiter. 'One here in Munich. One in
Berlin. One at the Berghof. I can't tell you what
my bills are like. A fortune. I pay for their silence,
of course. I wouldn't mind,' she went on, 'if they
were any good. Skirts. Trousers. Dirndls.' She
shook her head. 'Competent. But magic? They
don't have it in them.'

She bent down and picked up one of the Scotties,
lifting her chin so the dog could lick her. She

193

smiled, let him jump to the floor and turned to Ada.

'And you have magic, I see,' she said. She walked over to the green evening dress, ran her finger along its skirt, turned to Frau Weiter. 'Maliciousness. Lies. But why should truth stand in the way of gossip, Frau Weiter? Fitted,' she pivoted round, faced Ada. 'I want it fitted. Fanning below the knee. Like a mermaid.'

Douppioni was strong, would take a tail, but it didn't like to be stretched. *It watches sport*, she could hear Isidore say, *it doesn't play it*. The woman was slim but her calves were muscular, her shoulders square. She could see her playing tennis, or swimming, or in the Women's League of Health and Beauty back in London, navy knickers and a white blouse, backward flips and forward tumbles. The dress would have to be supple so it lived like skin, not tied taut, like a winding cloth.

'High neck,' she went on. 'Backless. And roses.' She pulled out some red fabric from the bag and showed it to Ada. Raw silk, a rich crimson. Rare. She crunched it up, pressed it against her throat to show Ada.

'Roses,' she said. 'Here, round my neck.'

Roses would be too fussy with a fantail skirt, would spoil the line, the simplicity that Ada had in mind. Roses would be a disaster. But a single rose, a large one, a *corsage*, centre left, just below the neckline, that would be *class*. She swallowed, took a deep breath and said nothing. This woman had poor taste. Ada would have to show her. Keep it pure, give it grace. More *soigné*. That was the magic. She hated herself for thinking this, needing to say, *Madame, perhaps this way* . . . Why did she care how this German woman looked? But it was the only thing she could do that was her own, that made her whole, a person.

'I will need to measure you, madame,' she said. 'Without clothes. For accuracy.'

'You'll have to undress, then,' Frau Weiter said, adding, 'don't worry. I'll stay with you.'

The woman shrugged. 'I know what needs to be done,' she said to Frau Weiter in a curt tone. 'You don't have to tell me.'

She bent down and fondled one of the dogs, rubbing it behind its ear. 'She doesn't have to tell me what I know, does she, my Stasile?' The dog rolled onto its back, its hind leg kicking as she scratched his stomach. '*Mutti*'s done this so many times.'

She stood up, unbuttoned her jacket, looked round for a hook, handed it to Frau Weiter instead as if she were a clothes' horse. Ada coughed to hide her smirk.

The woman stood in her satin underwear, a creamy brassiere and matching French knickers, the suspenders and the tops of her stockings showing just below the lacy hem. She was strong, this woman, sporty, no flab or spare about her. Ada took the measurements, over bust, under bust, bust. Upper hip, lower hip, length. Wrote them

195

down on a piece of paper. Nape to waist, waist to ankle and tucked the paper by the sewing machine with the other orders so it wouldn't get lost.

The bombing raids grew more intense that autumn. Ada watched the glowing skies, waiting for the *booms* of the bombs, counting between the light and the noise, as if it was a thunderstorm. *Eighteen miles away. Twelve. Nine.*

Christmas passed. She chalked it off. 1944. Her sixth. Most of them in this house. How many more would she have to spend here? Thomas would be four in February. She hoped he was safe and happy. Hoped Frau Weiss comforted him during the bombings, *It's all right, Tomichen, Mutti's here. Vati will look after you.*

The Widow Twanky and Obersturmbannführer Weiter and Anni weathered the raids in the basement, came up in the morning, dishevelled and angry. The Russians were getting closer, and the British. Americans, too. Ada had only ever heard how well Germany was doing, although she had wondered. If they were so successful, why were they still fighting? Now she knew the truth. Germany could lose, Germany was losing. She watched Frau Weiter's eyes narrow with hate, as if it was Ada's fault.

The boiler was in the basement, a black furnace that Ada had to stoke morning and night. That winter, 1944 to 1945, was bitter. Ada had never known it so cold. She shivered by day in her flimsy shift, lay on her cushions at night rubbing her legs to keep warm. She put on her habit, tunic, under-skirts, even the wimple, doubled the blanket over her, as well as Sister Jeanne's old habit, but she could still feel it, the frost creeping through the windows and icy draughts blowing across her face. *Boom. Boom.* Ada counted *eight, seven, six.* The bombs were coming closer. They rattled the doors and shook the house. Ada put on her crucifix, just for luck.

Frau Weiter's rash was still there. It left livid wheels round her waist which Anni had to dab with calamine. The doctor didn't know what caused it.

'What does he know?' Frau Weiter said, her voice high like a child's. She spat at Ada, a nasty gob of saliva which missed and fell to the floor with a *plop.* 'It's you. It's ringworm. Impetigo. Shingles. You're all filthy. Diseased.' She snatched the lotion from Anni, scratched the angry blisters, pulled up the shift and hitched the straps over her shoulders. Ada waited until she had left. *Widow Twanky.*

The washing froze on the line. Ada brought in the brittle sheets and draped them round the furnace in the basement. The snow was deep and had blown against the house up to the window sills. The sky was clear blue. Ada preferred it when it was heavy and yellow. It was warmer then, just before it snowed. The smoke from the factory in the nearby camp belched day and night, ugly black clouds that drifted across the garden and left gritty smuts on the ground. She heard noises from the camp which she hadn't heard before, lorries churning, orders shouted, *Raus! Beeilung!* The dull thud of people tramping. Something was changing. In the winter, when the trees were bare, she could spy the driveway to the camp from the far corner of the garden. Every morning as she hung out the washing, every evening when she took it in, more and more people were arriving. They looked hunched, exhausted. Someone fell and one of the guards stepped forward. There was a light, flimsy *crack* as if a twig had snapped. The man did not get up.

The camp. The factory. Ada had always thought of prisons as big Victorian buildings with bars at the window. She gripped the frozen sheet in her hand. This prison was different. She shivered. Something wasn't right about it. The smoke, the smell. The words the Germans used. *Untermensch. Ungeziefer.* Vermin. She'd heard once that they gassed sewer rats in London, burned their bodies.

Ada had almost given up on the woman with the *douppioni* and the dogs, but she reappeared one morning in January 1945 for a fitting, dressed in a simple skirt and twin-set, the two Scotties at her heels. There had been plenty of fabric for a fantail, but Ada had cut the dress straight, fitted, simple. Let her see it on. Let her appreciate its magic.

'And if you still wish for the fantail,' Ada said, 'I have enough.'

She had made up a single rose, cutting the silk on the cross, doubling, twisting so it curled and bloomed. She tacked it just below the neckline, to the left. The woman slipped into the dress while Ada hooked it together behind.

She stood there, the skin of her naked shoulders glowing ivory against the ebony silk, the rose at the neck, a luscious glimpse of crimson.

'There is no mirror,' Ada said. 'You have to go with Frau Weiter.'

Every customer had had to use the mirror upstairs in a bedroom, twisting in the reflection, one side to the other, back view, front, talking about the outfit away from Ada, as if Ada hadn't made it. Why they never let her have a mirror she didn't understand. Did they worry she would break it? Snatch a shard and hold it to their throats? She could do that more easily with the shears. Or were they too vain? They couldn't let her see that they *knew* they weren't worthy of Ada's creations?

'*Kommt*,' she said to the dogs.

'You can leave them,' Ada said. 'I'll look after them.' The woman hesitated, smiled.

'*Bleib!*' she said, raising her finger until the two dogs sat, then lay.

Ada waited until she had left before she called them over, their warm, wiry bodies and silky fur squirming under the touch, whimpering as they struggled to lick her face. She could feel the tickle of their beards and clutched them tight, kissing them on their foreheads as if they were the last living creatures she would ever know, the last affection she would share. She started to cry, wiped the tears from their fur, rubbed her hand to dry her cheeks.

'*Schön*,' the woman said as she walked back in. 'Elegant. *Perfekt*.'

The dogs rushed towards her.

'*Sitz*,' she said, and they sat, quivering, tail stumps thumping the floor.

'No fantail?' Ada said. 'And a single rose?'

'You were right. Thank you. *Danke*.'

Who had ever taken the trouble to thank her before? Ada swallowed. She hated to feel so grateful, it was pathetic, but kindnesses were to be clutched at.

'I need to hem it,' she said. 'Please, if you will, stand here.' Ada walked over and fetched her stool. 'On this. Mind how you go.'

The woman leant on her as she climbed onto the stool. Frau Weiter looked cross. Ada had never dared ask Frau Weiter to stand on the stool. She was too heavy, her legs too fat to lift. Ada pressed her finger into the soft of the woman's leg, just above the ankle.

'I think, madame,' she said, 'this would be the best length. Longer, it would trail the ground. Shorter, it is neither one thing nor another.'

She pinned the fabric, 'turn when I say,' pinned again as the woman circled with tiny steps so the hem was even all round. Ada had never spoken to the other women, not to Frau Weiss nor Frau Weiter, much less asked them, *Is this for a special occasion? Are you going somewhere nice?* She wasn't sure she could ask this woman, but what did she have to lose?

'The dress suits you, madame,' Ada said. 'May I ask what it's for?'

'*Nein,*' Frau Weiter shouted. 'How dare you.'

'Why shouldn't she ask?' the woman said. She turned to Ada. 'It's a secret.' She put her fingers to her lips. 'Let's say it's for the day that every woman dreams of.'

Widow Twanky was panting with fury. She could have a seizure, Ada thought. Any minute. Good. Ada could work for this woman then. Tell her black wasn't the right colour for *that special day*. More for a funeral.

'Wear heels,' Ada said. 'Your hair back, away from your face.'

She smiled. A kind, ordinary woman. 'The nun isn't speaking out of turn,' she said to Frau Weiter. 'You will not punish her.'

Frau Weiter sucked her breath, was silent for a moment. Ada revelled in her discomfort. 'So, you approve of my little dressmaker?' she said at last, her voice soapy and pliant.

'Very much,' the woman said. 'My boyfriend will like this gown. It will be his favourite, I have no doubt. And nothing to pay.' She laughed. 'He will like that most of all.'

She stepped down from the stool, stood on tiptoe, twirled.

'Send it to me when it's finished,' she said to

Frau Weiter. 'To Berlin. Perhaps, Sister Clara, we will meet again.'

She stepped out of the dress, back into her everyday clothes, called the dogs and left.

There was fabric left over. The woman had not asked for it back. A yard, maybe more. Enough for a small jacket, a bolero, short raglan sleeves, a splash of crimson on the left breast, enough raw silk for a small rose.

The aeroplanes came almost every night now. Sometimes there were flashes and explosions, other times they flew past without dropping bombs. Frau Weiter grew more agitated, the rash round her waist seeped blood that Ada had to wash from her slips. A horrid job, but it was worth it, to see her suffer. The Obersturmbannführer came home later each day. She understood that Obersturmbannführer Weiss was coming back, resuming his charge of the camp. She heard Frau Weiter screaming at her husband about him. And Thomas, Ada thought. Where is Thomas? Please let him be safe. Sent to the country somewhere, away from the bombs. The war was going badly for Germany. Ada listened as Frau Weiter screamed to Anni. The Germans had pushed back the Americans in France but it had taken everything they had, and now the Russians were coming closer. The Russians were beasts, ill-disciplined, vengeful. Who would protect them?

'Who is in charge?' she had screamed. 'What will happen to us? Who cares about us now?'

Evenings grew lighter, but the cold persisted. The ground was icy underfoot where Ada trod with the laundry and more than once she skidded and fell on her back and winded herself. Anni stayed in the kitchen and cooked, but food was scarce. The railways and the roads had been bombed. There was no transport. The British had blasted the fields and the factories, the aerodromes and munitions. *It must end soon.*

Hope made it worse. It had become an impatient horse that Ada needed to rein back each day. She wasn't sure she could hold on. Her hands trembled and she had bouts of weeping that she couldn't stop, standing over the sink, elbows in water, watching the tears fall hard as pebbles, breaking the surface and rippling in circles, just like Auntie Lily when she was attacked by nerves. Came and stayed with them then, days spent screaming and sobbing. Was Ada getting nerves too? Was she at breaking point? Now, when it was nearly over? When she'd held it in all these years?

They still had some vegetables that the prisoners had grown, but they were running short and the spring crop wasn't ready. A few onions, soft in the middle. Potatoes, starting to sprout. Cabbage, more leaf than heart. Ada had to feed herself from the peelings, but Anni still let Ada scrape the saucepans, drain the last dregs of soup. They were running out of tinned fish and the flour wouldn't last till the end of the month. Anni still made bread, but eked it out, a slice a day, and none for Ada. She made traps and laid them in the garden. She caught a pigeon, wrung its neck and plucked its feathers and added it to the stew. Ada had pains which made her nauseous, and she was constipated. She grew thinner and more frail. She had no strength for heavy washing, or ironing or mending. Frau Weiter shouted all the time, thumped and shoved Ada, walloped her with the strap. Her periods had stopped too, as if the effort would push her body over its limit, would waste its precious blood.

The black silk dress had been sent off to the woman. Ada had to finish the jacket. It should be lined, but there was nothing to line it with. It would fit. Whip the seams. *Douppioni* frayed, fine filaments that spun free from the weave. Like soldiers, Ada thought, close ranks, strong as an ox. But one by one, could be picked off, *crack*.

She came into the kitchen one morning, handed it to Anni, finger to her lip, *shush*. A gift. For you. Couldn't tell her it was the remnants from that woman, the only other person who had shown her kindness.

The snow began to melt. The grass was muddy and Ada had to take care she didn't drop the sheets in the dirt. Shoots of daffodils had begun to lighten the flower beds and the trees began to fuzz with a soft, luminous green as they had every year that Ada had been here.

Frau Weiter came into the scullery. 'Nun,' she said, 'what's your name?'

Ada thought a moment. 'Sister Clara.'

'Sister Clara,' she said. Frau Weiter had lost weight, they all had. She had loose skin on her cheeks and chin, the dirndls gaped at the waist. 'You have had no complaints here, have you? We have treated you well, Obersturmbannführer Weiter and I, don't you agree? Fed you, kept you warm? You are a nun. We have respected your calling. You have nothing against us, do you?'

Ada said nothing.

That night the whole house shook. Ada lay on her bed, wrapped the habit tighter round her, pulled the scapular over her eyes. Tremor after tremor, like an earthquake. Would the walls stand up? The roof hold? The glass in Ada's windows cracked, and a pane fell to the floor, smashing into small crystals. Ada could smell mortar dust and burning. She lowered the scapular and saw livid, scarlet flames shooting into the sky. It's close, Ada thought. A relentless *boom, boom, boom*. The ground shuddered round her and Ada heard the house crack.

Then it stopped. The aeroplanes droned into the distance, and faded from her hearing. The house was stiff and empty. The slow grey of dawn crept up and the lights from flickering fires backed off.

★　★　★

The April sun was low and frail, cast splindly shafts of light onto the thick slubs of black silk, turning it into a sea of ebony and jet, silver and slate. Ada watched as Anni ran her hand along the fine, crisp edges of the jacket, tracing the rich, warm threads and fingering the corsage as if the petals were tender blooms crafted from the filaments of nature. She was wearing it over a thick wool jumper and her cook's apron, so it pulled tight round the shoulders. *No*, Ada wanted to say, *not like that. It won't fit.* But she kept her mouth shut. She could see from Anni's face that the jacket was the most beautiful thing she had ever possessed.

She was holding the key to Ada's room in one hand, and a suitcase in the other.

'Goodbye, nun,' Anni said, throwing the key on the floor and kicking it towards Ada. '*Auf wiedersehen.*'

She walked away, leaving the door open.

Ada pushed herself up from her bed. It was a trick. They were testing her, waiting for her to run. Frau Weiter would be outside, ready to grab Ada as she rushed past. *You thought you'd escape, did you, nun?* The room was cold. Ada shuddered, could feel her heart pushing at her chest, churning her blood through her veins. She stumbled to the doorway, leant against the frame and looked towards the kitchen. It was silent now. No clang as Anni filled the kettle and heaved it to the stove, no slap of the wooden spoon against the blackened pot, no squeal of the larder door as it swung on its hinges. She looked towards the corridor. Anni had left the door to the hall ajar. Beyond it Ada could see that the big wooden front door was open, and beyond that, the outer door. The house was empty.

She tiptoed into the corridor and crept towards the hall, touching the walls as she went, ready to freeze if she heard anything. She peered over the threshold. There was no one there. It was as if a ghost had passed through and sucked the breath from the house. There was an unfastened bag at the foot of the stairs, scraps of clothing strewn across the floor, a hairbrush, one of Frau Weiter's shoes. Empty files lay on their sides and there were glowing ashes in the fireplace. Ada couldn't make sense of what she was seeing. They had left in a hurry, all of a sudden, run out of the door, *no time for that, no time for that.* Paris. Stanislaus. *Leave it. It'll slow us down.*

Something had happened. She could taste metal in her mouth, her stomach tightened. Her hands and armpits began to sweat. She was alone. They had gone. Her jaw was juddering, and her teeth *clip-clopping* together. Her body was shaking. They could come back. She was going to cry again. Her nerves. They staggered and lurched, threshed round inside her, locked in a macabre waltz, *left two three, right two three.*

She took another step. Her foot brushed a small

tube on the carpet which glinted as it rolled away. Lipstick. She twisted the base. A thin, flat tip of red came through. She looked up at the vacant stairs, at the deserted corridor behind her. There was no one here. She dabbed the stick on her lips and rubbed them together, smelling the sweet wax of the cosmetic. She dabbed again, pushing the lipstick from side to side, smacking her lips. Her breath came in short, frantic puffs. She pressed the back of her hand to her face, brought it down across her mouth, saw a smudge of red on her fingers.

Not a bird, not a dog. No cars, no aeroplanes. No voices, no words. No shutter swinging in the breeze, no door slamming shut. The wind held its breath, mute, lulled. She heard her bare feet on the floor as she walked towards the door. The sideboard was on her left. She reached out to steady herself, and paused. A large mirror hung on the wall above it.

An unknown face stared back at her, hollow-eyed and drawn, with a livid, red smudge across the centre. A dirty grey cloth bound the head, a scrawny neck like a giblet stuck from a shabby nun's habit. Ada lifted her hand and touched her cheek, saw the reflection do the same. She sank to the floor, her arms tight round her knees. She stared through the open door, into the void beyond. She was trembling, unable to stop, and from deep within her she heard a soft, palsied keening.

★　　★　　★

There were two soldiers in the doorframe pointing rifles into the house. Ada had watched them approach. She should get up and run, but her legs were heavy, like felled logs. It didn't matter anymore. She felt nothing. She was dead. How long had she been sitting here? All day? All night? She'd heard gunfire. The *ratatatat* of machine guns, the *boom* of explosions echoing in the distance. The soldiers stepped into the hall, syncopated, guns left, guns right. Their heavy boots scrunched on the floor and their webbing squeaked. They came closer. She smelled the metal of the muzzle as it pressed against her temple.

'Get up.' Was he speaking English? It sounded strange, foreign. It didn't belong. Not here, in the Commandant's house. She stared ahead, unblinking, her hands and legs jiggling, her lips quivering.

'Can you stand, lady?' This voice was closer, gentler. American. She opened her mouth, *Who are you?* She wasn't sure if the sound came out, if it was in English. The first soldier walked behind her. She flinched, felt his arms under hers as he hauled her to her feet.

'Who are you?' she said.

'Americans,' the soldier said. 'Sixth Army. You speak English?'

She looked from one to the other, at the drab, olive uniforms. *Americans.*

'I'm British,' Ada said. She leant on the soldier, feeling the coarse wool of his jacket. His body was firm and warm. She had forgotten what another body felt like. She pressed herself closer. 'Is it over?'

'What are you doing here?' The other soldier spoke.

'Is it over?' Ada said. 'Is it over?'

'Almost,' the first soldier said.

'What are you doing here?' the other one said again.

What *was* she doing here? She took a deep, shuddering breath. 'I want to go home,' she said. 'Take me home.' Her thoughts were confused, scrambled. Her hands were still trembling, her legs numb, her voice feeble, like a child's.

'Who are you?' the soldier said.

'Please, take me home.'

'You have to come with us.'

'Please.' She wanted to howl.

The first soldier spoke again. 'What's your name?'

She fingered the crucifix round her neck. Who was she? 'Sister Clara,' she said, biting her lip, tasting the sweet marzipan of the lipstick.

'What are you doing here?'

'They kept me,' she started to sob again. 'Frau Weiss. And the baby. My baby. Thomas. Where is he?'

'Who was Frau Weiss?'

'His wife. The Commandant's wife. And Frau Weiter. Thomas, I must find Thomas.' She pushed against the soldier, struggled to free herself from his grip. 'Let me go.'

The soldier's hand tightened round her arm. 'No, lady,' he said. 'You're coming with us. Now.'

He pushed her towards the door.

'My shoes,' Ada said. 'I need my shoes. And my dress. I must get them. It's not allowed.'

She struggled, pointing behind her, but the soldier held firm.

'It's a trick,' he said.

'Go with her,' the second soldier said, pointing his rifle at Ada. 'She can get her clothes.'

He released his grip, walked towards the corridor, rifle at the ready, checking it was clear before he entered and beckoned Ada to come after him. She sidled into her room, and the soldier followed. Her unmade bed was still on the floor, the blanket and Sister Jeanne's old habit in a dishevelled heap on the cushions. The glass from the shattered window lay in shards across the tiles.

'You can't come in,' she said. 'It's not permitted. *Es ist nicht gestattet.*'

The soldier came closer. 'You speak German,' he said, 'you're a fucking Nazi.' He gripped her chin in his hand, yanked her face close to his. He hadn't shaved that day, his stubble was coarse and there was a fleck of food on his cheek.

'You're a fucking Nazi,' he said. 'We'll get you for this.' He began to shout, waving his free arm in the direction of the camp. 'All of it.' Ada could hear him choke, almost sob. 'You did this. Fucking German. Fucking *bitch*.' He pinched her chin and pushed her away.

'No,' Ada said, rubbing her face. '*Nein*. I'm not a German. I'm British. *Britische*.'

'Yeah?' The soldier was snarling, flecks of spit appearing on his lips. 'Then you're a fucking collaborator. A traitor. You'll swing for this.'

'I don't understand.' What was she saying? She couldn't speak English. She had forgotten the words. '*Ich verstehe nicht*.'

The soldier pulled a pistol from his waist and pointed it at Ada. She stared at the gun, at the soldier. His arm was straight and steady, the muzzle aimed at her head.

'It'd be so fucking easy,' he said.

These weren't Americans. It was a trick. They were guards. From the camp. Impostors. They had come to get her. Frau Weiss had threatened it.

'My dress,' Ada said, 'I must wear my dress. Frau Weiter won't let me wear this habit.' She lifted the dress off the table, began to pull it over her head but the thick serge of the tunic bunched it up. She tore it off, heard it rip and flung it onto her bed on top of Sister Jeanne's crumpled habit.

The soldier stepped forward, his pistol closer.

'I'll sew it,' she said, bending down to retrieve it. 'I'll do it. Sister Jeanne's bag. I must find it. I must give it back.' She lifted up the habit, and the torn shift, rolled them with shaking hands and tucked them under her arm.

'What the fuck are you doing?' The gun clicked.

Ada winced. 'Help me,' she said. 'You must help

me find it. I have to take these back.' She could hear her words spilling out. She hadn't spoken English for so long, not out loud. The war was over. *Der Krieg ist vorbei*. The end. *Das Ende*. Over, for good? She had to think. Her head felt muzzy, her words drunk and slurred. She held out to the table to steady herself. She was dizzy.

'Get your shoes, Kraut,' the soldier was shouting.

Ada flinched. 'Yes, my shoes. I need my shoes. They're by my bed. Right here. Here.' She lifted them up to show the soldier, then put them on the ground. They had no laces, and the backs were broken. Ada slipped her feet into them.

'My mending,' she said. 'I have to mend my dress. Where did you put the mending? I must clear up the mess, and Frau Weiter's washing. Sister Jeanne's bag. I can't find it.' She heard herself whimper. It was under the table. Of course. She used it to store the remnants of material. She pulled it out, turned it upside down so the fabric fell free.

'Sister Jeanne's habit,' she said. 'I hope she won't be cross.' What was she thinking? She must sound mad, deranged. She couldn't stop herself. She shoved it into the bag but the bag was too small and the tunic bulged over the opening. The fabric was greasy. Ada hadn't noticed that before.

'Stop fucking me round,' the soldier screamed. 'German whore.'

Ada jolted at the words. 'No, no,' she said. 'I'm not. *Britische*.'

'You better be telling the fucking truth, so help me God.'

'Where are we going?' she said, looking round, spotting the sewing machine by the window. 'I need that. I can't go without it.'

'Leave it,' the soldier said. He clamped his arm on Ada's elbow.

She shook it free. 'I can't,' Ada said. 'I must put on the lid. Here it is. Here's the lid.' She slammed it over the machine, adjusted its fit, closed the catches.

'Leave it.' He was shouting, waving the pistol at her.

'No,' Ada said, 'you don't understand. I have to take it.' She lifted the machine off the table. Its weight pulled her over. She pushed herself up, grabbed the handle, dragged it towards the door.

The other soldier had entered the room. Ada hadn't seen him come in. He put his finger to his head and twisted it. 'She's gone crazy,' he said, adding, 'the Sarge is here.'

This soldier picked up the sewing machine and walked towards the hallway. Ada followed. There were two more soldiers there now.

'She's a Kraut,' the first soldier said. 'Speaks fucking German.'

They began to talk among themselves. Ada didn't know what they were saying. She picked up words that made no sense. They thought she was German. An enemy. Would they lock her away? Shoot her? She had to tell them who she was, why she was here. *I'm not German. They took me. I couldn't help it.* Why couldn't she find the words? Make them see the truth?

She stood in the centre of the hall, fingering her crucifix with one hand, holding Sister Jeanne's overflowing bag with the other. One of the new soldiers came towards her. He didn't have a rifle but Ada noticed he had a gun in a holster round his waist and three beige stripes sewn on his arm. A Sergeant.

'Say,' he said. 'You speak English?'

She nodded.

'Are you some kind of nun?'

No. Yes. Ada stared at him, her mouth open. 'What are you going to do with me?' she said. 'I'm not German. I'm not.'

'Well,' he said, stretching the word. 'We met a whole bunch of you nun folks in Munich yesterday.' He stepped closer. 'So, Sister, what's that red on your face?'

Ada's heart was pumping, a hard *da-dum* against her chest. She was light-headed, floating. The soldiers weren't real, they couldn't be. This couldn't be the end of the war. Just like that. Americans. She wasn't a German. She reached out and touched the Sergeant's hand, felt the hairs on the back of his fingers and the soft lie of his skin. The red on her face. Did she have red on her face?

'You want to tell me how you got here?' he said, not waiting for her answer. Ada jerked her head.

215

It jarred against her neck, a surge of pain shot through her skull. She began to stagger. The Sergeant caught her before she fell.

'When did you last eat?' He called over his shoulder. 'You got one of those D-bars?' His corporal fished out a small packet from his pocket and passed it over. 'Chocolate,' he said, pressing one in her hand.

Ada smelled the sugar and cocoa, sweet and bitter. She shook her head.

'It'll make you feel better,' the Sergeant coaxed. She stared at him. 'You want to tell me how you got here?' he said again.

'I'm not a German,' she said, 'believe me.'

'Tell me what you're doing here.'

She had never told anyone, not the full, true story, not even to herself, in her head. She wasn't sure how to, where to begin. It was so very long ago.

'The Germans came,' she began.

'Where were you?' the Sergeant said.

'In Belgium, Namur.' *No more.* Stanislaus.

'And?'

'They took us. The British nuns. Sent us here, to look after old people. Only Herr Weiss—' She could feel his arthritic hand clench over hers, pressing it down on his groin. '—sent me here.'

'Cushy number, here. Nice house.' he said. 'You sure you weren't a volunteer?'

'Volunteer?' Ada said. 'They made me.'

'You see, Sister,' he said. 'I gotta be sure you're telling the truth.'

216

'And my baby,' Ada said. 'I've lost my baby.'

The Sergeant stepped back. 'What she says figures,' he said. 'That's pretty much what the story the other nuns told.'

'Frau Weiss has my baby,' Ada said.

'Sure, Sister,' the Sergeant said, his voice smooth and gentle. 'You're a little confused.'

'They've gone,' Ada said. 'They've all gone.'

The Sergeant looked at her hard, then he smiled. 'What's your name again?'

'Sister Clara.'

'Well, Sister Clara,' he said. 'I'm taking a hunch on you. We should haul you in, make sure you're a bona fide prisoner and not some Kraut pretending, or some traitor with the shits under them, excuse my language, Sister.' He fished out the chocolate from his pocket and offered it again to Ada.

'You change your mind?'

Ada shook her head.

'That camp is no place for a nun,' he said. 'I can't send you there, with the other prisoners. Believe me, lady, you don't want to go there.' He paused, screwing his eyes in concentration. 'Now, those other nuns—' He bit his lip. 'Say, can you give me some of their names?'

'Sister Brigitte,' Ada said. 'Sister Agatha, Sister—'

'Sister Brigitte. Yeah. She's like the boss one, who speaks for you?'

Ada nodded.

'Well, Sister Brigitte says they're staying where they are. They can't abandon their old people. War or peace, makes no difference. They serve God, and their vocation.'

He held up both his hands and rolled his eyes. 'So why don't I restore you to your flock? We'll register and classify y'all later.'

'When can I go home?' Ada said. 'I must find my baby. Frau Weiss has my baby.'

'Sure,' the Sergeant said. 'Sure.' He turned to one of the soldiers. 'Get the jeep, and drive her there.' He pointed to the sewing machine on the floor. 'And take that, if it keeps her happy. I'll get Battelli to go with her.'

The soldier who had taken her to her room helped her into the back of the jeep, scowling the whole time. There was a tarpaulin stretched across the top and the sides, and a rough tail-board. He pointed to a seat, dumped the sewing machine by her feet and handed her a blanket. He backed away, turned towards the house. She could see the road ahead through the back of the vehicle. A pall of smoke hung, drifting thick as a cloud. There was a smell of burning, of rubber, the bitter stench of cordite.

Another soldier climbed on board, and sat down beside her. He was young, with thick, black hair and dark brown eyes. He seemed more friendly than the others. He smiled at her. 'Sister,' he said, 'my name's Francesco, but they call me Frank. I'm a Catholic too. I've been detailed to look after you.'

She stared past him, to the tarpaulin behind him. It had faded in the sun, streaked by rain. The eyelets were rusty and the tie ropes had turned brown. I'm not a nun. She should say it. Not Sister Clara. Not a Catholic. Not anymore. I'm nothing. She stared at her hands, riddled with veins, her knuckles sharp as mountain crags. Her skin was raw, her nails bitten to the quick. That's all that she was. Bones and veins. An empty carcass.

The driver started up the jeep and they jolted out of the driveway, passing army trucks, their dull green camouflage splattered with mud. On the left were the bombed-out ruins of a large building, dust and smoke hovering above the rubble and the warped remains of a train and a railway line, twisted like a broken hanger.

'Yeah,' Frank was saying. 'We got the big one. Munitions. Went up like Coney Island at Fourth of July.'

Was it last night? Or last month? *Boom, boom.* Ada winced at the meaning. Flashing sky. Explosions. The window pane belching from its frame, shattering on the stone floor, the death rattle of the stricken house. Munitions. The big one. It made sense.

Frank pulled out a packet of cigarettes. 'Old Gold', Ada read. He took one and lit it. She hadn't had a cigarette since those sour French Gauloise she and Stanislaus smoked in Paris all those years ago.

'Please,' she said. 'May I have one?'

Frank looked puzzled. 'I didn't think Sisters smoked,' he said. 'You sure you want one?'

Ada nodded.

He raised his eyebrows, and passed her the packet. 'I guess you might need it.' He winked at her. 'I won't tell Reverend Mother.' He leant forward and lit the cigarette. Ada took a deep drag. The tobacco tasted foul, and left flecks on her tongue. She felt the coarse hot smoke fill her lungs. She coughed, watched as the smoke furled through her nose.

'Say, don't inhale,' Frank said. 'Just puff. I guess you've never had one before.'

The cigarette made her even more light-headed than before, but it cleared her mind, opened a memory. A man, taking care of her, lighting her cigarette. This was *her*, Ada, coming back to life. A second cigarette wouldn't taste so bad.

They passed another factory. The gates were open. *Arbeit macht frei.* Of course, she had passed that when she first came, remembered the words. Work makes free. People were milling inside. Some were wearing striped jackets and trousers like the men in the house. She could see soldiers standing with clipboards.

'What happened there?' she said to Frank. 'What did they make?'

The muscles clenched in his jaw and he turned his face away. 'Corpses,' he said.

He pinched out the cigarette with his fingers and flung the stub out of the back of the jeep. 'It was a concentration camp.'

The camp. *That* was the camp.

The driver built up speed. Dachau was a bigger village than Ada remembered. They passed another railway station, its roof ripped off, a large crater on the platform. The windows and doors of the nearby houses had been blown out. They passed a church and a water tower, drove down long, curved cobbled streets with tall houses either side. There were soldiers on the road. Americans, Ada guessed from the colour of their uniforms. A man in a striped jacket staggered across the road, his face gaunt. Ada twisted to get a better look. Perhaps she had met him once, was one of *her* men. He turned, his expression vacant and ghostly. The jeep came to a stop. A crocodile of children were crossing the road. They wore identical shabby grey coats and scuffed shoes with socks concertinaed round their ankles.

Ada flung her cigarette away, scrambled towards the tailgate, lowered herself to the ground.

'Hey!' Frank called.

She hitched up her tunic and ran after the children, grabbing the last one by the sleeve and turning him round.

'Thomas,' she said. The little boy cried out and the teacher at the head of the crocodile stopped and walked towards her.

'Go away,' she said, her face twisted with fear. 'Let him go.'

'Thomas,' Ada said. 'I'm looking for Thomas.

221

Or Joachim. Yes, Joachim. That's his name. Is he here?' The children had stopped and were staring at her. She scanned the pallid faces, noting how their cheeks were chapped and their lips sore. They must have been eight or nine years old. Too old for Thomas.

'No,' Ada said. 'Where is he?'

Frank was beside her, taking her elbow, leading her away. 'Come with me,' he said. 'Don't ever do that again.'

He walked her towards the jeep, lowered the tailboard, helped her climb back in. Thomas was still a little boy. Such a very little boy. A war baby. That's all he'd ever known, the black thunder of war.

She shut her eyes. 'I thought I saw him,' she said. The driver moved forward. 'Where are you taking me?'

'Munich.'

The jeep was draughty and she pulled the blanket tight round her.

The road was full of potholes and the jeep had to swerve and slow. They had to stop twice for a checkpoint, *OK buddy, that's fine.* They passed a group of people, an old woman, and a younger woman with a boy. The younger woman was pushing a cart piled high with suitcases, an old man balanced on top of them. The countryside looked wintry. Patches of snow on brown, barren fields. The villages were deserted, the houses bleak and dowdy. They drove through a forest of beech, trees with mossy trunks and naked limbs as far as the eye could see.

'Am I free?' she said to Frank.

'Sure,' he said.

'Is it over?'

'Sure.'

Free.

'And Frau Weiter?' she said. 'And Anni?'

'I don't know who you're talking about.'

But the mending. She had to do the mending. She rummaged in Sister Jeanne's bag, pulled out the tatty habit. The bag was empty.

'I've left the mending,' she said. It was in the suitcase, on top of the wardrobe, with all the other samples back in Paris. Stanislaus had to stop the jeep. 'We have to go back.'

'Forget it,' Frank said.

'Please.'

'Why do you need the mending? It's over, Sister.' He laughed, *Ha ha.* 'You're a funny one.'

She shook her head. This wasn't Stanislaus. It was another man. 'Where am I?' she said. 'What's happening?'

The jeep slowed again and Ada saw they were in a wide street with houses set in large gardens. They had come to a town. Beyond the gardens Ada could see other buildings, a church spire, attic roofs.

'Nearly there,' Frank said. They turned the corner. The houses on one side of the road had been rended apart, as if an arm or a leg had been torn off, exposing the socket beneath. Sinews of wallpaper hung in shreds, a mattress tipped over the edge like a muscle ripped from its tendon, a table with jagged edges, snapped like a bone. Another corner. The shell of a church. A bronze lion knocked from its plinth, lying on its side, its paws clawing the air. There was dust everywhere, and smoke. And people, wandering, lost and silent. Buildings smouldered, piles of rubble tall as slag heaps. There was half a railway bridge, the tracks humped like a roller-coaster. They drove across a square. The buildings on all sides had been blasted of their windows and doors, gaped with empty eyes and hungry mouths. Debris everywhere. There were three tanks in the far corner, and soldiers leaning against them. Ada froze.

'It's OK, Sister,' Frank said, 'they're ours.'

Nothing was as she remembered it from that brief truck ride years ago. She guessed they were in the centre of Munich.

The geriatric home had survived. It had lost its gates and its walls, and the gardens were as bare as the fields, but she recognized it. Frank helped her down, took Sister Jeanne's bag and the sewing machine.

'After you,' he said. Ada walked towards the doors, opened them, stepped inside the hall with its chequered floor. Sister Brigitte was there.

'Sister Clara,' she said. She walked forward, her

arms open. Ada fell towards her and Sister Brigitte enfolded her, pulling her close.

'Thank God,' Sister Brigitte said. 'Thank God.'

Sister Brigitte burned Sister Jeanne's habit, Ada's too. 'You don't need to give it back,' she said, pushing Ada forward in the bed and plumping up the pillows behind her. 'Now lie back and stop fretting.'

'Herr Weiss?' she said. She could see him tapping his way into the room, lying on the bed beside her.

'Herr Weiss? He passed away, God rest his soul.'

God *rot* his soul.

'And the sewing machine?'

'The sewing machine is under your bed. No one can take it away.'

'Humour her,' Ada heard Sister Brigitte say to Sister Agatha. *Nervous exhaustion.* The war was properly over now. Hitler was dead. Germany had surrendered. Ada lay in a bed, covered in a soft eiderdown. A *Federbetten.* Frau Weiter had used one. Ada couldn't see how it kept you warm without blankets, but it did, cosy and snug. She was in a large, light room, could see the gardens through the windows. No guards there now. Just a spindly birch frothing with new leaves and a couple of old men with blankets over their shoulders, shuffling along on the arms of Sister Josephine. She was taller than them, her wimple fresh and white. It was a miracle that they had all survived, these old men, even Sister Thérèse, fingering her rosary with ancient, arthritic fingers and snoring gently at night. There were six beds in the room, one for each of them. Proper beds, on legs, with headboards and linen, frayed at the edges and threadbare in the centre, but clean. They woke at dawn, said their prayers, went off to do their duties, leaving Ada to doze.

She would look for Thomas, once she was back on her feet. He couldn't be far. She wrote home: 'Dear Mum and Dad, I hope you're well and gave Mr Hitler what for.' She could picture their faces when they got the letter. Everyone would know. Foreign stamp. The neighbours would talk. *I bet it's from their Ada. Give it here.* 'I'm fine.' She mustn't worry them. They'd have been frantic enough as it was. 'It's been a bit of an adventure here.' Better not say anything about Thomas, not yet. 'I'll tell you all about it when I'm home, which will be soon, I hope. Your loving daughter, Ada'.

'Frank was asking after you today,' Sister Brigitte said, placing a tray of soup on her lap. 'He comes twice a week, with the rations. Taken a shine to you, I reckon.'

Ada smiled. He was a good-looking man. 'May I have a mirror?' Ada said.

'No,' Sister Brigitte said, 'you may not. Not until you're better.' She sat on the edge of the bed so Ada had to grab the tray and steady it. 'I know you're not a nun, Sister Clara, but we're proud of you. You've been a credit to us all. What's your real name?'

'Ada,' she said, 'Ada Vaughan.' She said it softly, over and over. This is who she was, *Ada Vaughan*. She hadn't said those words since, since when? She scrolled the years, counting on her fingers. Since the Germans had captured her. 1940. Five years, almost to the day. She could be Ada again, be herself again, go back home, back to normal. *Dressmaker extraordinaire*. She could turn on the light when she wanted, wear nylons, wash her hair. She'd have to see what the new styles were. Dance. Meet a young man and settle down. She and Thomas. A little family. Hope.

'Well, Ada,' Sister Brigitte said, smiling at her. 'Have you considered a vocation?'

Ada couldn't help herself. She laughed, shaking the bed so the soup slurped out of the bowl onto the tray.

'Perhaps not,' Sister Brigitte said, 'after all.'

'No,' Ada said. 'Perhaps not.' She picked up her spoon and stirred the soup. She took a deep breath. 'When I'm better, Sister Brigitte—' she paused, unsure how to frame the question. 'I must find Thomas. Will you help me?'

Ada saw Sister Brigitte's face in profile. She had aged in the war, worry lines etched round her mouth.

'Don't raise your hopes, my dear,' she said. Her voice was quiet. 'Terrible things happened in this

227

war. We find out more and more each day. Please eat your soup.'

'I don't want it.' Ada lifted the tray.

'I insist,' Sister Brigitte said. 'You must build your strength. Physical and mental.' She nodded towards the soup and waited until Ada picked up her spoon. 'Little and often.'

She stood and walked to the window. 'We survived because we grew vegetables,' she said. 'And we kept a pig, chickens, ducks. People stole the chickens, and the ducks. They would have stolen the pig but it made too much noise. They know, pigs,' she went on. 'Intelligent animals. They know when their time is up. They don't go quietly.'

She looked at Ada. 'Even so, we had to dig up the garden to feed us all. Now it's the Americans who feed us. We'll plant flowers soon, back where they belong. So our old people can look on beauty. Have you finished?'

Ada nodded and Sister Brigitte took the tray, balancing it on her hip, supporting it with one arm. 'Father Friedel was killed,' she said.

'I know,' Ada said, 'for speaking out.'

'Well,' Sister Brigitte said, 'not in so many words. He was killed in reprisal for a bishop who spoke out. He was a little old, Father Friedel. I'm not sure he knew what was going on. They caught him the day your child was born.'

Ada lifted her hand to her mouth, sucked in air through tight lips.

'They don't think he had the baby with him, so we were told. But we have no idea what he did with him. We can't ask him now.'

'Perhaps he took him to an orphanage, to a Catholic orphanage,' Ada said.

Sister Brigitte frowned, took a deep breath and opened her mouth as if to say something, but then adjusted the tray on her hip instead.

'Yes,' Ada went on, before Sister Brigitte could speak again. She was so close to finding him now, holding him tight, weeping into his hair, *Thomas*. 'He must have. I'll go there. When I'm better.' An orphanage, of course. He wouldn't have just handed him over to Frau Weiss. 'Will you come with me?'

It was a moment before Sister Brigitte replied. 'Perhaps.' Her voice was hesitant and she paused again. 'The orphanage was bombed.' Ada let out a cry. 'The children were evacuated.'

'Where?'

'I understand they took over an institution somewhere.'

'Where?'

Sister Brigitte paused. 'In Dachau.'

It all made sense. Frau Weiss. She had picked Thomas. In Dachau. A beautiful baby. The children she had passed, they were orphans. She'd go back to Dachau, find the orphanage. They could tell her, help her find Thomas.

Her hair had grown and she had put on weight. Ada had been in bed for two weeks before she was allowed to stand, shaky at first, two feet on the floor, push off from the bed, *easy does it*, like a child learning to walk. She went a little further each day, round their dormitory, down the corridor, into the conservatory. Ada grew rigid with terror at the thought of seeing Herr Weiss there. *Come, my dear. Sit by my side.* Sister Brigitte had said that he was dead. *Suicide.* Slit his wrists with a cut-throat razor. Left a note addressed to his nephew, Obersturmbannführer Martin Weiss. *In accordance with the Führer's plans.* Ada kept walking. Into the garden. The weather was cold for May, but the midday sun held the promise of warmth. Sister Brigitte brought some clothes for her, a pair of shoes, an old-fashioned skirt that was too long and too large, a blouse of brushed cotton.

'Frank bought them. Paid good cigarettes for them, so he said.' Her face was serious. 'No one has food. They're desperate. They'll sell anything. Cigarettes are money.' She pointed to the sewing machine gathering dust under the bed. 'You can use that. Take them in, make them fit.'

'Did I bring that with me?' Ada said. 'What was I thinking?'

'You weren't,' Sister Brigitte said. 'You were deranged.'

Ada lifted the machine onto a table. It still had thread from the house in Dachau. It could do with a little oil but it worked like a dream. Nip and tuck.

230

'And a mirror?' Ada said. 'You promised.'

Sister Brigitte led her down the corridor to a storeroom. A large chevalier mirror stood in the corner, covered in dust. They wheeled it into the centre of the room and Sister Brigitte wiped it with the edge of her sleeve.

Ada stood before it. She couldn't see so well now, the sewing had made her eyes bad. Things far away blurred. She stepped closer. Her face was gaunt, the cheekbones sharp. She could see the shape of her skull beneath her skin. But her eyes were no longer hollow, haunted craters, her skin was pink and healthy, her hair thick, chin-length. She pulled it free of her face, tucked it behind her ear, piled it on top. She turned, to the left, to the right. Ada Vaughan. Thin as a rake. But lucky. *Lucky.*

Sister Brigitte stood behind her, and pulled out a small tube from her pocket. 'We found this in your tunic,' she said, pressing it into Ada's hand. The lipstick. Ada twisted it, leant forward to the mirror, traced it over her lips. 'Thank you,' she said, taking Sister Brigitte and pulling her close, kissing her on the cheek, leaving a large red imprint of her mouth.

'Wish it was all as easy as this,' the American lieutenant said, handing her the papers and the train ticket. 'There's plenty others not so straightforward.'

Ada took the documentation, read the title, *Distressed British Subject.* She traced her name with

231

her finger, *Ada Vaughan. British citizen, displaced in the course of conflict, eligible for repatriation to the United Kingdom.*

She'd heard how the Germans had bombed London. What if the house wasn't there? How would she find her family?

'It will be fine,' Sister Brigitte said. 'They'll be so happy to see you.'

She held her pass in her hand. *Keep these papers on you at all times. They are valuable documents. Non-transferable.*

She didn't have long.

The jeep had an open top. It was early June. The weather had turned and the air was soft and warm.

'It ain't a limousine, I know,' Frank said. He and Sister Brigitte were sitting in the front, Ada balanced on the small bench seat behind. 'Not built for ladies, I'll say that. But she's a sturdy little warhorse,' he patted the steering wheel affectionately. 'And she'll get us there.'

He turned round and grinned. 'I never thought you were a real nun,' he said. 'I knew when I first clapped eyes on you. You gotta be something else.'

He was driving fast and Ada had to hold tight to the back of his seat. He tooted his horn at an emaciated dog, veered round a hole in the road.

'Just would you believe it? I told the Sarge. You remember him? I said to the Sarge, guess what Sarge, you know that nun you rescued? Well, turns out she wasn't a nun. Just a regular dame. But say, Ada—' he turned round again. 'You're some looker.'

Ada smiled a *thank you*. An unfamiliar surge of heat crept up her face. Frank's hair was short and jagged beneath his cap. There were specks of dandruff on his collar. His hands gripped the wheel, dark hairs curled from the cuffs of his jacket.

'So, you're going back home,' he went on. 'Leaving me all alone.'

Munich was full of people. They were shabby and thin, wandered round with string bags in their hands, or packages wrapped in brown paper. One stopped an American soldier, pulled out a clock from the package. The soldier shook his head. Rubble had been bulldozed into mounds twenty or thirty feet high. Women and children were swarming over them, picking at the stones with bare hands, digging with bits of broken wood or scraping at the surface. A woman was pulling at something buried deep, tugging it out through the broken bricks which tumbled down the slope as she did so.

'What are you going to do there?' Frank said.

'Where?' Ada said.

'Back home.'

Ada shrugged. She hadn't thought, not beyond that first moment when she opened the door and saw them all, Mum, Dad and the rest.

'Come to America,' Frank said suddenly. 'I'd

look after you. Feed you up.' He glanced sideways to Sister Brigitte. 'As God and Sister Brigitte are my witnesses, I'd make an honest woman of you. We wouldn't be rich, but we'd do all right. Put all this behind you. Start a fresh. Land of opportunity. What do you say, Ada?' He turned round and grinned at her. 'Marry me.'

'Marry you?' Ada laughed. 'I don't know you.'

'What's that got to do with it?' Frank was shouting above the noise of the engine. 'I knew when I first clapped eyes on you. You're the one for me.'

'And Thomas?'

'Kids too, I love them all.'

Ada saw his shoulders rise, high enough to swallow the sky. *'If you were the only girl in the world, and I was the only boy.'* His voice soared above the clatter of the street, pure as a caress, clean enough for heaven itself. It reminded her of her father who sang like a nightingale. He used to sing this song too, standing round the piano in the pub, or serenading her mother in the kitchen on the good days when they weren't arguing. Ada had not heard anything so beautiful for a long time. Maybe she could follow that voice. *America.* Marry Frank.

He slowed down, turned and faced her again, *'Nothing else would matter in the world today. We could go on loving in the same old way.'* He stopped, concentrated on navigating his way through the broken street. A woman rushed up to them in a shabby skirt and a man's shirt and shoes, hammered on the side of the jeep.

'You fat Yanks,' she was yelling. 'What about us Germans?'

Ada looked away, took a deep breath and opened her mouth.

'A garden of Eden just made for two
With nothing to mar our joy.'

Sing, Frank. Sing, please.

They had left the city and were on the open road to Dachau. Here and there a farmer was ploughing the land, or sowing seeds, coaxing the countryside back to life. There were orchards with small pellets of new-born fruit. Apples, Ada guessed, or cherries. Villages with wooden houses and heavy, over-hanging roofs. One or two of the houses had geraniums in boxes on the balconies, gaudy red blossoms against the black, seasoned wood behind. *Thomas.*

'Ada, I don't think you should raise your hopes,' Sister Brigitte cautioned. 'I don't want to see you disappointed. Or hurt.' She turned round in her seat and faced Ada. 'Maybe best to leave it.'

'I can't,' Ada said. 'I must know.' She had lived with the heartache of Thomas, with the dread and despair of losing him. She couldn't stop her search now, before she had even begun. 'What if Father Friedel didn't go to the orphanage? Gave him straight to Frau Weiss. We must be able to trace her.'

'You have no proof that child was Thomas. Just

235

because you wanted it to be true doesn't make it so. Have you thought of that?'

If Sister Brigitte thought she was on a fool's errand, she would prove her wrong. Ada knew, as only a mother could know, that the child was Thomas. She would find him. Rescue him. The orphanage would tell her where he was. Frau Weiss would be traced. Thomas would recognize her. He'd come with her. She'd have to teach him English, but he'd pick it up fast enough. Knock at the door in Theed Street. *Ada? Ada, is that you? Oh my lawd! And who's this little lad?* Tommy. This is Tommy. She'd look behind, beckon him to come. *Oh, I nearly forgot. This is Frank, Mum. We're getting married.*

'Here we are,' Frank said, steering the jeep up a driveway towards a large house. He stopped the car, helped Sister Brigitte down, then Ada. He leant against the bonnet, and fished out his cigarettes from his pocket. 'I'll wait here.'

Ada squeezed Sister Brigitte's hand. *This is it.* They pulled the bell and heard it ring inside, a deep sonorous *gong*, like a cymbal. No one came. They rang again. Ada looked at Frank, called over to him, 'Are you sure this is the place?'

'As far as I know.'

'Wait,' Ada said. She leant towards the door, ear flat against the wood. 'Someone's coming.'

They heard bolts wrenched back and a key turn. A woman in a grey dress and a stiff white apron and cap opened the door.

'*Ja? Was wollen sie?*'

Ada took a breath. She hadn't spoken German for a month, and wasn't sure how to start. 'I'm looking for a child,' she said. 'A little boy. *My* little boy. I believe he may have come here. As a baby.'

'Believe?' the nurse said. 'May? Did he or didn't he?' She narrowed her eyes at Ada. 'You're not German, are you?'

'No,' Ada said, 'I'm British.'

'How could we have a British baby here?'

'You wouldn't know he was British,' she said. 'A priest, Father Friedel, brought him. He'd just been born.' Still bloody from the birth, the cord tied with an old piece of string. Ada saw him now, his limbs spread-eagled, a little frog with bulging eyes. 'In 1941, February 1941.'

The nurse snorted. 'So long ago.'

'But you'll have records,' Ada said. 'You could check.'

'Records? They were destroyed in the bombing. Ask him.' She tilted her head at Frank. 'Ask the Americans where the records are.'

'But do you remember?' Ada said. 'Father Friedel. He was old. He would have had the baby in his bag.'

'How would I know?' she said. 'I wasn't here then.' She turned to Frank, shouted at him. 'We need food, medicine. The children are ill. Typhus. We need help.' She faced Ada again. 'Not time-wasters.'

She stepped inside and began to close the door. Ada slipped her foot onto the threshold.

237

'He had a teddy bear,' Ada said. 'A little knitted bear.'

The nurse rolled her eyes. 'Every child has a knitted bear.'

'A brown one.'

'Brown ones.' She squeezed the door against Ada's foot. Ada winced. She could not give up.

'Frau Weiss,' she said. 'Do you know Frau Weiss?'

'Weiss?'

'The Commandant's wife?'

'The Commandant?' she said, 'Oh no. I don't have anything to do with that lot. Never have. Nazis? I was never a Nazi. No, you can't accuse me.' She pushed the door harder.

'I've lost my son,' Ada's voice was cracking. Keep calm. *Calm.* 'She had a little boy. She and the Obersturmbannführer.'

'I'll tell you this for free,' the nurse snorted again, 'Martin Weiss was never married.'

'He was.' Ada knew, for sure.

'No.' The nurse was shaking her head. She squinted at Ada, leant forward and whispered, '*Sodomite.*' Ada clasped her hands to her lips. Sister Brigitte looked puzzled and Ada wasn't sure if she had heard.

'He used to hang round here,' the nurse went on in a soft voice. 'I wasn't born yesterday. I put a stop to that. Nearly cost me my job.' The nurse had let go of the door and was standing with arms akimbo.

'No,' Ada said again. 'That's not possible. He had a wife. He had a son.'

'I don't know who the floozy was in that big house,' the nurse said. 'But she wasn't his wife. And that wasn't his son, unless he strapped his member to a toothbrush.'

She kicked Ada's foot away and slammed the door. The sound reverberated through Ada's body, snapping her hope in half, strewing it across the barren gravel of the road. There was no wife, no Frau Weiss. She was some other woman with no name, vanished forever.

'I'm sorry,' Sister Brigitte was saying, leading Ada back to the car. 'I'm so sorry.'

'But Frau Weiss—'

'An alias,' Frank said. 'Whoever was living with him has skedaddled. It's a lost cause.' He stood by the jeep shuffling his feet. 'No papers. No record. No nothing. Needle in a haystack.'

'You can't be sure,' Ada raised her voice. Frank had no right to say such cruel things. She saw it now. She could never go to America. Not without Thomas. She had to stay here, search for him.

'Ada,' Sister Brigitte said, taking her hand and stroking it. 'You've done as much as you can.'

'The Sister's right,' Frank said. 'Come back again, when everything's back to normal. In a year or so. Look for him then. People don't know nothing now.'

Ada looked at Frank. 'You have him,' she said. 'You told me. You Americans have him. He's a prisoner. Weiss. Ask him. What's her name? Where is she?'

239

'Listen, Ada,' he said, squinting into the sun so his face screwed tight. 'I'm sorry for your loss and all that. But I think we got bigger questions to put to Weiss than his girlfriend's name.' He pronounced it 'goil'. His *goilfriend's* name.

Thomas had been taken from her four years, four months and ten days ago. He was alive.

'Ada.'

She ran down the driveway, back into the road. She could see the chimney of the camp over the rooftops. The streets were crowded with people and she had to dart and dodge, watching her step on the uneven cobbles and churned-up road. She could hear Frank's jeep behind her. He was blasting the horn, revving the engine. She turned a corner.

And there he was.

In a brown trilby hat and a beige trenchcoat. Moustache, spectacles, smile. *Hello Ada.*

'Stanislaus,' she shouted, 'Stanislaus.'

He crossed the road. She raced after him, her breath surging in short, painful thrusts. She was weak, about to collapse. She had to catch him. Talk to him. *Tell me you got lost. Tell me you looked for me. Dreamed about me, every day. You and me Ada, when the war's over, we'll make a go of it.* She'd thought about him every day, thoughts hurling like a Catherine wheel, sparks of love and hate. Stanislaus and Thomas. Her family.

He was gone. She stopped, panting. She must be imagining things.

TWO

LONDON, JULY 1945

Ada sat in the Ladies Only compartment of the train, staring at the peppered mirror opposite and the advertisements for Eastbourne and Bexhill-on-Sea, poster-blue skies and bright yellow sands. Southern Railways. The train was dirty, the windows thick with sooty smuts. She smiled at the other women with their curled sandwiches in greaseproof paper. *Fish paste. Liver paste. Pilchards.* The young lady from the Women's Voluntary Service, a comely figure in green uniform and pink lipstick, had given them the sandwiches when they climbed on board. It was a long time since Ada had seen someone like that, someone *womanly*. She ran her hand down the hollows of her body. She went *in* where she should have gone *out*. No bosom. No hips. She was fatter than she had been before, thanks to Sister Brigitte, but she could still count her ribs. The other women in the carriage were thin too, all DBS's like her. Distressed British Subjects. That's what they called them. She thought she'd been a prisoner or an internee. That, at least, gave her a character, a persona with a past, after all these years. But a DBS? Who was that?

Home. Should she knock? Open the door and walk right in? *Hello. Only me. It's our Ada. She's back.* Cissie, her sister. She was eleven when Ada left. She'd be a young woman now. Out at work. Their big sister, safely home. All together again. Alf and Fred, Bill and Gladys, Mum and Dad. Sitting in that kitchen, warm from the range and steamy from the washing draped to dry. *Ada, love, put the kettle on. Let's have a cup of tea.* Maybe Dad would send Fred to the pub for a jug of stout. *Good to have you back, girl.* Mum fussing. Neck of lamb from O'Connor's. Pearl barley. Dumplings. *You could do with some weight, bit of feeding up.*

Ada rubbed the window with her cuff but the dirt was on the outside and it was difficult to see through. They shunted through dilapidated towns and dog-eared villages. England was poorer than she remembered. The fields in between the towns flared ochre and green in the bright July sun, glowed with life and colour. There were woodlands, heavy oaks and beech and more houses. Suburbs. *Chuggety-chug,* semi-detached houses covered in pebbledash. *Chuggety-chug* through allotments and gardens with bean frames and early potatoes. Mum had always wanted to move to a place like this. Purley. Purley Oaks. Sanderstead. Her friend Blanche had moved to the suburbs. *Petit bourgeois,* Dad had said. *Nobody lives in Purley.*

The train was down to a dawdle. Balham. Clapham Junction. This was London? Whole streets gone, nothing but empty façades and lopsided walls. Anxiety began to scratch at her gut. Ada pressed her nose against the glass. Some of the ruins had been fenced off and displayed clumsy notices *Keep Off* and *Danger*. She could see children climbing through the stones, holding their fingers like guns. *Bang bang.* Battersea, the power station still standing. Vauxhall. There was the Thames, in full view. It was low tide, the banks brown as slugs, the river a dirty worm, busy with tugs and barges and dredgers. She pulled down the window. She could hear their hooters, echoing from side to side. She'd heard them as a child, melancholy trumpets of loss.

County Hall. That was still there and Big Ben. She sat forward. The river. This was wrong. You shouldn't be able to see the river, not from here. Where had all the works gone? The timber yards and brickmakers? The Tramways Department and the printers? The storage and the wharfs? Where were the gantries? Where was Belvedere Road?

Her mouth tasted dry, the metallic salt of panic. What about their house, their street? What if they weren't there? Had her family been killed? Blasted away, their gnarled limbs and tortured bodies dug from the broken bricks and twisted boards? Or what if they'd moved? How would she find them?

The train pulled into Waterloo. The sewing machine had been too heavy to lift into the luggage rack, and there hadn't been a porter to hand so Ada had pushed it under the seat. She picked it up, stepped down. They were hustled off the platform and into a makeshift office with 'Joint War Organisation' pinned to the door. The woman in charge was busty, her chest straining at the buttons of her grey uniform. Her skirt was drawn tight across her hips, creased round the groin where she sat. She was huffing, shuffling papers, annoyed, as if Ada was disturbing her.

'If you were a soldier,' she said, slamming the files on her desk, 'a proper prisoner of war, I'd know what's what. I wouldn't be dealing with you for a start. But civilians.' She curled her lip. '*Women.* What do we do with you?'

'I don't mean to be a nuisance,' Ada said, looking behind her at the other women in the queue. 'I'm not the only one.'

The busty woman looked at Ada and shook her head. 'More's the pity.' She pulled out a large, black money box from a drawer and slapped it on the desk. 'There's not much we can do for any of you, except give you the fare home.' She fished out four half-crowns and handed them to Ada. '*Ex gratia,*' she said.

Ada didn't know what that meant but it felt like charity. Didn't see why she should be made to feel like a tramp.

'You have got somewhere to go, I take it?'

'Oh yes,' Ada said, looking the woman in the eye. 'Yes.' She placed the coins back on the table. 'It's all right. I don't need them. I only live round the corner.'

The woman raised an eyebrow. 'Take it,' she said. 'It's all you're going to get. You can apply for your coupons. Over there.' She pointed to some forms. 'Are you single?'

Ada nodded.

'Hmm.' The woman snorted, leant to one side and, looking over Ada's shoulder, called, 'Next.'

Ada took the money, picked up her sewing machine and walked out into the station concourse. Waterloo. She wanted to pinch herself. Here she was, at last. Home. The machine was heavy. She fingered a half-crown. Left Luggage. She'd collect it later. Get Dad to carry it for her, or Alf or Fred. *What you doing with this, Ada? Bring it all the way back, did you?*

She stepped out into Waterloo Road, free of the machine. St John's Church was there. And the Lying-In Hospital. Stamford Street, Peabody Buildings. *All present and correct, sir, but a bit worse for wear, if you don't mind me saying so, sir.* If those buildings were all right, her street must be too. She crossed the road. Exton Street. Roupell Street. The houses were standing. All of them. One or two had their windows boarded up. The lace curtains were tatty and the windows and doors could do with a lick of paint, but they hadn't been bombed. It was all right. It would be all right. She began to run, her eyes misting up. She stopped and wiped her face. *Mustn't do to be crying.* Home. Round the corner. Theed Street. The terrace of little cottages with their even doors and windows with old-fashioned square panes.

Clip-clop along the uneven pavement, past where the Chapmans lived and the O'Connors, front doors *still* open to the street so you could see inside, respectable houses, good homes. Things hadn't changed, after all. She was smiling. Maybe someone would come out of these houses, recognize her. *Good Gawd, if it ain't Ada Vaughan.*

And there it was. Number 11. Home. Ada curled her fist and knocked, a soft *tap-tap* on the shabby wood. She breathed in and took hold of the handle. Turned. Pushed. The hallway was much smaller than she remembered, but it was the same faded, flowery wallpaper, the same dirty marks up the stairs and the chipped, green skirting boards. The door to the kitchen opened and her mother came through, wiping her hands on her apron, squinting at Ada as if she didn't know her.

'Who's there?'

Ada bit her lip. 'It's me.' Her voice was tight as a tripwire. 'Ada.'

Her mother took two strides and grabbed Ada's arm, pinching her elbow. 'You've got a bleeding nerve,' she said, 'waltzing in here after all this time.'

Ada flinched, not understanding. She had been

ready to hug her mother, bury her face in her hair, smell her sweat and the peach of her skin. Here she was, her daughter, missing presumed dead, back from the grave. A bloody miracle. But not so much as a *hello* from her mother, much less a hug.

'Causing your father and me no end of worry,' her mother went on. 'It killed him, you know that? Dropped dead. Just like that.'

Dad? Dead? Her bowels churned and her mouth filled with iron. This was not how she dreamed it. Dad, dead? She hadn't thought of that, not really. She swallowed hard, fighting back the tears. She'd never told him she loved him. Never said goodbye. Never said, *thank you, Dad.*

'When?' she managed to say.

'Left me to carry on,' her mother ignored her. 'No idea where you were, whether you were a goner or alive. Not a word from you. Not. A. Word.'

'That wasn't true,' Ada whipped a reply. 'Stanislaus sent you a telegram.'

'Stanislaus? Was that what he was called? Bloody German.'

His name slipped out. She hadn't wanted to talk about him.

'He—' she corrected herself, made it sound better. '*We* sent you a telegram. Saying I was all right. Not to worry.'

'Well, it never got here.'

'It was sent to Mrs B. She was going to tell you.'

'You mean you didn't even have the common

decency to send it to me? Mrs B. never told me about no telegram. Had her on my doorstep, the day war broke out. The *very* day. Is Ada back? Only she didn't come into work today. First we heard about it. Upped and gone to Paris with a fancy man. The disgrace of it. To think a daughter of mine would *do* such a thing.'

That was so long ago, *years* ago. So much had happened since, and here was her mother dredging it up as if it was yesterday, as if it was the most important thing, as if she hadn't missed her at all. Ada looked at her. She had grown bitter, worry lines along her forehead and round her mouth, her lips thin and mean.

'I sent you a letter when it was over,' Ada said. 'I couldn't before.'

'Fine letter that was. A bit of an adventure, you said. *An adventure,* I ask you. Have you any idea what it was like for us?' Her mother's face was close to hers, her breath musty and stale. 'While you were living it up, we were going through hell. *Hell.* What with the bombing, and the rationing and then the doodlebugs. We all had to do our bit. Pull our weight. But you? You lived off the fat of the land, you and your Nazi boyfriend.'

'No,' Ada said. 'It wasn't like that. I had it bad, too—'

'You had it bad? You've no idea the suffering we went through.'

'I was interned.'

Her mother snorted. 'What does that mean, when it's at home?'

'A prisoner. I was kept a prisoner.'

'Prison? Safe and sound, I bet. Not a care in the world.'

Ada didn't know what to say. How could she describe what she had lived through? What she'd seen? All she'd ever wanted was to come home, but she was being treated like a traitor. She wasn't a traitor. Would her mother believe her? Would *anyone* believe her?

'Did you ever spare a thought for your father and I?' Her mother continued. 'And your brothers? And your sisters?'

Ada needed to sit down. Her bones were loose and disconnected, her head was spinning. 'How are they?'

'Now you ask.' Spittle frothed at the corner of her mother's mouth. 'Fred was killed at Alamein. Gave his life for the likes of you.' She spat on Ada's shoes. Ada had never known her mother like this, not with her. Her father used to get the sharp end of her mother's tongue and gave back as good as he got. But now Ada was the target for her venom. 'Alf's all right. And the girls. But you? You always were the selfish one. Deceitful. You broke our hearts.'

Ada rubbed her fingers over her forehead. Her father gone left such a crater inside. She had wanted to breathe in his tobacco skin, feel him squeeze her close, smell his sweat as his lips brushed the top of her head, know that she was loved again. *You've always been my favourite, Ada.*

'I'm sorry,' she said. 'I couldn't help it.' Her voice was cracking and she was holding back the tears.

'Sorry?' Her mother's voice was at boiling point. 'Too bloody late for sorry. You're not welcome here. So you can get out. Now.'

'Out?' Ada couldn't understand what her mother was saying. 'Can't I stay?'

'No, you bloody can't.'

'I've nowhere to go.'

'You should have thought of that before.' Her mother twisted Ada's arm, forcing her towards the door. 'Think yourself lucky you're not trailing a bastard. Or are you? I wouldn't put it past you. Nothing would surprise me.'

Her mother pushed her. 'Clear off. And don't you ever darken this door again.' She shoved and Ada lurched to the door, feeling the wind as her mother slammed it hard behind her.

Ada stood on the doorstep, in the neat arc her mother had scrubbed round the threshold. She took a deep breath. *Pull yourself together.* Her mother was upset. It was the shock of seeing Ada again. That was all. She always had a temper. Even so, she might have been a bit more under-standing. She hadn't seen Ada for nearly six years. You'd think she'd be pleased. She'd calm down, would be sorry for her outburst. Give her time. All that worry, bottled up, ready to explode. A few more minutes. She'd knock on the door again. *Mum, please.*

Some children had chalked a hopscotch on the cobbles. Ada picked up a stone and threw it on the ground. *Hop, hop, hop, double, hop hop.* She balanced on one leg, picked up the stone, threw it again.

A window opened above her and her mother leant out. 'You heard me,' she shouted. 'Piss off.' She slammed the sash back again.

Ada let the stone drop to the ground. Mum could be funny like that. Had a temper hot enough to brew a cup of tea. And unforgiving. Kept a fight going for years. Ada knew she wouldn't change her mind, not today. Well, she thought, if that's what she wants, she can have it. Her loss.

She turned and walked down the street. Her legs were frail and her hands were shaking. She had no home, no clothes, no friends, no money, except ten bob from the Red Cross. Nine and eleven now, after a penny for the Left Luggage. She fingered the ticket. *Collect on day of issue. Uncollected items will be disposed of.* All she had in the world was a sewing machine. You couldn't sleep under that.

She'd lost everyone. Her son. Her mother. Her father. Stanislaus. *Good riddance.* And Frank. She could have gone to America. She could have had a good life. Frank had been a kind man, honest too. He'd reminded her of her father. She stopped, breathed in. She didn't even know where her father was buried. *Oh, Ada,* she could hear him. *No use crying over spilt milk*. There was nothing she could do now to make it better. *Your mother feeds on grudges like a gannet in a trough.* Well, she could do without that. She'd survived the war. She'd survive now. She remembered a song from her childhood, heard her father sing it in her head. *Pack up your troubles in your old kit bag and smile, smile, smile.* But it wasn't like that anymore. War had changed everything.

A troop train must have come in. Waterloo Road was full of soldiers and airmen in blue uniforms holding duffle bags. They were going home. War was about men. Heroes. Lucky them. They had their place. But the wives and the women, who cared about them? Nobody listened. How would Mum understand Ada's war? How would anyone? It had been a different war. Caught up in its flow, like a single scrap of flotsam and jetsam, alone.

There was a newspaper vendor by the entrance to the train station, a short, plump man, with a ruddy face and thick, white hair. He was leaning on a crutch. He held out a copy of the *Evening News*. She shook her head.

'Cheer up,' he grinned. 'It could be worse.'

It was the first time anyone had smiled at her since she had got back to London. She swallowed hard, felt her forehead pucker. *No use feeling sorry for yourself, Ada girl.*

The vendor limped forward. He had a kind face, happy lines round his eyes.

'Beautiful girl like you,' he said, 'you should be on top of the world.'

'I've nowhere to go,' Ada said. 'Would you believe that?'

'Where you from?' he said. 'Manchester? Just arrived in London?'

She looked at him. 'Yes,' she said.

'Try Ada Lewis House,' he said, 'New Kent Road. It's a hostel. For good girls, if you know my meaning.' He turned and handed out a copy of the paper to a man in a suit and bowler hat. 'You can get a bus over there.' He pointed to the stop on the opposite side of the street.

'Thank you,' Ada said.

She guessed it must be about five o'clock. She was hungry and needed a bed for the night. She went into the station, collected the sewing machine, and began to walk to the bus stop.

'Can I help you, miss?'

A soldier.

'Thank you.'

'Where are you heading?'

Ada pointed to the stop. Any bus to the Elephant, walk from there, the man had said. Perhaps the soldier was going that way too. She could do with the company and his help. She joined the queue and he placed the machine on the pavement.

'Toodle-oo,' he said.

She caught the number 12. *Dulwich*, she remembered. *Posh*. The conductor took the sewing machine and placed it in the cubbyhole under the stairs. She sat on the long bench just inside the bus, looking out of the window, at the once-familiar streets now bleak and battered. She craned her neck. There were pockets of bombed-out houses. The old Bedlam was still there. And the convent, Notre Dame. The buildings next to it, where were they? The tube was there, and the South London Press building. Half of it, the other half a mince of bricks and mortar. But the rest? The Tabernacle. The Trocadero?

She stepped off the bus, banging her shin with the machine. It took a moment to get her bearings before she could head off down the New Kent Road. Ten paces. Stop. Change hands. The machine was heavy, she could barely carry it. Nobody helped. She limped along, heaving the machine, looking at the name plates. The terrace on her left was a mound of fetid rubble and blackened bricks, split doors and distempered plaster shafts, long since picked over, desperate women pulling free from the rubble a battered saucepan, a photo album, the piss-pot for boiling beetroot. She'd seen it in Munich, but she didn't think she'd see it here. They looked as poor now as they did before the war. Women fishing for the last potato that had rolled beneath the cupboard. Boys with scabby knees thundering up the stairs *Mum, what's to eat?* Starving and old before their years. *I used to know you.* This was what she had come home to.

The site was fenced off with sheets of rusty

corrugated iron. 'Bill posters will be prosecuted' was written in white paint which had run down the ridges. Behind the fencing, a single house was still standing, a wall ripped away, its naked rooms poised sideways like a coquette, one above the other. Rags of wallpaper could be seen and a mirror still hanging on a wall, crooked. There was a table missing a leg, kneeling like a beggar. Along from the house a remnant of a brick wall was still standing. Someone had painted a Mr Chad in black, written 'Wot? No sugar?' beneath it. Ada could see the stump of a burnt-out chestnut tree, its dead roots bulging through the tarmac like buried veins, cleaving the pavement in two.

She picked up her sewing machine. Ada Lewis House.

It was a tall, brick building, with long, rounded windows. A cubicle was a reasonable price and meals were included. It would do, until she got on her feet. No children or animals allowed. She'd have to get a job. And then a proper home, for Tommy. She only had four bob after she'd paid two nights' board and lodging.

'What sort of work do you do?' the warden had asked.

Ada took a deep breath. 'I'm a dressmaker,' she said. 'A ladies' tailor.' *Modiste.*

The warden pulled a face. 'Not much call for that anymore,' she said. 'It's all off-the-peg now. Ready-made. You should try the factories in the East End. Whitechapel, that sort of way.'

Factory. *Arbeit macht frei*. Frank had told her about the bodies. She couldn't work in a factory, not after that. Besides, she hadn't survived the war only to work in a sweatshop.

'You get your coupons sorted out,' the warden had said. 'You can owe us till then.'

Tea was at six o'clock. Tripe and onions. Carrots and potatoes. Tasty. Ada wolfed it down. Cup of tea. *A cup of tea*. Thick and stewed. Good job she didn't like sugar.

She was up early that morning, took the tube to Green Park. She'd forgotten how hot the Underground was, how it smelt of soot and stale air, how crowded too, crammed between strangers, tight enough to crush her. She pushed her way free of the doors and out into the balmy July air, to Dover Street. If Mrs B. wouldn't take her on, she'd go to see Isidore. She was good at her job, had lots of experience now.

But the house in Dover Street was a bombed-out wreck. Other buildings in the street were intact. The bomb had hit just this one. A man jostled her on the pavement. His suit was cheap and baggy, his felt hat mottled with age. He had a pipe in his mouth.

Ada grabbed his sleeve as he walked past. 'Excuse me,' she said. 'Do you know what happened here? Are the people all right?'

He shrugged, sauntered away, leaving a scented trail of sweet tobacco.

Perhaps Mrs B. had moved. Ada walked along the street, squinting at the name plates on the doors, then went back to the ruin. Ada had no idea where Mrs B. lived. She crossed her fingers, shut her eyes. *Let her be alive.* She opened them, expecting Mrs B. to be standing there with her painted lips and powdered cheeks, but the street was empty. She wandered along Bond Street, into Oxford Street. Those big stores now had storeys boarded up, or missing parts, like old, wounded soldiers. John Lewis. Ada stared. Nothing but black, scorched remains. Scrawny buddleias had taken root and tufts of grass had pushed up through the rubble. This was not the London she knew anymore. She wasn't sure she belonged here.

Hanover Square Gardens had been dug up. Isidore's basement was still there but the plate on the door had gone. Ada stepped down and peered through the windows. It was empty, apart from a crate and some old newspapers scattered on the floor. She staggered through Hanover Street, along Regent Street. Dickins & Jones. The scars of battle were everywhere. The Café Royal. She stopped underneath the awning, looking at the revolving doors. How could she have been so stupid? Taken in by a common con-man, Stanislaus von Lieben. If it hadn't been for him, she'd be all right now. Would never have had all this pain and heartbreak. *Bastard.* What she wouldn't do to him if she saw him again. Perhaps there was a bit of her mother in her. She'd do more than give him a tongue lashing. She'd bloody *murder* him.

She nodded at the flunkey by the Café Royal door and walked further on. There were some young women in Piccadilly Circus, circling the statue of Eros with their rouged lips and low-cut blouses, smoking. She'd seen them in Munich as well. Sometimes they were there with their mothers. *Yankee, you want?* They did it for cigarettes. Was it like this here too?

Ada wondered what it must be like, a different man, every hour. No man would look at her these days, with her flat chest and shapeless waist. No one would *desire* her, would touch her face with tender fingers, and pull her close, kiss her with the soft promise of love. No one would love her now, not even her family. A rush of loss and sadness let loose inside her and she swallowed back tears. That vendor man was full of banter, would call every woman beautiful. Ada knew his sort. It didn't mean a thing. She wasn't beautiful, not anymore.

She left the rouged girls behind and stepped into Haymarket. Stucco had broken loose and scaffolding propped up porticoes. Many of the façades were boarded up and covered with posters. The Theatre Royal was intact. *Lady Windermere's Fan.* What sort of a play was that? Left into Trafalgar Square. *Victory Over Germany,* she read, *1945.* It was still early in the morning but the square was crowded with soldiers in uniform, sauntering across with their girls. There were workers in shabby suits, young girls in smart shoes and slim skirts. One or two were sitting on the sides of the fountains eating sandwiches, brushing away the pigeons who hovered for scraps. One woman held a cup of tea in one hand, a thermos in the other. A cup of tea. Ada spotted the Lyons Corner House opposite Charing Cross. They used to make a good cup of tea. She fished in her pocket. She had enough.

There was a notice in the window. 'Waitresses wanted. Enquire Within'. A burst of hope. She could be a waitress, a little nippy, until she got a proper job. Ada pushed open the door. Panelled walls in rich, deep brown wood and lighting hidden behind thick panes of glass. She had forgotten how sumptuous it was in here. There were couples sitting at the wooden tables leaning forward, deep in conversation. Married couples, Ada thought, nice day out, back from the war. There were single women too, with ankles crossed, staring through the window. One was smoking, a packet of Players beside her on the table, another was reading a book. You lucky people, she thought.

Ada walked to an empty table in the middle, passing a plump middle-aged woman and her elderly companion. 'Stick-thin,' she heard her say as she passed, 'Consumption'. The waitress came towards her, smart black uniform, clean white apron and collar, sharp white cap with a black trim.

261

'Can I help?'

'Yes,' Ada didn't hesitate. 'I'm enquiring after a job.'

The waitress tucked her lips together. 'You'll have to see the manageress,' she said. 'Do you want anything else?'

'A cup of tea, please.'

The manageress was behind a desk, and signalled to Ada to sit, pointing to a high-backed chair, the same that they used in the restaurant, hard spokes and a shiny seat.

'Don't mind my asking,' she said, leaning forward across the desk, 'but you're awfully thin. Have you been ill?'

'No,' Ada said.

'Only if it was a communicable disease, we couldn't take you on.'

'No, nothing like that.'

'No nervous trouble?'

Ada shook her head. *I had a bad war, that's all.* What could she say? The manageress couldn't begin to imagine it. Ada had already sensed that nobody wanted to hear about it.

'No,' Ada said, 'I just lost my appetite.'

'Oh dear,' the manageress said. 'How unfortunate. I hope you've got it back now.'

Ada nodded. 'Eat like a horse.'

'Glad to hear it. Have you ever done anything like this before?'

'No. But I learn fast,' adding, 'I'm ever so keen.'

262

'When can you start?'

'Straight away.'

'Two pound ten a week wages, uniform included. Laundry your responsibility, apart from the cap and apron. Make sure your hair is clean and tied back, fingernails short. What size?'

'Size?' Ada said.

'For the uniform. Not sure we've got anything small enough for you. Are you handy with the needle?'

'Yes,' Ada said, 'as a matter of fact, I am.'

'Then you might be able to take it in. Come with me.'

Ada wrapped the uniforms over her arm. *Lucky.* The wages weren't bad and she might have some over at the end of the week. Once she got her coupons sorted, she'd run herself up a few things. She needed new underwear, soap, toothpaste. The necessities. Perhaps she'd make some friends. Lots of girls worked there. She'd have to walk to work, and back, at least for the first week. She looked at the clock at Charing Cross. Ten past three.

It took her thirty-five minutes to walk. In her cubicle, she laid out the uniform on the bed. It had a good hem and the seams were generous. The white collar was detachable, so she could wash that out overnight, if needs be. She unbuttoned her blouse and slipped off her skirt. Her slip felt damp. She twisted it round to the front.

Blood. *Blood.* She couldn't remember the last time she'd had a period. She yelped, and laughed. She wanted to fling open the window and bawl out. *It's all right. It'll be all right.* Here she was, Ada Vaughan, a woman again. She was coming back to life. Fit to call herself a mother. A few more pounds, she'd have her figure back. It'd take a month or two, but she was on her way. She'd be all right. She was going to live. *On her way.* She opened her purse. She'd need to go to Boots, get the necessities.

That first Christmas was the worst. But there were other girls, from the north, who were staying in London without their families. The warden gave them a good dinner, chicken with all the trimmings, sage and onion stuffing, gravy, even a Christmas pudding. They pulled crackers, read out silly jokes, crammed the paper hats on their heads. They gave each other little presents wrapped in crêpe paper left over from the paper chains they'd made for decoration. A bath cube. A hair-comb. Ten Woodbines.

Ada wondered if her mother had told the others she'd come back, wondered what her family were doing right now. Dad and Fred, *God rest their souls.* Ada. *What happened to her?* Unlike her mother not to vent her spleen. *Don't talk to me about her.* Ada had tried, had gone round one Sunday in late November, caught Mum after Mass. Her mother looked through her as if she wasn't there. Ada

264

waited till she had turned a corner before she leant against the wall and sobbed. God knows, she'd tried.

She came on regular as clockwork now, had fleshed out, still slender like a mannequin but with a figure again. She needed glasses too, couldn't see distance, the doctor said, writing out his prescription. Could barely catch the number of the bus until it was on top of her, had to squint to read her own writing. *You'll get wrinkles, screwing your eyes like that*, the manageress had said. Ada couldn't tell her why her eyes were bad. She saved up for specs, a nice, modish pair she'd seen in an old copy of *Everywoman*. 'You can be pretty and wear glasses,' it said. 'Glamour with glasses.'

Ada couldn't afford a perm, but she bought a bottle of peroxide to bleach her hair, and ragged it each night so it fell out crimped in the morning, rolled it back and up and pinned into a curl, front, sides, back. Perhaps she'd catch a young man's fancy one of these days, even though she was twenty-five, and a bit old. But wiser. She wouldn't fall for someone like Stanislaus again.

She was doing all right, what with the basic and the tips. She divvied up the money each week. So much for board, so much for necessities, so much for shoes and stockings, so much for clothes, so much for etceteras. She tried to put some aside for a rainy day, and for Tommy, but it was tricky. She'd had to save her coupons for

265

months to make a winter jacket and buy a pair of decent shoes, and the glasses had eaten into her necessities budget. But she'd never had to borrow, or ask the manageress for an advance. Now that Christmas was well over, and she had the essentials, maybe she could try and make the money stretch just a little further. She only had the one skirt that the Red Cross had given her, so she needed another. And a dress. But that was eleven coupons. Blouses. She was lucky she had a uniform for work.

Berwick Street Market. That was the place. She could get there and back in her lunch hour.

It hadn't changed from before the war – *Best caulis, two a penny* – same stalls, same stallholders. Only *her* man didn't recognize her, not at first.

'Cor, love a duck, Ada.' He narrowed his eyes, as if to reassure himself. 'You look different. Specs. Dyed your hair and all. Suits you, that does, blonde. Mind you,' he'd leant over the stall, 'what you done to yourself? You're all skin and bone. You could do with some feeding up.'

She ended up with some good offcuts of fabric and a little bit of make-weight too, along with some parachute silk, now the war was over, for a new slip and undies.

There was a sewing room at the hostel and Ada was allowed to leave her machine there. She ran up a couple of skirts, pencil-thin, kick-pleat. A blouse, spread out on the table, particular with her measuring and cutting, finishing and hemming. It attracted an audience.

'Can you make one for me, Ada?'

'And me, if I give you the material?'

She charged them too. Just that little bit extra, but it made all the difference. She had to start somewhere. The girls here weren't the clients she'd prefer, and she didn't want to do it on the black market. But rationing couldn't go on forever. She'd save. Put a deposit on premises somewhere. Give herself a few years. All good practice in the meantime. Start a business. House of Vaughan. Get a home. If she ever met Stanislaus again, she'd show him. *Bounced back, like a rubber ball. You couldn't get rid of me.* She'd like that. Meet him again. *You thought I was done for. I've got news for you.* Yes.

It was early summer in 1946 when the man in the Berwick Street market beckoned her aside and pulled a bolt of cobalt moiré from underneath his stall. She'd been back in London now for almost a year.

'Look a treat on you,' he said. 'Suits a blonde and all.'

Ada hadn't seen anything like this since before the war. The watermarks danced arabesques in the sun, promising light and mystery and elegance.

'Pricey, mind,' the coster said. Ada ran her fingers over the fabric. Silk was stubborn, would resist. You had to be firm with silk.

She gave him what coupons she had, and some

extra in cash. Ada knew he'd slipped in a generous length. It was worth it, whatever it cost. *On the black*. Everyone did it now. She poured over pages of *Everywoman* and *Woman's Weekly* for inspiration on the latest fashions, checked out *Vogue* in the library. Cobalt moiré was not for everyday. She closed the magazines and shut her eyes. Slim fit, no fuss, a single diagonal shoulder strap. It would flatter her bosom, show off the slenderness of her neck, her now flawless skin, the sharp of her shoulders and the jut of her collarbone. Invisible zip. The design needed care, one false move and it would be ruined. She doubted she'd get more moiré, not this side of a decade, the way the government were talking.

It fitted like a smooth film of water flowing with her body, eddying round her breasts and pouring over the angles of her hips like a wave on the rocks. Ada hung it in her cupboard, slipped it on each night, ran her hands over it. Once silk was brought to heel, it obeyed like a faithful servant. She wasn't sure when she'd ever wear it but it was good to dream. Life was no fun. Nothing but *work, work, work*. She didn't have the money to go out, not unless she dipped into her savings. The other nippies only wanted to hang round Leicester Square and drink tea and where was the fun in that? Besides, she was older than they were. They'd been kids in the war.

Tommy wouldn't want a stick-in-the mud for a mother, or a bitter, frustrated woman. And Ada didn't want to turn into her mother, angry and ill-tempered. It wouldn't hurt to go out once in a while. She had enough in her savings and ration book for a pair of sandals to match the dress. Tommy would understand. He would be getting to be a big boy now. Five years old. Losing his baby teeth. He'd want his mother to be happy. She'd put the money back next week.

She took the dress with her into work, and the sandals, hung it up in her locker and changed at the end of the day.

'Going somewhere nice?' one of the other nippies said. 'You don't half look gorgeous. Got a man?'

Ada was leaning towards the mirror, putting on her lipstick, a new one she'd bought in Woolworth's, Poppy Red.

'I'm not saying.'

'Where are you going then?'

'I'm not saying,' she said, enjoying the mystery.

She sauntered up the Strand, swinging her handbag. Men were looking at her. It had been so long since she'd felt that gaze. She smiled as she walked. This was like the old days. Ada Vaughan. Mannequin. *Modiste*. She still had the magic, a tap of her wand and the drab became dramatic, the body a landscape of dreams and desire. She turned right, off the Strand, to the doors of Smith's Hotel. The flunkeys tilted their heads and led her inside. Ada glided into the foyer, a slender, blue butterfly drinking nectar.

Nothing had changed. They still had the crystal chandeliers and bevelled mirrors, the chequered floor and sweep of stairs, the panelled hall and leather chesterfields. The Manhattan Bar, she remembered, was to the left. She walked up the staircase.

The maître d' stood at the top behind a slim lectern. He nodded as she approached, head to one side. *Smarmy*, Dad would have said, *lackey of the bourgeoisie*. But Ada understood. They were in this together. Two toughs against the toffs. Class warfare.

'Are you meeting someone, madam?'

Madam. Ada smiled. No longer a *miss*. A mature woman.

'Oh no,' Ada said, peering over his shoulder at the glass and chrome of the bar in the distance.

'I'm sorry,' the maitre d' said, 'but we don't allow single ladies entry.'

Ada drew her gaze back to his. 'What?' She corrected herself. 'Excuse me?'

'It's our policy,' he said. 'Unaccompanied women are not permitted in the bar area.'

Ada hadn't reckoned on this. She couldn't go back now. She'd be the laughing stock.

'If you were meeting someone,' he went on, 'that would be different.'

He tapped a tattoo with his fingers on the lectern, *dum, du-dum, dum, du-dum*, stared at the wall behind her.

'I just remembered,' Ada said, recognizing his

meaning. 'I am meeting someone.' He turned and faced her, drumming with one hand, while the other delved into his pocket. He made no move, and neither did Ada. He coughed, a polite *hem-hem*, looked pointedly at his hand still beating a rhythm on the hollow lectern.

He wanted a tip. Bloody cheek. She had dipped into her savings for this night out, brought enough cash to pay for a cocktail and the bus fare home and a little extra just in case. She didn't think she'd have to spend it, not on a flunkey. But what else could she do? She opened her handbag and took out her purse. He didn't look like the sort of man who'd take brown money. She pulled out a silver sixpence, and placed it on the lectern. The maitre d' pinned his finger over it and pressed down, splaying his fingertip so it covered the coin. He dragged it to the bottom and slipped the money into his pocket. *You've done this before,* Ada thought.

He led her to a corner table on the right. There was a mirror in the centre of the wall and Ada caught a glimpse of herself as she walked towards it, her long blonde hair falling in coiled tresses on her naked shoulders. Her figure twisted as she walked, *in* at the waist, *out* at the hip, the practised rolling gait of the catwalk. She sidled into the bench, placed her bag beside her, and thanked the maître d'.

One cocktail. That's all. If she sipped it slowly, she could make it last. She knew what she would

271

have. Not too sweet. Gin. Lemons. Cointreau. The room was shabbier than she remembered, the carpet threadbare in places. The mirrors were the same, bright and angular, and the walls a nicotine-stained custard, darker in the crevices where the walls joined the ceiling. Ada leant back on the blue velvet bench, ran her palm over the soft velour. Strange rule to have, no single women. She'd always been with Stanislaus when they came before the war, had never noticed that only couples were allowed in.

The waiter brought her drink over, flipped down a small linen mat, placed the glass on top. A White Lady. She waited until he had gone, then lifted it to her lips, smelling the sharp acid of the citrus and the dry juniper of the gin. She'd have to be careful. She hadn't had a drink for years. Not since that beer in Namur, *no more*. She leant back and took out ten Senior Service, another birthday present to herself. She laid them on the table, blue sailing ship uppermost, took out a cigarette, held it between her fingers. She didn't have her matches. The waiter would have a light. She'd ask him when he came by.

'May I?' She hadn't seen the man walk over. She looked up. His nose had a cleft at the tip, matched the one on his chin. His hair was red, his lashes fair, his eyes grey. He was smiling at her, flicking a silver lighter. She put the cigarette to her lips, breathed in.

'Are you waiting for someone?' he said. He was

in his thirties, at least, wore a blazer and a checked
Viyella shirt, a navy blue tie with insignia on it.
His regiment, Ada thought. Must have served in
the war. An officer, by the look of him. He had a
glass in one hand.

'I don't think they're going to come now,' Ada
said, sniffing. 'They're very late.'

'Would you care for some company?'

'That would be nice,' Ada said. 'Just for a little
while.'

He sat down, placed the glass on the table, fished
into his pocket for his cigarettes.

'My name's William.' He stretched his hand
across the table. Ada dipped her fingers inside
his. He squeezed them gently, his hand was
warm.

'Whoever you were waiting for is a fool to stand
you up,' he said. 'They obviously don't know what
they're missing.'

Ada smiled. He spoke smooth, like a gentleman,
saying the sort of things they say in films. She
didn't believe him for a minute, but it was good
to hear.

'What's your name?' he said.

Ada. A two-a-penny, common-as-muck name.

'Ava,' she said.

'Like the film star?'

'Not quite. Same initials.' She posed her lips into
a pout and looked at him from beneath her lashes.
'No, I'm an ordinary Ava.' She thought fast. 'Ava
Gordon.'

'Well, I can assure you there is nothing ordinary about you, my dear.' He lifted his glass into the air. 'Chin, chin.'

He had been an officer. RAF, Berlin, at the end of the war. Never seen anything like it. *Must have been terrible.* Mentioned in dispatches, up for a medal. Didn't do anything to earn it. *I bet you were ever so brave.* It was difficult back in Civvy Street. No one wants to talk about the war. *Shame, that is.*

'Were you in the services?' he went on. 'I can see you as a WREN, with the backroom boys.'

'No,' Ada said.

'A Land Girl?' He laughed. 'You don't look hardy enough.'

Ada shook her head.

'Well, you must have done something.'

'I can't talk about it,' she said. It was the truth.

He stubbed out his cigarette and leant towards her. 'How jolly exciting. Were you a spy? You'd make a stunning Mata Hari.'

'What do you do now?' she said.

'I say, are you changing the subject?'

'Yes. What do you do?'

Farming. Mainly arable, sugar beet, barley. Ada was drinking faster than she wanted. His parents ran the farm while he was away but they needed to retire. He was happy to take over, a country boy at heart. He was in London to talk to the bank. No money in farming. Needed to re-mortgage, invest.

'Drink up,' he said. 'Let me get you another.'

He was old-fashioned, with his blazer and brogues, but he made Ada laugh. She couldn't remember the last time she'd laughed with a man, had had fun. He was good-looking, in his way, even though he had ginger hair. His face was lined but he was slim, with broad shoulders.

'Are you hungry?' he said. 'Let's have dinner.'

Smith's Grill. White tablecloths. Starched. Ada ran her fingers over the shiny folds, checked the stitching at the edge. Drawn threads. Someone stitched those. Alone, hunched over, into the night. Her fingers turned cold and clammy at the memory. She pushed it away, picked up her napkin, dabbed at her mouth, leaving a smudge of lipstick.

She smiled at William. 'I like Smith's Grill,' she said.

Sole meunière. Ada'd never had it before. Made with real butter, too.

'Would you care to come up for a nightcap?'

They'd had wine with the meal. She shouldn't have anything more to drink but she was enjoying herself. The evening had turned out better than she thought. She'd rather go back to the bar but he seemed a nice enough fellow, not the sort to try anything on. They took the lift to the fourth floor, walked along the corridor. He opened the door, 'After you.'

She was barely inside when he grabbed her shoulders, pulled her close and kissed her, tongue and all.

275

She pulled away. 'That's a bit fast, William.'

'Don't tease me.'

'I'm not. You said a nightcap.'

'In time,' he said. He held her face in his hands. 'You really are the most beautiful creature, Ava.'

Gentleman's talk, farmer's hands. The skin was rough, but the flesh firm. It smelt of soap. He pulled her closer again. He was breathing hard, and she felt the power of his chest as it rose and fell, the vigour and life in his arms as he closed them round her. It had been so long since anyone had held her, had desired her this way. His strength brought life into her muted body, made her young and lusty again.

He held her hand and led her to the bed. She thought of the hotel room in Paris. This would have a bathroom too. He pulled her down on the satin bedspread and rolled her close to him. She lay in his arms, the rough cloth of his jacket scratching against her cheek. She was warm and wanted. He'd called her beautiful. She felt his fingers search for her zip, slip them inside her bodice, reaching for her breasts. He was a fast worker, she'd say that. He must think she was loose. She tried to push his hand away but he held it firm. It was warm on her flesh, soft. It disturbed her, excited her. Why shove him away? She wasn't a virgin. Why pretend to be good when she knew she wasn't? She wanted this, she wanted love, tenderness, affection. She wanted to forget her war, its pain and loss and loneliness, to immerse herself in another human being, to be coddled and nurtured, to smell the musk of a male body, and wallow in its warmth. To live again. She kissed him back.

He snapped on the light, checked his watch. 'You should go,' he said.

She knew she couldn't stay. Wouldn't do to spend the night with him. She rolled off the bed, gathered up her clothes and padded to the bathroom. There were some salts by the bath, neat little cubes in silver foil. She was tempted to pick a couple up, but she didn't want to be exposed as a thief. It was bad enough being in a guest's bedroom after hours. She liked him. He'd caressed her, been tender and careful. *If you were the only girl in the world.* She'd like to see him again. He seemed a good man. She dressed, brushed her hair with her fingers, dabbed on some lipstick and came out. He had pulled on a dressing gown and was standing by the door, her handbag in one hand, jangling some coins in the other.

'Two bob for a taxi,' he said, pressing the coins into her hands. 'And two for the doorman's troubles. Off you go.'

'I can walk,' she said. 'It's not very far. And this is too much.'

'You'll be safer in a cab.'

'Thank you, William,' she said. 'And thank you for this evening.' He wasn't saying anything about a rendezvous. 'I really enjoyed it,' she added.

'Please go now,' he said. 'I have a busy day tomorrow.'

It would be too forward to ask to see him again, and she couldn't very well tell him where she lived, in a hostel for working girls. He opened the door, waved for Ada to go through. He'd grown cold. Had she done something wrong? She supposed if he wanted to see her again, he'd find a means. Or she would. Ask for his full name at the desk, and his address.

In the lobby, one of the doormen approached her. 'Would you like me to find you a taxi, miss?' he said.

She nodded.

'Do you have anything to give me for my trouble?'

She wanted to say *not really, no.* She could get a taxi herself. This lot didn't stand back when it came to extras. What with the tip for the maître d' and now the doorman, this evening was working out expensive. He stood still, his gloved hands folded behind his back. But William had given her the money, so it wasn't costing her anything.

She handed him a florin and he ushered her through the revolving door, whistled for a taxi.

'Just tell the cabbie where you're going.'

'Not often I do that journey,' the cabbie said. 'Smith's to Ada Lewis House. You had a good time, ducks?'

He set her down at the hostel. She had a late key and let herself in, taking off her sandals and tiptoeing up the stairs, along the corridor, into her cubicle. She shouldn't switch on the light. She'd wake the others. She slipped out of her clothes and crawled beneath the sheets.

From the brightness of the sun, Ada guessed she had overslept. It must be midday. She'd drunk too much and had a headache. Ada pulled her bag towards her for a cigarette and opened it. There was a five-pound note folded inside.

She pulled it out, held it up to the light. She'd never had a fiver before. A thick line was embedded in the note. It was real. William. William must have put it there last night for some reason. She'd have to return it, of course. She'd get his address that way, too. *Dear William, thank you for that lovely evening but I believe the enclosed is yours and I am returning it forthwith. Must have been some kind of mistake. I do hope we meet again soon.* She couldn't give her address, Ada Lewis House. She'd get a Post Office box. That way he wouldn't know. Were they expensive?

Though perhaps it was a present. He intended her to have it, would be insulted if she gave it back. Strange present, money, especially after the amount he'd spent on her all evening. Generous.

Oh my lawd. He had *paid* her. Should have realized sooner. Would have too if her head hadn't throbbed so much. Thought she was on the game. She laughed out loud, spluttered on her cigarette, stubbed it out on the ashtray. That's why he changed, afterwards. Had to get her out. He'd

279

have to pay double for the room otherwise, and then his wife would find out. *His wife.* The bastard, probably had children too. A boy and a girl. She could see them, on his farm, a tough little boy in a Fair Isle pullover, a sturdy girl with her hair in plaits. He knew the ropes. Money in the bag. Cash for the doorman. William probably wasn't even his real name.

She fingered the note. This was twice what she earned in a week at Lyons. She'd have to open a Post Office account now, deposit it safe. Pay back what she'd taken from her savings for the night out, then add some more each week. Little by little.

Ada lit another cigarette, and thought.

She'd had a nice time. It wasn't really payment, this, more an appreciation, for her company. She hadn't *prostituted* herself. Not like those creatures who hung round Eros, or those skinny wrecks in Munich who'd do anything for a cigarette. No, she and William, they'd had a pleasant time. He'd worn a rubber. She'd probably never see him again, but he had found her alluring, desirable. What harm had been done?

She could go again. Maybe she would meet someone else, someone permanent. She could wear her blue dress. *Lucky.* And if she didn't, if the man wasn't looking for that? It was a lot of money for nothing, really. She knew the ropes now. Sixpence for the maître d'. Two bob for the doorman, if she ended up in the room. If she went each month, she'd save money fast. She'd need more clothes, would have to use some of those savings, spend money to make money, but it would be worth it. She wouldn't go with anyone she didn't fancy. Smith's attracted a good class of people, nobody rough. She'd be fussy, lay down the terms. Five pounds in the handbag, four bob in coins for expenses. Nothing she didn't feel comfortable with. Must wear a rubber. If she went twice a month, that would be a tenner. She counted the money. She'd be able to move out of the hostel, find a little bedsit. Tommy would need a home. She'd do it up lovely for him. Paint cars on the walls, give him a football. She could find some premises, a workshop. Somewhere smart. Put up a sign that read: 'Vaughan, *Modiste*'. She had her sewing machine, solid little work-horse that was. Get a table. Tools of the trade. Proper shears. She'd have to advertise. 'Ladies. Make your clothing coupons stretch further.' What was that magazine Mrs B. kept in the waiting room? *The Lady.* She'd put an advert there. It'd cost, but she could afford it. She'd enjoy herself in the meantime, make money. She couldn't lose.

Not full-time. Those girls round Eros looked coarse and common. She didn't want to be like them. But twice a month. Week off for her period. She'd stay working at Lyons until she was on her feet and could open up shop. She liked the girls. They were a laugh, and she didn't have much other company. The hostel was all right, but if she was in a bedsit, she might get lonely. Work in the day. Saturday nights out.

Three times a month was fifteen pounds.

It had only taken her three months but she had the deposit in hand, and the key money, and a week's rent, in advance. The landlady was a racketeer, had ratcheted up the price, but it was a good bedsit, in Floral Street. Four flights up, wouldn't be bothered by the costers from the market pissing in the basement.

'No gentleman callers,' the landlady had said.

'What if I have a fiancé?' Ada said.

'Do you?'

'I live in hope.'

The landlady smiled.

'Actually,' Ada said. 'I'm a widow. I have a little boy. I just need a nice place till I can get back on my feet.'

'And where's your kiddie?' the landlady said. 'Only I don't allow children.'

'He's being looked after.'

'Well, this is a respectable house,' the landlady continued as if Ada hadn't told her anything. 'Can't be too careful. *Nice* girls don't live on their own. They live with their *people*.' She added, 'Unless they live a long way away.'

It was a big room, across the whole of the top floor, with what the landlady called a 'kitchenette', a ledge with a single electric ring, Baby Belling embellished on its side, and a basin. There was running water. There were shelves for her cups and plates, a hook for her saucepan, a small cupboard for the tins and perishables. The room came with a bed, an easy chair, a Utility table and wardrobe. The bed would be big enough for Tommy, too, for the time being. When he got bigger, she'd have to buy another one. She'd talk the landlady round into allowing him. Run the old black-out curtain across the room for him. It wouldn't do to share a bedroom.

There was a lavatory on the second floor, and a bathroom with a geyser that you paid for and a big notice. 'Guests. Remember. No more than two inches of water in the bath.'

Ada used her coupons and the last of her savings to make the room homely. She didn't have enough for new curtains, but she bought some flannelette sheets, and a second-hand candlewick bedspread that matched and a calendar for 1946 with a picture of a dog. The manageress had given her a busy lizzie in full bloom, which would have to do until she could buy flowers in the summer. It was handy having the market so near.

'Where've you got the money for this?' the manageress had asked.

'My grandmother died,' Ada said. 'Left me a little nest-egg.'

She managed to acquire, cash only, a couple of plates and cups and cutlery, a pot and a frying pan, and made a mat for the table so the sewing machine didn't scratch the wood. Ada procured a wireless. It was second-hand, occupied all the space on top of the food cupboard, took five minutes for the valves to warm up but it was company in the evenings when she was alone. Sometimes she missed the noises of the dormitory, Beryl talking in her sleep, incoherent ramblings that they teased her about in the morning, Maureen with adenoids two cubicles down, snoring like a train. Still, she could always talk to Scarlett in the basement if she got too lonely.

She would wake occasionally in the early hours. There were voices outside. A woman's voice. Shouting. Frau Weiss? Her heart began to pound. Frau Weiter? She rolled over and reached for her cross, bracing herself. *Nun. Get up.* Her fingers tangled in the sheets. The cross had gone. She patted the mattress. She was in a bed, not on the floor. She was here in her room, in London. Of course. She listened. What language were they speaking? Who was talking? Her ears grew attuned. It was Scarlett. She heard a man's voice. *Stanislaus. It was Stanislaus.* What was he saying? Was he asking for her? *All right, all right, all right.* No, it wasn't him. Who was it? Was he coming or going?

Going. Scarlett stopped work at midnight. Shutters down. Closed for business.

'Like a shop, see,' she'd said to Ada. 'But I'm a late bird so pop in, if you see a light on. We'll have some cocoa.'

Every Saturday, in the early hours of the

284

morning, kicking off their high heels together, plastering on the cold cream, peeling away their make-up. Scarlett looked dowdy in flat shoes and without her paint. Ordinary. She was like a chameleon, drab as a cobblestone by day, bright as neon by night. Men couldn't change the way women could, pull on a new dress and slap on the powder, dab on the lipstick and rouge up their faces. Her real name was Joyce, but she called herself Scarlett.

'Scarlett?' Ada said. 'What kind of name is that?'

'Don't you know?' Scarlett's voice was high in disbelief. 'Scarlett O'Hara. *Gone with the Wind?*'

'What's that?'

'*What's that?* The best bloody film I've ever seen, that's what that is. Clark Gable. My heartthrob?'

'Don't know it.'

'Blimey. Where was you in the war?'

Ada hesitated. 'Far away,' she said. 'In the country.'

'Well,' Scarlett said. 'You must have been in Scapa bloody Flow not to have seen *Gone with the Wind.*'

Ada clasped her chipped mug of hot cocoa and looked over at Scarlett sitting cross-legged on her bed, her dress pulled tight across her knees, a packet of Woodbines nestling in the valley between. Her fingers were brown with nicotine and her voice was rough, but Ada liked her.

Scarlett sorted her rubbers, three for two bob and told Ada to make sure they put the money in the bag *before* they got anything.

'You being a beginner and all might not appreciate that. We need to stick together, us women.'

Ada ran her up a skirt from an offcut she got in the market, by way of thanks. Soft, pink check Dayella, 'Does Not Shrink'.

Two years, she'd do this. That was all. Then she'd have saved enough.

Ada had a routine. Up in the morning with her nippy's uniform, smart black frock and stiff white collar and apron, *clip-clopping* down the Strand to J. Lyons. It was convenient, she could go home in her lunch hour if she wanted, though she preferred to sit with the other girls and have a laugh before she went back to work, sashaying between the tables with her pinny and cap. *Two pots of tea and a scone. Coming up.* She saw the men looking at her. She was a cut above this. She knew it, and they knew it too, she could tell.

She preferred the restaurant to the snack bar. The work wasn't so hectic and it was a different class of client, older, better paid, gave good tips. There were regulars, office workers, managers most likely, who came in their lunch hour, sat by themselves with a newspaper and ordered from the carvery, roast pork and apple sauce, ham and piccalilli. Wednesdays was early closing so it was shop girls out for a treat, steak and kidney pie, sausages and chips. Mondays and Fridays, women with time and money, out for luncheon with their friends, went home to Beckenham or Turnham

Green to get their hubbies' tea. She liked these women the best, smart frocks, hats and gloves, *ever so, ever so.* Ada knew them all. Had charladies, children who went to private prep schools in the suburbs. They had dressmakers, too, a little lady round the corner.

The woman smiled at Ada as she stood up from the table, tugging at her dress so it hung straight. She had a good figure, slender and lithe, and a pretty peaches-and-cream face. The dress was rayon, a pale apricot, with tucks round the bust and pleats on the hip.

'Always rucks up,' she said, running her hands over her hips, 'and clings.'

Ada wasn't sure who she was talking too. Her friend was putting on powder, holding her compact to the light and dabbing at her nose. The dress was badly fitting. Too tight round the hip; too loose round the bust. The woman scooped up her bag and gloves and headed off to the Ladies. The nippies weren't allowed to go there. Ada checked no one was looking and followed her in.

'If you don't mind my saying so, madam,' Ada said, 'it's the pleats. They don't give enough.'

The woman turned in surprise. 'You'd know, would you?' Her voice was sarcastic. *What does this little nippy know?*

'As a matter of fact,' Ada said, 'I do. If you pleat on the horizontal it tightens the fabric. You need to give it a bit of rein, make allowances.'

'You're a dressmaker, are you?' Her voice sneered, but she was paying attention now.

Ada put her heels together and stood straight. 'I am,' she said, 'a good one too.' The woman looked at her watch. 'I'm just doing this to make money,' Ada added, pointing to her apron. The woman was in a rush, anxious not to miss the 3.10 from Charing Cross, or the tube from Embankment. 'I want to set up in business.'

The woman threaded her arm through the handle of her bag. 'Could you alter this?' she said.

'I'd have to see it first,' Ada said. 'How much slack there was in the seam. Wouldn't take much. Quarter of an inch either side. Loosen the darts.'

'I hardly ever wear it as it is,' the woman said. 'But I can't throw it away. I'll bring it to you next week.' She placed a ha'penny in the saucer by the basin. 'What can I lose?'

Her name was Bottomley, Mrs Bottomley. She brought the dress in the following Monday. Ada turned it inside out, looked at how it was made. The seamstress who'd made this didn't know about fabric, couldn't even sew a straight line. The pleats were crooked, the folds caught in the stitches.

'Leave it with me,' Ada said. 'I'll bring it back next week.'

Mrs Bottomley tried it on again the next week, returned to her table, the dress folded back in its wrapper.

'Perfect,' she said. 'Do you have a card?'

'No,' Ada said. A card? Even Mrs B. didn't have cards. 'But you can get hold of me here.'

'For a fitting?' Mrs Bottomley said.

Ada held down her smile. 'I can give you my address,' she said. 'It's just round the corner. We can discuss terms.' She liked that word. 'I work halfday on a Thursday.'

Mrs Bottomley took out her address book, a slim volume bound in leather. 'Your name?'

Ada spelled it out, VAUGHAN. Added, *Modiste*.

A tweed suit for Mrs Bottomley and a cotton dress for her daughter. A best dress for the daughter's friend's mother to wear at a christening. Sensible clothes with honest cloth. Nothing to shine, but it was a start.

Ada listened to the news on the Home Service. She had to be on top of things, *au fait* with current affairs because sometimes her gentleman friends talked about them. Not that they expected her to know anything about the wider world, but Ada was interested. Trouble in Palestine and India. Trials in Nuremberg and Dachau. It was strange to think she'd been there, in enemy territory. To think she'd made clothes for the Fraus, kept house for the Commandant. She could never tell anyone that, it would have to stay a secret now, forever. Obersturmbannführer Weiter had committed suicide and Martin Weiss had been hanged – she saw it in the *Daily Herald* – but there had been nothing about his wife and family. Perhaps Frau Weiss, or whoever it was, changed her name and Joachim's. How would Ada ever find them? And Stanislaus. She knew it had been him in Munich on the street that day. He was alive, at least. Munich seemed so long ago. And London, before the war. She couldn't always remember what it had been like before the bombs flattened it to rubble. Couldn't always remember Stanislaus. Sometimes she thought her memory played tricks, or she'd made him up. She wasn't sure she'd recognize him now.

She'd never known a winter so bitter, even in Germany. January 1947. The snow was waist-deep along the Strand. There were photos in *Picture Post* of drifts in the countryside, banks of heavy white snow smothering the fields and forest, the railways and roads. Her room had a gas fire, but it was old, the firebricks were cracked and not all the jets ran clean. It was difficult to control the gas, and the heat gave Ada chilblains. The windows were draughty and a gale blew under the door, until Ada found some sacking in the market, and made a sausage stuffed with newspaper and shoved it underneath. She bought a stone hot-water bottle and wrapped it in her towel and laid it in the bed to fight off the icy damp.

Ada's coster friend understood how she was placed. His stall was laid out with Utility fabrics, hard-wearing material, good value for money, CC41 stamped through the selvedge. But he kept bolts of cloth underneath which he'd pull out when no one was watching. Ada had the means now. The blue moiré was fine in the summer but she had to ring the changes of clothes, and now the weather was so bitter, she needed a proper outfit or two. She didn't think twice about the navy petersham for her winter coat, nor about the black jersey for a new dress, even though it meant another week she wasn't able to save. She'd pay it back.

Jersey was greedy, grew above its station, spread where it shouldn't. She worked on it by candlelight when the power went off, no thanks to Manny bloody Shinwell. It was hard on her eyes, but if she held the work close she could make do, as she used to in Dachau. She sewed at the weekends while she listened to the wireless, the *Dick Barton* omnibus on a Saturday morning, *Much-Binding-in-the-Marsh* on a Sunday afternoon. Three-quarter sleeves, a sweetheart neck that she'd seen in *Everywoman*, peplum – Ada had some coat lining left over, so she inserted it as inlay in case the skirt seated and grew baggy.

Saturday night, the first of February. Ada took care as she stepped on the pavement with her high heels, along Floral Street, round by the actor's church, through the slush and broken cabbage leaves of the market, down South Street, *careful does it*, to the Strand. The snow seeped into her shoes. The soles of her stockings were wet and the backs of her legs splashed with icy mud. Ada wiped them clean in the Ladies' lavatory, looked at herself in the long mirror of the powder room. The padded shoulders made her look tall, and the jersey clung tight without a pucker. The sweetheart neck emphasized her bosom, the peplum her hips, her waist a slender valley between. She fingered a roll of her hair and tucked it under. *Ava Gordon*. Even with glasses, she scrubbed up well. She folded her coat over her arm, handed it into the cloakroom and walked up to the Manhattan Bar. Slipped her usual sixpence to the maître d', and allowed herself to be seated.

The room was quiet. 'It's the weather,' the barman said, 'the snow. People can't get in or out. And the strike at the Savoy. Puts people off. Frightened it'll spread. The usual?'

The routine was the same. She'd sip her White Lady, lay out a packet of cigarettes on the table, pull out one and roll it between her fingers. She never sat at the bar. That was cheap. Nor did she look round to see who was there, whose eye she should catch. That was obvious. Wait for a gentleman and see if the barman winked. *Has a room here*. Take off her glasses, put them in her bag, and wait some more.

Once their trousers were down, men were all the same little boys.

'Immoral,' Scarlett said, 'the lot of them. Sometimes I see them with their wives and kiddies and I think how can you do this?'

One or two of the men wanted her to do things they wouldn't do with their wives, disgusting things, funny peculiar. Ada thought she was a good judge of character these days, could sum a fellow up just by looking at them. But you never knew, really.

'Charge them more,' Scarlett said. 'Those types talk to you ever so nice but as soon as they get you alone, they're like rats in holes.'

'No,' Ada said. She was a good-time girl, not a professional, not like Scarlett. She'd up and leave then, pocket the money. She knew they couldn't complain.

They liked to talk, all of them. Things they couldn't tell their families. Poor sods. Sometimes Ada thought she should have been one of those new-fangled trick-cyclists. D-Day. Alamein. Scared out of their wits. No one understood, no one wanted to listen. Gone so long their children didn't recognize them, their wives didn't want them. Civvy life was tough. *Had a good war?* Didn't do to say *No.* Who'd ever had a good war? Ada understood. *I know how you feel.* Crammed it inside, cork rammed down so hard she thought she'd crack. *You're the first person I've been able to talk to about it*, they always said. She wished she could have someone to talk to, let it all out.

'You can trust me,' Ada would say. Could have made a fortune in the war selling secrets. Could have made a fortune now if she charged extra for listening. *A penny for your thoughts.* Set up in business as an agony aunt, *a problem shared is a problem halved.* Their minds cowered from the memories of the dead they never knew but had blasted to pieces. War never went away. Not the hidden war, the unspoken war. It festered like a shameful, weeping wound, tormenting in silence. Ada knew all about that.

She offered them a service, that's what. They could afford it too, with their army gratuities.

'Allow me.' He had a book of matches with 'Smith's' on the cover. His hair was wavy, parted and smoothed to the side, thick with Brylcreem. He was a heavy man, dark and swarthy, but with a chubby, infant face, like one of those Cow & Gate babies that you see in the advert. Must have been out of the army for some time. Most of the other men she'd met still had the gaunt frames and hungry faces of service rations. He cupped the flame, leant towards Ada. Tufts of black silky hair showed below the cuffs of his jacket. His suit was well cut, neither demob nor Utility. Businessman.

'Thank you,' Ada said.

'Are you waiting for someone?' He spoke with an accent she couldn't place. Italian. Or Spanish.

Ada knew the patter. *I am. They're late. Yes, I'd be delighted if you'd keep me company for a while.* She could turn anyone away if she didn't like him. But this man was attractive, in his way.

'Is this your first time in London?'

'No,' he said. 'I've lived here for many years. I think of myself as a Londoner now. And you?'

'Well,' Ada said, 'as a matter of fact, so am I.'

'Well, there we are,' he said, 'we have a lot in common already. Gino Messina.' He stretched out his hand, took hers and brought it to his lips.

'Where are you from?'

'Malta,' he said, 'a little island in the Mediterranean.'

'I bet it's hot down there then,' Ada said. 'Is that why you look so dark?'

He laughed. She laughed with him, *ha ha ha*. She felt relaxed.

'And your name?'

'Ava,' she said. *Modiste*. 'Ava Gordon.'

'Ava Gordon.'

He'd had a good war, nothing to complain about.

'But I don't like to talk about those times.'

'Me neither,' Ada said, relieved. *That* made a change from the others. 'Look to the future, I always say.'

She crossed her legs, tucked down her skirt where it had rumpled. The snow had left a mark on her shoes. A bit of polish would sort that out.

She didn't demand up-front like the girls at the bar, but left her bag unclipped, *discreet*. Checked that all was there, taxi, doorman, fee. She liked that word, *fee*. Mrs B. had charged a fee for her services, so did the doctor.

'Are you here every Saturday?' Gino said as she was dressing to leave.

'Most Saturdays.'

'What about next week, then?' Gino said. 'Save my place in the queue.'

'There's no queue.'

'I'm glad to hear that. In which case, save yourself for me.'

He was smooth, suave even, *continental* charm, and a baby-face smile.

She nodded.

That week Ada knitted a V-necked cardigan in pink which she unravelled from an old cardigan she'd picked up in a jumble sale. Sat by the fire, *knit one, pearl one*, listening to a play on the wireless. Gino wanted to see *her*. She'd wear her blue moiré but she needed a woolly in this weather. She'd take it off when he arrived, but she might as well be warm while she waited. Couldn't risk a clashing blue, and black was too sombre. The pink was a real find.

She asked to be seated on the velvet bench in the far corner, away from the draughts by the window. She sipped her White Lady, making it last.

'No, thank you,' she said to a tall gentleman who came over with a gold lighter and lit her cigarette. 'I'm waiting for someone.'

She was telling the truth this time. Only he *was* late. Ada finished her drink and ordered another. Perhaps he had forgotten. She should give him another half hour. She kept an eye on the tall man who was talking to one of the girls at the bar. He kept looking her way. She only had to smile, and she'd lure him back over. She couldn't afford to lose a fiver, just like that. How long should she give Gino? It would serve him right if she did go with someone else. He shouldn't keep a girl waiting, keep *her* hanging about, as if she had nothing else to do. It was rude. No, it was more than that. He was showing her who was in charge. You wait for me, Ava. Not me for you. Well, Gino Messina, Ava Gordon had news for him.

She fished her glasses out of her bag and put them on, spotting anew the sharp features of the faces, the stains on the carpet, smoke unfurling in the air. She slipped off her cardigan and pulled another cigarette out of its packet, rolling it between her fingers, eyeing the man at the bar.

'You did wait then.' She hadn't seen Gino come in, flick open the matchbook, strike a light. 'Didn't recognize you in your spectacles.' She saw him clearly now, with her glasses, in the bright light of the bar. His eyes were black, still like a hammer pond, deep enough to see herself reflected. His mouth and forehead were creased. Well fed. Foreign. A voice inside her whispered, *Don't trust them. Haven't you learned?*

'I was about to give up on you,' Ada said. 'Thought you weren't coming.'

He reached across and pulled out a cigarette from her packet as if it belonged to him. *Bloody cheek*. 'I apologize for that. I was delayed.'

'So I see,' Ada said. 'What kept you?'

'Business,' he said. 'Nothing you'd understand.'

'And what is your business?'

He tapped the side of his nose. 'In my country, we have a saying. *Chi presto denta, presto sdenta.* Curiosity killed the cat.'

She'd run out of things to wear. It was one thing going with different men. They'd never see you in the same thing twice. But she and Gino were going regular now and she needed more outfits. She liked that idea, her and Gino, regular, like they were stepping out together. He was a man of the world, she could see that, well travelled, polished. He had class, old-fashioned chivalry.

'That's what you need,' Scarlett said. 'Regular clientele.'

'Clientele?' Ada said. 'I'm not what you think I am.' She didn't *fish* like Scarlett did, stand in the street until she hooked one in.

Scarlett guffawed. 'The law might see different.'

Gino wasn't clientele. More like her young man. He treated her well, spoilt her really, the high life, wine and port afterwards, never kicked her out, not like some of them who couldn't wait to get rid of her, as if she'd made a nasty mess in the bed.

Her coster friend had some wool crepe. 'Only a

remnant this week, Ada, couple of yards, but fifty-four inch wide. I'll let you have it cheap.'

Burgundy, wool crepe. Ada remembered Frau Weiss, that first time, wool crepe with a white Peter Pan collar, slim fit, cigarette-holder. She'd had blonde hair too, glowing like the fresh-born sun, set off by the ruby fabric. She'd never forgotten that, such elegance and beauty in the face of ugliness and squalor.

She cut it out that night. Not enough to make on the cross, but a simple frock, straight down, fitted sleeves and a diamond cut out below the neck band, a hint of cleavage, tasteful, nothing common, just right for Smith's.

The maître d' nodded approval when she slipped him the sixpence that night. The barman brought her drink. 'You're looking gorgeous tonight, Ava,' he said. 'Quite fancy you myself. Meeting the same gentleman? Only that's five weeks on the trot. Might say you were courting.'

Ada liked that thought. She liked Gino and he liked her, she knew, as his eyes scrolled down her figure and he slipped his arm round her waist.

'Beautiful,' he said. '*Bella.* You have exquisite taste.'

'Thank you,' Ada said.

'Where do you shop for these dresses?'

'Shop?' she said. 'I don't *shop*, Gino, I *make* my clothes. Design, everything.'

'Well, you have a rare talent, Ava Gordon. It could be couture, straight from Paris.'

'I'd like to do more,' she said. 'You know, set myself up in business. Have my own clients, my own name.'

'You would do well.'

'I could make it work. I've got clients already.' Mrs Bottomley had introduced her to another lady who wanted an outfit for her son's wedding. *Something classic. So it won't date.* And she had recommended Ada to someone who was looking for a dressmaker. Said she'd write her a testimonial any time she wanted. *Miss Vaughan is a woman of sound character, pleasant disposition and exemplary dressmaking skills.*

'You'd have to have capital,' he said. 'Backing.'

'I know,' Ada said. 'But I'll do it, one day. Just watch me.'

He laughed. 'I like a girl with ambition.' He squeezed her waist. 'We'll have to see what we can do, won't we?'

We. Gino and her. He had money, she could see. Maybe he could be her patron, wouldn't take much for a man like him, put her in business. He'd hinted as much, after all.

This time in her bag there was a packet of stockings as well as the money. Bear Brand hosiery, fully-fashioned, fine-gauge nylons.

Gino flicked the ash from his cigarette onto the carpet. 'A present for you, Ava.'

'Oh, *thank* you, Gino.' Nylons were a treat, and this was a gift from Gino.

'Well, I know how hard it is for you ladies, getting the little things you like.'

He took a deep drag at his cigarette so the smoke blew out through his nose like a stallion.

'I guessed a size 9.' He smiled, a crooked, half-curl of his lip. 'There are plenty more where these came from.'

'Really?' Ada said. 'How?'

'Questions, questions.' He tapped the side of his nose. 'As a matter of fact,' he said. 'I've got a few to spare with me right now. Bear Brand. Park Lane. You could make a nice profit here. My contact sells them to me, I sell them to you, you sell them to your friends. What do you say, Ava?'

Ada thought about the girls at work. If the price was right, she could probably sell a few pairs. She'd have to keep it quiet from the manageress. She didn't want to end up in front of the magistrate, although she could always say she had an American boyfriend. But it was no big deal, really. Everyone got stuff on the black.

'Buy them for sixpence,' Gino was saying. 'Sell them on for a shilling. A hundred per cent profit. That's a good deal, Ava. And a good price for nylons.'

If she couldn't sell them, she could always keep them. You had to be so careful with nylons. One snag and that was it.

'Give me a couple of pairs,' Ada said. 'I'll try it out.'

Gino pulled two boxes from his case and handed them to her. 'I trust you, Ava,' he said. 'I'll see you next week. Same time, same place. You can give me the money then.'

'And if I haven't sold them?'

'Sale or return. No hard feelings. I'll make sure my man understands. Here,' Gino said. 'put them between the pages of this. We don't want anyone asking questions.' He handed her a copy of the *Evening News* and Ada slipped the boxes inside the folded paper.

'And should anyone ask,' he said, 'say you got them from a Yankee seaman.'

She tucked the nylons under her arm.

Ada could have sold twenty pairs without even trying.

'I can't promise,' she said, making a note of the girls' sizes in the tea break at work the next week. Saturday night she handed Gino the money she'd collected, and an order for twenty pairs of nylons.

'Out of their boxes,' he said, handing them to her, 'but genuine.' She slipped them between the pages of the *Evening News*, checked her handbag for the fee. 'Same time next week, Ava. Same place. Let me have your order.'

'I can't put in an order every week,' she said. The girls at work didn't earn a lot. Nylons were a treat, not routine, except maybe for Scarlett or Ada who had a little to spare.

'I thought you were good at your job. These are a bargain, Ava.'

He was sitting in the chair, a towel wrapped round his waist. He stood up, walked towards the wardrobe, reached for his suitcase, leather, expensive, travelled, with chrome clips. He opened it and fished out a bottle of nail polish.

'If you can give me an order,' he said, 'there may be something in it for you.' He held out the bottle towards her.

'And if I can't?'

'You'll find a way.'

She took the nail polish, Dura-Gloss, American Beauty.

She handed the doorman his florin, and walked back through the market. Funny thing, money, the way it worked, a cut for the maître d' and the doorman, a cut for her landlady. A cut for Ada flogging nylons, a cut for Gino supplying them, and a cut for his contact. Who had done the work here? What did they get for their labours? *Bloody parasites,* she could hear her father say. *Capitalism.* But that's what capitalism was like, had a life of its own.

She took an order for eleven pairs of nylons that week, and a request for clothing coupons if her boyfriend's contact had any to spare, or bread coupons if he could get them.

'We'll see how it goes, Ava,' he said. 'See how it goes.'

He met her again and again in the following weeks. He wasn't like the other men. She was growing fond of him. He seemed fond of her too, though he made sure it was all professional, the fee in her bag, no questions asked, the buying and selling. Commission is what he called it. *Commission.*

Dorchester and the Savoy, Smith's and the Ritz. He had almost the same haunts as Stanislaus. He always had plenty of cash. His business, whatever it was, was profitable. She was curious about it, but he never said a thing.

'You're too pretty to bother with my work, Ava,' he'd say. 'It's a man's world.'

Martinis, Pink Ladies, Mint Juleps. He was an attractive man, knew how to treat a woman well, even though she knew he didn't *love* women, not the way William had done. She was getting used to his body, close and familiar to her. He was still an enigma. She couldn't slot him in, but maybe that was because he was a continental. Only this time, she told herself, she was wise, a different woman from the one she'd been before the war. She'd get the measure of the likes of Gino Messina, sooner or later.

'You do me proud,' he said. 'People turn their heads when they see you and me together. What's that old man got, they say, that I haven't? How is it the ugly men get the beautiful women?'

He probably had other women, other nights of the week. Sometimes a fist of jealousy punched her in the ribs, caught her unawares. *Can we make a deal, Gino? I'll only go with you, if you only go with me?* She knew he was married. They all were. He said his wife didn't understand him.

'I'd like a divorce, but she won't have it, for the kiddy's sake.'

'How many do you have, Gino?'

'One,' he said. 'A little boy.'

'How old is he?'

'Six.'

The same age as Tommy.

'What's his name?'

'Gerardo,' Gino said, 'but we call him Jerry. Born in the Blitz. My friend, the one I told you about, my contact, he said call him Jerry, after Adolf's fuckers. *Fokkers.*' It sounded funny, with his accent, all rolling *rrrs* and stretched vowels. He spoke perfect English, otherwise. Goodness knows where he'd learned it. He was laughing, *ha ha ha*. Ada had never told him about Tommy, wasn't sure she should bring it up now. He might not like it. He thought she was foot loose and fancy-free. Independent, he'd said. *That's what I like about you, Ava. Ambitious, too. Want to get on in the world.*

The manageress had a nephew, a little boy. She said they were affectionate, much more than girls, would fling their arms round you and crawl onto your lap, *I love you.* Ada could still remember the German. *Ich liebe dich.* She mustn't forget her German. *Mutti.* She thought of Thomas, every day. She was doing this for him.

'I can get you material,' Gino said. 'Direct. From my contact. No middle man.'

'Oh yes?' She *had* got the measure of him. Utility with the mark blacked out most likely. 'Get me coupons,' Ada said. She'd use them to buy from her coster. He sold the real McCoy.

Perhaps she could set herself up in business sooner than she thought. Ada Vaughan, *modiste*. Do what she knew best, what she had dreamed of long ago. Her coster friend seemed to know where to get the material. Everyone was sick of the war, of rationing and belt-tightening, of Utility and austerity. She'd make clothes to lift the spirits. Lace and batiste, georgette and sateen, tulle and zibeline. Clothes that swung and danced, that sung and laughed. Clothes that became the body, transformed it into living sculpture. Drape the toile, left for bias, right for straight. *Never be afraid*, Isidore would say, *the cloth is not the enemy*. Shrink and stretch, steam and shape. It's the invisible work that counts, that lifts a dress from the doldrums into paradise.

She'd have to sell them on the black market, but Gino and his friend would be able to help. It would have to be word-of-mouth. Nothing wrong with that. It had got her a few clients already and Mrs B. had done very well through word-of-mouth. Best publicity, she used to say. Much better than paid advertising, that was for the likes of off-the-peg, pay-by-instalment frocks, or C & A. Hers would be *bespoke*, a mode for the mood. She liked that. House of Vaughan, *a mode for every mood.* Mrs Bottomley always said as much. *Your clothes,* she said, *help put a spring in my step.* Things would be back to normal soon.

'Coupons?' Gino said.

'Yes,' Ada said. 'I could use them, make things, sell them. I know I could get rid of them. Easier to hide than nylons, easier all round.'

'What makes you think he can get coupons?'

'He seems able to get most other things.' She hesitated. She had to say it. 'I'd like to start up in business, Gino. Would you help me? Be my patron? It could be a loan. I'd pay you back.'

Gino lit a cigarette and lay back on the bed, pursing his lips and blowing rings into the air with a quiet *putt, putt.* 'Perhaps,' he said. 'We would have to put things on a more professional basis.'

'Of course.' Perhaps Gino wanted a better return on his money. He split the profits on the nylons fifty-fifty, so he said. Maybe he'd want a bigger cut on the coupons, for more of a risk. Or a cut in the business.

'You could be a partner,' Ada said. 'I wouldn't mind. I could make it work, I know it.'

Gino watched as the smoke rings drifted and dissolved. 'Well,' he said, his words slow and liquid. 'I don't mean that, exactly.'

'What do you mean, then?'

'These Saturday nights. A hazard, wouldn't you say?'

'I don't understand.'

'You never know who you might meet. Beautiful woman like you. How do I know what you do when I'm not around? Who you talk to? I'm putting myself at risk.'

'There's nobody, Gino,' Ada said, 'only you.'

'How can I be sure?'

'You have my word.'

'Your word doesn't mean a thing. How can you *guarantee* that I'm the only one for you?'

What was he insinuating, that she couldn't be trusted? Ada could feel a surge of irritation bubble up. 'You have to believe me, Gino.'

He stubbed out the cigarette on the ashtray, pushing the ash into a mound in the centre. 'Why don't I pay you a retainer?' Gino said.

'A retainer?'

'So much a week. Reserve yourself, just for me.'

Scarlett was right. Ada thought she had a lover. But he was a client, a regular client. *Clientele.* Two could play at that. If she was going to be a kept woman, it had to be worth her while.

'How much?'

'Ten pounds,' he said.

She shook her head.

'That's a generous offer, Ava,' he said. 'It's dangerous, your line of business. You should think about protection.'

There were some awkward customers out there, kinky with it, no scruples. She knew from Scarlett that not all the girls got away with it, and she'd

308

had some dodgy moments. Ada had been careful, but she'd also been lucky. She had to be safe for Tommy. What good would she be to him dead? She needed the money too, had to make a home for her little boy. Those things didn't come cheap, and she was on her own.

'Just one thing,' he said. 'I want to use your place.'

'What's wrong with Smith's?'

'Change of scenery,' he said.

It was only once a week, Ada explained to the landlady, on a Saturday. *No gentleman visitors.* Gino was her fiancé. *With a name like that? Don't have truck with Eyeties.* He'd be gone by midnight. *No gentlemen after ten, fiancé or not.* The landlady must have been young once. Ten was a bit early. Ada hadn't caused her any bother. Paid her rent on time. Was never noisy, or disorderly. Not like Scarlett in the basement whose visitors came and went, or the so-called clairvoyant on the first floor who had clients at all hours. It seemed cruel to kick him out at ten. *Eleven, at the latest.* Eleven would be fine. *Only I'll have to charge extra, to defray expenses.* Expenses? *If I'm charged with running a brothel.*

'No,' Ada said, 'it's not like that. There's only the one for me, and that's Gino Messina.'

'Glad to hear it then,' the landlady said. 'Only I'm still putting your rent up. Four quid a week.'

'Four quid? That's more than double the price.'

'You'll have to work harder then, won't you?' the landlady said. 'You and Gino.'

'I'm not what you think I am,' Ada said. 'I work at Lyons. I can't afford that kind of money.' Wanted to add, *racketeer*. Wanted to threaten her with the police, but knew she couldn't, in case they nabbed her too.

'We'll see,' the landlady said, 'what this fiancé of yours gets up to.'

The snow melted, the floods drained, the skies turned from grey to blue. Motes danced in the April air, picked out the dust lining the cupboard tops and skirting boards. The room needed a spring clean. Ada wanted to keep her home pure, had been saving it for her and Tommy. He was growing up fast. It could be difficult to track him down now. Six years was a long time. She wasn't sure Covent Garden was the best place to bring up a child. It was rough, what with the costers and the all-night pubs, and the girls from Shaftesbury Avenue and Seven Dials round the back of the actor's church. It was handy, though, for work, and the costers knew her and would toss her some carrots or a cauliflower at the end of the day, even though they were trade.

She didn't like Gino there in her room. He made himself at home, so it didn't belong to her anymore. Took off his shoes and padded round in grey socks, put the kettle on without asking.

'That costs money,' Ada said.

'I'll make a cup of tea whenever I want,' he said. 'Just remember who's paying your bills.'

He didn't like her going out, not even with the girls from work.

'I have spies, you know,' he said and ran his finger across his throat.

She wondered whether this was a price worth paying. Maybe she'd been better off before, when she was on her own and in control. But she didn't know how to get out of it now. Gino would calm down, once he was sure of her.

'Besides,' he said, 'this place is a dump. I have property. Holdings, in Mayfair. I could let you have a little flat, somewhere nice, Stafford Street, Shepherd Street. You might have to share it, but you'd have company, so you wouldn't get lonely.'

Ada liked living by herself. Her bedsit might be small, but it was home. She didn't want to move.

'It's all right,' Ada said. 'Thank you.'

'I don't think you understand me, Ava,' he said. 'Girl on her own. Think of the dangers.'

Stafford Street. That would be expensive. Twice what she paid here, and that was pricey enough. She could never afford it, let alone save.

'Watch it,' Scarlett said. 'He'll pimp you next. That's how they all start.'

'Who?'

'Oh lovey, you are *green*. Pimps. Ever so nice to their girls then, *wham*, they turn the screws, make you work for them, live off of us.'

'Gino wouldn't do that.'

'Mark my words, he's a pimp. *We* choose our ponces, not them.'

'But I'm not a prostitute.'

'Too bloody right. You're an amateur. You're no threat, not to me.'

Gino wasn't like that. He was just a bit moody, possessive.

Ada felt lonely that spring. Her mother had kept to her word, refused to see her, even though Ada went round there once a month, sometimes more. She had sent her brothers and sisters her new address, but they never made contact either. She had nobody to care if she came home or not. No one to know if she was thrown off a pier, to claim her body if she was found dead in the river. The manageress might report her missing if she didn't turn up for work, but the girls were always walking out on the job. She wouldn't think Ada had done any different.

Ada had woken early. A baby was crying, a loud, vibrating wail that wove its way between the drums of the night carts on the cobbles and the shouts of the early-morning traders. It had been crying some time, worked itself up into a steady rhythmic *waagh, waagh, waagh*. She shut her eyes, tried to conjure Thomas's face and his new-born mewl. She had forgotten what he looked like, it had been so long. Had he cried at all? He'd been asleep, such a quiet baby. Tired from being born. It must have been hard work for him.

Gino said his friend could lay his hands on ration books. Clothing. Bread. Sugar. Things were tighter than in the war and there was more demand than ever. Ada had no problem passing them on, handing over the money, receiving her cut, giving him the orders for next week. It was regular earnings, and gave her a bit extra to put aside for Tommy, and the business.

'Only the way I see it, Gino,' Ada said, curling into his chest and walking her fingers up towards his neck. 'Since I take all the risks at work flogging it on, I think I deserve a bit more of the share.'

'Don't be greedy, Ava,' he said.

'I'm not. I just mean more of a *stake* in the business.'

'Meaning?'

'We could go into partnership, you, me and your friend,' she said. Took in her breath. 'He supplies, I sell. Clothing, dresses. I thought that was what you wanted. Set me up in a little firm.'

He pushed her arm aside and reached for a cigarette, lay back in bed, smoking it with slow, deliberate drags.

'Maybe you haven't quite grasped the nature of business,' he said, blowing rings in the air. 'How can I put it in words you'll understand?' He leant over and flicked the ash on the floor. He could have used an ashtray, but made a mess to show who was in charge.

'Let's say me and my friend are Mr Marshall and Mr Snelgrove. Or Mr Dickins and Mr Jones.' Ada knew he wasn't going to agree, could read it in his body, chest tight, muscles clamped. 'Big stores. Lots of departments,' he went on. 'Different goods. We'd see you as one of our workers. Haberdashery, let's say. You're talented, Ava. We might even see you as head of that department. You keep the orders coming, you pay on time. But a partner?' He reached for the ashtray and stubbed the cigarette hard in the centre. 'No. This isn't the bleeding Co-op, or John Lewis.'

He pushed her away and swung his legs over the side of the bed. He pulled on his clothes and opened the door. She heard his footsteps on the stairs, the soft click of the outside door. *Let's get this right, Ava. I'm in charge here, and don't you forget that.*

Forget-me-not. Cornflower blue. Ada hummed at the price.

'I know you, Ada.' The coster wet his middle finger and drummed it against the palm of his other hand, as if he was counting through a coupon book. 'Worth every penny.' He'd pinned a picture of Princess Margaret on the side of his stall. It showed her sitting in a dress with a tight, trim bodice, and a long, full skirt that billowed round her.

'Organza,' he said, 'that's what this is.' He thumped the bolts of fabric. 'New Look, they call it. But if it's good enough for the likes of her,' he rolled his thumb towards the picture, 'it's good enough for the likes of you, Ada.'

She had been planning to sell the coupons to the girls at work, set the money aside for Tommy.

'Of course, with this bloody rationing,' the coster was saying, 'no one likes to look extravagant. But it doesn't bother that lot.' He tilted his head backwards.

She'd have enough with her coupons, if she kept them. She never asked Gino where his friend got them from and the coster in Berwick Street never looked too closely. Three yards for the skirt. One and a half for the bodice. Plus lining. Notions. Thread. Zipper.

She looked carefully at the picture of Princess Margaret while the coster cut the cloth. Cross-over bodice, raglan sleeves. The skirt would be easy enough. She'd make the lining first, as a mock-up. Organza was feeble, needed nursing. She'd start at the weekend, in the daylight.

'Making yourself something nice, Ava?' Gino peered closer at the machine. 'A Naumann. That name sounds foreign. German.'

Most Saturdays Ada put the machine away when Gino came round but it was heavy and awkward, and she was in the middle of sewing. Never occurred to her he'd look at it.

'A Singer isn't good enough for you?' This was nothing to do with Gino. He had no right to criticize. She shrugged.

'Where did you get it?'

'What's it to you?' she said, her voice light and airy, an *organza* voice.

'I don't want to be consorting with the enemy, that's what it is to me.'

'Well, you're not,' Ada said. Her voice had an edge. She hoped Gino picked up on it.

'Where did you get it?' He grabbed her arm, squeezed it hard. This was not his business. Why did he care? 'Who gave it to you?'

'You're hurting me, Gino.'

'Well?'

'If you must know.' He relaxed his hold and she shook her arm free, rubbed it with her other hand. It would leave a bruise, a thumb and four fingers, would show below the sleeves of her uniform when she went to work. She took a deep breath. 'If you must know, my brother brought it back for me. From the war. He was in Germany.' Ada warmed to her story. 'Bought it for five cigarettes. Poor buggers. He said they were desperate. Would sell anything. Even their daughters. But it's a good machine.'

The sunlight was behind him and his face was in silhouette, dark and featureless.

'Where in Germany?' he said.

'Munich,' Ada said. 'He was in Munich.'

'So he's American, your brother?'

316

'No, why?'

'It was the Americans who were in Munich.'

'Oh.' Ada thought for a minute. 'Well, maybe not Munich. Maybe somewhere else. I was never good at geography.'

Gino stepped forward, and sat down in the easy chair. 'No, but you're good at other things.' He patted his knee and signalled for Ada to sit on it.

'As a matter of fact,' he said, running his finger up her skirt. 'I know someone who was in Munich at the end of the war. A little town outside Munich.'

Ada pushed his hand away. 'Do you now.' She tried to control her voice but it came out high and thin. 'That's how you'll know then, about the Americans.' She studied his face, the dark, sombre eyes, the curl of his lip, the groove of his skin lines. 'What was he doing there?'

'Business,' he said, adding, 'army business.' He began to laugh. 'I know where you can get the parts.' He tipped his head towards the sewing machine. 'If you ever need them.' He pushed her off his knee, tapping her bottom as she stood up.

The bodice fitted like a membrane, slick and smooth. Forget-me-not blue. She made a pair of shields for under her arms. Wouldn't do to spoil it with sweat. She thought of poor Anni, the Weiter's cook. Anni. Where was she now? Probably living in some bed-sit in Munich. Ada tried not

317

to think about those days. They'd had a friend-
ship, of sorts. Never a word, a different kind of
language. Anni had kept her alive. Anni understood, maybe even loved.

Ada stood on tiptoes and turned, faster and faster
as the skirt floated higher and higher, like the rings
of Saturn. The dress made her a woman, made her
free, to dance and pirouette, to *be*. She was sublime,
flying through the heavens, a celestial being of
happiness and joy. She steadied herself on the chair,
waited for the dizziness to pass. Pulled on her
shoes, the same sandals she'd worn with the cobalt
moiré. Blue was a *lucky* colour.

Clip-clop. Trafalgar Square. Pall Mall. Haymarket.
Piccadilly. Swathes of organza like angel's wings
swirling in fans as she swung her body this way,
that, her waist rippling with the movement. She
spotted the men's eyes, lustful, envious. The war
was over. She had survived. She'd play Gino along
for now, but she'd get rid of him soon enough.
She hadn't survived the prison in Dachau only to
become a prisoner again, in her own home. She
wanted freedom to soar, to dance in a lapis sky,
she and the moon.

He said his contact wanted to meet her. Talk
business. Gino winked as he'd said it.

House of Vaughan, Ada thought.

Café Royal. She hadn't been there since before
the war. It wasn't one of Gino's usual haunts. *No*

rooms, you understand? He said he'd wait for her in the Grill Room. She had a sixpence ready, in case she was early and they had the same rigmarole here as in Smith's. She'd have a champagne while she waited, fizzing elegant on her tongue, popping in her nose. Sit on the gilt chair surrounded by mirrors, losing herself in her own reflections.

He was already there, talking to another man who was slouched in a chair, tie loose round his neck, the top button of his shirt undone. He wore small, round glasses. Hair short, slicked back.

'Here she is,' Gino said, beckoning her over.

The man turned. Behind the glasses his eyes were soft and pale. *Duck-egg blue*, Ada thought, airy enough to see through. A cold stream of dread coursed through her nerves. *Stanislaus*. There was no mistaking.

'Meet Stanley, Ava.'

She froze as he tried to stand up, leaning on his arm which buckled beneath him, knocking the table so the glasses teetered. He looked past her, with vacant, glazed eyes.

'This is Ava Gordon,' Gino said.

'Ava Gordon. Invergordon. Pleased to meet you,' he said, slurring his words and slumping back into his seat. He tried to focus his eyes, but the lids hung heavy and his chin dropped onto his chest. *Stanislaus*. She had changed, she knew, thin as a matchstick, blonde hair, glasses. But he didn't recognize her. He was too drunk. Did he call

himself Stanley now? He didn't sound foreign
anymore. Same eyes, but the rims were red and
swollen and his face was lined. It had been over
seven years since she'd seen him. He'd put on a
bit of weight, hadn't aged well. But, she realized
now, it *had* been him in Munich, hat down, collar
up. She hadn't been wrong. Her hands turned
clammy and she began to sweat. *Keep calm. Pretend.
Act normal.*

Gino signalled to the waiter. 'A Manhattan for
me. A Pink Lady for madame here.'

Ada wanted champagne, but he didn't ask her.
Gino waited for the drinks to arrive, then leant
forward. 'Well, Ava,' he said. 'We have something
to celebrate here.'

'Oh?'

'Your ship has come in, so to speak.'

'Really?' she said. She knew what he was going
to say. He was going to put money in her business. He and Stanley. She didn't want their money
now. She could feel the panic rising. *Pretend,*
she told herself, pretend you don't know him. She
needed time to think. 'Do you want to tell me
about it?'

'Not yet,' Gino said. He had an unlit cigarette
between his lips that bobbed as he spoke. He was
looking at her hard, without a smile. 'But I've great
hopes for you, Ada.'

Stanley's head fell forward and he jerked it back,
awake. He was very drunk.

'Tell me,' Ada said.

'Not yet, no.' He picked up the matches and lit his cigarette, dragging on it so a catkin of ash hovered at the end. He didn't lift his eyes for a moment.

'You look very lovely tonight, if I might say,' he said. 'Turning heads as always.' He turned to Stanley. 'I hand-pick my girls. Only the best.'

He flicked his cigarette in the ashtray and smirked. 'You play your cards right with Stanley,' he said. 'Who knows where it might lead?'

'Meaning?' Ada said, eyeing Stanley – Stanislaus – who was nodding like a marionette and grinning. *He must know who I am.*

'Him and me,' he said. 'Invest in you. Start you up in business.'

'See,' Stanley said, leaning forward and propping his elbows on the table. 'You're legit.' His arm stretched into a long arc as he pointed his finger at her. 'It's the marriage of bloody Cana.' He drooled as he spoke, wiped his cuff across his mouth, and peered at her again, his lids low and sluggish, his eyes bleary and unfocused. 'You turn water into wine. Metal into gold.' He broke off from what he was saying, his head lolling to one side.

'Coupons into clothes. Dirty money into clean,' Gino continued. 'You cooperate with Stanley tonight, and it's all yours.'

'Cooperate?' Ada said.

'Ava, don't play the innocent. It doesn't flatter you.'

Scarlett's warning rang in her ears.

'You go with Stanley tonight,' Gino said. 'Do whatever he wants, and who knows where it will lead?'

'No, Gino. No. I'm with you.'

'You're with me on Saturday night,' Gino said. His chubby face curled into a snarl and his black eyes grew sharp and pointed. 'But the rest of the nights you're with whoever I tell you to go with.'

'No.' Ada stood up sharp, knocking the table so the glasses wobbled. Gino grabbed her arm, pulled her back down.

'You're my present to him. His reward for loyalty.' He dug his thumb into the soft bones of her wrist hard enough to break them. 'You're part of my *family* now. Do I need to teach you a lesson in obedience?'

Ada cried out from the pain. Scarlett had been right. He was pimping her. Had gifted her to Stanley as if she was a bottle of cheap booze. *Words, words.* She had to ditch Gino. She wasn't sure how she'd give him the slip, but she'd find a way. And Stanislaus. He didn't recognize her. She could leave him.

'Be a good girl,' Gino was saying, 'or there will be consequences.'

He stood up, adjusted his tie, and walked out of the room. Stanley pushed back in his chair, leant forward to Ada.

'Me and Gino,' he said. His speech was still

slurred, his eyes glazed and confused. He crossed his fingers and waved them in front of her face. 'That close. Like brothers. We go back a long time. Before the war.'

Ada sat, too stunned to speak. Stanislaus. Here, in London. After all these years.

'London. Paris. Belgium,' he went on. Ada's hands stiffened round her glass. 'Don't suppose you've ever been to Paris, have you?' Stanley sniffed, finished his drink, signalled to the waiter. 'We're going to have a good time tonight,' he said, not waiting for her reply. 'You and me. Drink up.'

Run, now. He'd be too drunk to catch her. She stood up, turned, ready to make a dash for it.

Gino was standing in the doorway, watching.

He needed help out of the restaurant. Two doormen down the stairs. He stumbled and tripped on his feet. He had pulled his tie looser and his jacket was falling off his shoulders. He put his arm round her, leant on her with all his weight, moved with uncertain steps, one foot dragging behind the other.

'I think you should go home,' Ada said as they drew close to Charing Cross. 'You're in no fit state.'

'Home is where you are.' He spoke his words like a ventriloquist, slow and articulated. 'I'm not leaving you here. You're mine. Tonight.' The station clock said half past nine, and the day was fading, the sun's sleeping rays turning the sky a rich, deep indigo. It was still warm and Ada was hot in her dress, wished she'd made the sleeves shorter.

Stanley was heavy. He weighed down on her, gripping her shoulder hard. She could barely support him. If she moved away, he'd keel over, fall flat on his face. She could escape then, leave him to it. The police would sober him up in a cell. She tried to prise open his fingers and push his hand away, but he wouldn't let go. She twisted sharply to break his hold, but he squeezed tighter and slammed his free fist into her chest, winding her. She was no match for him, drunk though he was. And Gino? Was he still watching her? What would he do if she didn't obey? Gino was a big man, strong. He knew where she lived. Knew where she worked. He'd sniff her out. She'd have to move house. Find another flat. *Consequences*, he'd said. *Consequences.*

She had to help Stanley up the stairs to her room. He tumbled onto the bed. Ada put the kettle on, sat in the dark watching his chest rise and fall, sipped her tea. She could slip away now. Find Scarlett, she'd know what to do.

He patted the bed. 'Come over here, Ava,' he said, running his words together. 'Give us a cuddle.'

She could make a run for it.

'Now.' His voice cracked like a pistol. He might be drunk, but she heard the menace in his voice. He could throw himself at her from the bed, cut off her exit. 'Or I tell Gino.'

Gino pays you for this. She was trapped. She walked towards the bed, one slow foot after another.

'That's a good girl,' Stanley said.

She slipped out of her dress and laid it over the end of the bed.

'I've seen some things in my time,' he slurred, 'but nothing as lovely as you.'

She climbed on the bed and lay down beside him. Gino had tricked her when he said they'd start her in business. He didn't mean dressmaking. This was the business he had in mind. And now here she was, side by side with Stanislaus. Only he called himself Stanley. *Cockney* Stanley. Not *Count* Stanislaus.

'I'm glad the war's over.' His words were sluggish. 'Don't get me wrong. But it gave me a chance in life, a leg-up, as it were.'

His voice was flat, melancholy from the alcohol. She'd heard it before. They had to talk, these men. Even Stanley. Get it out of their system. Tell their stories. Stanislaus. Stanley. Who was he?

'What *did* you do in the war, Stanley?' She could see him in Namur, his shadow in the doorway. She could remember the way his collar was turned up in Munich, his hat pulled low. She needed to know where he'd been in between. She'd never get another chance to find out.

'I have a dodgy ticker,' he said. 'Rheumatic fever. When I was a nipper.'

'Really?' Ada said. *Humour him.*

'Yeah,' his voice was far away. 'They signed me off. I'd have liked to have fought.'

Ada could feel her heart hammering against her chest. She was sure Stanislaus must hear it.

'What did you do instead?' Her words came out high, strangled.

'I was in business.' He tapped the side of his nose. *Business, Ada, business.*

'You didn't have any adventures then?' Ada said. She knew how fast these drunken moods could swing, she had to ask now. She *had* to know what happened.

'No,' he said, 'not really.' He pushed himself up on one elbow. She could smell the whisky on his breath. 'Mind you,' he said. 'I was in Belgium when the Germans invaded. That was a bit of an episode.'

The blood drained from her head, cascaded down her spine. *Bit* of an *episode.* The bombs thundering in her head, her flesh flaying in the heat and dust as she ran, alone, for sanctuary. Her life destroyed and all he could say was that it was a *bit* of an *episode.*

'Oh?' Her voice was thin.

'Yeah,' Stanley reached for a cigarette, lit it and leant back, one arm behind his head. 'I was in Namur, as a matter of fact.'

She wanted to grab his shoulders and shake him so hard his tongue would loll in his mouth and his brain would crash against the hard of his skull. She wanted to scream *Don't you recognize me?*

Namur, *as a matter of fact*, as if nothing had taken place.

'Managed to get the last boat out,' Stanley went on. 'It was a close shave, I can tell you.'

'Namur is a long way from the sea.'

'I was lucky. I'm a lucky man, Ava, I tell you. Last train, last boat. Last-chance saloon, that's me.'

He blew cigarette rings that silhouetted in the dark, round ghosts of memory that hovered like grey haloes. 'Lots of buggers didn't make it. Refugees. Standing on the quays, begging. They'd have sold their grandmother if it'd got them out.'

I didn't make it, Ada thought. *You didn't save me. You don't even recognize me.*

'The world owes no one a favour, Ava girl,' Stanley was saying. 'If you don't have the money or the nous, why should you expect others to help you out? Every man jack for himself. That's my motto in life.'

The drink had made him talkative, a burst of energy before the crash.

'Were you by yourself?' Ada said. She was quivering, hoped he hadn't noticed. She'd say she was cold, lying here, all naked.

'Why do you ask?'

'I just wondered.'

He stubbed out his cigarette, blowing the last of the smoke free. It smelt bitter.

'There was some empty-headed tart who'd latched onto me.' He lay back on the bed, resting his head on the pillow. 'Could have made good

327

money off of her, but I ran into a spot of bother. Glad to be shot of the bitch.'

Ada swallowed. 'What happened to her?'

'How should I know? I left her in Namur. Right pain she was. As a matter of fact,' he pushed himself up and looked down at her, 'you remind me of her. Funny that.'

The bastard. Abandoned her. Never cared for her. Empty-headed tart. He hadn't recognized her. Hadn't *cared* enough to remember her. Probably never given her a second thought.

'What about you, Ava?' he was saying. 'What did you do in the war?' Stanley was calmer now.

She pushed herself up from the bed, walked over to the window. The night was clear and she could see the speckled lights of the Milky Way a million miles away. 'You don't remember me?'

'No,' Stanley said, 'should I?'

'Ada Vaughan?'

'Name rings a bell.' He smacked his lips, as if he hadn't a care in the world.

She walked back to the bed and stood over him. 'I was the girl in Namur. You took me to Paris, promised me a life, then you left me. In Namur.'

He pushed himself up on both elbows and looked at her, his eyes icy and hard.

'Really?' He laughed, a hollow, bitter cackle. 'Thought you looked familiar.' She felt her head tighten, her thoughts spin, like a child's top teetering out of control. 'Yes, I remember you now.

328

Got my wires crossed a bit there,' Stanley went on. 'It was French tarts in London that make the money, not English tarts in Paris. I'll say this.' He was opening his mouth wide so his words would come out square. 'At least you've gone up in the world since then. One of Gino Messina's tarts. Fancy that.'

Ada gasped, raised her hand to slap him, but Stanley grabbed her arm and pulled her back on the bed. He roped his hand through her hair, pulling it hard so Ada yelped with pain.

'You *bastard*,' she shouted, hurt and anger and bewilderment ricocheting in her head, her words wrenched from the deep. 'I thought you loved me. I stayed with you. Then you left me. *Why?* You told me your name was Stanislaus. Stanislaus von Lieben. *Why?*'

'Fancy you remembering that,' he said. 'We had a nice time in Paris, didn't we?' He was nodding, grinning. 'Yeah, I was Stanislaus that time. I had lots of names, all foreign Johnnies. Good run, mind,' he said. 'Papers, all that.'

He had her pinned to the bed.

All of her blood and warmth drained away, leaving a cold, empty imprint of hate. She had never felt such loathing. 'You abandoned me,' she said, 'and our son. His name was Thomas. *Thomas.*'

'Son? Nothing to do with me. You should have used a rubber,' he said, pulling her close, 'like the professional you are. Besides,' He began to kiss her, clumsy wet lips that smelled of whisky and wine, tobacco and stale breath, 'I thought you girls knew how to take care of things like that.' She tried to push him away, but he rammed her down harder on the bed. She squirmed beneath him, pressing her hand against his chin, digging her nails in his cheeks. He slapped her hard on the face, and forced himself into her.

Namur. It was Namur. He didn't wear a rubber.

He lay on his stomach, one arm sprawled over her, out cold. She wriggled free from beneath it. He didn't stir. She pulled on her dressing gown, opened the door, holding the handle tight, turning it so it didn't click and wake him, and padded down to the lavatory.

Stanley Lovekin. Stanislaus von Lieben. She had the measure of him all right. Abandoned her in the middle of a war. *Every man jack for himself.* Didn't care about her. Had never cared about her. And she thought she had loved him. She yanked the lavatory chain so hard it spun back out of her hand. She wrapped the dressing gown round herself and pulled the belt tight. And Gino. Cut from the same cloth. They controlled her, she could see now. Scarlett was right. Was that what Stanislaus had planned for her in Paris, or Namur? White slave trade? Was he going to set up a brothel? Had he known the Germans would invade? *Ein wunderschönes junges Mädchen, Herr Beamter.* He had been lining himself up to be her pimp. Of course. All that niceness, sucking her in so she needed him. Like Gino, now. Him and Gino. He said they went back a long time. Paris. Perhaps he'd gone to meet Gino in Belgium, in Namur.

She went back into the bedroom. She'd tell him to get out. Yell at him, scream, *Never come back*. Had a mind to report him to the police. He was out for the count. She went over to the sink for some water. Throw it over him. Bring him to.

Or leave him. He wouldn't wake for hours. She slipped off her dressing gown, grabbed her dress from the end of the bed and pulled it over her head. Stanislaus fidgeted in his sleep. Ada froze. He settled back into a steady state and began to snore, an oily rumble from his throat. She pushed her feet into her shoes, balancing on one foot, then the other, pulling up the ankle strap, placed her bag on the bed. He coughed, and twitched. She held the bedpost for balance and watched.

He lay there sleeping, as if nothing had happened. She had suffered beyond all reason, all because of him. Always a man, she thought. It's always been a bloody man. Stanislaus. Herr Weiss. Gino. If she were shot of the lot of them, what then? She could be her own woman, the master of her fate. She snorted. A long time since she'd thought of that poem. *I am the captain of my soul.* Yes. *The* mistress *of her fate.* Sweet revenge. She deserved it, for all her suffering over the years. Now it was their turn to suffer. She was sweating, her armpits clammy. She stared at Stanislaus, his face silver in the moonlight. The jagged edges of memories began to grind, filling her head with their frenzied clamour. Thomas, lying still as a dream in the priest's brown bag. Ada, alone in Dachau, starving, as her skin flaked away and her flesh devoured itself. Bombs falling round her, blasting the skies and hammering the earth. She felt the bitter gall of terror burst and spread like poison through her veins and nerves. Stanislaus had destroyed her life, and Thomas's. An eye for an eye. Her mouth tasted the tart tin of blood. He was still asleep, snuffling like a baby. She would be free of him forever. Ada Vaughan. She'd find Tommy then, bring him home, start her life afresh.

She picked up her handbag and tiptoed across the room. She pulled the curtains, holding the sliders high on their metal tracks so they didn't squeak, tucking the ends of the fabric into the window sill and folding the sides together so no chink of light came through.

Ada paused to let her eyes became accustomed to the dark. Stanley was snoring, the bed frame trembling with his breath. She stepped closer, waiting for his hand to come and grab her but he lay still. She waited, counting, *one, two, three*. She stepped to the fire, *four, five, six*, took a deep breath, *seven, eight, nine*. She turned on the gas, heard its hiss, smelt the sour sulphur of its fumes. She picked up her bag, tiptoed out, closing the door behind her, and pushed the sausage hard against it so the gas didn't seep through into the hallway. *Ten.*

Down the stairs, four flights, out. She'd been holding her breath and now she let the air rush in hard and fast so it hurtled round her lungs and crashed against her ribs. She heaved across the pavement.

'You all right, love?' A woman's voice.

'Yes, thank you,' she said. 'I just winded myself.'

Stand up. Walk away. Like nothing happened. *Walk.*

Her legs were strings and tendrils, one foot flailing in front of the other. She stumbled to the end of Floral Street and into Garrick Street, pausing for breath on the corner, one hand steadying herself on the wall of a building. She was shaking, her frame rattling beneath her skin. But she was free, at last. She could go with whoever she wanted. Beholden to no man. Never again. No more. *Namur.*

She glanced at the clock in the Strand. Eleven o'clock. Not too late. The flunkey at Smith's opened the door, raised an eyebrow. *Clip-clopped* to the powder room. Her hair was a mess. She took the comb from her bag, teased it back into shape, roll on the top, underneath, down the sides. She rummaged for her lipstick, dabbed it on, smacked her lips together. Good as new. Like nothing happened. Up the stairs. She had her money ready.

The maître d' was still there, the same one from before.

'Haven't seen you for a while,' he said.

'I've been busy.' Ada slapped the sixpence on the lectern.

The maître d' picked it up. 'It's gone up,' he said. *I have spies, you know,* she could hear Gino saying. 'Silence is golden, if you get my meaning.'

'I don't think so,' Ada said, 'not anymore.'

She swept past him into the bar, took her usual seat, ordered a White Lady. She brought out her cigarettes, laid them on the table, took one out and rolled it between her fingers. She hadn't forgotten.

She lit it, sucked, a deep drag that stirred her lungs. She drank her cocktail in two gulps, the bitter alcohol burning her throat as she swallowed.

'Would you like another?' The voice was soft. She tried to focus on the man by her side in a tweed jacket and corduroy trousers. He must be sweltering in that outfit. He was looking down at her, smiling, a pipe in one hand, its stem resting on his lips. There was something homely about him, fatherly. A kind man. A man to come back for, warm slippers by the fire. 'You look like you need it.'

Ada stared at him in a daze, said nothing as he called the waiter over. *Another one.*

'You look like you've seen a ghost,' he went on. 'Do you want to talk about it?'

She shook her head.

'It helps to talk sometimes. You're such a pretty woman. I can't bear to see you looking troubled.'

'You don't know me,' Ada said. 'Why should you care?'

'If the war taught me one thing,' he said, 'it was that we need to look out for each other. I'm not trying to pick you up,' he added. 'Don't get the wrong idea.'

Ada laughed, an angry, bitter *ha ha*.

'Please yourself,' he said, moving away, 'I was only trying to help.'

'No,' Ada said, 'stay.'

He pulled out the chair and sat down. 'I'm Norman,' he said.

Ada looked at him.

'Ada,' she said, 'Ada Vaughan.' It felt good. *Ada Vaughan. Modiste.*

The waiter brought her another drink, and a martini for the man.

'Cheerio, Ada,' he said, raising the glass. 'Down the hatch.'

A wave of weariness swept over her. She didn't want to talk. She didn't want company. She wanted to be by herself.

'Actually,' she said, 'would you mind leaving me alone?'

He raised an eyebrow, looking puzzled and hurt. He shrugged, stood up and walked away, without saying a word. The scent from his pipe drifted towards her. *St Bruno.* Her father smoked that. *Rough cut.* Norman was a good man, Ada thought, any other time and I could have had him. Why do the nice men always come at the wrong time?

She was the last out of the bar at four in the morning. The maître d' held her elbow as she walked down the stairs.

'No tricks tonight, eh?' he said. 'You're not in a good way. Have you far to go?'

'No,' Ada said. 'No.'

She stumbled past the doorman. The maître d' was shaking his head. *No cut this time.* Through the heavy revolving doors, into the soft, fresh light of early dawn. The lemon sun cast shadows and the pale topaz sky promised moisture.

'Need a storm,' the doorman said, 'clear the air.'

Her head was light. She leant a hand against the glass of the shop on the corner. *Fairy* light. She giggled, retched, vomited on the pavement. She stepped aside. It had splashed on her shoes and the hem of her dress. She'd have to wash it. Plunge it up and down in her tiny basin. Organza may be feeble but it fought for its life. She'd have to punch it to stay still, push it under till it drowned. Her feet were slipping in her shoes, so she tried to take them off, hopping on one foot, then the other, pulling at the straps and kicking them free. She picked them up. *Tiptoe, through the tulips.*

★   ★   ★

336

There was a policeman standing on the door-step to her building, a right old bluebottle. *I know a fat old policeman, he's always on our street.* Her father used to sing this to them when they were kiddies. *Fat, jolly red-faced man, he really is a treat.*

She swung close to him, 'Constable.'

'You can't go in there, miss,' he said. 'There's been a fatality.'

'And what's that, when it's at home?'

'A murder,' the policeman said, 'in plain English.'

'Oo-er.' Ada blinked hard. 'But I live there.' She took a step back and pointed in the air. 'Up there. Right at the top.'

'And you are?'

'Ada,' she said, her mouth open wide so the sound came loud and clear, all elocuted, *electro-cuted.* Pissed as a newt. *Language, Ada, language.* 'Or Ava.' Her teeth bit into her bottom lip. 'You pays your money,' she hiccupped, 'you takes your choice.' She staggered and grabbed the policeman for balance.

He gripped her wrist. 'Surname?'

Ada blinked. He wasn't friendly, this copper. 'Vaughan,' she said, 'Ada Vaughan.'

'Well, Ada Vaughan,' he said, 'I think you'd better come with me to the station.'

'Station?' He was still holding her with one hand, fishing in his pocket with the other. He produced a pair of handcuffs, and clapped them over Ada's wrists.

'Ada!' Scarlett was rushing towards her. 'Oh, Ada, plead guilty,' she said. 'Makes it easier. You just get a fine.'

Ada was confused. Then a sober slash of memory cut through her mind. Stanislaus. She'd left the gas on. He would be dead.

'I did it,' she said. 'I killed him.'

The policeman walked her across the road and into the police van. She sat on the hard bench, her head spinning. Had he thrashed round, gasping for air as his lungs burned to a cinder and his throat clinched tight? Did he try and claw his way up the wall, block the jets of gas? Would the stench of his flesh linger in the chimneys?

'De-li-ber-ate-ly,' she added.

He got everything he deserved.

THREE

LONDON, NOVEMBER 1947

She'd had to wait months after the arraignment for her trial date, cooped up in that cell with its white tiles and sooty grout and the barred window high in the wall. She was let out once a day to empty slops and walk round the yard. She'd almost rather be busy in the Commandant's house than numbed in prison here, no one to visit her, not even Scarlett because Mr Wallis said she might be a witness so she couldn't.

'Not guilty,' she'd said to her barrister, Mr Wallis. She'd done it, confessed to it and all, but she wouldn't want to swing for Stanley Lovekin, give up *her* life for *his*. He wasn't worth it.

Mr Wallis was young, looked like a schoolboy. He couldn't pronounce his 's's and they came out thick and dribbly. He licked his lips, sucking back the spit, looked at Ada. This was his first murder case, he told her, but he was the only one who'd do her for free. She had to come to court in her prison uniform, a grey skirt that sagged at the back and a limp green blouse. She'd liked to have worn her own clothes, but Mr Wallis said her landlady had cleared everything out as soon as the police were done. The only thing she had was the blue organza dress she had been wearing, and the coppers took that as evidence. Right pair they looked, Ada and Mr Wallis. Him barely out of short trousers, and her in her prison uniform and ugly lace-up shoes. Not even a dab of lipstick.

The gallery was packed even though it was November. The fog outside so thick the conductors had to walk in front of their buses. So many people there to watch the case, as if it was some public spectacle. Her mother must know she was up for trial. Mr Wallis had said it was all over the papers. She wondered whether she'd be there, had forgiven her. *Come what may, Ada, you are my daughter and I love you through thick and thin.* More likely her mother would disown her. *No, you're mistaken. It's another Ada Vaughan. My Ada went missing, before the war.* Perhaps her father could see her from above, *It's all right, Ada girl, I had a word with your union rep up here.* Grinning, winking. She thought of Thomas. Nearly seven years old. The gallery was on a mezzanine above her, and she couldn't see who was there, not from where she stood. If she got off the charge of murder, and Mr Wallis said she had a good chance, she'd do her time and then go to Germany, find Thomas, finally.

The jury sat to her left. Twelve men, middle-aged judging from the grey in their hair. They'd have to be *somebody*, these men, own property, or have a decent lease, a good address. Mr Wallis said it was helpful to have men. Women hardly ever did jury service but they could be bitchy, especially to another woman. She could charm men, easy, togged up in glad rags and heels. Her blue moiré, her black crepe. Would these men consider her beautiful, in her flat shoes and green prison blouse? No powder, no lipstick? Her hair had grown out and three inches of brown roots made the blonde ends brassy and common. She had styled it into a victory roll, pinned with Kirby grips. At least from the front it looked neat, wholesome. She'd do her best. Stand tall.

She'd had to go to the lavvy three times already today. Mr Wallis had told Ada the case would be difficult. The jury would need a lot of persuading. He'd do his best, but he couldn't make promises. This judge was hard, and Mr Wallis was young and inexperienced. He said no one had ever used this sort of defence for a case like hers. Provocation, he called it. Except the provocation wasn't a single blow, one violent act that hit like a see-saw, down and up, but instead a long, slow fuse that burned like a taper across years, the powder keg invisible until finally one spark set the place ablaze, triggered a fire-storm that sucked reason into its vortex.

They rose as the judge came in, the same one as at the arraignment three months ago. He was old, had a face like a skull, sunken eyes and jagged cheeks. Half-glasses toppled on the end of his nose, two craggy hands hovered beneath his gown. He looked like a cadaver. Ada wondered if he was ill, crabs eating his soul, gnawing at his heart. She curled her hands round the wooden rail of the dock, fingers on the top, thumb underneath. It was rough, splintered by other people's thumb nails, clawing for their lives. She was going to be sick.

'Please give the court your full name.'

'Ada,' she said. 'Ada Margaret Vaughan.' Margaret, after her mother.

The clerk read out the charge: '. . . in the Central Criminal Court, Rex versus Ada Vaughan . . . on the charge of unlawfully killing Stanley John Lovekin, on the night of the 14th June 1947 . . .'

The ceiling pressed down and the panelled walls closed in. She felt frail and small, the judge high on his bench and the jury on theirs, Mr Wallis in the pit and Mr Harris-Jones, the prosecutor, swaggering as if he'd won the case already. Harris-Jones was older than Wallis, more experienced, you could tell, the way he rocked on his heels and his grown-up hands collared the edge of his gown.

She began to quiver, legs like she needed callipers to keep them strong and straight. She wasn't sure she could stand up. She understood what that phrase meant now, the *weight of the law*. Not the copper's heavy hand on your shoulder, *You'd better come along, miss*, but the gravity of justice crushing her into the ground and grinding her to dust. She looked up at the windows in search of earth and sky and the horizon in between, but the windows were set high in the wall and all she saw was the thick, green phlegm that blew in smelly squats through the lanes and round the towers of the City.

'How do you plead?' the judge said.

She could say guilty, have it over and done with, go back to her cell. But she'd hang if she did, and Stanley Lovekin wasn't going to have that over her. She was going to survive. She was a survivor. *Lucky*.

'Not guilty,' she said quietly.

'Speak up.' The judge's voice. The room was hollow, she'd have to project. *From the diaphragm*. She could hear Miss Skinner's voice in her head all those years ago. *You can look like a swan but if you talk like a sparrow, who will take you seriously?*

'Not guilty.' *E-nun-ci-ate.*

The judge leant towards Mr Wallis.

'Not guilty of murder but guilty of manslaughter through provocation,' Mr Wallis said.

'Thank you.' He wrote something on the pad in front of him. His pen was gold. Must be worth a bob or two.

'This is a most *unusual* defence,' the judge said, turning towards Harris-Jones. 'I trust you have acquainted the prosecution with the law on provocation, as it stands?'

'Yes,' Mr Wallis said.

The judge turned to address the jury. 'The jury must decide whether the person charged has been so provoked as to lose self-control, that is, provoked *beyond reason*. Normally,' – the judge paused, eyed the jurors one by one, eyed Ada, head bowed, picking at the skin on the side of her nail – 'the provocation would fall under the following expectations.' He held up his hand, fingers splayed wide. 'First, by witnessing the sodomy of his son.' He took a deep breath, pulled down his index finger. 'Second, by witnessing the adultery of his wife.' He smacked his lips tight, bent his middle finger over. 'Or, third, the unlawful arrest of an Englishman, and, fourth, the mistreatment of a relative.' He said the last bit all in one breath, as if he was singing, his voice higher and higher, pulling down his third and fourth fingers simultaneously, turning as he did so to Mr Wallis again.

'Yes, your honour,' Mr Wallis said.

'And there is only one possible line of defence left? A most unusual line?'

'Yes, your honour.'

'Of a grossly insulting assault?'

'Yes, your honour.'

'Very well.' The judge grunted like a walrus.

The jury were looking at her. Judging already. Appearances matter, Ada knew that, better than them all. *I thought you were one of the customers, looking so smart.* They'd see her in prison togs, *looking* guilty, condemn her before they began the trial. The jury foreman had a moustache and a row of ribbons across his top pocket. War hero. Ada never trusted men with moustaches, not after Stanislaus. She put her hand to her hair, made sure that it was in place, watched as Mr Harris-Jones stood up, stacked his folders on the desk before him and turned to face the jury.

'The case for the prosecution,' he said, looking at the jurors, 'is straightforward. There is no issue that the deceased was unlawfully killed by the administration of gas when he was unconscious. There is a confession, corroborated by the evidence, which can be taken quickly. The only issue is whether there was a *grossly insulting assault* causing her to lose control in circumstances where a *reasonable* person in her position and with her background would have done so.'

Fear. She remembered how it tasted, how it charged through her body like an engine and left her quivering in its tracks. There was a policeman who stood behind her in the dock. She turned, wanted to catch his eye, snatch a crumb of sympathy, but he was staring straight ahead, expressionless.

'The case for this *grossly insulting assault,* members of the jury,' he spoke the words slowly, carefully, like it was a foreign language that no one understood, 'goes back some ten years, to the start of the war.'

Mr Harris-Jones laid it out: Stanislaus von

Lieben. Seducer. A cad and a coward, undoubtedly. But did he abuse her? Assault or insult her? He twisted his hand in a so-so manner. 'Did he abandon her? Or were they separated in the anarchy of war, through no one's fault?'

He laid out her life like a corpse, dissecting it. Here's the head, here's the feet, large intestine, small intestine. But there was nothing about love or guts or heartache or fear, nothing about the *inside* of her, Ada Vaughan.

Internment by the Nazis. Secret pregnancy and a birth. Herr Weiss. Years locked up in that room. Perhaps scared, hungry. A little boy, Thomas, *Thomas*, in German. *German*, members of the jury. The loss of this child.

'Was she so haunted by his memory? *Driven* to murder by it?' His voice was sarcastic.

He was looking at her, directing the jury to follow his eyes, to see her dressed as a common-or-garden villain, incapable of knowing right from wrong.

Lovekin. Stanley Lovekin. Stanislaus von Lieben. Had he been the architect of her torments for the last ten years, the cause of her suffering? Her fall from grace, into a life of sin and despair? *Abandon hope all ye who enter here.* Or was he simply a man like any other?

'What was the nature of the assault? That he had reappeared?' He paused and looked at the jury, man to man, eyeing each one, before he stared back at Ada. She stood in the dock barely above the railing, like a caged animal, or a lunatic. 'If, indeed, it was him.'

'It was,' Ada shouted out.

'Silence,' the judge said.

He had no heart, this man, Ada could see.

The jury had her confession. *I, Ada Margaret Vaughan* ... She had signed it. A policeman said how he found the body on the bed, wearing only a shirt and vest, no trousers. Reeked of whisky. A detective said that the sole fingerprints on the gas tap were Ada's, and on the window frame, where she'd closed the gaps in the curtains, and on the bottom of the door where she had wedged the draught excluder. Those were the facts of the case. Incontestable. Guilty of murder. But manslaughter? Provocation? *Grossly. Insulting. Assault?*

Sister Brigitte had plumped up since the war. She stood in the witness box with a clean, starched wimple and dark grey scapular over her black tunic, her brass crucifix glinting under the electric lights. It was odd, seeing her here in London. It seemed as if she belonged somewhere else, on the Continent, in war.

Yes, Ada had sought refuge in the Mother House in Namur. They understood she had been separated from her husband, Stanislaus von Lieben. After the Nazi occupation of Belgium the British nuns had been interned, taken to Munich, forced to nurse the elderly.

Sister Brigitte. Hearing her words breathed life
into Ada's memories, reanimated the corpse which
Mr Harris-Jones had laid out. Ada knew she was
trembling. She could hear the bombs and the
shouting, smell the cordite and the burning, and
the fear that had surrounded her that day in
Namur.

'If you had refused to nurse them,' Mr Harris-
Jones said. 'Would you have been shot?'

'Possibly,' Sister Brigitte said. 'We never put it
to the test.'

'You made no attempt to resist?'

She looked hard at Mr Harris-Jones, as if she
could see through him to his soul.

'Our vocation,' she said, 'is to nurse the elderly,
wherever and whenever it is needed. Our vocation knows neither politics nor war. Nor does
old age.'

'High principles,' Mr Harris-Jones said.
'Convenient, in the face of the most evil regime
in history, would you not say?'

'Only those without principles resort to cyni-
cism,' Sister Brigitte said, eyes level with his. She
stared until he looked away to his notes. Sister
Brigitte had faced the Nazis down. She wasn't
fazed by a smarmy barrister, even if he was a
King's Counsel.

'I understand you stayed on in Munich for
several months after the war was over,' Mr Harris-
Jones said. 'Can you tell me why?'

'We couldn't abandon our old people. Not until

we were sure that their welfare would be taken care of.'

'The defendant, Ada Vaughan—' Mr Harris-Jones said.

'Sister Clara.'

'Sister Clara. That was how she was known?'

'Yes.'

'Did she work?'

'Yes. She wasn't a trained nurse, but she could carry out the menial tasks.'

'And she behaved as a nun?'

'Yes,' Sister Brigitte said, 'obviously.'

'And the Nazis never guessed she was not whom she claimed to be? Even though she was pregnant?'

'She wore a borrowed habit, from a nun much larger than herself. It did not show.'

'And when she gave birth?'

'Fortunately, there were no complications. The baby came in the night. Our dormitory cell was out of earshot of the guards.'

'Coincidence?'

'No, good fortune.' Sister Brigitte smiled. 'We had prayed.' Ada knew that smile. 'The Virgin Mary was looking after us.'

'And the baby? What happened?'

Sister Brigitte swallowed, looked over to Ada. Who did she see in the dock? What was she thinking?

'The baby was born dead.'

★ ★ ★

No. His delicate skin, marbled purple and blue, like the inside cover of a prayer book. She'd pulled the edge of the towel from his face, so she would remember it. His eyes were closed and puffy, deep folds round the sockets. His hands were clutched in little fists, pressed to either side of his cheeks. He was bald, his head slicked with blood and mucous. He lay there with naked shoulders and creases in his neck. He was sleeping.

He was alive.

Ada remembered the black stole fluttering in Father Friedel's bag from Thomas's breath, his nostrils flaring as the air filled his lungs, as he moved his chest, *in out, in out.* It was his breath, not the breeze from the bag as she clicked it shut.

Sister Brigitte had baptized him, so he didn't go to Limbo, had held Ada's hand as Father Friedel left. 'May his little soul rest in peace. Say it with me, Sister Clara.'

'No,' Ada had said. 'He's not dead.'

'Say it with me, Sister Clara, *may the souls of the faithful departed, through the mercy of God, rest in peace, Amen.*'

No. Thomas was alive and kicking.

'He was alive,' Ada screamed out. 'Sister Brigitte, he was alive.'

'Miss Vaughan,' the judge said, 'silence.'

'What happened then?'

'The priest helped us. He smuggled the baby's body away.'

'Where?'

Sister Brigitte shrugged. 'We don't know.'

'How did he dispose of the body?'

'We don't know. But there were funerals almost every day. He could slip the baby's body in one of the old people's coffins. No one would know.'

'And Sister Clara?'

Sister Brigitte looked towards Ada. Tenderness was there, contrition too. 'She found it difficult to accept.'

'That he was dead?'

'Yes.'

'What did you do?'

'Postpartum depression is a terrible condition as is,' Sister Brigitte said. 'We couldn't have it get any worse. It was prudent all round to humour her.'

'Lie to her, you mean? Let her believe the baby was alive?'

'Sometimes a white lie is for the best, for the greater good. God forgives those little venial sins.'

No, Ada thought, *no*. This wasn't what happened. Thomas was alive. Sister Brigitte knew this. Why was she saying this?

'And when she returned at the end of the war, did you continue with the white lie?'

'We had to,' Sister Brigitte said. 'She was in a dreadful state. She was half dead, out of her mind. She couldn't take that news.'

'Did she try to find her son?'

'Yes.'

'Did you not tell her then?'

'We thought it best that she try to find him, and learn for herself that he couldn't be traced, rather than have us tell her he was dead. We thought if she still had hope, it would help her recovery.'

'You knew she was lying, didn't you?'

'I beg your pardon?'

'About being married.'

'I didn't take a judgement on that.'

'You were told by Sister Monica that Ada Vaughan was not married to Stanislaus von Lieben. Her passport was in the name of Vaughan. Vaughan was her maiden name. We have an affidavit from Sister Monica to attest to that. Jury,' he turned to the men sitting in rows, hands poised on their files. 'Item 1 in your bundle. Ada Vaughan wore a curtain ring as a wedding band. You must have known that she was a liar. A fantasist.'

'It was war,' Sister Brigitte said. 'It was all confusing. Terrible. People do anything to survive. I wouldn't condemn someone for that.'

'You said that you were above war.'

'You're twisting my words. I said old age does not know war.'

That's what they did, these lawyers. Show the facts out of context, so they sat skewed, like a picture hanging crooked on a wall, or one of those mirrors in a fairground that show you squat or stretched. Ada wanted to shout out to the jury, *Can't you see what he's doing?*

'Did Ada Vaughan visit you after your return to England?'

'Sadly not,' Sister Brigitte shook her head. 'She would have been welcome.'

'Let me ask one more time. You are certain that her baby died?'

'There was no pulse, no heartbeat, no breath. The baby was born dead. Without doubt.'

'Ada Vaughan would be lying when she said he was alive.'

'She would be deluded. There is a difference.'

'Fantasist,' Mr Harris-Jones said. 'No difference.'

Sister Brigitte stepped down from the witness box, kissed her crucifix, left the room without a backward glance. Ada should have gone to visit, she should have. But what would they have talked about? *Do you remember when . . .?* There was no joy there, no happiness to look back on. Just emptiness and sadness.

Ada was back in her cell at the end of the first day. Mr Wallis came with a packet of sandwiches and a bottle of ginger beer, face like a wounded weasel.

'The baby was dead,' he said. 'You didn't tell me that.'

'I didn't know it,' Ada said. Sister Brigitte's words

clanged in her head. She wanted to crash her skull against the wall, drive out the demons that had settled there.

'I can't defend you if you don't tell me what happened.'

'I swear to God,' Ada said, 'I never knew.'

'Or you just denied it, to yourself?'

'Why would I do that?' Ada said. Her voice quivered. 'I couldn't.'

'Couldn't?' It was a cruel question. Mr Wallis bit into his sandwich and Ada watched as his tiny mouth rotated. She couldn't eat, not now. All she saw were the empty pits and the mottled skin of the cadavers buried underground. Little Thomas lay stretched out in a coffin with a stranger, an old man who'd emptied his life and flushed away his love.

'Death.' She sat with her hands clasped round her waist, rocked herself, forwards and back, forwards and back, as if her mind was splitting in two, the memories of hopelessness driving a wedge between the parts. 'Death and darkness.'

'Talk to me, Ada,' Mr Wallis said. 'Tell me what happened.'

Ada shook her head, rocking, rocking.

The next morning the gallery was just as full. Ada twisted in the dock, tried to see who was there. Maybe her mother had come today.

Mr Wallis had warned her that the prosecution would jump round in time, like a jack-in-the-box, calling witnesses so that the jury saw her in a certain way. It was their job to prove that there was no provocation. He'd said that Scarlett would be called, though Ada didn't see why. Scarlett had nothing to do with the war, or Stanislaus; she didn't even know about Thomas, hadn't seen a thing that evening when Stanley Lovekin died. Ada stood in the dock, nervous and on edge.

Scarlett entered the courtroom. Low-heeled shoes, shabby checked coat, headscarf knotted at the front, not a trace of face paint. She could be anybody, a plain, anonymous woman.

'Would you tell me your name?' Mr Harris-Jones said.

'Joyce Matheson.' It was the first Ada had heard her real name.

'Your relationship with the defendant, Ada Vaughan?'

'Friends.'

'Good friends?'

'Yeah, well. We help each other out.'

'And your occupation?'

Scarlett stuck out her chin and looked the jury square-on. 'I'm a prostitute.' Scarlett wasn't afraid of the law, *so what*. She had been in front of the beak more times than Ada'd had hot dinners.

'Is Joyce Matheson your only name?'

'Sometimes I call myself Scarlett. When I'm working.'

'And do all prostitutes use an alias?' Mr Harris-Jones asked.

'Some do.'

'Did Ada Vaughan?'

Ada took in her breath sharp. They were making her out to be a whore. Two of the jurymen were shaking their heads. She knew their types. Bloody Christians. Baptists. She felt like shouting, *Let him who is without sin cast the first stone.* She was on a helter-skelter, up and down and round and round, frightened of what else would come.

'Oh yes,' Scarlett was saying. 'She called herself Ava Gordon. Ava, after the film star, you know, Ava Gardner.' Mr Harris-Jones nodded, letting her talk. 'Don't know where the Gordon came from. Gin, perhaps. She liked her Pink Ladies.' She smiled, warming to her theme. 'Scarlett's from *Gone with the Wind.* Have you seen it?'

Harris-Jones was stitching her up and now he'd laid a trap and Scarlett had fallen into it. She could see Scarlett fidgeting on her feet.

'Would you describe Ada Vaughan as a common prostitute?'

'Not common,' Scarlett said, looking across at Ada. 'Classy. Charged more than the girls up West.' She smiled, a satisfied pout. She was *proud* of Ada, proud to be her friend. 'But then it wasn't just a fifteen-minute job she gave them. She worked out of Smith's.'

'As I said,' Mr Harris-Jones sneered, 'a common prostitute.'

'No,' Scarlett said. Her cheeks had gone red and Ada could see she was riled. 'She wasn't a street-walker. Didn't solicit. Nothing like that. I mean, she only did it for pin money. There's nothing wrong with that.'

'Pin money or a regular living, it doesn't matter. Selling your body for sex is prostitution.'

'She was a good-time girl,' Scarlett said. 'That's all. Heart of Gold. Her gentlemen showed appreciation.'

'In cash?'

Mr Harris-Jones's silver hair curled below his barrister's wig. She could see him in Smith's. *Are you alone? May I join you?* She'd had a few barristers. Judges too. Perhaps he'd been one of them, she'd never recognize him in his wig. He looked the sort. Acted it and all. Guilty after-wards, blaming Ada for his sins, as if it was her fault he'd left his wife at home with the house-keeping and a little extra. What was that, if it wasn't payment? That's all marriage did. Made sex legal. It was hypocrisy. She wasn't having that. She was as good as any of their wives. She hadn't killed Stanley because she was a prosti-tute. She'd killed him because he was an evil, deceitful bastard.

'What was the relationship between Ada Vaughan and the deceased?'

Scarlett fidgeted. 'I never met him,' she said.

'But you knew about him?'

Scarlett shrugged. 'No.'

'What was the nature of the relationship?'

'What do you think?' Scarlett snapped.

'Thank you.' Mr Harris-Jones looked down at his notes, lifted his head and looked Scarlett in the eye. 'One further question. Did Ada Vaughan ever mention what she did in the war?'

Of course not, Ada wanted to shout. Why should she? She always kept herself to herself.

'No,' Scarlett said. 'We never talked about the war. Best put that behind us, that's what we said.'

'Thank you, Miss Matheson,' Mr Harris-Jones said. 'No further questions.'

Scarlett caught Ada's eye, gave her a look of sympathy. *Sorry, love. I did my best.* She had to give evidence, Mr Wallis said, couldn't wriggle out of it. Still, Ada couldn't see why she was there, telling the jury what she did for a bit of extra.

'I did it for Thomas,' Ada shouted. 'I was saving for him, to bring him home. But you think he's dead now.'

'Miss Vaughan,' the judge leant forward, 'my patience is wearing thin. You will have an opportunity to put your defence later. Until then, you must be silent, or I will evict you from the court.'

Mr Wallis said he had no questions.

The landlady was standing in the witness box next, holding the Bible, swearing to Almighty God. Ada hadn't forgiven her for throwing out her things, leaving Ada with nothing to wear. She'd paid for that room, up-front. She had no right to get rid of her stuff. She'd probably let it out again. Racketeer.

Mr Harris-Jones stood up. 'Were you aware of the defendant's occupation when you rented out a room to her?'

'You only get done for brothel-keeping if every room's used,' the landlady said. 'I was going clean.'

'I know the law on this,' Mr Harris-Jones said. 'I asked you if you were aware of her occupation.'

'She said she worked in Lyons,' the landlady said. 'I did wonder, mind, how she could afford the room on a nippy's wages, but she went out every morning in her uniform so I didn't question it.'

'When did you discover the truth?'

'Well,' she said, 'when she started bringing back her pimp. Or her ponce. Whoever.'

'Stanley Lovekin?'

'No, another one. Foreign name. A *negro*.' She said it through her nose, stretched the vowels, a *neee grow*.

The judge leant forward, *ahemed*. 'Would this be Gino Messina you are referring to?'

'Yeah, that's the one.'

She knew what the jury was thinking already. Only prostitutes go with black men. Loose morals. The landlady said that on purpose. Gino wasn't a negro. Ada'd only ever said he was her fiancé. The landlady wouldn't know anything more. She was making it up.

'Why did you think that pimping was the nature of their relationship?'

'My bedroom's just below hers. All sorts came up, I can tell you. That bed brayed like a donkey with a sore tooth.'

'It never,' Ada shouted. The cheek of the woman. Gino and her didn't even always have sex, not every week. Now here was this woman implying she was at it all night, every night, with any Tom, Dick or Harry.

'Miss Vaughan,' the judge said, glowering over his glasses. 'Another warning.' He nodded to Mr Harris-Jones, 'Continue.'

'What else did you hear?' Mr Harris-Jones said.

'Rows. Terrible rows. You could've heard them across the river.'

'What were the rows about?'

'Money. Every time. Either she wasn't giving him enough, or he wasn't giving her enough.'

'You're lying,' Ada shouted.

'Miss Vaughan,' the judge said, his voice toned to a deep timbre. 'No more outbursts, otherwise you *will* be removed from the court.'

'But the nosey cow must have had her ear pinned to the door,' Ada said, caught the judge's frown. 'Sorry.'

Mr Harris-Jones had been looking at the judge. He turned back to the landlady. 'And the night of the murder?'

'Well,' the landlady pursed her lips together and shook her head. 'Whoever it was she brought up had had a skinful. You could tell. Stumbling up the stairs. I heard her shouting, then it went all quiet. Eerie, if you know what I mean. Not like normal. Bed creaked a bit. I thought they was asleep. I heard her go to the lavvy, see, because it's just down the stairs, at the back. I never heard no more, then I smelt gas.'

'And?'

'I looked up the stairs and saw this sausage thing, that she used to block the draughts, stuffed outside. I hammered on the door, but there was no reply. I didn't want to go in. So I rushed back down the stairs, straight to the White Lion. Got them to ring the police and the fire brigade.'

'You're sure no one else was with them, had entered or left the room?'

'No,' the landlady said, 'it was only the two of them. They have to go past my flat. I hear everything. *Everything.*'

Ada knew the landlady would have queued to be a witness against Ada. Anything to put the boot in. Probably kept all Ada's clothes and sold them on for profit. Mr Wallis shook his head, like he was too scared to put it over the parapet and challenge the woman. Couldn't he see she was lying? He should do one of those clever tricks lawyers do with words and get her to tell the truth. But Wallis stood up, flipped his gown like she'd seen Mr Harris-Jones do. Barristers must do that, made them feel big.

'Do you like a drink?' he said.

'I like a glass of porter of an evening,' she said. 'It helps me sleep.'

'Thank you.' Mr Wallis smiled, as if he'd won an argument. Didn't bother to ask anything more.

'They won't call Gino, will they?' Ada asked Wallis in the adjournment. 'I couldn't bear to see him. I don't know what I'd do.'

'They would have liked to,' Mr Wallis said, 'but he refused to testify.'

'Why?' Ada knew he'd never cared for her but perhaps there was some decency in him after all. He didn't want to sully her name.

'You don't know?' Mr Wallis said. 'He's in prison.'

'Prison? What for?'

'Got three years for beating up a prostitute in Mayfair.' *Consequences, Ava, consequences.* He must have beaten her pretty hard if he was sent to prison for that long.

'Is she all right?' Ada said. 'The woman. Is she all right?'

'I think so,' Mr Wallis said. 'But if he testified in court now, he'd risk being done for living off immoral earnings.'

Ada shut her eyes and clenched her fists. She had been so stupid. So bloody *stupid*.

The manageress came next. Dressed up, smart black suit, black-heeled Utility shoes. Had the nerve to wear the nylons Ada'd sold her. Ada wanted to ask her, so the whole courtroom would hear, *Where did you get those stockings?*

The manageress confirmed that Ada worked as a nippy, wondered how she could afford a bedsit, on her own. Wondered how she got it, what with the housing shortage and all.

'And what did the defendant tell you?'

'Her grandmother had died. Left her a little nest-egg.'

'Did you believe her?'

The manageress pulled her jacket straight, looked Ada in the eye. 'No.'

'Do you think she was lying?'

'Must have been.'

Hypocrite. She'd come with a busy lizzie, had a cup of tea, *Nice place you've got here, Ada.*

Ada sold the other nippies nylons, she said. Clothing coupons. Bread coupons. No end of supplies.

'Did she say where she got her goods?'

'No,' the manageress said. She shifted her weight. She shouldn't have been receiving the stuff. '*I* never took it, you understand,' she added. 'Never on the black.' Ada opened her mouth, *Liar*, but the sound gargled in her throat. The judge frowned. 'It was never done on the premises,' she was saying, 'not in the Corner House. Not in Lyons.'

'Stick to the question. Where did she get her supplies?'

'I believe she had a boyfriend.'

'One final question,' Mr Harris-Jones said. 'Did the defendant ever talk to you about where she was during the war?'

'No. It's all news to me.'

She looked across at Ada, like she'd never seen her before. Stepped down from the stand. Ada watched as she walked away, a small ladder in the back of her stockings, near the ankle, stopped with a blob of red nail polish.

Ada wondered how many more so-called witnesses Mr Harris-Jones would bring on to twist the truth. He was painting Ada as nothing better than a common, greedy prostitute. She expected her mother any minute. *My daughter? Running off with a fancy man? Deceitful, through and through.* Miss Skinner. *Ada Vaughan? The sparrow who wanted to be a swan? Pure fantasy.* Her gentlemen friends wouldn't vouch for her. *Lucky escape there, I can tell you.* And what would they tell their wives? Mrs Bottomley and her friends would drop her like a hot coal. *Never knew the woman.* Snooty cows. Mrs B. at least would have been able to vouch for her. Only Mr Wallis said they'd made inquiries and she'd died in the war, in the shop when the Luftwaffe bombed. *Madame DuChamps, modiste.* The one person who might have believed Ada, believed in her. Blown to pieces.

'I daresay Ada Vaughan told lies to get a passport,' Mr Harris-Jones was saying. 'Probably forged her father's signature. She lied to the nuns, to her boss, to her landlady. And not once did she talk about her war experiences. Why?'

Why? Ada wanted to scream. *I didn't say a word because nobody would have listened.* There's only so much anyone wants to know about the war, and *nothing* if your story didn't fit. Better to keep your mouth shut.

'Women can't keep secrets.' Mr Harris-Jones was smirking as he spoke, man-of-the-world addressing other men. 'We know women. Tittle-tattle is what they do. But not once did Ada Vaughan mention these things. Including the *loss of a child.*'

He paused, face clouding with solemnity. He's an actor, Ada thought, nothing more, treating the jury like this was a play and they were the audience. All make-believe.

'What kind of mother never speaks of her grief? She never spoke about losing her son in the war. She brushed him under the mat as if he were dirt. A bastard, because that, gentlemen of the jury, is what he was. Could this have been the cornerstone of Stanley Lovekin's provocation, to the extent that she forfeited all self-control? And murdered him? Because of this child, of whom not one word was ever uttered, about whom, we must construe, she did not care?'

He took a deep breath. 'Furthermore,' he added, 'she would wish you to believe that the deceased, Stanley Lovekin, was no other than Stanislaus von

Lieben, a Hungarian national with whom she allegedly had a long-term grievance that went back to her wartime experiences, these same experiences about which she never spoke. She never mentioned Stanislaus von Lieben, not once, until now, in the courtroom. He is a silent, absent witness. They're sometimes the best, those witnesses who cannot testify.'

He picked up his folder. 'Please refer to item 2 in your bundle. As you see, Stanley Lovekin's records show that he was born in Bermondsey, south London, in 1900 and has never been out of this country.'

Well, they wouldn't, she wanted to yell, *he didn't have a passport. Not a British one.* His passport was stolen, foreign. He'd made her get one before they went, to be on the safe side, so he could piggy-back on her. She knew that now.

'This was, of course, another fantasy,' Mr Harris-Jones was saying, 'invented by the defendant to excuse herself. There is no evidence that Lovekin and von Lieben were one and the same, much less that he took her abroad and abandoned her. If there is, it must be a bigger secret than the making of the atom bomb.' He paused, looking at the jury again, waiting for them to nod. He flung his gown behind him, and sat down.

Mr Wallis had his work cut out, Ada could see. *It will be all right,* he'd said to her, in that interview room at the end of that day, the sound of the metal gates echoing shut down the corridor. *Keep calm*. The true story would stack up, like bricks, one by one. Stanislaus, Stanley. How he'd left her, thrown her in at the deep end, without a care. How Ada still felt these things, fretted, worried at them like a rabbit in a snare – for eight long years. Ada couldn't fight Stanley when she met him again. Couldn't even run away, not with Gino Messina behind her. She had to bide her time, wait for the moment. You'll see, he said, when we put you in the witness box.

Ada made an effort as best she could. Borrowed some rouge from one of the wardresses, washed her hair and brushed it till it shone, rolled it back and under and pinned it in place. Wore a cardigan over her blouse, buttoned to the neck, and dabbed at the gravy stain on her skirt so it looked clean and presentable. Spat on her shoes and rubbed them so they gleamed. Confidence comes from the inside. Appearances matter.

She had never had to make a speech before. Never had to talk. *Be yourself*, Mr Wallis said, *tell them what you know*. She'd told it to herself every night since Thomas was born, over and over in her head. But not out loud. She'd never told her story out loud.

Mr Wallis prompted and coached, *Let's start at the beginning, Miss Vaughan*. Her voice snagged more than once, caught like rayon on the ragged fringes of memory, pulling the threads tight.

'And Thomas,' Mr Wallis said, 'tell us about baby Thomas.'

369

Ada gripped the witness box, braced herself.

'Was he born dead, or alive?'

She didn't often cry, but she felt the tears welling behind her eyes, knew that the mention of him would send them cascading to the floor. She'd never talked about Thomas, never even said his name out loud, not till now, when she'd had to tell Mr Wallis about him, and everything, *everything* that went on in her war, a woman's war, far away from her mother's war, *You've no idea the suffering we went through.* It was far away from the soldier's war with their heroes and cripples and *Mentioned in despatches, meritorious action in the face of the enemy.* A war that had never existed. No one had listened till now. No one had cared.

'I don't know,' she shuddered back the tears.

'Why don't you know?' he said.

She paused, looked at the jury. Was that sympathy in their eyes? *You could have been my daughter. Just an ordinary girl, caught up in tragedy.*

'Have you ever lived with death?' she said. 'Not the everyday death of ordinary times. But death, every day, every hour. To live and work with cadavers belching gas and fumes, to watch skin shrivel and ferment, to wash flesh and feel it fall away into your hands.'

They were listening, Ada could tell. The words emerged from somewhere buried far into the deep.

'I was nineteen, twenty years old,' she said. 'A child. I couldn't vote, or marry. But I could be held a prisoner, sleep with the stench of death, dream of rot and decay.' She groped for words. 'Have you ever been there? The valley of the shadow of death? Except by a graveside, safe, on top, with the priest in his robes?'

One of the men nodded when she spoke the words of the psalm, looked at her straight. She'd caught his eye. She turned to the man on his left, spoke to him direct too.

'Death was inside me, and all round me. I lived and breathed it, carried it with me like bones in a butcher's bag. Death was within me.'

Ada kept her gaze steady. '*Within me*,' she said. 'I carried death within me. And I gave birth in a factory of death.'

She was crying. She'd left her handkerchief behind. She wiped her nose on the cusp of her hand. 'But I wanted to give birth to life,' she said. 'I wanted to hope, to live. In all of this hell, I wanted to produce life, a soul, a living mass of tissue and fibre and blood and love. Have you ever needed that?'

Mr Wallis was watching her, nodding.

'Have you *ever* needed life so bad that you would conquer death for it?'

She didn't know where these words had come from, except from far inside, love and emotion buried so deep she never thought she'd see them again.

'And then?' Mr Wallis prompted.

'Thomas lived,' Ada said. 'He lived in my mind and in my memory. Not a day went by when I

371

didn't see my son, didn't touch the down of his head, smell his new-born scent. I watched him grow up, I sang him songs. *She was as beautiful as a butterfly, and as proud as a Queen.* I saw him take his first steps, heard his first words. I kissed his cuts better, dabbed witch hazel on his bumps. My son Thomas kept *me* alive. Nobody can tell me he was dead. He did not die.'

She looked at the other men of the jury, one by one, the bald man with the demob suit, the squat man with red hair in a tweed jacket, the foreman with his handlebar moustache in a grey coat and army ribbons. She was tall and dignified. She was no tart, no common prostitute. She was a woman whose pain drilled to the reach of the earth, who had screamed to the horizon, and no one had heard. A woman who had survived, despite everything.

'And Dachau?' Mr Wallis said.

'Dachau,' Ada said. *Dachau.* She talked. She told them what her war had been like, *her* Dachau, the beatings and starvation, the stench from its chimneys, the gases from its pores, walking in the wretchedness of evil.

'What happened to Stanislaus von Lieben? Did you ever see him again?'

'He was in Dachau,' Ada said. 'The town of Dachau. At the end of the war.'

'What was he doing there?'

'I didn't know at the time. I only learned later. Business, I was told.'

'Did you talk to him?'

'I saw him. Crossing a street. I ran after him, but he'd disappeared. There were too many people.'

'You were sure it was him?'

'Yes.'

'And Stanley Lovekin. What makes you think he and Stanislaus von Lieben were one and the same?'

Ada began to fiddle with her cuff, unravelling a yarn that dangled like a coiled spring. 'I recognized him,' she said. 'He had the same voice, only without an accent. Except when Stanislaus got excited, his accent went, and he spoke sometimes like a Londoner. I wondered, even then.'

'Did he look the same?'

'He was a bit fatter,' she said. 'Lost some hair. But his eyes were the same colour.'

'Anything else?'

Ada rolled her weight over onto the side of one shoe. Hard to admit this, given what Harris-Jones had thrown at her, but she had to show the jury she was right.

'Yes,' she said, her voice soft.

'Please tell the jury what made you so sure Stanley Lovekin and Stanislaus von Lieben were one and the same.'

A swarm of heat circled her neck, threw her cheeks into florid, red flushes. She licked her lips, swallowed. Didn't want to say the word but Mr Wallis said she *must*. Shouldn't be embarrassed. 'He was circumcised,' she said. 'He never said he was Jewish. I mean, it's not only Jews who get circumcised. But Stanley was. So was Stanislaus. And not many men are.' She bit back the words but they tumbled out. 'That I know of.'

The foreman was scowling, and the man in the demob suit, the one she thought was probably a Baptist, spluttered.

She couldn't help it. 'Didn't mean to cause offence,' she said, looking at them.

'Anything else?'

'He told me he'd been in Namur when the Germans invaded,' she said, 'with someone else. He called her an empty-headed tart. That was me.'

'He hadn't recognized you?'

'He said I reminded him of her. But I'd changed, too. War does that to you. I have to wear glasses now. I'd dyed my hair, too. Blonde. I was thinner.'

'And how did you feel when he told you this?'

'It was like he pulled a trigger,' Ada said. 'All those years at Dachau, the loss of Thomas, my baby, *our* baby, coming back, the rejection. Years of misery and unhappiness. It all blew out, like a bazooka.'

Mr Wallis nodded. Ada was breathing hard, gripping the handrail of the witness box, her knuckles glowing white through the magnolia skin.

'And what happened next? What were you thinking?'

'He'd been drinking. Heavily. Called me names.

374

Shocking. Denied he'd put me in the family way. Insulting me.'

'How?'

'He said I was a tart. Only I never was,' Ada said, looking hard at the foreman. 'I never was a prostitute. But that's what he took me for.'

'And?'

'I thought then that perhaps that's what Stanislaus had wanted me to do. In Paris. It made sense. He knew Gino Messina, before the war, during the war, only something happened and his plans fell apart.'

'And then what?'

'I wanted to run away, but I knew he'd find me, or tell Gino. They had spies, that's what they told me. I'd be done for then. I thought, it's him or me. That's what I thought. And he was out cold. I couldn't stop myself. I turned on the gas. It was the only way to get free of him, and Gino, to escape.'

There, she'd admitted it again. But he'd asked for it. Couldn't they understand that he had?

'Don't you see? He drove me to it. He insulted me. He—' she hesitated, but she had to say it. '—he *abused* me, assaulted me. He had *raped* me. I couldn't think straight.'

The jury foreman raised his eyebrows, and the man in the demob suit adjusted his tie. The judge peered at her over his glasses, nodded to Mr Wallis to continue.

'Did you see Stanislaus's passport?' Mr Wallis said.

'He didn't have one,' Ada said, 'not a British one. He had some kind of papers, but they were stolen ones.'

Stanislaus and Stanley. One and the same. Her knees buckled beneath her and she sank to the floor, her face streaked with tears, her nose running. The policeman helped her up.

'Thank you, Miss Vaughan,' Mr Wallis said. He smiled at her, a beam of pride, affection almost. *Well done,* she read it there, in his eyes. *Well done.* Provocation. Slow-burning provocation. *Grossly. Insulting. Assault.*

The next day Ada looked again into the public gallery. Third time lucky. But the people on the front bench were the same strangers who had been there the day before and the day before that. Her mother wasn't coming, would never come, she knew that now.

It was Mr Harris-Jones's turn to question her. *He'll play dirty,* Mr Wallis said. *It's his job.* She'd told her story. Wasn't that enough? The jury had to believe her. They'd heard the truth now. *Manslaughter.* Three years. Maybe four. Good behaviour.

'Dachau,' Harris-Jones said. 'You weren't actually in the concentration camp, were you, Miss Vaughan?'

'No,' Ada said. 'I worked in the house of the Commandant.'

'And who was that?'

'Obersturmbannführer Weiss. Then, after he left, Obersturmbannführer Weiter.'

'The nature of your work there?'

'It was forced labour. Day and night. Sewing. Washing. Ironing.'

'Nothing strenuous then?'

Ada glared at him. 'Have you ever done house-work?' she said. 'Have you ever scrubbed and rinsed heavy linen sheets, wrung them out by hand, hung them on the line? Ironed them?'

He smirked. 'You're talking the kind of work that every married woman in England does as her duty to her husband and family.'

'No,' Ada said, 'it was more than that. I spent all day with my arms in scalding water and borax, all night sewing and mending.' But the men in the jury wouldn't understand that. It wasn't *men's* work, that.

'The more you tell me, Miss Vaughan,' Harris-Jones still smirking at the jury, 'the more normal it sounds.'

'I ruined my eyesight. I nearly starved. I barely slept. I was alone.'

'But you didn't starve, Miss Vaughan,' he said. 'You didn't die. You weren't in the camp. Those poor wretches knew the nature of forced labour, of starvation. How many was it died at Dachau? Do you even know?'

He faced the jury, spun round on his heel to Ada. 'Upwards of thirty-two thousand docu-mented deaths. *Thirty-two thousand people.* And you're complaining about a little borax and poor food.'

He turned once more to the jury. 'The Germans eat a lot of sauerkraut,' he said. 'Pickled cabbage. Can't stand the stuff myself, but Captain Cook took it on his explorations. Not a single sailor died from scurvy on his expeditions. Not one.'

Pivoted back to Ada, like a cuckoo in a clock. 'Your war was rather easy, wasn't it, Miss Vaughan?'

'No. It was hard work, *hard* labour. On cabbage soup, nothing more.'

'Did you try to escape?'

'No.'

'Why not?'

'I was locked in my room. There were bars at the window.'

'Were you in your room all the time? Did they ever let you out?'

'I was let out to do the laundry. Hang it on the line. Empty my bucket.'

'And why didn't you run?'

'I was under guard,' Ada said, 'all the time.' Not that Anni would have stopped her, but she didn't say. Anyway, where would she have gone? She'd have been captured in no time and shot.

'You performed your duties well?'

'I was punished if I didn't.'

'How?'

'The belt. I was beaten.'

'You did nothing to resist? Fight back against the Germans?'

'How could I?' Ada said, adding, 'I tried.'

'How did you try, Miss Vaughan?'

She puffed air out of her lips, breathed it back in. Her hands were sticky. One of her suspenders had worked free and her stocking was drooping at the front, cutting across her thigh. 'I'd try to contaminate the clothes,' she said. 'I'd put them on before I handed them over, rubbed them against my skin so flakes would stick in the seams and the weave. I knew they were disgusted by me.'

'That's it?'

'I put rose hips in the gussets and gathers of Frau Weiter's clothes.' Ada turned to the jury again. 'She wore dirndl skirts and blouses, so there were lots of creases. It made her sore.'

He laughed then. Harris-Jones *laughed*. 'Do you see, gentlemen of the jury? While our boys were fighting Hitler, sacrificing their lives in the cause of freedom, Ada Vaughan was trying on clothes and putting itching powder in the laundry.' He turned to Ada. 'Well done, Miss Vaughan. That made a big difference to the war effort.'

A church bell struck outside, a sonorous, *gong gong*. St Sepulchre's. *When will you pay me, said the bells of Old Bailey.* She counted. Twelve o'clock. The judge said nothing. She only heard the *scritch* of his bristles as he rubbed his hand against his chin. She shifted her weight. The thick stockings, 'H.M. Prison Holloway' stamped across the top,

379

itched her calves and she lifted one foot and rubbed it against her leg. The laces on her left shoe had come undone. He was making her look small, mocking her.

'It wasn't like that.' Ada had had enough. 'You don't know what it was like. I was their slave. At their mercy. Locked away. Day in, day out. No one to talk to. No hope. No escape. Hard labour. Really *hard*. Have you ever been a slave? Have you?'

'That's quite enough, Miss Vaughan,' the judge said, leaning forward, peering over his nose like a crow over carrion. 'You have been warned many times.'

'I was by myself,' Ada said, ignoring the judge, staring at Harris-Jones. 'I did what I could. What would you have done?'

'I'm sure you did your best, Miss Vaughan.' Harris-Jones's voice was laden with irony. 'I'm sure you did.'

He flicked through the papers on his desk, pulled one free of its folder and put it, face down, next to him. She wished he'd move on, talk about Stanley Lovekin, or Stanislaus, what he was like, what a bastard he was.

'Could you tell me, Miss Vaughan, how you came to be at the Commandant's house?'

'I don't know,' Ada said. 'I was taken out one day and driven there.'

'Did you go voluntarily?'

'I had no choice.'

'What can you tell me of Herr Weiss?'

His scrawny face flooded her vision. She could feel his trembling fingers enclosing hers. She shuddered and flicked her wrists to shake off the sensation.

'He was one of the old men we nursed.'

'What was the nature of this nursing?'

'We made sure the old people were clean and fed, given their medicines. The usual.'

'Was there anything special about Herr Weiss that caused you to treat him differently?'

'He had been a school teacher. He had a lot of respect, from the guards, especially. And he spoke English.' Why all these questions about Herr Weiss? She looked at Mr Wallis for guidance but he was concentrating on his notes. 'He asked me to speak English with him, so he could improve it.'

'Did you take advantage of this?'

'How do you mean?'

'Did you exploit his attention?'

'He taught me German in return. I was grateful to him for that.'

'Anything else?'

'No,' Ada said.

'You didn't give him services of a more intimate nature?'

He was guessing. He must be. Ada had never said, not to anyone, ever.

'Answer the question, Miss Vaughan,' the judge rattled from the dais.

'He was a bit frisky sometimes,' Ada said. 'Forced me to hold him while he did his business.'

'Did his business. Did you enjoy that?'

'Of course not.'

'He was well connected, was he not? In Dachau. In the Nazi party.'

'He was a relative of Martin Weiss, the Commandant.'

'And did you ask him to get you moved into the household of the Commandant, in exchange for sexual favours?'

'No,' Ada said.

No. She had never asked. 'Life can be easier for you, *meine Nönnerl.* Did you know that?' Whispered in her ear so she felt his breath warm on her cheek, his bristles rough against her skin.

What was her life now but the steady drip of death among the dying?

'Just one small favour,' he'd said, 'and it can be arranged.'

Did she agree? What choice was there?

His flesh hung loose over his bones, like a coat too big for him.

'And you,' he said, picking up his stick and flicking the hem of her habit. 'Take off your clothes. Let me watch.'

His skin was oily, rubbed against hers, rubbed into hers. He was kissing her, crinkled tongue in her mouth. She lay still.

'I won't hurt,' Herr Weiss said. *'Adelheid.* Ada.

How can I give you pleasure? Tell me what to do.'

She wanted to say, *Leave me alone*. She didn't know what he meant. His lips were close to hers, dribbling over her.

'I forget,' he said. 'You are a nun. But you're not a virgin, are you, *meine Nönnlein*?'

She felt him as he thrust into her, heard him grinding his teeth, concentrating. His body was soft and heavy on top of her.

'I am a man of honour,' he said. 'I always keep my word. I will make your life agreeable. You will like that.'

He pushed himself free and rolled to one side, one arm behind his head like a younger man.

'I know someone who needs a dressmaker. Would you like that?'

'A dressmaker?'

'*Ja*,' he said. 'This will be our little secret, *Adelheid*. Mine and yours.'

Ada pulled her shift towards her, clutched it against her breasts.

He watched while she dressed, gave her the key. 'Open the door.'

She walked through, into the corridor. He'd seen a person behind the flesh. *Adelheid. Ada.* A woman. No one had done that in a long time.

And a dressmaker.

'Even back then,' Mr Harris-Jones was saying, 'you'd sell your body for a better life. Your soul,

383

too. Body and soul. To the Nazis. A pact Faust would have been proud of.'

'How would you understand?' she said. 'How *could* you?'

Her life wasn't easier at the Commandant's house. She'd wondered more than once whether she wouldn't have been better off with the nuns in the home. She'd have had company, companionship, protection.

'Was the Commandant married?' Mr Harris-Jones said.

'There was a woman there, with a child.' Her voice hitched up again. Poor little mite. Screaming and screaming till he burst a blood vessel.

'His wife?'

'I found out, after, that he wasn't married. I don't know who she was.'

'You made her clothes. Did you make anybody else's clothes?'

'She brought her friends along.'

'And you made their clothes too?'

'Yes.'

'Talk me through how it went, Miss Vaughan. A typical day.'

This had nothing to do with provocation, or Stanislaus. He was wasting the jury's time, everybody's time. Well, she could do that too. He wasn't the only one who could drag it out.

'I'd wake up,' she said. 'Daylight would wake me. I'd put my bedding in order, use the bucket. I'd pick up whatever sewing I had. Perhaps some mending. Or a hem. Wait until I was let out. Sometimes it would be quite soon. Sometimes I'd have to wait until midday. No breakfast then. Nothing to eat or drink. I'd pick up my bucket, make sure it didn't slop, because sometimes it was quite full, go outside to—'

'Spare us those details,' Harris-Jones said. 'We want to hear about dressmaking. What happened when the women came to the house?'

'They'd come with their material. And a photograph or a picture of a dress. I'd have to make it for them.'

'What did that involve?'

'Measuring them,' Ada said, 'advising. Suggesting. Designing a dress, to suit. Making a toile, a pattern. Cutting. Tacking. Sewing. Finishing.'

'Designing. *Bespoke*. Making a toile,' Mr Harris-Jones said. 'That's some skill. You weren't an ordinary seamstress, were you, Miss Vaughan? You were a couturière.'

He was playing on her vanity, Ada knew, but she enjoyed the recognition, couldn't help it.

'I suppose.'

'You suppose? You built up quite a following in Dachau. This woman, whom you thought was Frau Weiss, was your front man, front of house. A mannequin, was she? Quite a business. The dressmaker of Dachau, couturière to the Nazis.'

'No.' Ada scratched at the loose skin of her thumb. '*No*.'

'Your own *atelier*.'

'That's not it. I don't know why you're saying this, what it's got to do with Stanislaus.'

'Did you take pride in what you did?'

Her thumb was bleeding. She sucked at the blood, wiped her nail against her skirt.

'It kept me alive,' she said, 'the dressmaking.'

'I asked if you took pride in your work,' Mr Harris-Jones said.

'Yes,' Ada said, jerking her head high and glaring at him. 'Yes, I took pride in what I did. It made me human.' She clenched her teeth, hissed through them. 'What would you understand?' She turned to the jury. 'I wasn't given a choice. I was trapped there. I was never paid. How could I be? Not even any special favours. So what if Frau Weiss got me work, wore my creations, she and her friends. *So what.* It kept me alive. I did what I had to, to survive.'

'You did your best for those women, didn't you, Miss Vaughan? You hung on their praises, lapped up their plaudits.'

'They never spoke to me. Only one of them was ever kind to me and yes, I lapped that up. I craved love. I don't expect you to understand that.'

Mr Harris-Jones was lifting up the paper he had pulled out of his folder, and laid it on the table, face down.

'Item 9, in your bundle,' he said to the jury, walking over and handing Ada the paper he'd extracted earlier. It was a photograph. Ada stared at it, the features drifting in and out of focus, *now you see it, now you don't.* There was no mistake.

And the dogs. Ada struggled to remember their names. Little Scotties. Negus, Stasi.

'Did you know this woman, Miss Vaughan?'

'Yes,' Ada said.

'Who is she?'

'She was one of the women who came to me.'

'Do you know her name?'

'No,' Ada shook her head. 'I didn't know anybody's name.'

'Have you heard of Eva Braun?' Harris-Jones said.

Ada swallowed. 'Eva Braun?'

'Yes. Eva Braun.'

'Wasn't she something to do with the Nazis?'

'Are you feigning ignorance, Miss Vaughan?'

'I don't understand.'

'Eva Braun,' Harris-Jones said, rocking on his heels, satisfaction scrawling across his face, 'was Adolf Hitler's mistress.'

Ada had heard something about it on the wireless, but it was a while ago. She didn't often see the papers, never looked at the pictures. She didn't want to live in the past.

'I repeat. Did you know this woman?' He held the photograph high with both hands.

'I told you,' Ada said. 'I met her.'

'This woman,' Harris-Jones puffed out his chest so his voice ricocheted round the courtroom, 'is Eva Braun.'

His words hit her like a steam train. Ada stumbled with the recoil, grabbed the rail for balance.

'I didn't know who she was,' she said. 'Nobody ever said her name in front of me.'

'Did nobody tell you?'

'No. Why should they?' Ada said. 'People didn't talk to me. They never called her by her name. Sometimes they talked about a Fräulein, *that* Fräulein. Like she was scum, common. They never said who she was. Not Hitler's mistress. Not then.'

Mr Harris-Jones raised an eyebrow. 'Really?' he said. 'Your circle was well connected. Hitler's mistress? Whom he married the night before they committed suicide? *Nobody* gossiped?'

Ada swallowed. Eva Braun had thanked her, complimented her. She had lapped it up, and all along she was Hitler's mistress. Ada hadn't known a thing.

'Do you recognize the dress in the photograph, Miss Vaughan?'

Ada knew it well, every dart and stitch, the distinctive corsage. She was tempted to lie. *No. Never seen it.* But Harris-Jones must know, otherwise he wouldn't be showing this to her. *Whatever you do,* Mr Wallis said, *don't lie.*

'Yes,' Ada said.

'You made it, didn't you?'

Ada nodded.

'Speak up.'

'Yes.'

'Designed, cut, sewed. *Bespoke.* Showed Eva Braun how to wear it, where to place the corsage.

This was the dress Eva Braun wore when she married Adolf Hitler. She wore the same dress, without the corsage, when she died with him.'

Someone in the jury box coughed. Ada watched as the foreman fidgeted, crossing and uncrossing his legs, shuffling his feet.

'How does it feel to be Eva Braun's dressmaker, Miss Vaughan? To have made her bridal gown, and her shroud?'

Ada didn't know. She never knew.

'Eva Braun,' Harris-Jones was saying. 'Mistress of the most powerful man in Europe, if not the world. Certainly the most evil. Are you still proud of your work?'

This wasn't the point.

'Was this your contribution to our war effort?'

This wasn't how it was. She'd done nothing.

'Or to the *enemy* war effort?'

'I was trying to stay alive,' she said. 'I had no choice.'

'Just obeying orders, were you, Miss Vaughan?'

'No,' Ada held her head in her hands. 'No. You're twisting things. It wasn't like that.'

'You were a collaborator, Miss Vaughan.'

'No.' She was shouting. She didn't know she had so much sound inside her. 'I was forced. I was a prisoner. I didn't do this voluntarily.' She turned to the jury, sitting there, angry eyes drilling into her. 'You have to believe me. Facts don't tell you the truth, don't tell you what happened. You didn't know what it was like there, in that house.'

The foreman with the medals was nodding. Maybe he understood.

'War,' she went on, 'it's a mess. A muddle. We do things in war, to survive, from one day to the next. There's no future in war. I never believed in the Nazis. But I had to live with them. Is that collaboration? What if I had resisted, Sister Brigitte could have been shot. Could I have lived with that? Would that have been moral?'

Mr Harris-Jones raised an eyebrow.

'Are you so pure?' she said, glaring at him, then across to the jury. 'So moral? With your guns and your bombing? Trading cigarettes for family heir-looms, or a little girl's body? I saw that. Our boys did that too.'

She heard the judge draw in his breath, as if he was about to speak. This was too much. She knew she was crossing a line, but she had to.

'They say all's fair in love and war. But not if you're a woman.' Ada slammed her fist onto the witness box. 'I thought I was being tried for murder. Not treason. This has nothing to do with Stanley Lovekin. You're stringing me up like a Nazi at Nuremberg.'

She turned to the jury, sitting tight-lipped, jackets buttoned up, fingers itching in their pockets. They'd shave her head, if they could, strip her naked and parade her through the streets.

'I never betrayed my country. *Never.*'

✱   ✱   ✱

The foreman had had a good war. They all had. Done their bit for king and country, if not in this war, then the last. Old comrades, all of them. The jurymen, Harris-Jones, the judge. Spoke the same language, of old soldiers, of men. They understood each other. She could see them looking down their noses at Mr Wallis. *What did* you *do in the war, sonny boy?*

Mr Harris-Jones swaggered towards the jury, radiating success. *Man to man.* He looked down on Mr Wallis, as if he were the class dunce.

'Grossly insulting assault,' he began, an eyebrow raised into a question mark, nodding at Ada, at the jury. 'This, from the woman who made Eva Braun's wedding dress. Took pride in her work for the Nazis.' He stretched the words *prrride*, and *Naazis* so the jury would not forget.

'This is a very long way from the murder of Stanley Lovekin through asphyxiation by coal gas. A particularly unpleasant death, it should be said.'

He tapped his pen on the desk, looked at the clock. *He thinks he's got it all in the bag, sewn up tight*, Ada thought. One or two of the men in the jury were looking at her while he talked, though she wasn't sure they were searching for innocence. She was tempted to glare back at them, but knew she had to be contrite.

'This was not a matter of self-defence. Nor could it be a matter of provocation,' Mr Harris-Jones was saying. 'Ada Vaughan is a liar. She lies to anyone foolish enough to listen. She lies to further

391

her advancement. She lies to herself. There was no Stanislaus von Lieben. There was no baby. There was no Frau Weiss. There is no evidence for any of it. There *was* a dressmaking business. There *was* Eva Braun. There *was* prostitution and black marketeering. Ada Vaughan pursued her own interests in an amoral, immoral and ruthless manner.'

He sipped his water from the glass on his table, glimpsed his notes, looked up.

'The facts of the matter are straightforward. Ada Vaughan, also known as Ava Gordon, on the night of the fourteenth of June 1947, unlawfully killed Stanley Lovekin at number 17, Floral Street, Covent Garden. The defendant admitted her guilt at the scene, and subsequently signed a written confession at the police station. The forensic evidence demonstrates that the confession is true. There were no mitigating circumstances or issues of self-defence which could explain her actions.'

That's all right, Ada thought. If he just sticks to the facts and leaves me out, that gives Mr Wallis a chance to put my case. It's not *what* happened, but why.

'This wasn't even a lover's tiff. This was a dispute between felons squabbling over the proceeds of their crimes. Ada Vaughan, a woman without morals or sensibility, an inveterate liar and fantasist, was in cahoots with Stanley Lovekin, running a black-market business and, with his partner in crime, Gino Messina, a vice ring. His murder was the result of a squalid quarrel between a pimp and a prostitute, a spiv and a fence over money, which resulted in the defendant, with malice aforethought, turning on the gas, which Stanley Lovekin inhaled and which killed him. A grossly insulting assault? Provocation? We're talking about a tart here, not a nun.'

'It wasn't like that,' Ada was shouting. 'You can't think that.' She faced the jury. 'I can see how it looks, the way he puts it. But it wasn't like that.'

'Miss Vaughan,' the judge's voice rang loud.

'But that's not what happened,' she said. 'Let me say it.'

'Miss Vaughan. This is your final warning.' The judge nodded to Mr Harris-Jones to continue.

'Ada Vaughan waited until Stanley Lovekin was insensible, then turned on the gas and withdrew, sealing the gaps in the windows and door as she went. She intended for him to die.'

Harris-Jones looked over to the judge, like they were equals, in cahoots. 'Loss of self-control is instantaneous. It can only be *of the moment*. When the provocation, whatever it is, is so acute that it drives reason out of the door. There cannot be provocation by instalments. It cannot come years later. It is not like purchasing a frock on the never-never, or building a wall, course by course. It happens,' Mr Harris-Jones snapped his fingers, 'like that. In an instant.'

He sat down, peered at Mr Wallis along the table.

Mr Wallis stuttered. He started crooked, tripped on his consonants, choked on his vowels, staggered on his 's's. Ada could see his hands trembling. He coughed, blinked, paused.

'Let me start again,' he said, 'from the beginning.' He took a big breath and now his words came out rounded and formed, like he'd found his voice, and the story behind it, all together, ripe for the telling. Mr Wallis was good with words, she'd give him that, used proper, long ones. She held her breath, crossed her fingers behind her back, hoped.

'A bazooka,' Mr Wallis was saying. He licked his lips, sucking back the spit. 'Those were Ada Vaughan's words. "*It was like he pulled a trigger. It all blew out, like a bazooka.*"' He squinted, catching each juryman's eye. '"*He drove me to it.*" Stanley Lovekin's provocation was such that any *reasonable* man,' he paused, turning to Ada, 'or *woman*, would lose self-control. In other words, gentlemen of the jury, had you been in Ada Vaughan's position, you too would have behaved as she did.'

He was breathing through his open mouth, gathering wind. 'Grossly. Insulting. Assault.' Mr Wallis slithered out the words. 'Such that any reasonable *man*,' he spoke it like he didn't see how a *woman* would be reasonable, 'would lose self-control.'

'Miss Vaughan did not witness an act of sodomy,

394

adultery or violence upon a relative. She wasn't a husband or a father. She wasn't witnessing an *Englishman* being unlawfully deprived of his liberty. This was Floral Street,' Mr Wallis went on, 'not Burma. Or Italy.'

The juryman in the demob suit smirked. Mr Wallis adjusted his gown, lifted his head, hunched his shoulders as if it made him look grown up.

'The normal expectations of provocation do not apply here. Nor, moreover, did she grab an axe, or a kitchen knife, or a heavy-bottomed saucepan and kill Stanley Lovekin in a frenzy.'

He paused, gathering his breath, and tilted his head towards Ada. *He's acting, too*, she thought. *Putting on a show.*

'But neither did she calculate to kill him.' Mr Wallis stuck out his chest. 'There was not a *single* act, a grossly insulting assault, that provoked her.' He shook his head with fatherly concern. 'That's not how women think. Their reason works in a different way.'

Ada thought he might be putting ideas in the jury's head, not taking them away.

'This was the legacy of an abuse that had lain dormant for seven years. It was reignited by Stanley Lovekin. Stanislaus von Lieben. One and the same person. The physical evidence matched. The behaviour matched. He was in Munich, he confessed to abandoning her in Namur. He had ruined her life. He was a man with neither empathy nor remorse.'

Mr Harris-Jones blew his nose, a noisy trumpet that sliced through the silence of the courtroom, breaking the concentration. He returned the handkerchief to his pocket in a contemptuous flourish, hoisting up his gown, pulling it back down. Mr Wallis waited.

'The pain that Miss Vaughan had undergone in the loss of her child,' he went on, 'and as a victim of the Nazi programme of forced labour, was a pain no one was prepared to listen to. Had she been a soldier, a prisoner of war, had she returned from Colditz or Burma, she might have had an audience. But she had to bury it inside her, where it grew like a fistula, drained her reason, so that when Stanley Lovekin confessed *and* dismissed her as an empty-headed tart – an insult by any standards, but one that was a particularly gross and insulting assault given its heritage – and *then* abused her, she turned on the gas, knowing that it would cause him to die. She did not think about it. There was no *distance of time* between his confession and her actions. She lost self-control in that very moment. The *provocation*, on the other hand, had grown in the *passage of time*. Historic wrongs have a way of festering. She does not deny killing Stanley Lovekin unlawfully.'

The foreman of the jury was leaning forward. The cadaverous judge was rifling through his file.

Mr Wallis waited and the judge focused his eyes back onto the court. 'She pleads not guilty to murder.' He spoke deliberately and carefully, shoving out his words like he was pushing a boulder up a hill. 'But to manslaughter, under the duress of provocation.'

Bit her nails to the quick in an hour. That's all it took. Ada knew, the moment the foreman stood up, shoulders back, chest forward, hero's ribbons striped across his lapels. She didn't stand a chance. Could have spared herself the trouble. She could have pleaded guilty and had it over and done with by now.

'Will you visit me, Mr Wallis?' Night was closing in and the single bulb in her cell was high in the ceiling, dribbled a dim brown light and cast long shadows across the walls. She had no one left in the world. 'Before I go?'

She knew she'd never see him again.

The wardresses were kind to her. They had nothing to lose. Nor did Ada. She couldn't run away. The cell was big. Had her own bathroom, *bathroom*, with a bath and a proper lavatory. Table. Wardrobe, not that she had anything to put in it.

She could only sit and count the days. Wished they had done it there and then, not made her wait. Time on her hands. The last of time. The trial. Funny way of looking at the past. Facts. This way, or that, white or black. Where was the in-between? The *truth*, that connected one fact to

397

another? The twilight? If you read about it in the papers, or in a history book, it wouldn't tell what went on, what really happened. Ada's war would be forgotten.

'An exercise book?' the day wardress said. She was an older woman, old enough to have been her mother. Her bosoms sagged and her stomach was soft. Ada wanted to tell her she should wear a girdle and get a better brassiere, but that would have been a cheek.

'And a pencil,' Ada said, 'or two.'

'No sharpeners allowed,' the wardress said. Ada knew why. Unpick the screws, take the blade and *swish*, the gallows man would be out of a job. Albert Pierrepoint. She knew his name.

'Albert Pierrepoint. He does them all,' the night wardress had said. They chatted at night. Ada couldn't sleep, and they wouldn't turn the lights off. 'Nice, clean job. Skill. Nothing to worry about.'

He'd looked a jolly man, ordinary, like a shop-keeper, a grocer perhaps. Ada could see him in a brown gaberdine overall behind a counter. *Coupons? Thank you. Two ounces cheddar. One of butter. Quarter tea.* Yorkshire accent. Smoked a pipe while he sized her up. What kind of a living was that? Took his jacket off. Ada expected him to have a tape measure round his neck, like a tailor, neck size 13 inches, knot, like a corsage, just so. *Drop*, this much, *slack*, so much. Never knew a rope could have so many sides.

Ada had filled one book, written small along the

lines. No one else would tell the truth, tell her story, *her* war. This was what she wanted to say. It happened, like this. The wardress had brought her another book, a rubber too.

'Even though you didn't ask for it.' Six HB pencils. She'd tried not to rub out too much because it left smears across the page. She got a bump on her middle finger with all that writing, and the side of her palm was grey with lead.

She had more fittings with Mr Pierrepoint than she ever did at Mrs B.'s. All in a week. Was this her last?

'I used to be a dressmaker,' she said. 'Neck to waist, I know about measuring.'

He didn't say anything, gripped his pipe between his teeth, flecks of saliva on his lips, the pungent fug of Capstan Navy Cut tucking itself into her nostrils.

'House of Vaughan,' she said. 'I was going to call it House of Vaughan. Like Chanel. Signature style, too, like her. Mine was a corsage. A large red corsage. Like—' Why was she telling him this? He didn't care. The wardress nodded, smiled at her. She'd talk to her, tell her the stories.

'I dreamed of Paris,' she said. 'Rue Cambon. Have you ever been there? Cut on the cross, too. My dresses. Once this rationing is over, that's what I'll do.'

She stopped, corrected herself. That's what she would have done.

That's what she should have done. She wished she'd never met him. She might have been rich without him. Successful and happy. Worked hard. House of Vaughan. Paris. London. And Thomas, Thomas. Her baby. Her beloved son. If he had lived, she would have cared for him, given him a home, with his own bed. *Your father died in the war.* That's all she would say. Like Sister Brigitte said, sometimes you have to tell white lies. He'd never know. They would have been happy, just the two of them. A little family.

The wardress's hand gripped her elbow. 'I'll take you to the lavatory,' she said. Ada shuffled into the bathroom. White tiles, horizontal, no lock on the door.

'I don't need to go.'

'Be on the safe side,' the wardress said, *before you leave*, like Ada was going on a journey.

'I'm sorry,' the wardress said, 'you have to put these on.'

Padded calico drawers.

'Do you know how to?'

'Yes,' Ada said. Her fingers were shaking as she pulled the tapes, wound them round, tight. They'd leave a mark.

'How long will it take?'

'You won't feel a thing,' the wardress said.

'Where will they bury me?'

'In the prison.'

'Can't I be buried with Thomas?'

'We'll find him,' the wardress said. 'We'll find

400

his grave. Bring him to you. We'll make sure of it.' She was a kind woman.

'Thank you.'

'A priest is here,' the wardress said.

'I don't want him,' Ada said. What had the church ever done for her? Her mother hadn't visited. Not once. Nor her brothers and sisters. Too busy being Catholic to be Christian. Scarlett had been the only one who'd come to visit and she hadn't set foot inside a church for twenty years. *Well I never*, she'd said. *You were a dark horse.* Added, *Mind you, I'd have done the same.*

Ada took off her glasses. 'I won't be needing these,' she said. Placed them on the table with the exercise books.

The wardress took Ada's hand, shook it. 'Good bye, Ada,' she said.

Ada heard the door open, saw Mr Pierrepoint come in. He nodded to Ada, walked over to the far wall.

Mr Pierrepoint released a catch and pushed the wardrobe aside. It had been on runners, Ada never knew. There was a door, into another room. He opened it, held it for her, beckoned her to go first, as if he was escorting her to dinner. The room was empty. The brick walls were painted green, dark below the halfway mark, pale above. The floor was concrete, polished so it shone. There was a small window high up, with bars, and the February sun shone through, casting a feeble light. This can't be the last time to see the sun, to see a morning. It made no sense. No light. Ada couldn't think. Why was the room empty? Where was he taking her? There was another door ahead of her. He opened it, took her elbow, led her through.

She could see the knot of the rope, knew where it would go, just so, at the point below her ear, could see the unvarnished wood of the trapdoor in the polished stone floor. She was sweating. She was cold. Why didn't they have the radiators on? The cord on her knickers, just above her right knee, was too tight. It pinched when she walked, pressed in, on a nerve. It was uncomfortable. She had to loosen it. Mr Pierrepoint was fiddling with something at the back of her head. She'd ask him. When he'd finished. She'd like to bend down, please, and release the cord.

The wardress was standing by the door.

'There's the notebooks,' Ada said. 'I kept them. Everything's in it. It's the truth. My truth.'

'Are you ready?'

'No,' she said. 'No.'

HISTORICAL NOTE

While the Second World War forms the backdrop to this novel, the story and the personas given to the historical characters are fictional.

The concentration camp in Dachau was opened in March 1933, within weeks of the Nazis coming to power, and served as a prototype for other camps. It was originally built for political prisoners but later expanded to house others, including religious, sexual and ethnic minorities, Jews and Allied prisoners of war. The numbers swelled dramatically in the last months of the war as inmates from camps in the line of the Allied advance were moved to Dachau, arriving sick and emaciated, and exacerbating the overcrowding and unhygienic conditions already there. Although it was not an extermination camp, tens of thousands of inmates died within it, the corpses cremated in large ovens. Dachau, and its satellite camps, was the second to be liberated, but the first to allow reporters in and it holds an emblematic place in the history of Nazi atrocities.

Civilian prisoners of war in Germany, many of

whom were brought from occupied territories, were used as slave labour in factories, hospitals and even homes. I do not know if the Commandant of Dachau's household used such labour. This is my invention. But I do know that my aunt, a nun, was captured when the Nazis occupied France and set to work nursing old people, although this geriatric home of the novel, and its location, are my own creation and do not necessarily represent an accurate portrayal of old age care in the Third Reich.

Martin Weiss was the Commandant of Dachau from January 1942 to September 1943, and again, briefly, in April 1945. Wilhelm Eduard Weiter was the Commandant from September 1943 to April 1945. Weiss was later executed for war crimes; Weiter committed suicide. Weiss never married. His mistress is a fictional character, as is Herr Dieter Weiss, Frau Weiter and other members of their households, including, of course, Ada. There is no record that I know of for a dressmaker of Dachau.

Sources in the National Archives on the logistics of repatriation for British civilians (or Distressed British Subjects as they were called) interned in Germany or in occupied Europe revealed that British nationals married to Germans who wished to return to the UK after the war were treated as immigrants for ration purposes. For them, and for others, the family was required to pay for the repatriation of their relative. If they were unable (or unwilling) to pay, then the Red Cross had the responsibility for the journey home of DBSs, and provided emergency clothing if necessary; the British consulate made the travel arrangements and notified relatives of the impending return; the repatriation of British nationals interned in Germany took place by ship from Cuxhaven to Hull; the clearance from Hull to the destination was paid for by the Red Cross and the Central Office for Refugees. On arrival in the United Kingdom (at the port, not the railway station), they would complete their national registration and be given a civilian ration book. The Assistance Board would help with weekly maintenance and hostel accommodation in cases of destitution; the Ministry of Health or a D.P.A.C. (Displaced Persons Assembly Centre) officer would provide clothing coupons if there was an immediate need. British-born women, however, had to make their own arrangements for their reception in the United Kingdom.

I took liberties with the procedures, because I wanted Ada to see the River Thames as she arrived home, a view visible from the train from Southampton, but not from Hull.

The Messina family ran brothels in Mayfair and trafficked women from across Europe. Of the five brothers, Eugene (Gino) Messina was the most ruthless. He operated out of London, Brussels and Paris, and was found guilty on 24 June 1947 of grievous bodily harm, but it was not until 1956 that a Brussels court sentenced him to six years in prison for procuring women for prostitution. His wife and son are imaginary.

The Britain that Ada returned to, and particularly the London she found, had been ravaged by war. Churchill's wartime government had been overturned in 1945 in a landslide victory for the socialist Labour Party who promised change and an end to the inequalities of pre-war Britain. They put in place sweeping reforms, nationalizing key industries, instituting a welfare state and a National Health Service (in 1948), opening up educational opportunity and (in 1949) legal aid. While these institutions were popular (the welfare state and NHS broadly speaking remain in place, albeit under increasing attack), the continuing policies of austerity, including the rationing of clothing and food, were not and the Labour government was voted out of office in 1951. People were sick of hardship and drabness. The black market, providing both essentials and luxuries, including forged clothing and other coupons, thrived.

Although the 1945 reforms were designed to make Britain a fairer and more equitable society, post-war Britain was desperately poor and remained hidebound by the same class, gender and racial prejudices which had characterized it before the war. Working class women, in particular, were doubly discriminated against and women who found themselves caught up in the judicial system fared badly. They would stand trial not just for the crime, but for a crime against gender as the trials of Edith Thompson in 1922, or Ruth Ellis in 1955, attest. Both women were charged with murder (of a husband and lover, respectively); although there were serious issues surrounding the veracity of their testimony and the conduct of the trials, both were found guilty and hung. Ada's clients, respectable and middle class, would *never* have befriended Ada nor, given the charges, have defended her. On the contrary, they would have sought to put as large a distance as possible between themselves, and her.

Ada's London no longer exists. Working-class neighbourhoods in London, before and after the war, were further stratified by occupation and status. Cottages in Theed Street and in nearby Roupell Street and Whittlesey Street were known, colloquially and locally, as the 'white curtain streets', although the white net curtains were rarely white for long. Streets along the banks of the River Thames were notorious for their noxious industries and trades and intolerable levels of pollution. Ada's neighbourhood was inhabited by 'respectable' working-class families of labour aristocracy – skilled men with regular employment, who could afford to rent a whole house and provide three references for a landlord. Their wives would not have gone out to work (although they may have taken in work to do at home) and would mark their status, and signal their cleanliness, by scrubbing their doorsteps and the pavements, polishing the thresholds red with Cardinal's polish, or marking out an arc in white around them.

Ada was typical in her desire for self-improvement. The school-leaving age was raised to fifteen in 1936, but most working-class children had an elementary education only. There was a hunger for further education, and institutions arose to satisfy it, among which was the Borough Polytechnic Institute which provided evening classes in a range of vocational, academic and recreational subjects. The original building – along with Theed Street and the neighbouring streets – survived the bombing in the Second World War. The Borough – a neighbourhood of London bordering the south side of the Thames, and obliquely opposite the City on the north, the financial centre of London – is now best known for its gourmet food market. Then, it was a working-class area of London, with pockets of respectability and of roughness.

Finally, the judicial system in 1947 was stiff, formal and misogynist. The jury, the judge and the barristers would have been male and anti-German sentiments would have run high so soon after the ending of the Second World War. Before the Legal Aid and Advice Act of 1949 (part of the welfare reforms of the post-war Labour government in Britain), poor defendants had no entitlement for legal representation and relied on the goodwill of lawyers. It is quite likely that Ada would have had a young, inexperienced barrister who provided his services *pro bono*, in order to further his legal experience and career. The defence he ran at the trial fell under the law of provocation as it then stood, an archaic and gendered piece of legislation which has now been revised. Ada didn't stand a chance.